CHELSEA M. CAMERON

Sweet Surrenderings

www.chelseamcameron.com

ISBN: 978-1492893905

Edited by Jen Hendricks
Interior Design by Novel Ninjutsu

Chapter One

How in the name of everything holy did I end up on my back on the polished mahogany table in the boardroom, getting the daylights fucked out of me by one of the sexiest men alive?

Wait, wait, wait. That's not the place to start the story. Let me rewind a little for you. . .

Dad called me on the phone first thing on Monday morning, and he didn't sound happy. One thing about working at the same company as your father is that you never know if you're in trouble for something work-related, or if it's something else. I locked my computer and strolled down the hallway to his office, trying to keep my face blank. I usually wore a blank face at work so I could never be accused of being "too young and emotional" to do my job. I knocked softly on Dad's door.

"Come in," he said, and it sounded like the voice of doom. I scrolled through anything I could have possibly done wrong. I was paranoid, so this was a long list. I'd also only heard him use this particular voice when he fired people, or he called them out for screwing things up royally. Wait, could he fire me?

"What's wrong?" I said, wanting to get this over with as quickly as possible. One cut.

He held up a folder with papers in it. My heart beat erratically at the sight of the folder. For all I knew it could have been nuclear launch codes, or that fourth grade test I cheated on that he never found out about. Until now?

"Have you seen this?" he said. His face was drawn and serious. This worried me even more.

I crossed my legs and cleared my throat. "I'm not sure, what is it?" Just get it over with. I almost closed my eyes and braced for the blow.

"I was just going over some of the expense reports and something popped out at me. See what you think."

Wait, what? Expense reports? Who gave a fuck about expense reports? I mean, normally I did, but at this moment? I couldn't find any fucks to give.

But I opened the folder and tried to calm my heart and find what he wanted me to see in the sea of numbers that were doing this weird swirly thing that they probably shouldn't be doing.

"See that?" he said when I obviously wasn't immediately picking up on what he thought should be patently obvious.

"Yeah, look at that," I said, not sounding convincing.

"The sixth line down. Does that look right to you?" I looked at it. Okay, yeah, that did look odd.

"Did we really go through that much toner? That seems like an awful lot. Do you have the other months here?" He pointed and I thumbed through and saw that we'd been going up and down, but steadily ordering more and more. Not enough to make a huge red flag, but once I thought about it, it seemed like a lot.

"Has anyone been looking over these?" There were people whose entire job it was to check these things over and make sure they made sense and that everything was accounted for.

"That's just it. Seems that the reports have been altered. I haven't told anyone else, but I wanted to make sure that I had something to go on before I said a word, so I needed your eye."

"What are you going to do?"

He sighed and sat back in his chair.

"Well, the problem is that clearly, if this is something, it's an internal thing, which means that I can't make a big deal of it, or whoever it is will be tipped off. For right now I'm going to keep my eye on it, and if you could do that as well, I would appreciate it."

"Yeah, absolutely." He didn't need to tell me to keep my mouth shut about it, so I handed him the files back and he put them back in his desk and then locked it and put the key back in his pocket. His face changed and morphed back into the one I knew so well.

"Thanks, Rory. I'm so lucky to have you." He got up from his desk and gave me a hug. I hugged him back and I held on a little too long.

It's funny how something that seems so insignificant, so unconnected to your life, can alter the course of it so dramatically.

Sal Martin had worked for my father's software company, Clarke Enterprises, as an administrative assistant since the very beginning. He'd been a friend of my father's, and when he'd needed a job, Dad hired him. Dad was always like that. A nepotist, through and through.

Sal had started out low on the totem pole and had worked his way up. When his mind started to go, I took him on as my assistant once I joined the company after college, because I knew how much he valued his job, and the company. I kept his workload light, but soon his mind was in the grips of Alzheimer's and there was nothing we could do. It was absolutely heartbreaking, and more than once I caught Dad crying in his office about it, and I'd shed more than a few tears, watching his decline.

I planned a retirement party for him, and in the meantime started looking for a new assistant.

I was all for promoting from within the company, and that's what Dad would have done, but I still put an advertisement online, just in case there were any stunning applicants.

"Anyone strike your fancy?" Dad said, finding me alone in the room we used for interviews, my head resting in the desk. I loved, loved, loved my job as Vice President, but being one of the only women in the company was challenging. Especially in times like these. Being the boss' daughter didn't help either. People either thought I was an entitled airhead, or were so scared of me they couldn't speak. All three of my interviews had been some variation on those two themes.

I lifted my head as Dad put his arm around me. In spite of looking like a man who never hugged his children, Dad had always been affectionate. Just not in front of the whole office. He'd made sure my door was closed before he'd hugged me.

"Not yet. I think I'm going to look at some of the applications after lunch. See if anyone pops out."

"Go with your gut, Rory," he said, using my childhood nickname. It made me smile.

"I always do." That was one piece of Dad's advice that I always, without fail, followed.

After a quick lunch at my desk while I scanned the new quarterly report for typos, I went back to the applications that had been submitted online. A knock at my door brought me out of my work haze.

It was Mrs. Andrews, Dad's current administrative assistant and another one of his oldest friends. Nepotism, I tell you.

"Um, Miss Clarke? There is a gentleman to see you." I pulled up my calendar on my email and scanned. I'd been so frazzled lately, that I could have forgotten I had a meeting. But I was coming up blank. Mrs. Andrews was nervously hovering, half-in and half-out of my office. What was with her?

"I don't see a meeting. Did I forget to put one on my calendar?" It had happened before.

She looked over her shoulder and then came all the way in and closed the door, as if someone was chasing her.

"What's wrong?" Mrs. Andrews leaned over my desk and spoke quietly, as if someone was listening in. What was going on?

"It's . . . someone to see you about the assistant job. I don't know how he talked his way in, but he's insistent that he has to speak with you."

"Has he sent in his résumé?"

She shook her head. "He's got it with him."

"I'm not sure how I feel about that. He sounds . . . pushy."

"I'd say he's the kind of fellow who is used to getting what he wants. If you know what I mean." Yes, I most certainly did. Growing up with money meant that I practically had a degree in Men Who Don't Understand The Word No.

I sighed. This really wasn't something I wanted to deal with, but if it came down to it, security was only a button push away. I also didn't think Mrs. Andrews should have to deal with this douche, whoever he was. I'd put him in his place faster than you could say "privileged."

"I'll take care of it," I said, getting up and straightening my black peplum jacket, which was buttoned over a white shirt. I'd chosen to wear a black skirt that matched the jacket, and now I was regretting that. He'd probably see the skirt and think I was just a woman, and he could push me around. My stature didn't help either. Unless he was under average height, I'd be looking up at him, which was why I wore monster heels most of the time, especially when we had stockholder meetings, and today was no exception. Dad always called them my stilts.

Checking to make sure my honey blonde hair was still pulled out of my face, I strutted out of my office, Mrs. Andrews in my wake.

My bright red heels clicked pleasantly on the floor, alerting everyone that I was on a mission. I strolled with purpose down the end of the hall, turning the corner to get to the reception area where I stopped in my tracks. A man, with his back to me, leaned against the desk. My first impression was of a well-tailored dark-blue, nearly black suit. I'd seen a hell of a lot of suits in my life, and I can spot a custom-tailored one a mile away. I also saw a shock of dark auburn hair that was combed back, but was probably unruly most of the time, because little strands were starting to curl from the July humidity outside.

Then he turned around and I almost choked on the words I was about to spew at him. He seized my moment of silence and spoke first.

"Are you Aurora Clarke? I'm Lucas Blaine and I'm here to apply for the administrative assistant position. I was hoping to speak with you about it in person." His voice was deeper than I thought it would be. It reminded me a bit of a country singer I couldn't name at the moment. It was the kind of voice that made me quiver, deep down inside, and I hoped he didn't notice.

I finally let my eyes travel from his sleek black tie up to his face, where I nearly gulped when I saw that he had a chin dimple. He had a dusting of freckles on his nose to go with the hair, and then I met a set of eyes that were a strange color in between blue and gray. Like wet stones I used to collect on the beach at our vacation home in Maine. Or the color of the clouds before a storm.

I gaped like an out-of-bowl goldfish for a second and he held his hand out. I kicked myself as I stared at it, as if I'd never seen one before.

Shake his hand, Rory.

No! Don't shake his hand! You're here to yell at him, not ogle his chin dimple. This was only happening because I hadn't gotten laid in months. I was just a little sex starved, that was all. Looked like it was time for another session with Mr. Buzzy, my favorite vibrator. A long session.

I finally found my voice. "Listen, I'm sure you're more than qualified for this position, but that doesn't mean you can come in here and harass Mrs. Andrews. It doesn't really start you off on the right foot, you know." I tried to turn on what I liked to call my "bitch voice." It was the one I used when I had to talk over a bunch of men who all thought they were right, but none of them were. I'd dealt with far worse than this, so why was it so hard to think when I was looking in his eyes.

Stop looking at his eyes.

"I figured you'd see it as assertive," he said. "Being assertive is a good quality to have in an employee, don't you think?" He sort of turned his head to the side and, once again, I was speechless.

Oh, fuck me.

"Well, do you have your résumé with you?" He had a briefcase in one hand and I could see a white piece of paper.

"Signed, sealed, delivered," he said, holding it out as the Stevie Wonder song floated through my head. I took it from him and pretended to scan it, though it could be written in Chinese for all I took in of it, but I had to keep up appearances. He waited while I pretended read, just barely tapping his briefcase against his thigh. That could get irritating. Fast.

Finally I had to say something, so I cleared my throat and nearly choked in my own spit. Smooth, Rory.

"Well, Mr. Blaine, this a bit unorthodox, but I've been having some trouble finding a suitable candidate and I do have some free time now, so why don't you come with me and we can do an interview right now?" I wondered if he could spot all the lies. Firstly, I didn't have free time. I had a meeting I had to prepare for. Second, there was no way I could interview this guy without doing something stupid.

It had to be the cursed chin dimple. It was rendering me incapable of behaving normally.

I'd taken shit from men ever since I started at this company as an intern in high school. There was no way this guy was going to come out on top, so I rolled my shoulders back and motioned for him to follow me.

I made extra sure that my heels were loud as we marched back to the interview room, Mrs. Andrews gaping at me from where she'd been eavesdropping in the hallway. I gave her a look that told her I had everything under control and opened the door to admit Mr. Blaine.

This . . . could be interesting.

Chapter Two

"May I offer you some water? Coffee?" I motioned to the little table that had a mini water cooler and a Keurig on it. I turned my back to him for a brief second to pour myself a glass of cool water, and I could feel his eyes staring at my ass. Granted, it did look great in this skirt, but you're not supposed to ogle your future boss.

"To be honest, I'd like a Scotch on the rocks, or even a Whiskey, but I'm guessing that would be frowned upon." He was trying to throw me off; I could feel it. Two could play at that game. I turned slowly, sipping my water. I set a glass down in front of him and sucked my bottom lip into my mouth to get off the last of the water.

He watched me without blinking and I could almost see the wheels in his head turning under that gorgeous mop of hair. Something sparked in his earlobe, and for the first time I noticed a tiny diamond stud in his left ear that was out of place, given the office setting, but somehow suited him.

"Sorry to disappoint you, but this is an alcohol-free building. Unless, of course, it's one of the corporate dinners. Then all bets are off." I sat down across from him, making sure my back was as straight as possible, crossed my ankles and rested my hands on the table.

"Would I get to see you go a little wild? Let your hair down?" He motioned to my tight chignon. Oh, he knew absolutely nothing about me.

"How about we talk about you, Mr. Blaine, since you're the one that needs a job?" I put emphasis on the word "job". Mr. Blaine leaned back in his chair as if he were in his living room and gave me a whisper of a smile.

"Aren't you a little ray of sunshine?"

I fumbled with my list of normal interview questions and could only come up with a few.

"Where do you see yourself in five years?" He smirked at me for a second, as if he was going to give me a wiseass answer and then changed his mind.

"I see myself being happy. Having a job I love and working with people who are reaching for the same goals. Despite my earlier comments, I'm not a slacker. I work hard and I don't take no for an answer. I just see it as an incentive to make someone say yes." He leaned forward then, placing his forearms on the table and I saw his arms flexing under the jacket. One sleeve slid up and a watch glinted on his wrist. I pulled my eyes away from the watch and back up to his eyes, which were blazing now.

The storm was raging. This . . . this was a passionate man. Was he passionate in all areas of his life, I wanted to ask, but I already knew the answer.

Unequivocally, yes.

I re-crossed my ankles and cleared my throat again, moving on to my second question.

He answered it the same way as the first, with a sincerity that was hard not to believe. I moved on to a few more questions and I realized that it was growing hot in the room, and I was wishing I could open one of the windows without making a fuss.

"So," he said when I was done with all the normal questions I could think of and was groping for something else to say, "where do you see yourself in five years, Miss Clarke?"

That was none of his business. This was his damn interview, not mine. I'd already gone through one of those. Several, actually, as I worked my way up. Being the boss' daughter only got me so far. In fact, I was pretty sure being Walter Clarke's daughter made it even harder to get where I was.

"But we're not talking about me, Mr. Blaine. This is your interview." A beat of silence followed what I said and he was studying me in a way that made me both uncomfortable and a little intrigued. He stared so openly, so confidently. Not in a gross way, more in a way that said he was just as interested in me as I was in him.

"Why can't we talk about you? Yes, I am the one who needs the job, but wouldn't it be good to see if we are . . . compatible? We will be working very closely together." Was it just me, or did he mean to make that sound dirty? To make my mind play a little fantasy of the two of us getting close? As soon as I thought it, I was picturing it.

I swear to God, I was going to kill Royce Winkle for cheating on me and forcing me to break up with him, so I wasn't getting regular sex anymore. The fact that his last name was Winkle should have been my first red flag, but he was charming and rich and liked to pay for dinner when we went out. That was before I found out that he was just after my money (big shocker) because he had a gambling problem and owed a lot of people a lot of money. He was also banging a bartender on the side, but that was just the straw that broke this camel's back.

"I suppose you have a point there. What, do you want to play twenty questions?" This was already an off-the-wall interview. Why not make it even more so?

He didn't answer so I sighed, looking up at the ceiling as if it would tell me how to deal with this guy.

"I see myself being president of this company. Dad wants to retire and sail around the world with Mom on his boat and I want nothing more than to make that happen."

What. The. Fuck.

I'd meant to give him a vague answer, but I'd told him exactly the truth.

SERIOUSLY, WHAT WAS WRONG WITH ME?!

I blushed and waited for his reaction.

"That's very . . . sweet." He finally said.

"I'm sorry," I said, although I didn't know what I was apologizing for. Being sweet? There were a lot of people who would never call me sweet. Raging bitch monster was more like it.

Awkward silence followed as he continued to study me and I tried not to squirm and show him that I was uncomfortable.

"Well," I said, finally snapping back into business mode. "I'll look over your résumé again, and have Mrs. Andrews give you a call."

I stood and stuck out my hand, as is customary at the end of an interview.

He stood slowly, as if he didn't want this to be over yet, but gave me a nice firm handshake that didn't linger. Hm. Most men were worried about crushing my delicate lady hands so I was used to the dead fish handshake.

"Thank you for coming in and we'll let you know," I said, because I didn't know what else to say.

"I look forward to it, Miss Clarke. Very much." He gave me a wink, gathered his briefcase and was out the door, shutting it behind him.

Je-sus Christ.

I had to sit back down and stare at the wall for a minute to recover. One thing was for sure. Actually, two things.

One, I needed to get laid. Soon.

Two, there was absolutely NO WAY I could hire Lucas Blaine.

No. Way.

Chapter Three

Part of me wanted to take the rest of the afternoon off so I could go home and have some quality time with Mr. Buzzy, but I had meetings and my revisions on the quarterly report were due at midnight or else the board would have my hide, and I didn't need to give them any more reasons to dislike me.

To top it off, I kept getting interrupted by assholes who thought that somehow, it was in my job description to do their work as well as my own. Sometimes I thought it would be better if I could do their jobs as well as my own because I'd do it right. I wrote four terse emails, asking ONCE AGAIN for various projects/reports/files that I needed yesterday, or last week, or even last month. Some people liked to put smiley faces and so forth in their emails to make them seem less mean, or terse. I didn't believe in that. Smiley faces didn't get anything done. People being afraid of you did.

But they weren't all bad.

Dad believed that no company could run without everyone being accountable, even him, which was why he had a board of trustees to make sure that happened. The only problem was that they were (mostly) a bunch of old white dudes that would be content going back to the 1950s to make sure women stayed in the kitchen and out of the boardroom. Ironic, considering they worked at a software company that was all about reaching for the future.

I took a cab back to my apartment, even though I could have taken the T. Dad had tried to make me use a driver, but I kept paying him off and then ditching him, so Dad had given up and compromised by buying me a car that I only used when I drove up to the summer house in Maine.

I'd grown up just outside Boston in a nice suburb, but had always longed for the noise and cacophony of living here. People said New York was the greatest city of all, but it was definitely Boston, hands down.

The other thing Dad had tried to insist on was a lavish apartment, on which I had relented, but only as long as my best friend from college, Sloane, could live with me. Dad adored Sloane, so it was easy to convince him.

"I'm home," I called as I slipped out of my heels and set my bag down by the door. "You will never believe the kind of day I had," I said, walking into the kitchen where Sloane was making . . . something.

"Rough day?" she said, handing me a glass of white wine. There were many reasons I loved Sloane, and this was one of them.

"Thank you. Um, you could say that." I told her everything about the interviews and then started the story about meeting Lucas Blaine as she stirred steaming and bubbling pots and pans on our six burner stove, her dyed blacker-than-night ponytail bobbing around.

She'd been on a floral kick lately, and was wearing an ankle-length halter dress with a huge tropical flower print on the front. She'd accented it with chunky gold jewelry and gladiator sandals. I wished I could pull off her outfits, but I just couldn't.

Sloane was a fashion designer now, but when we'd met, she'd just been a girl from a bad family trying to get through college at an Ivy League university by the skin of her teeth. She'd made it and since then had been building a fashion empire, most of which had been spawned in this very apartment. She was brilliant, passionate and very persuasive, which is how she managed to fund everything. Even Dad wrote her a check. Anonymously, of course. She would never take money from me, and insisted on paying rent and utilities. And having the final say on all decorating decisions. Our place was cozy and cluttered, but everything fit together anyway. Bright and fun, we had lots of knickknacks and throw pillows and picture frames arranged to make the place feel welcoming.

Her blue eyes widened as I told her about Mr. Blaine. I was determined to call him that and not by his first name.

"So yeah. I am not hiring him. No way." I sipped the last of the wine and poured myself another. I was a bit of a lightweight, but this was a two-glasses-of-wine kind of night.

"Why not? I would. Then you could stare at him all day and pretend it's for work."

But how would I get any actual work done?

I sighed and decided to change the subject.

"What are you making?"

"Truffle mac, garlic asparagus, and mango sticky rice for dessert." In addition to being a fashion genius, Sloane was also an unbelievable cook. She was one of those people who was good at everything she tried. I always told her that she needed to open up her own restaurant, but she didn't want to. Her heart and soul were in fashion. Cooking was just a hobby.

I used to try to help, but Sloane is a bit of a control freak, and I hadn't been able to master her stirring technique, even after all the years I'd been trying. So I sat at the bar and rested my forehead against the cool of the granite countertop.

"So you want to go out on Friday? Open mic night at the bar." She just calls it the bar, because it's the one we frequent. Any other place is called by name.

"Listening to douches with guitars that think they can sing and girls with too many feelings trying to pour them into crappy lyrics? I am there," I said, raising my head.

"Oh come on. You're not still upset about King Douchebag, are you?" Sloane had started calling my ex that, because of the whole cheating thing. It made me laugh, and it was an accurate portrayal, so I called him that too.

"Not really. I just . . . I miss being in a relationship. I miss having something to look forward to. A reason to get pretty."

"Babe, you don't need to get pretty for anyone but yourself. How many times have I told you that?"

"Too many to count." It was true that I could live very easily without a man, and had done so for nearly my entire college career. I'd been too focused on working my way up in the company and maintaining my GPA to deal with guys.

"So we'll get pretty, you'll borrow something from my new collection, and we'll go out and have a girl's night. Just us. Oh, and Marisol. And Chloe," she said, taking one of the pots off the heat as she mentioned the other two girls in our little friend group. I'd always found it funny that girls seemed to hang out in groups of four, but it worked.

Through some strange coincidence, all four of us were currently single. That had never happened, and we were taking full advantage of it, having as much fun without worrying about men as possible. Or women, in Chloe's case.

"I'm in," I said, finally smiling as she held out a spoon for me to taste.

"That's my girl. Now, back to this Lucas fellow. I want details, and I want them *right now*."

This was going to be one of those nights.

After I told Sloane any and every detail of Mr. Lucas Blaine, down to this earring and chin dimple (mmm . . .), I made her let me off the hook by putting in a movie and volunteering to paint her toenails. And, of course, there was more wine involved.

"Have you ever, you know, thought about doing a no strings attached kind of thing? Just to scratch that itch?" she said as I added topcoat with precision.

"Not really. I don't know if I could have sex with someone without getting my emotions into it. I have a tendency to bond with whoever I'm having sex with."

Sloane raised her eyebrow, because we both knew that was an understatement.

"Okay, okay. I have issues where that's concerned, but I don't think a fuck buddy is going to help any."

"No, but it would get you laid. I mean, can you imagine how many guys would want to rock your world? Enough to start a waiting list, that's how many."

"But they just want to sleep with me to get at my money, or to get to my dad, or whatever." Been there, done that.

"Well, why don't you invent a secret identity? Dress down and have a new name and then they wouldn't know. You could just be a regular girl."

I'd tried that too. In college for a little while I'd gone by my first and middle name, becoming Rory Abigail, but people had found out anyway. You can't hide who you are, as much as you try. I'd need witness protection and a serious makeover.

"I don't know. Maybe being alone will be good for me. I can . . . pick up some new hobbies. Maybe try hot yoga. Or knitting. I've always wanted to learn how to do that."

Sloane rolled her eyes.

"Knitting is no substitute for some quick, dirty sex." She was right and we both knew it, but thankfully she dropped the topic and shifted to talking (again) about Chloe's recent (and volatile) breakup with her girlfriend. Let's just say that Chloe listened to every Miranda Lambert breakup song and acted them all out, including tossing Harmony's clothes out the window of their apartment. It was like watching a movie, only it was much more horrible when it was real.

I hadn't been that dramatic when I broke up with Royce. I'd been more stoic, but there had been a lot of crying in the shower and moping, but I was over that. I was ready to move on.

Chapter Four

"I'm pretty sure I've gotten really intimate with at least ten strangers already," Sloane said on Friday night as we squeezed our way inside the bar. We were holding hands so we didn't get shoved around too much. Sloane was in front because she was the tallest, with me bringing up the rear, because I was the shortest, though not by much. Like kids in school holding onto each other when they cross the street.

We squeezed through the crowd, which was a fantastic cross section of Bostonians. Men in pressed suits getting a cold one after a hard day of meetings and yelling at people, and construction workers doing the same in dirty white t-shirts. People who were down on their luck, nursing drinks they couldn't afford, a bachelorette party that was in full swing, and all kinds of friend groups. It was very much come as you are.

We always went for casual, and I had my favorite jeans on, the dark wash ones that made me look a size smaller than I was, and a bright pink silk top that clung in the right places and was loose in others. My hair was down around my shoulders, but it would be up in the pony band I kept on my wrist in about an hour. I was so used to wearing my hair up, that wearing it down almost felt uncomfortable.

Sloane battered her way through the crowd, the rest of us in tow and somehow found a high top table in a dark corner and commandeered five tall chairs to go with it. The open mic night hadn't started yet, but the noise was enough to drown out most conversation.

Marisol was scoping out some of the suits, and Chloe was still down in the dumps about her breakup. Our plan was to convince her to get onstage and sing. She had a killer voice and it always made her feel better, but she met Harmony after one of the mic nights here, so that might not be a good idea, considering.

Sometimes people mistook Marisol and I for sisters since we both had blonde hair and were short. But her face was rounder and sweeter than mine, and her personality was a lot sweeter too. Chloe was just a few inches shorter than Sloane and she was always changing her hair color and style. Right now she was rocking a red asymmetrical cut, but I'd seen it just about every color of the rainbow, and she was fond of extensions.

"Okay, I'm going to get drinks." Sloane was always our drink girl because of her height and her inability to take no for an answer.

She took our orders and memorized them. I went with a gin and tonic, because it was quick for the bartender to make and almost always good. Sloane pushed her way to the bar, leaving a trail of people with newly forming bruises in her wake. I swore sometimes she had the reincarnated soul of an Amazon.

"Are you doing okay?" I leaned over to Chloe. She looked so sad that it broke my heart.

"Yeah, I guess." She attempted a smile, but it fell from her face. I put my arm around her and gave her a little hug.

"We can cut out early if you want. No pressure."

"No, no, I'll be fine. Just call me Eeyore from now on." I kissed her cheek as the first person took the stage. It was a girl who looked like she watched some videos of Woodstock and tried to emulate them, complete with a flower in her hair. Her hands shook as she settled her guitar in place. I always tried to judge how people were going to sound based on their appearance. It led to me being surprised more often than not.

I decided that this one was going to be tone deaf, and I was mostly right. She hit one note and sounded like a screeching cat, but unlike in other bars, she didn't get booed offstage. Everyone just kind of gave her halfhearted encouragement and clapped politely when she left the stage.

Sloane came back with our drinks and we sipped and listened to the next few performers. There was a guy with a banjo who wasn't half bad and then another girl with a guitar who sang an original song that actually had the lyrics, "you're the sun in my sky, the apple of my eye," and by the time I was on my second drink, it looked like open mic night was going to crash and burn.

"Excuse me," one of the bartenders said, tapping my shoulder and holding out another gin and tonic. "The gentleman at the end of the bar wanted to send his regards." I'd been bought drinks before, but usually not by anyone I'd want to be bought drinks by. All four of use craned our necks to see who it was.

Lucas. Fucking. Blaine.

It took me a second to realize it was him, because he was completely dressed down in a flannel shirt and jeans. When he caught me looking, he raised his glass and I swear he winked.

"Who the hell is that?" Sloane hissed in my ear as the bartender set the drink down. "If you don't want him, I call dibs."

The other girls leaned in as the bartender went back to his post.

"Lucas. Blaine." I said slowly, because I could feel him watching us and waiting for my reaction.

"Shut up," Sloane said as the other girls finally got it. Of course Sloane had told them all about it. Not that I hadn't asked her to, but still. They were making a scene. Or maybe it just felt that way.

I bet he was getting a kick out of this. Bastard. If this was some weird way to get in my good graces so I'd hire him, he had another thing coming.

I pushed the drink aside, hoping he would see it.

"You're not going to let perfectly good alcohol go to waste, are you?" Sloane said as another douche with a guitar took the stage and murdered a John Mayer song. Slowly. Painfully.

I looked up to see if he was watching, but he was gone. I searched the rest of the bar, but it was too crowded to see. Well, a drink was a drink.

Taking the drink away from Sloane, I downed it and shoved the glass away so even if he looked over, he wouldn't see the empty glass.

"Way to go," Marisol gives me a thumbs up and a smile as the John Mayer wannabe finally exited the stage. "I'm not sure if my ears are going to recover from that. Why do we do this to ourselves?" She rubbed her ears as if to rub the last song out of them.

"Because we're young and hot and it's Friday night in Boston," Sloane said, mimicking the heavy accent so many people around here had. Mine only came out every now and then, but I definitely had a tendency to drop the R's in certain words.

I could feel the effect of the alcohol starting to take hold of me after the next two acts. I became pretty much cool with everyone and everything and I couldn't stop touching everyone's faces.

"Um, you should look at the stage right now, Ror," Sloane said, moving my head for me.

It was him. Lucas Blaine. He was holding a guitar, had swapped out his diamond ear stud for a silver hoop and his hair was falling all over the place. Add the guitar and flannel shirt and he was one bow tie, pair of nerd glasses and a set of suspenders away from being a hipster. I'd personally never seen the appeal, but Lucas Blaine could make a duck costume sexy.

Damn him. Damn all good looking guys and their chin dimples and well-proportioned muscles and their hair that you want to touch so bad you can barely sit still.

Damn them all to the fiery pits of hell.

The announcer started to introduce him, but Lucas whispered in his ear, and then the announcer spoke into the mic. "Our next act is Lucas Blaine. Give him a hand everyone."

Lucas pulled a stool forward and adjusted the mic as Sloane and Marisol talked about the various sexual things they'd like to do to him. Chloe just stared into her drink.

"Do you want to go?" I asked her, hoping she'd say yes so I had an out.

She shrugged.

"I'm good for now." Crap.

I decided that I wasn't going to watch. Nope.

But then the bastard started singing, "Sooner Surrender" by Matt Nathanson and my head snapped around at the sound of his voice.

Oh, fuck me. Again.

His eyes were half closed, his hair falling in front of them. And his voice. Oh, his voice touched me in places that a voice shouldn't have access to.

His voice crawled down my body and under my clothes and teased me, taunted me, pleasured me. Like he was making love with music.

Alcohol. It had to be the alcohol causing me to be more turned on by a song than I'd ever been before. Everything else faded into the background as my entire being focused on him on that stage.

The song ended, and the spell was broken, almost with a snap, and I was back to reality.

And everyone was staring at me as my face flamed up.

"You, um," Sloane said, taking a sip of her drink, "you didn't tell us he could sing."

"I . . . I didn't know." He sure didn't put that on his résumé. Not that it would have made a difference.

My throat was dry, but I was out of drinks. I should have gotten a glass of water.

"I'm, I'm going to get another drink," I said, getting up and hurrying to the bar without asking if anyone else wanted anything. I just needed to get away for a minute. Try to clear my head.

"What did you think?" a voice said behind me as a warm hand lightly touched my back to tell me that he was here.

I froze and didn't answer, instead concentrating on trying to get one of the bartenders' attention.

"You seemed to, ah, like it," he said, removing his hand, but he was still close. The fact that the bar was so packed could have been responsible, but I didn't think it was.

The bartender was completely ignoring me, and I had to get away from Lucas Blaine if it was the last thing I did, so I whirled around so fast, I nearly knocked him completely off balance and announced, "I have to pee."

There were worse things I could have said, I suppose, but the way he smiled in response to my declaration morphed his irresistible face into something that was somehow even more irresistible.

Abort, Abort! I needed to bail, so I shoved him aside and headed for the ladies' room. I swore I heard him chuckling behind me.

Of course there was a line at the ladies', so I was stuck standing behind two girls that were trying to prop each other up and doing that whisper-yell thing that drunk people do.

I really didn't want to break the seal and be peeing all night, but I had no choice. Once I was done, I snuck a peek back at the bar before I walked back to my table. No sign of Lucas Blaine. My eyes did a quick sweep of the rest of the room and found him in a worse place than at the bar.

He was standing next to the table I had vacated a few moments ago, smiling and clearly flirting with all of my friends.

They were all smiling and laughing at some joke he'd probably made and it was all I could do not to grab a pitcher of beer from the next table and pour it on his head. He probably would have loved that.

"There you are! I thought you'd fallen in," Marisol said when I finally made my way back to the table. I had no choice.

Lucas' eyes swept up and down my body, as if he'd just seen me for the first time instead of staring at me for hours.

"Nope," I said and moved to get back in my chair, which Lucas just happened to be standing next to. I went to pull the chair out, but he did it for me.

"Need a boost?" He was making fun of me, the jerk.

"No, I'm fine," I said as I used the bar attached to the legs of the stool to vault myself into it. Doing so was none too graceful, but I had short legs and I was not accepting help from him.

"So Lucas was just telling us all the reasons you should hire him. I swear, if you don't want him, I could use an assistant," Sloane said, looking at Lucas like she was going to lick him up and down. I gave her a death glare that he couldn't see, standing on my other side, and she kicked me under the table.

"You have an assistant," I said, because it was true. She had plenty of college students that would work for nothing just for the chance at making it in the fashion world.

"Mmm, but my assistants are usually female or gay and don't look like him." Lucas seemed to be swelling with the praise.

"My God, if you make his head any bigger he's going to fall over, and that wouldn't be very attractive," I said.

"The only praise that would make my head swell would come from you, Miss Clarke," he whispered so low my friends couldn't hear it. Ugh, I hated how he called me "Miss Clarke" outside of the office. What was this, 1953?

"Secrets don't make friends," Sloane said, leaning in, as if he was going to share what he told me with her.

He did lean over to her and whisper something, but I didn't think it was what he told me, because she gave him a look and then started laughing.

"You're right," she said, nodding.

What? What was he right about? Oh, this man was infuriating.

"Can I buy you a drink?" he said after I kicked Sloane under the table. She was going to be spilling her guts later when we got home.

"You already did that," I said, my voice flat. Even Chloe had dragged herself out of her breakup misery to watch my interaction with Lucas. We must be entertaining.

"I could buy you another. Just say the word."

"Actually," I said, turning toward him, "I'm a little tired, so I think I'm going to go home. *Sloane*, why don't you come with me?" I grabbed her arm, forcing her to get off the chair and pulling her through the crowd.

"Hey, it was just getting good," she whined and pulled back against me. Where strength was concerned, Sloane would win, but I could always take her out at the kneecaps.

"Please? Can we go?" She shook her head and dug her heels in.

"I will go after you let him buy you a drink."

"He already bought me one."

"Let him buy you another. It's not going to kill you."

Oh, Jesus Christ, Mary and Joseph. I was going to murder her.

"One. Drink." She beamed and dragged me back to the table where Lucas was wearing a similar grin. I wanted to slap it right off his face.

Chapter Five

Sometimes, you say you're going to have one drink and you have one drink. Go home and wake up refreshed and hangover-free.

And then sometimes you say you're going to have one drink and one drink turns into two and the guy who has been buying you drinks and touching your back and your hair and making flutters in your stomach suggests that you go back to his place, and that also seems like a good idea (because of the drinks) and then you're in a cab, on the way to his apartment with no idea how it happened. One drink. It was just going to be one drink.

"I've wanted to do this ever since you walked around that corner in those red heels," he said and reached for me across the backseat of the cab where I'd tried to put as much distance between us as possible while I tried to come to my senses.

One of his hands reached out and gripped my chin, and he moved his face so close that I could count the freckles on his nose and smell the faintest hint of Scotch on his breath.

"Don't move," he said and then his lips met with mine in a kiss so sweet, I was twelve again and at my first dance. Feather light and brief, he pulled away and the space between us was back. He looked away from me and out the window.

The fuck?

That was it? One little innocent kiss? That's all he's got? What was *with* this guy?

I was fuming. Sitting in my seat with my arms crossed and fuming. All that teasing for nothing. He had to be screwing with me, but I wasn't going to let him get away with it. I leaned forward to speak to the driver and tell him there was a change of plans before I gave him my address.

"Change your mind?" he said when he heard me tell the driver that I wanted to go to my own place. The driver sighed and looked for a place to make a U turn. This was probably for the best. This guy was not going to get the upper hand. This time I was shutting him down.

This was the last time I was going to see him. I would rip up his résumé. I wouldn't even have Mrs. Andrews call him to say that he didn't get the job. It was a bitchy move, but I needed this guy out of my life. He made me feel unstable, and I did not like feeling unstable.

"Yes. This was a mistake. I shouldn't have even let you buy me a drink, but Sloane made me."

"Oh, so this is Sloane's fault. I see." Now he was mocking me.

"Look, I'm going back to my apartment and you're going back to yours and I never want to see your face again." *Especially your chin dimple. And your eyes. And your hair.*

"Fine, fine with me."

He shrugged and went back to looking out the window. We were nearly to my place.

"There is something seriously, seriously wrong with you," I said.

"Why do you say that?" He turned to me with a little smile.

"Are you serious? You barge your way into my office and turn my interview upside down. Then you won't leave me alone at the bar. You buy me drinks, suggest that we go back to your place, tell me that you've wanted to kiss me since you first saw me, and then you do kiss me—the most tame kiss ever—and now you're acting like this is completely normal behavior. Yes, there is something seriously wrong with you."

"You thought the kiss was tame? Well, if you're such an expert, why don't you show me how I should have kissed you." His eyes sparkled in the light of oncoming headlights. Ah, so this was his game. Okay, two could play at that. It was time to get the upper hand, so to speak.

"Okay, Lucas Blaine, I'll show you a good kiss."

I knew it was a terrible idea, but I had something to prove to him.

Slowly, I crawled across the space between us and he turned as I climbed into his lap. Ha. I hadn't even done anything and he was hard. I could feel it pressing against his jeans as I straddled him, putting both hands on his shoulders and then moving them down his chest. I let one hand rest on the growing bulge in his pants, and I shifted a little, so he was pressing harder against me. I wanted to get a little something out of this, too.

Air hissed between his teeth as I moved the hand on his jeans and ground my hips, just a little. My other hand moved back up to his face, going around and tangling in his hair, wrapping my fingers in it.

Yes, it was soft as I thought it would be. I pulled a little, moving his head back, and he made a sound in his throat.

Good boy.

I was pretty sure the cabbie had already passed my place, but he was probably getting as much out of this as we were.

I lowered my mouth, but I didn't kiss him. Not yet. First I kissed his cheek and then inched my lips a tiny bit lower until I was at the corner of his mouth. Then I switched to the other side. I could feel his muscles tensing and quivering under me. I was playing him like a violin. I was owning him.

I sucked on his bottom lip and it was like something in him broke. I was thrown backward on the seat until he was the one on top.

"I swear, if you don't come back to my place with me, right now, and let me fuck the hell out of you, I am going to lose it, and you don't want to see me lose it."

Our eyes locked and he started moving his hips against me. Damn. I missed having a man pressed against me, passionate, and lusty. Sometimes Royce would come visit me at work and we'd sneak away. But it hadn't lasted. The fire had burned out in only a few weeks, and then it was like a chore. Royce was also more conventional than I was in bed. I'd suggest all kinds of things to spice things up, but he'd looked at me like I was a deviant and so I dropped it and tried to be content with missionary.

Something told me Lucas Blaine would be game for anything and everything.

The driver announced my stop and I had a decision. Lucas waited for me, pressing a little harder and making his intentions even clearer.

"I changed my mind," I heard myself say to the cabbie.

"Drive," Lucas said. His head dipped down, and I put my hand up to stop him from kissing me.

"So I'm a good kisser then?" I said innocently as he opened his mouth and I slid my finger in.

"I'll let you know in the morning," he said, licking the tip of my finger and giving me a devilish smile.

In order to get out of the cab and up to his apartment, Lucas to climb off me; our legs got a little tangled and it was hard to do with grace. Red-faced Lucas gave the cabbie a fifty and told him to keep the change. I give him a wink and I definitely heard him chuckle as I tried to walk with some sort of dignity. It was a bit easier for me, because I wasn't the one pitching a tent in my jeans. I laughed a little and shifted so I was standing in front of him as a few people passed by. Lucas used me as a shield, which made me start laughing and then I couldn't stop.

I doubled over, because I just couldn't help it.

"Well, this is a bit of an ego blow. You'd think this was my first time," he said behind me, and I heard a tinge of embarrassment in his voice. Trying to keep a straight face I stood, turning around. It was dark, but I swore I could see him blushing.

He was *blushing*. How unexpectedly adorable.

There was a lurch in the bottom of my stomach that I didn't really understand, but it made me stop giggling as if I'd been dunked in a bucket of cold water.

"Something wrong?" he said, taking a step back from me, regardless of what was going on in his pants. "Not having second thoughts?"

Oh, hell no. The sex was happening. I'd shut the door on my common sense about three drinks ago. Even though I knew it was a bad idea.

"None," I said, grabbing his shirt and yanking his mouth onto mine. Luckily, our teeth didn't collide, but I almost sliced his lip open.

I wrenched my mouth away after one fast, hot kiss that had me tingling from the tips of my hair to the ends of my toes and everywhere in between. It was a fire-starting kiss.

"Let's go," I said, wobbling on my feet a bit and hoping he didn't notice. I had been a hell of a lot more confident in the cab.

He took my hand and I stared up at the building.

"Wow, swanky." It was a doorman building. A really nice doorman building. What the hell was he doing applying for an assistant job if he lived here? I didn't even have a doorman and my building was pretty nice. Dad wouldn't allow me to go "slumming" as he said it.

"Let's get you upstairs and into my bed, hmm?" It was like he was singing again, the way his voice slipped and slid over and under my skin.

"Sounds good," I said as he tugged me toward the door where the doorman gave him a smile and a "Nice to see you, Mr. Blaine."

I prayed that my hand wasn't sweaty as he yanked me toward the elevator and pushed the button.

"Maybe we could just take the stairs?" I said as we both stared up, waiting for it to come to us.

"I live on the fourteenth floor," he said with a grin. Now that we were out of the cab I was feeling shy and apprehensive. I must have left the vixen who'd climbed onto his lap in the cab. I kind of needed her back.

"Finally," he muttered when the elevator door opened. A woman exited and was nearly run over by Lucas as he dragged me inside. She made a huffy sound, but he didn't apologize.

As soon as the door closed, he shoved me so hard up against the back wall that I knew I was going to have a bruise. But I really, really didn't care as his mouth claimed mine and I was pressed and connected with every inch of him.

His hands held onto my face, as if he was desperate not to lose me. It felt So. Damn. Good. I hadn't had anyone who'd wanted me this much in a long time, and I burned with it.

We drank each other in and I barely noticed when the elevator opened and we were on his floor. He broke the kiss long enough to pick me up in his arms and stride with purpose toward his door.

Of course, in his haste to get me into bed, he forgot that he had to unlock his door, so he ended up having to put me down to get his keys out, and he fumbled with them.

It was such a sweet moment that I almost started laughing again. But as I was about to cheer when the lock clicked and he kicked the door open, I was swept up in his arms again.

I had a brief look at an open floor plan and lots of white and black and chrome before he kicked another door open and I was tossed on a giant bed covered in silky black cotton sheets, and then he was diving on top of me.

It was like we were horny teenagers and he was worried that any moment his mom was going to come in. He seemed sure in some ways, but his fingers fumbled a little, and it just made me kiss him harder.

Normally, I liked being with a guy who was willing to take control, who knew exactly what he wanted and how to get it, but I liked this. It was new. It was like our first time ever and that made it better somehow, instead of awkward.

In his haste to get my top off, he ended up ripping my shirt as he tried to pull it over my head.

"Sorry," he said against my lips.

"No big," I said. Who cared about the damn shirt? I could just buy another one. I couldn't buy the way his hands raced over my exposed skin, or how it goose bumped in response. Now he was the one who had me eating out of the palm of his hand.

He pressed his face in between my breasts and breathed me in. Oh God, I was hot already and he'd barely done anything. He slid the straps off my shoulders and kissed my skin through the lace of my bra, sucking and biting here and there. Yup, my skin would bear the marks of his mouth tomorrow. He raised his head and went back to my mouth, his hands going to my nipples, rolling them between his fingers as they ached for more.

His shirt was giving me an issue. Too many damn buttons. I made a sound of frustration and his lips left mine.

"Do you need some help?" His face was a smirk.

"No, I got it. You just have a lot of buttons, and I'm a little distracted, okay? And I've been drinking. And I'm not really the kind of girl who has sex with guys she's just met." And now I was the girl who babbles during sex. To be honest, I hadn't been this nervous about sex in a very long time.

"We'll take it slow. Nice. And. Slow." He stroked the front of my jeans with every word, and I finally got the last button undone and pushed the shirt off his shoulders. He had one of those white tank tops on underneath. How frustrating. I just wanted him to be shirtless. It took another few seconds for me to get the damn tank top off and then I finally got to really look at him. "Let's Get It On" started playing in my head. I was kind of a fan of sex to music.

"Enjoying the view?"

"Maybe," I said, and that was a total lie. His body was even better than I thought it would be, and I wanted to taste and touch every inch of it. He had freckles dusted all across his well-formed chest, and his left nipple had a silver hoop through it. Yet something else that was completely unexpected.

I went for the nipple ring first, sucking on it and pulling it a little with my teeth. I was satisfied when he groaned deep in his throat.

"I knew I got that for a reason. I didn't know it would take nine years to find out that reason."

I kissed my way down his chest, and paused where the band of his underwear peeked out of his jeans. Of course, he had a belt on, so I went to work on that, but his hands stopped me.

"Slow. Nice and slow." He took both of my hands and put them over my head and pressed his now naked chest against mine, and went back to kissing me.

Slow. Okay. I could do slow.

I let myself melt back into the kiss, and it was easy. He was a damn good kisser. Must have had lots of kissing lessons in his youth.

"That's it," he said, breaking the kiss once more to reach around my back and undo my bra clasp with one hand before removing it completely. He paused for a moment to stare at me and then he was kissing down my neck and back to my nipples. My hands went into his hair as my back arched, trying to get closer to his sweet mouth.

I bit the corner of my lip to keep from moaning. I tended to be really loud when it came to sex. I'd bought poor Sloane the most expensive noise-cancelling headphones when I'd first started dating Royce, before our sex had gotten so boring I barely made a sound.

He dragged my left nipple through his teeth and I couldn't help it. At the sound of my moan, he laughed a little and did it again.

"I like that sound," he said, propping his chin between my breasts and smiling at me. "I think I'd like to hear it all night long. I think I'd like to save it and make it my ringtone."

"You would not," I said and he laughed as he kissed his way down my stomach.

"I might," he said as he paused at the top of my jeans before unbuttoning them and pulling the zipper down a millimeter at a time.

He was killing me. I was already coming undone, and he hadn't even touched my lower half. This guy was good. Or maybe I was just wound up from not getting any for months.

Or both.

Once he had the zipper undone, he slowly pushed my jeans down my hips, pausing briefly to admire my lace underwear before exposing me completely.

"Lovely," he said as he pulled my jeans off my legs and kissed his way down my belly again. I was just waiting for him to discover…

"You're pierced?" he breathed.

It had been a spur of the moment thing after I'd broken up with Royce. I hadn't told anyone, not even Sloane, that I'd done it. I'd thought about getting a VCH genital piercing for years, but Royce had always thought it was gross, and, like an idiot, I'd listened to him.

Lucas paused, studying the diamond barbell that pierced the hood of my clit. I waited for his reaction. This could end the evening right here.

He raised his eyes until they were locked on mine as he stuck his tongue out and licked my clit and then sucked the piercing into his mouth.

"Oh, *God*," I said as my entire body shook with want and need and lust and everything that had been pent up for months.

Lucas licked and sucked with his mouth, and then slid one of his hands up the inside of my thigh before plunging one, and then two fingers inside me, working them in tandem with his mouth.

"Don't stop," I said, pushing my hips toward his mouth and pulling on his hair so hard I swore I yanked some of it out. He didn't seem to notice or care.

He crooked his fingers against my inner walls and that in conjunction with his mouth sucking on my clit brought me to the most forceful (and quick) orgasm I'd had in . . . God, who cares?

I cried out and I heard him laughing as he slowed his movements, bringing me back down from the edge of the cliff. He removed his finger and gave my piercing one last little kiss before climbing up my body and grinning at me as if he deserved a gold star.

"You taste even better than I thought." Well, good thing. I'd been a little worried about that since it was the reason Royce never would go down on me.

"Good job," I said, still panting as I patted him on the shoulder. I was still recovering when he kissed me, sticking his tongue in my mouth so I could taste myself. That was something that always turned me on with my first boyfriend, but Royce said it was disgusting. Clearly, Lucas didn't think so.

Now that he'd taken care of me, it was my turn, so my hands inched their way down to undo his belt, and then unzip his pants.

I shoved my hands down the back of his pants and grabbed his ass. Perfect. It was perfect. He slid out of his pants and paused for the first time. Something crossed his face that wasn't exactly reluctance, but it was something. Something that didn't match what was currently happening.

"Are you sure?" I gave him an "are you fucking serious?" face and then reached out and took him into my hand, stroking once and then gripping him at the base where his dick met his body. I tightened my grip.

"I swear to God, if you don't fuck me the rest of the way, I'm going to twist." His eyes flew wide and his mouth dropped open.

"I'm serious," I said, twitching my wrist just a little bit. He was still hard as a rock, which made me want to laugh.

Then he smiled and reached over me to a drawer in his nightstand. I kept my hand on his dick as it pulsed in my hand and I moved my hand up and down as I heard him groan a bit. Ha. I am the master of hand jobs. My hands are just that fantastic when a penis is placed in one of them. I could teach a damn class on this. Probably because my blow job skills left a little to be desired. I couldn't help it if I had a gag reflex.

"Good thing we came to my place," he said, holding up the familiar square packet.

"Safety first," I said, squeezing his balls a little as he tried to rip the thing open.

"If you slip between her thighs, condomize," he said and I moved my hand so he could roll the condom on. I was so distracted watching him do it that I almost missed what he said.

"Come again?"

He looked up and grinned at me and I swear I wanted to fuck that smile. Yes, I know that's not possible. I mean, he did fuck me with his mouth, but this was something different.

"I'm sincerely hoping you will. It's my mission," he said, positioning himself over me as I adjusted my hips and he hovered at my entrance. I was wet, I was ready and he was teasing me. He held his dick in one hand and moved it up and down my entrance.

"Do you want me inside you?" He spoke the words against my lips and I tried to kiss him, but he pulled back.

"Yes," I said. Had I not made that clear by the penis grabbing incident earlier? Did he want an invitation? I Cordially Invite You To Enter My Vagina.

"Tell me you want me inside you," he said, stroking me with his dick again. This was cruel. I should sue him. I knew a lot of good lawyers.

"I want you inside me. I want you to fuck me, *right now*." I grabbed his head and pulled his mouth toward mine and he plunged his tongue into my mouth, but didn't plunge where I wanted him most.

Oh screw me with a rusty spoon.

"All you had to do was ask," he said with a dark smile as he slowly slid inside of me and I expanded to accommodate him.

"Christ," he said, going all the way in as I lifted up to meet him. "You feel amazing."

So did he. His mouth reunited with mine as he pulled nearly all the way out and thrust in again, harder this time. I hooked my ankles around him so he could get deeper and he did.

His tongue matched the rhythm of his thrusts and it was like he was fucking me in two places and it was the hottest thing I'd ever done. I moaned and met him stroke for stroke, and it was like our bodies were singing the exact same song and I could feel a second orgasm building as he slipped one hand down to work at my clit.

This guy deserved gold stars. Lots of them. Stars and . . .

"Don't you come yet," he said, feeling the onset of my second orgasm. "I can't hold out if you come. I've barely kept it together so far and I want to draw this out." With that, he slowed his pace and it was agonizing.

"You're trying to kill me," I moaned, but I wasn't sure he understood what I was saying. Hell, I couldn't even remember my name.

He chuckled and I looked into eyes that were staring at me as if I was the sexiest, most beautiful thing he'd ever seen.

At that moment, I felt it, and then he slammed into me harder and faster and I was coming, stars exploding, and fireworks, and all those other exploding things I couldn't think of because I was having a fucking amazing orgasm, and this guy was beautiful and sexy and he was coming now too, with one last, "Fuck."

He made sure not to crush me when he let himself down and laid his head on my chest.

We were both covered in sweat and breathing hard. Good workout. Now I didn't need to go to the gym. Yet another perk of sex.

"That was . . ." he said, tilting his face so he could look at me.

"Yeah," I said. "I don't think I can move."

He finally pulled out and I almost reached out to grab him and pull him back. I liked having him inside me. Probably like how a socket feels having a plug snugly inserted into it. Or maybe not. I have no idea how sockets feel.

"So does this mean you'll take another look at my résumé?"

Chapter Six

I didn't mean to fall asleep. I really, really didn't, but after the brilliant sex and ;seeing Lucas' sweet face and sex hair next to me on the pillow, I couldn't leave. By the time I knew it, the sun was creeping under the curtains and an alarm was blaring and I was wondering where the hell my underwear was and if he had an extra toothbrush and if he didn't, was I comfortable enough to use his?

His arm reached over me and slapped at the alarm clock as he groaned and moved closer to me, resting his head right on my breast.

"What time is it?" I mumbled.

"Six-thirty," he said, his voice muffled by said breast. His tongue flicked out and licked my nipple and I could feel his morning wood under the covers. I'd never been much for morning sex. Mostly because I hated mornings and I always felt kind of gross. But maybe I could change my mind . . .

"Why are you getting up at six-thirty?" I said, looking around the room for my clothes. My head was only a little achy from the drinks

I'd consumed last night. Yes, I was one of those bitches who almost never got hung over. As long as I wasn't drinking wine. That had me leaning over the toilet in no time.

"Forgot alarm. Coffee. Need coffee before talk." He'd been reduced to a Neanderthal. Any moment he was going to start banging his chest and then go out to slaughter a wildebeest and proudly drag the bloody carcass back to me.

He sighed heavily and got vertical, walking out of the bedroom still naked and I watched him go, admiring his more-than-perfect ass.

As soon as I was sure he wasn't coming back, I wrapped the blanket around myself and did a search for my clothes. I found them all, crumpled on the floor. My shirt would need to be steamed to look good, and there was a rip I'd need Sloane to fix, but I didn't really have a choice. This is why I should always carry extra clothes in my purse.

I nearly jumped out of my skin when I heard him behind me.

"Coffee?" I was crouched on the floor, gathering my shirt, so when I turned my head, I was staring straight at his one-eyed snake, and it was staring right back at me. Well. How about that?

I looked up and he arched an eyebrow at me as he held two cups of coffee, one in each hand. I had two options. I could stand up, take the cup of coffee and do the walk of shame while I got my ass out of here as quick as I possibly could . . .

Or, I could move my head just a little . . .

"Oh, shit," he said when my tongue darted out and circled the head of his dick. He was bigger than anyone I'd been with, so my chances of deep throating like a champ were slim to none, but I could at least give it a go.

I licked up and down his length and I could feel him quivering like a plucked guitar string, which made me smile. Using my hand

and mouth, I sucked him off the best I could and somewhere along the line his hands went into my hair and I wondered where the coffee had gone, but it didn't really matter.

"I'm going to come. You need to stop unless you want me to do it in your mouth." His voice was ragged and he was coming undone and I was thinking maybe I wasn't so bad at this after all and then his hand tightened on the back of my head and it was too late. I swallowed and then grinned up at him.

"Spitters are quitters." I rose to my feet as he collapsed on the bed again. "Where's the coffee?"

He pointed to two broken cups sitting in a couple of giant wet spots on the floor. Funny, I missed that part.

"It's official," he said, staring at the ceiling. "You are the sexiest woman alive. I mean, I knew it when I saw you the first time and again when you walked into the bar and again when I was getting you off and again when I was inside you, but . . . *Fuck*." He turned his head to the side and grinned. I gathered my clothes and lay down on the bed next to him.

"You're not so bad yourself."

Our eyes met and we both smiled. I was feeling goofy happy and satiated and maybe a little hung over and I knew this was a bad idea, but right then I was going to bask in it.

"So I was serious about the résumé thing. I know this," he motioned between us and I thought he meant the sex, "would make things a little more interesting, but I think I'm adult enough to be able to work with you without this getting in the way." Yeah, he was adult enough. Now if I said I wasn't okay with it I looked like a moron who let sex get in the way of work. I was not that girl. It didn't mean that I was going to hire him. Hell would freeze over first.

"You're being very nice to me. You weren't so nice during the interview," I said. He wouldn't stop smiling sexily.

"You should mark this in your calendar. I'm only nice a few days of the year, and you just happened to catch me on one of them. As soon as I've had my coffee, I'll go right back to being a dick, I promise."

I had to look away from the smile. It was making me feel all sexy again.

"I should go. Because . . . I should go." I had a lot of reasons, but none of them came to mind. I mean, obviously I had to get dressed first, but still. I wanted to leave with as little awkwardness as possible.

"No coffee?" The way he said it, I was thinking he didn't mean . . . coffee. I stared at him and he smirked and winked at me. Yup, he didn't mean actual coffee.

"No, I gotta go. Um, thanks. For the sex."

"Thanks for the coffee, Sunshine." He wiggled his eyebrows and I had the urge to smack him with a pillow, but I hustled my butt to the bathroom. By the time I got out the door, he was nowhere to be found.

A solitary round of applause greeted me as I tried to sneak into my apartment and past Sloane. No such luck. She was sitting at the bar, a plate of croissants and two cups of coffee in front of her, as if she'd been waiting for me. My phone had died sometime during the night and I hadn't had a chance to charge it.

"Welcome home, you sex bunny." I'd tried to fix my hair, but it was kind of a lost cause. Plus, the wrinkled shirt and smudged makeup didn't help.

"Shut up," I said and went for the coffee. I took a sip and sighed in bliss. It wasn't coffee; it was my absolute favorite, dirty chai. Yeah, yeah, I know. It was basically a chai with an espresso shot. My favorite was vanilla peppermint and that was what Sloane has gotten me.

"Who's your favorite roommate?" She put her hand to her ear, as if she was waiting to hear my answer.

"You are," I mumbled into my cup as she handed me a croissant. God, I was starving. Sex could do that to you.

"Okay, so now that you've had your fix, I demand details!" She smacked her hand on the counter and I wished she had something better to do with her time.

I sighed and sat down at the table and gave Sloane all the details she could possibly want. We had a very open relationship, so if I didn't tell her every single detail, including the blowjob, she'd find some way to shake it out of me somehow.

As soon as I was finished with my chai, croissant and cock story sharing, I was languishing in a long hot shower.

Of course my mind went immediately back to last night. I slipped my hand between my legs and remembered Lucas' face as he went down on me and I had to hold onto the shower wall because my knees were trembling. Hooray for new masturbation material.

When the water finally started getting cold, I got out and toweled off and I definitely needed more caffeine. I got dressed and went out to the living room to find Sloane with her head bent over my ripped shirt and a needle and thread in her hand.

"What would you do without my services?" she said, not looking up.

"Pay a lot of money for alterations and mending," I said, sitting down next to her.

"You want to do anything? I was figuring you'd want to spend the day here. Pizza and movies? My treat?" Have I mentioned that Sloane is the best roommate ever?

I leaned my head on the couch and smiled.

"You're my favorite."

"I know."

Hours later, we were both stuffing our faces with pizza and watching *While You Were Sleeping.* Every time we did movies, we had to pick a theme, and tonight was Sandra Bullock night. We'd already made our way through *Practical Magic, Miss Congeniality* and *Speed.* Next up was *Hope Floats*, and then if we could stay awake, *The Blind Side.* We liked to get a good variety of funny, romantic and tear-jerky.

My phone rang and it was my Dad, so I took it into the kitchen. Sloane didn't mind when I talked during the movie, but I had no idea how long this call was going to last.

"Hey, Dad." I was going to see him tomorrow for dinner, so it was a bit unusual that he was calling me and my mind went immediately to a dark place.

"Hey, Rory girl. I was just calling to make sure you were on for dinner tomorrow." We had dinner on Sunday nights at my parents' house every week, barring some catastrophe, and have done so since I could remember.

Something was up and I didn't think I was going to like it.

"Is tomorrow Sunday?" I said, trying to keep my voice light.

"Is that a trick question?" Sometimes Dad had a hard time with my sarcasm. It was actually kind of fun messing with him.

"Of course I'm coming over. Why wouldn't I?"

"Oh, no reason. Your mother just wanted to make sure." Sloane was giving me a questioning look, but I waved her off. She paused the movie so she could eavesdrop.

"I'll be there."

"Fantastic. Well, see you tomorrow." He hung up before I could say good-bye.

I stared at my phone for a second.

"What's up?"

"That was my dad. He's being really weird and shifty about dinner tomorrow, and I think I know what that means," I said.

"Fin's in town," Sloane said, stating the obvious.

"Must be."

Time for a little backstory. Fintan "Fin" Herald and I had known each other since we were in diapers and went to the same school until sophomore year when he transferred. Fin's dad and my dad played golf, our mothers went shopping and we grew up not that far from one another. So, of course, we were destined to fall madly in love and get married and make adorable babies per both our sets of parents' wishes.

Only problem in that charming little picture was that Fin and I . . . just . . . weren't. I mean, I was only sixteen when Mom had forced us to try to date, but I was smart enough to know that we would never work.

"Yup, Fin must be back in town. I smell a setup." I'd been there, done that, saw the movie, read the book, saw the crappy sequel. Besides, I hadn't seen the guy in years. We'd somehow missed each other on breaks and during the summer, and I'd been able to weasel my way out of every other setup my mother had planned since high school. We weren't even friends on Facebook.

"You could tell them you're seeing someone," Sloane suggested.

"But then they're going to want details, and I can't give them. You know my parents. They have been trained in interrogation techniques. I swear, those people could get anything out of anyone."

I sighed and turned my phone off and sat back down with Sloane. I didn't have to think about how my parents were going to pitch Fin to me as a prospective mate right now. I'd deal with it tomorrow.

"So, Fin's back from France for a few weeks to see his parents," Mom said just as we were starting our salads. Wow, we didn't even get to the main course before she ambushed me. I thought I was at least going to make it that far before having to defend myself. They'd brought out the big guns and now I had to dive into a foxhole and take cover and try to think of a new strategy before the artillery shells started falling.

I got nothing.

"That's great. I bet they're really happy to see him." Fin worked for his father's PR firm and traveled all around the world to work specifically with foreign companies to help them make it in the US markets. I only knew that because Mom liked to keep me apprised of his doings.

"Maybe the two of you could catch up. I'm sure he'd love to see you," Mom said, as subtle as an air raid.

She shared most of my looks, but I had my father's eyes at least. Eva Clarke was one of those women who made any outfit shine. Seriously, we could put on the same thing and she would look like she was ready to stroll the runway or be in a magazine and I would look like a homeless person.

Tonight she was casual in a burgundy skirt and crisp white shirt. How that woman could eat an entire three-course dinner and not get anything on her shirt was beyond me, but I could count the times my mother had ever spilled anything on a white shirt on one hand.

Why didn't inherit this gift?, I asked myself as I dropped a cucumber slice down the front of my (not white) shirt and into my lap.

"Sure, maybe we will." I fought the urge to roll my eyes. Mom hated it when I did that.

"Well, I took the liberty of giving him your new cell phone number, so expect a call from him anytime," she said, spearing the last leaf of lettuce on her plate and popping it in her mouth.

"Mom!" I ended up dropping my fork and having to fish for it under the table. Yes, my parents had money, but they were not multiple fork people, only had a person come in once a week to clean, and there was no personal chef in sight. My parents took turns cooking, and it was actually really funny to watch when they tried to cook together.

They always ended up in a fight about tarragon vs. saffron and I was stuck in the middle and would have to decide if I'm Team Tarragon or Team Saffron. It could be exhausting.

"I haven't seen the guy since high school. I don't even know what he looks like." The last time I'd seen him, he was as tall and thin as a beanpole and had braces. Not bad-looking; there was definitely potential, but he just wasn't my type. I liked them more . . . redheaded . . .

"I thought you were friends on Facebook," Dad finally chimed in. He always let Mom go first and then came in after with the cavalry. Time for evasive maneuvers.

"No, we aren't. Listen, I'm kind of seeing someone." They both stared at me, and I willed myself to pull this off. I didn't have a backup plan. This was my one shot.

I gave myself a brief Braveheart-esque pep talk and then plunged ahead.

"Yeah, I went to the bar the other night with the girls and I met this guy there. His name is Blaine and we've been on a few dates. Everything is so new and that's why I didn't tell you." I stopped firing and waited for the response. Mom and Dad shared one of those parent looks that you can never quite figure out and Mom dabbed her mouth with her napkin.

"I don't see why Blaine would have any problem with you having lunch with an old friend. He's not one of those possessive boys is he? Because I don't want you dating someone like that." Dad nodded his agreement.

I had to go easy, or else they'd smell my fear.

"He's not possessive. I just . . . I don't want to make it seem like I'm going out with a bunch of guys. Plus, have you asked if Fin is seeing anyone?" Ha! Bet they didn't think about that.

My brief moment of victory was stomped on when Mom got up to go get the rest of the dishes for the main course of her fabulous pork chops, mashed potatoes and garlic green beans.

"For your information, Fin is not seeing anyone and I don't think it would do any harm to have coffee with him. Just coffee, Rory." Coffee. I was NOT "having coffee" with Fin the way I'd "had coffee" with Lucas.

"What's so funny?" Dad got up to help her with the dishes and I started clearing the salad plates.

"Nothing."

They both stared at me, and my defenses started crumbling. I was no match for them.

"Okay, okay. Coffee." I waved my pitiful white flag and started treating the wounded. There were many causalities.

But then Mom was beaming and Dad was jolly and the rest of the dinner they were all glowy and happy and I'd get over it. This was what happened when you were an only child. Your parents teamed up against you.

Hopefully it would be just actual coffee with Fin and it would be boring and we would both agree never to do it again and then that would be it for at least five years.

This was the plan.

Of course, the plan only worked in my head because as soon as I walked in the door from my parents' house, my phone rang with an unknown number. I went to my bedroom, passing a curious Sloane before I shut the door and put the phone to my ear.

"Hello?" I didn't usually answer unknown numbers, but I figured this was probably Fin, and I was right.

"Hello, this is Fin Herald." I almost dropped the phone. The Fin Herald I remembered did not sound like that. This guy had a deep voice. Puberty had been good to him.

"Hi, Fin, this is Rory. Wow, you didn't waste any time." Stupid words. Why must you come out of my mouth at the wrong time? Just because I think you, doesn't mean I need to say you out loud.

He laughed.

"Yeah, my mother wasn't going to let a day go by. Look, I'm really sorry about this. Not that I haven't wondered what you've been up to, but I don't want you to feel awkward about this."

I sat down on my bed and slipped my shoes off. "So your parents ambushed you, too?"

"Something like that. They did all but strap me down in the chair and hold a gun to my head to call you and ask you to coffee. You seriously don't have to say yes." Huh. The guy I remembered was not this confident. Or funny.

"No, it's fine. If we don't do this, they'll never get it out of their systems," I said.

"Good point. So, um, what have you been up to since high school?"

Thus began the catch up. He loved his job and he got to travel a lot and I told him about mine and how much crap I got for having a vagina and being in the tech field and we laughed and it was like we'd been close for years. We never got along this well in high school.

"Well, it sounds like this coffee thing is going to be no problem. I think we've got this," he said twenty minutes later. Sloane was probably dying on the other side of the door.

"Thank God. I was hoping I wasn't going to have to fake a broken ankle, or park my car in a no parking zone so it gets towed on purpose."

He paused for a minute.

"You know, that's actually not a bad idea. Thanks for that."

"Anytime." We finalized the details of our coffee date for the following Wednesday. I just had one meeting in the afternoon and then I could leave early and meet him.

I hung up and set my phone down. "Well, what do you do know about that?" I said and shook my head. There was a frantic knocking at my bedroom door.

"Well?" Sloane had been camped out on the other side and now was bursting for details. Because my life was her life.

"We're going for coffee," I said, pushing the door open. "That's it. He actually was kind of funny and it wasn't too awkward, so it might not totally suck." Sloane raised and lowered her eyebrows and I pushed past her.

"Don't get any ideas, Miss Sloane." Too late.

"Rory's got her very own love triangle. God, I'm jealous." I got a coffee cup from the cupboard, filled it with water and put it in the microwave to make some Kava tea. I needed a little something to help me sleep.

"Oh come on! Let me live vicariously," she whined. "All I have is work and nothing else to occupy my mind. Take one for the team."

Take what? What team was she talking about?

"Have you been sniffing too much fabric glue again?" This one time in college she'd had a project due and not enough time to sew it and had to glue a lot of the seams together and she'd gotten totally looped out on glue. I wished I had a video of it.

"It's either this, or suffer through marathons of reality television, and not the kind you like." Ugh, spare me.

The microwave dinged and I took my tea to my room without another word.

Chapter Seven

"Have you narrowed down your candidates for assistant yet?" Dad said when he stopped by my desk the next morning. He usually tried to see me at least once during the day and sometimes we had lunch together.

I'd been so busy trying to put out fires and rearrange a meeting that had already been postponed twice that I hadn't had a chance to even think about it.

"I will this afternoon."

"I heard you had a very enthusiastic fellow that came highly recommended." I looked up from my exploding inbox and blinked at him a few times.

"A young man by the name of Lucas Blaine?" How had he found out about this guy? Probably Mrs. Andrews.

"Oh?" I pretended I wasn't super interested.

"I must say he doesn't seem like the kind of boy to be interested in this type of position, but maybe he's been looking to make his mark here and start moving up. He seems like a valuable asset. Something tells me that he's going places. Anyway, I don't want to tell you what to do, but I think he'd do really well here. Mrs. Andrews was also very impressed with him." My phone rang, but I ignored it.

"Well, I haven't made my decision yet, and I don't think he would . . . fit well." Really? That was all I could come up with? It wasn't like I could tell Dad that I had amazing one-night-stand sex and I didn't think I could ever look him in the face as my employee.

"Well, just something to consider. Not that I'm telling you what to do. Go with your gut. Coffee this afternoon?"

I quickly scanned my schedule.

"No can do. I'm booked today. Tomorrow?"

"It's a date." He looked around before he gave me a kiss on the top of my head.

"Dad, stop," I said, smiling as he chuckled and walked back to his office.

I finally had a moment that afternoon to look over the applications and nothing jumped out at me until I got to Lucas' résumé. Holy Hell. He was only twenty-five and he had a record that would make someone nearly twice his age look good. Valedictorian, Magna Cum Laude, charity work, academic honors, athletic honors, awards from every job he'd ever had. Jesus. I was beginning to feel inadequate. His references were all from prestigious companies as well, including from our biggest competitor.

It was all . . . too perfect.

Yes, I know how that sounded, but I needed a reason not to hire this guy and other than the sex, this was all I had.

Plus, I knew for a fact that people pad their résumés and I wouldn't put it past him. Maybe a little call to some of his references would clear that up.

I really didn't have time to do this, but I was going to do it anyway. I wanted the satisfaction of having a good reason (other than the sex) for saying no to this guy. Because really, he was the best candidate by a long shot.

I was picking up the phone to call the first one when my cell phone started dinging. Damn. I'd completely forgotten about the monthly meeting with the board of directors. Fantastic. I groaned inwardly and was glad I'd worn my absolute highest and shiniest black pumps. They definitely weren't the kind of shoes you could reasonably run in, or even walk briskly, but I didn't really care. I was a bitch on heels.

I ducked into the ladies' room to make sure I looked good, hair smooth, shirt tucked into my gray pinstriped pencil skirt and deodorant still working.

Check, check, check. I took one breath and grabbed my notebook as I headed to the boardroom.

Forty minutes later, I was trying to keep my attention on the meeting while everyone argued about which pens we should order for the company. These ones wrote better but were $.02 cents more expensive than these ones. I swear, they could turn this into a marathon meeting if they wanted to.

They finally settled on the more expensive ones and that was the final item on the agenda. About time. We were dismissed, but I was accosted by Hal Marksman before I could make my escape. Hal was the oldest member of the board, and had the most clout (and the most money). Usually, if he decided something, there would be a quick battle and then everyone else would change his or her minds and vote in his favor. He was also not my biggest fan.

"Miss Clarke?" Just his voice made me want to cringe and roll my eyes. Why was it that I felt like a teenager again when he talked to me? A stupid, ignorant teenager.

"Yes, Mr. Marksman, how are you?" I plastered a sweet smile on my face and pretended to give a damn. Kissing the collective asses of the members of the board is one of the less pleasant parts of my job.

"Doing well, doing well." He nodded as he said it, but didn't ask how I was. Jerk. I kept my smile in place and begged him with my mind to make this quick. Everyone else was milling around, fighting over the last of the coffee and pastries.

"I hear that you're hiring a new secretary." Obviously. He'd been at Sal's retirement party.

"I am," I said and waited for him to get to the damn point. He stroked the front of his shirt, smoothing it over his potbelly.

"Well, I happen to know that there is a young and very eager fellow named Lucas Blaine that has applied and I strongly suggest that you hire him."

Was he fucking serious? How the hell did he know about Lucas?

WHO WAS THIS LUCAS BLAINE AND WHY WOULDN'T HE LEAVE ME ALONE?

"Oh," I said, because, hell.

"I've heard about him from your father and if I could hire him myself, I would. I'm positively jealous of you." He chuckled and I laughed as well, using my patented "polite fake laugh."

"I, um, I'm just a little flummoxed by your interest in him." Actually, I was a lot flummoxed.

Hal leaned in, as if to share a confidence. Like everyone wasn't listening.

"We've been trying to get him away from . . . the company that shall not be named, for years now. I don't know why he left them, but we want him, and this is the best way to get him here. Start him out easy and then we can slide him right where we want him. You can put in a good word for him with Walter, and before you know it, we'll have him on our side, working for us." God, some of that sounded dirty, and I had to fight the urge to laugh. I'd slid him right where I wanted him on Saturday, but I was pretty sure Hal wasn't thinking about the same thing.

"This company needs him, Miss Clarke." Now it was my turn to talk again. "And working with you is the best place."

"I'll consider him," I said, knowing that it was already a done deal. What the board wanted, the board got.

"You need to do what's best for you, but remember that the needs of the many overpower the needs of the few." Oh my God. He was using Spock Logic on me and he probably didn't even know it. I stifled another laugh as a cough and nodded and tried and stop myself from telling him to live long and prosper as he gave me one last hard look before he went to take the Danish that someone has saved for him.

Dad gave me a look and then followed me back to my office.

"What was that about?"

"Oh nothing, he just 'strongly suggested' that I hire Lucas as my assistant and by 'strongly suggested' I mean he said I had to because the company needs him." I sat down in my chair in a huff and pinched the bridge of my nose with my hand. This day needed to be over two hours ago.

"Yes, Hal and I had a chat about him, and I have to agree with him. There's no one else that's so overqualified. We would be lucky to have him." Lucas Blaine should have changed his name to Jesus Christ, because everyone seemed to be worshipping him. What I didn't get was why he wanted this dinky little assistant job, if he was qualified, and he obviously didn't need money. It just wasn't adding up.

Dad interrupted my wonderings. "Unless you have any overwhelming reasons not to hire him?" Other than the fact that I'd slept with him?

"None at all," I said with another smile that made my teeth hurt.

"Good. I'll be glad to have someone to pick up the slack for you. You're working too hard again." Dad always thought I was working too hard because I was still his little princess and I always would be. I also couldn't say no to him.

"I'm fine. I'll just check his references and call him with the good news." I would rather swallow five very large and venomous spiders than call Lucas and tell him he'd gotten the job. I could ask Mrs. Andrews to do it for me, but that would have made me look like a coward. I had to do this for the good of the company. My company.

Mr. Craig, one of the other Vice Presidents who also had a billion other titles, was waiting for me when I got back to my office. I wasn't in the best mood, and I just gave him a terse nod as I walked back into my office. Of course he followed me in.

"Can I help you?"

"Oh, no. I was just wondering how the meeting went." He had been curiously absent, but Mr. Craig wasn't a big fan of meetings. He liked to spend as much company time on the golf course wooing clients as he could. He wasn't a bad guy, just lazy.

"We went with the fancy pens. Anything else is in the minutes they send around." Somehow, files had started multiplying on my desk like rabbits.

"Oh well. I just wanted to check in." Why was he checking in WITH ME? He snapped his fingers as if he had just remembered something.

"Could you let Walter know I need to leave early today? I have an appointment with my acupuncturist. My sciatica's been acting up," he said, holding his back and cringing in a comical way. Yeah, maybe you should stop playing so much fucking golf.

I was in rare form due to the Lucas Blaine situation. I might have also been PMS-ing. And, it wasn't my freaking job to tell my dad that he had to leave early. Grow a pair and do it yourself. But I didn't tell him to do that. Instead, I said, "sure, I'll tell him." Mr. Craig gave me the thumbs up and strolled back to his office, whistling as I banged my head on my desk.

Lucas Blaine had quite a fan club. All of his references ranted and raved and sang his praises and I was beginning to wonder if they had also slept with him.

I hung up with the last one, a woman who praised him like the second coming, and then it was time.

Of course I had to organize my drawers, arrange my pens, get more coffee and reapply my makeup before I did it. I put it off as long as I could, but I was really drowning under my work here. I had been completely avoiding my voicemail box.

Taking one deep breath, I picked up the phone and willed my voice to be steady, and my brain to provide me with the appropriate words.

"Hello?"

Mmm, that voice. I paused for a second and forgot what I was supposed to be doing, so I cleared my throat.

"Hello, may I please speak to Lucas Blaine?" I knew it was him, but I didn't want him to know I recognized his voice from just the hello.

"This is he." Swoon.

"Hi, Mr. Blaine, this is Aurora Clarke from Clarke Enterprises. I was just calling to tell you that you got the assistant job."

"Hello again, Aurora Clarke." Oh, the way his voice caressed my name made me quiver.

Stop that.

"That is very good news to hear. I have been sitting here and waiting for your call." There were sounds in the background and I could tell he wasn't at home.

"I'm sure you were," I said sarcastically, dropping all pretense of being professional.

He laughed and I wanted to strangle him through the phone.

"So, when do I start?"

I gritted my teeth before I answered.

"How about tomorrow? We can get you set up on the company software and Mrs. Andrews can show the ropes. Be here at eight."

"I'll be there. How do you take your . . . coffee?" Oh, he was going to make this a miserable experience, wasn't he?

"Look, whatever happened, happened and I think we're both grown-up enough to put it behind us. Besides," I said with a smirk I hoped he would hear in my voice, "if it's a choice between he said, she said, I win. Cream and sugar. Eight o'clock."

Before he could say anything else, I hung up on him, slamming the phone into the receiver, but I swear I could still hear him laughing.

Chapter Eight

As fate would have it, I was running late the next morning. Traffic was horrendous due to some construction and I skidded into the lobby, nearly wiping out on the smooth floor. A hand reached out and prevented my face-plant.

"Good morning, Miss Clarke." I peered into those blue/gray eyes and they were smiling and laughing at me.

Damn, he looked good in the morning. I stood up and adjusted myself, trying to gain composure.

"Coffee?" he said, holding out a tray with two cups on it. "The one with the happy face is yours."

I give him a look and took the happy face cup. I hadn't had a chance to have my fix yet, and I was jonesing.

"Shall we?" he said after I took a sip. He turned and didn't wait before striding toward the elevator and hitting the Up button. I sighed to myself and followed him. This time he was dressed in a perfect gray suit and sapphire tie, and the diamond stud was back in his ear.

"I never wear my nipple ring to the office, if that's what you're wondering," he said when he caught me staring at his chest and wondering that very thing. My face flamed red and I tried to glare at him.

"I wasn't thinking that."

Yes I was.

"Yes you were."

"Shut up." *Wow, brilliant response, Rory. You sound exactly sixteen years old.*

He just grinned and handed me a bag.

"Cheese Danish, cherry Danish, croissant and donut with strawberry frosting and sprinkles. I wasn't sure what you liked." His face was smug and I wanted to smack it and then smack a kiss on it.

He seemed to read my thoughts again and turned his head to the side and moved his face closer to mine. I was captivated by his eyes and the enclosed space of the elevator and his smell and . . .

The elevator dinged and the doors slid open, cutting off the moment. Lucas pulled back and shook his head and tried to hand me the bag again. I snatched it from him.

I was going to eat every single pastry in that bag. I was an equal opportunity pastry eater, but the strawberry donut was my first choice, though I wasn't going to tell Lucas that.

He said hello to Mrs. Andrews as he walked past her desk and she gave him a genuine smile, as if she was happy to see him. God, not her, too.

I showed him around the office again, the break room, bathrooms, copier, etc., and he was too close for comfort, even though he was almost completely silent.

He followed me all the way to my desk and I was about to snap at him to stop following me, but then I realized I hadn't showed him to his desk.

Get your head in the game, Clarke.

I set down my coffee and the bag of pastries.

"Your, um, desk is right over there," I said, pointing to the desk that was right in the middle of the hallway across from my office. Granted, I had a door in between us, but I almost never closed it (BLB, Before Lucas Blaine) unless I needed privacy, and that was rare. So basically, we'd be facing each other. All day. Every day.

Those stormy eyes would be staring at me for at least forty hours a week. More if we had a big project to work on.

He faced me and walked backwards to his desk with a come hither smile. He wasn't making this easy. Well, I could make it hard.

Head in the game, Clarke.

I tried to snap my spine straight and made sure my heels made the maximum amount of noise as I crossed the space between us and started explaining everything.

We did have a dedicated person whose job it was to train new employees, but I was a bit of a control freak and I'd rather teach him once and have him do it the way I wanted, than have to spend time making him unlearn one way and relearn my way.

This meant there was a lot of leaning over his shoulder and trying not to breathe in his scent too much, or let our faces get close when he turned to ask me a question. I'm pretty sure he did that on purpose, along with leaning back in his chair and bumping into me, and the half-dozen chest grazes.

It was evident within a few minutes that he was smart, he learned fast and he could remember it. I'd had a little hope that he'd turn out to be a moron, but he was sharp and took everything I could throw at him. I needed some space, so I started him out with the task of going through my inbox and flagging anything that might be important and deleting all the chain emails that were against company policy, but still seemed to make the rounds anyway.

"I've got this, boss," he said with another smirk as I walked back to my desk and I could feel his searing gaze on my ass. I tossed my hair back and closed the door behind me, breathing a small sigh of relief before going for my coffee and belated breakfast.

An hour later I was knee deep in approving a presentation and wondering why it was that the people I worked with could speak html and CSS, but not English when there was a knock at my door. Wonder who that could be?

I crumpled the empty pastry bag and shoved it in the trash bin before answering. For some reason I didn't want him to know I'd binged and eaten everything due to the fact that he stressed the hell out of me.

"Yes?" I kept my voice calm and cool and glued my eyes to the computer screen before the doorknob turned and he poked his head in.

"I'm sorry to interrupt. I just wanted to know if you needed anything. Coffee, or . . ." he trailed off with a smile. Bad boy.

"I think I'm all set for now, but thank you. How are the emails coming?" I pretend to type something on the computer so I had an excuse not to look at his face. His freckles were especially cute today.

"You seem to have a lot of spam coming in, so I reconfigured your filters. I hope you don't mind." That made me look up. I hadn't messed with that in months, and not since the last software upgrade.

You'd think, living my entire life inside this company, I would be on top of something like that.

"Oh, thank you. Yeah, I have noticed a lot of funny stuff getting through, but I've been so swamped I haven't been able to deal with it."

He gave me a smile and it was like I'd given him another gold star.

"You're welcome. Anytime. Just let me know if or when you need something, Miss Clarke." He managed to make the last part sound just a little bit dirty.

"Thank you, Mr. Blaine." I called my last assistant Sal, but that was because he treated me like a granddaughter and that was just the way things were. I would have to keep the boundaries very clear with this one so he didn't get any ideas.

And so I didn't get any ideas, either.

Sloane texted me and asked if I wanted to have a lunch date, and I was thrilled because I needed her. I needed my best friend to vent to.

I gathered up my purse and locked my computer and walked myself to Lucas' desk. Mr. Blaine's desk.

I wanted to smash my head on his desk.

I swear, everything I thought turned dirty in his presence. I shoved it aside as he looked up from the computer. His earring winked at me.

"I'm going to lunch. When I come back, you can go. You, can, um call me if there's an emergency, but I'm sure Mrs. Andrews would be able to help you out with whatever you need."

"Thank you very much, Miss Clarke. I hope you have a wonderful lunch," he said with such a sweet voice and such a sweet smile I knew he was messing with me. Well, it was about time.

"Thank you, Mr. Blaine, I'm suuuurrreee I will." With a wink, I strutted slowly away from the desk and I knew he was watching me and I hoped he was remembering how awesome in bed I was because that was NEVER happening again.

"You look all hot and bothered," Sloane said as I sat down and she shoved a mimosa across the tablecloth at me.

"Do I?" God, I hoped not. I didn't want anyone at the office getting wind of my history with Mr. Blaine. I pulled out my compact and checked my face for signs of hotness or botheredness. My eyes were a little wide, but other than that I looked the same. Warm blonde hair, brown eyes, small nose.

"Jesus, take a Valium, why don't you?" I picked up the mimosa glass instead as the waiter made his way over and I ordered a pear and goat cheese salad and a bowl of minestrone. I figured it was the healthiest option since I'd had so many pastries this morning. My ass couldn't deal with too many more calories.

"So, how is it going?" Sloane said as she dug into her steak sandwich. Yes, she was one of those bitches who could eat ANYTHING and stay skinny without purging. Feel free to hate her for it.

"It's fine so far, although he has ogled my ass so many times, I feel like I should walk in slow motion so he can better admire it. Or maybe I should play sexy slow motion walking music *while* I walk in slow motion." I was babbling and Sloane listened without interruption. This was our thing.

When I was done she made a sympathetic face.

"Well, I don't know him, but I know you and I know that you take your job seriously and you won't let anything get in the way of it. So I know that you're going to put on your big girl panties and go back to work and be a goddamn professional." She raised her glass and I clinked it with mine.

That's right. I was a goddamn professional.

No guy with stormy eyes and a fuck me smile and a magic tongue was going to stand in the way of that.

Because I was a goddamn professional.

My confidence in my ability to be professional lasted as long as it took for me to walk to his desk and tell him that he could take his break.

The second I met those eyes and saw that mouth forming words, I was lost again.

"You okay?" He caught on, of course.

"Yeah, I just had a mimosa and I think it went to my head." *Wow, brilliant save there Rory.*

"Or maybe you're just going to swoon in my presence. Would you like me to catch you and then fetch the smelling salts?" And just like that, I was wondering how I ever found him attractive.

"You get a half hour. No more. Be back here at one-thirty or you're fired." I stomped back to my office and shut the door. Seconds later, I heard his footsteps walking toward the elevator. I turned on my computer and threw myself back into work. Ah, work. My sanctuary.

I went back to working on the presentation, but checked the clock every few seconds. At one-thirty on the dot, there was a knock at my door. Damn.

"I'm back, Miss Clarke," he said, actually coming into the office this time and closing the door behind him. The place felt like it grew increasingly smaller until it was barely a closet.

"Thank you for your punctuality, Mr. Blaine." I straightened some papers on my desk, trying to breathe normally.

"You are most welcome, Miss Clarke," he said, sauntering toward the desk and resting his hands on it and leaning forward. "And please, if there's *anything* I can do for you, *anything*, all you have to do is ask." His voice dipped into a lower register that made my insides do funny backflips and cartwheels as his face came within a foot of mine.

"Anything," he breathed.

I found myself involuntarily leaning forward and our lips were a whisper away . . .

And there was a knock at the door and we broke apart like teenagers getting busted under the bleachers. I banged my knee on the desk and he nearly crashed into the credenza near the door trying to put space between us.

"Come in," I said, rubbing my knee and trying not to wince too much as Lucas (Mr. Blaine) straightened his tie.

"Sorry to bother you, dear, but I just had a call for you and I didn't see Mr. Blaine at his desk, but clearly he is here. Would you like me to transfer it?" Mrs. Andrews, bless her heart, seemed totally oblivious that she'd walked into a wall of sexual tension. Still, it's a little strange that she walked all the way down here to tell me about a call when she could have just called my extension and the put the call through. Huh.

"Who is it?"

"It's Fintan Herald." Fabulous.

"Sure, you can transfer him, Mrs. Andrews." I gave her a smile and she nodded, her hand still on the doorknob.

"Of course, dear."

"Nice to see you, Mrs. Andrews," Mr. Blaine said to her.

"It's nice to see you as well, Mr. Blaine. I hear we have high expectations for you." Obviously, she'd talked to Dad about him. I would have been surprised if they hadn't talked about him.

"I will do my best to live up to those expectations and exceed them."

"You'd better," Mrs. Andrews said with a mock straight face. Yup, she was part of his fan club. She gave me a smile before leaving. A few seconds later my phone rang with the transferred call from Fin.

"I need to take this," I said, as Lucas (JE-SUS CHRIST, MR. BLAINE!) started to back out of the office and got back to his desk.

"Of course, of course." He seemed a little stunned, and I wasn't sure if it was to do with nearly running into the credenza, or if it was something else. Ten seconds ago, he was ready to leap over the desk and molest me.

Something I'd learned when I was very young still rang true.

Boys are weird.

I shook my head as my phone rang and I picked up Fin's call.

The second call with Fin was shorter than the first; he seemed busy so we decided to meet up on Friday afternoon instead because he couldn't do Wednesday. He let me pick the place, which was considerate.

I hung up and realized I wasn't actually dreading our little coffee date. I was also dying to know what he looked like now, but I wasn't going to creep on the internet and spoil it.

A sharp rap sounded at my door.

"Yes?"

It was Mr. Blaine and he was looking distinctly grumpy. His forehead was all furrowed, which, actually, was kind of . . .

"Your mail is here, Miss Clarke," he said, holding up a few of interoffice envelopes that probably needed my signature. It was nothing that required him to knock on my door. I would have gotten them later.

"Thanks, Mr. Blaine, you can put them right there," I said, indicating the basket on the edge of my desk for those very things. It was even marked MAIL.

He dropped them in the basket and his grumpy face didn't change. I wanted to jokingly ask him what he'd got his panties in a twist about, but I was determined to make this a professional relationship from now on, at least on my side.

"Would you, um, mind bringing me some coffee, Mr. Blaine?" If anything, the grumpy look deepened. I didn't ask for a kidney.

"Cream and sugar?"

"Yes, please. Thank you." He turned on his heel and walked out. I shook my head and started sorting through the mail.

He came back a few minutes later and slammed the coffee down on my desk, so much so that it sloshed out of the cup. That was it. I waved good-bye to any semblance of being professional.

"What is your problem?" I said, jumping up and grabbing some tissues from the top desk drawer to blot the coffee puddle that was racing toward some very important papers.

"Shit, shit, stop!" I said, blotting the coffee and trying to talk it out of ruining everything. A hand reached out and shoved the papers to the side as I mopped up the rest of the coffee, which was pretty damn hot, by the way.

I dropped the soggy tissues in the trash and pulled out a cleaning wipe from the container that I also kept in my desk.

"I'm so sorry," he said when I finally looked up and saw him trying to fix the mess that had been made of my desk.

"It's not a big deal," I said, even though I was kind of pissed. "Is there something wrong?" I tossed the wipe and took the papers from him. He didn't know my arranging system yet.

"No, nothing. I'm so sorry." He moved around the other side of the desk, as if he was leaving.

"It's okay, Lucas. Mr. Blaine. Are you sure you're okay?" He stopped and gave me a tight smile that didn't reach those gorgeous eyes.

"It's nothing, I promise. I'll get over it."

"I hope so, because I'm not sure my desk can take any more." I was very fond of my desk. It had been a present from Dad when I got promoted and I planned on taking it with me, even if I changed offices.

"I'm sorry," he said, and then he left as if he was running away from something, and I was left wondering what the hell that was all about.

Chapter Nine

"I thought you would need this," Sloane said, handing me a glass of wine when I stumbled in the door that night. I hadn't been that tired after work since I'd pulled a few all-nighters a month ago.

"You're my favorite," I said, and gulped the wine. Ah, sweet elixir.

"I also took the liberty of ordering takeout," she said, holding out her arm like a bimbo from a game show presenting a brand new stove as she gestured to the bags and boxes on the counter.

I collapsed on the couch and downed the rest of the wine.

"I didn't know sexual tension would make me so tired. I mean, it's not like we were ready to rip each other's clothes off in a fit of lust, but it definitely wasn't easy." Watching his mouth as he talked, remembering what it could do on my body . . .

"You're such a liar. You totally were ready to rip each other's clothes off in a fit of lust. I bet you eye fucked each other all day. I know I would. He's not really my type, but damn. I'd be on my back on the desk for him." I gave her a look and went to stuff my face with takeout, which included pizza, a tortellini salad from my favorite Italian place, chow mein and baklava. Our tastes were eclectic.

"You're being so nice to me lately," I said when I sat down on the couch again with a full plate.

"I'm just buttering you up to ask you a favor."

"It must be a big one. What do you want?"

She took a big bite of chow mein and chewed it before she answered.

"I need your body." Ah, that was what I figured. Sloane had all sorts of mannequins and models for her clothes, but sometimes she wanted to try them on a real person. I was usually her guinea pig, but she normally just started putting the stuff on me without asking.

"Okay, why the big production. You know I never say no."

"Well . . . here's the thing. I'm working on a new line. Of undergarments, but ones for real women." She wouldn't look at me.

"So you're saying you need me for my ass." I guess I should have been offended, but I had no delusions about my body or the size of it.

"Not just your ass. I need your tits as well," she said, smiling. I set my food on the coffee table and stood up in a huff.

"You only want me for my body. I thought I meant more to you than that!" I pretended to cry and Sloane got up and hugged me.

"I love your sexy mind, but I really only need your bod. Please?"

I sighed like it was the hardest thing in the world, but turned around.

"Fine. But you'd better buy me some flowers afterward and call me the next day."

She clapped her hands and I knew that the food would have to wait. Fashion waited for no man. Or woman, in this case.

"What is that?" I said, pointing to the mess of black lace and red ribbons that was laid out on Sloane's cutting table.

"That is the first piece I've been working on. See, here's the thing. I was thinking that I'm good at the clothes part, right? But what about what's under them? What if I could sell someone an entire outfit, down to the undergarments? Why wouldn't I? Plus, the lingerie market is huge and it requires a lot less material, in theory, and it gives me a chance to be a little naughty. So. Here it is!" She picked it up and I saw that it was basically a bra with panties attached by crisscrossing red ribbons, with little bows on the ends where they meet the bra and panties. It's more of an outfit than a set of underwear.

"How the hell do I get into it?" It looked impossible. Like half the moves in the Kama Sutra, or going to Coach without buying something.

"You're such a drama queen. Here, you can snap the ribbon part off. So it's like a little extra. You can wear the bra and panties without it." She showed me how to get the ribbon part off, leaving just the bra and panties, which were cute on their own.

"You're going to make me try it on now, aren't you?"

"Yup," Sloane said, shoving me toward my bedroom. I would also be expected to model as well, and I hoped the panties would be big enough to cover everything they need to cover. Good thing I got waxed on a regular basis.

I stripped down and slid on the panties first. Success! I almost did a little victory dance in front of the mirror. The bra was also my exact size, with no spillage. I got myself situated and then snapped on the ribbon parts and checked myself out.

Wow. It actually looked good. Sexy. Like my body was a nice little present to unwrap. I turned and it looked good from the back too. Not bad, not bad. I bent over and stood up and twisted side to side. It was actually pretty comfortable. Not as binding as I'd thought it would be.

There was a frantic knock at the door.

"How does it look?" I rolled my eyes and opened the door and Sloane dragged me out. I stood still as she stepped back, came forward and adjusted, and walked around me like I was a mannequin. I was used to this. If I moved she'd get mad, so I stayed as still as I could until she finished her inspection.

"What do you think? Does it fit well? Do you feel comfortable in it?" I shrugged my shoulders and twisted again and met Sloane's worried eyes.

"I love it. I feel totally sexy."

"Fabulous!" Her smile was a mile wide and she clapped her hands. "You look smoking hot, by the way. Like, if I swung the other way, I would have made my move already. All you need are those red heels and you're in business."

The red shoes would be awesome with this.

"Okay, I'm going to put my clothes on now, because I'm hungry and it's a little cold in here."

Sloane gave me the thumbs up and I heard her going to the kitchen and putting things in the microwave as I went back to my bedroom.

Once I was dressed again, we finished our dinner and continued our Sandra Bullock marathon. Sloane was twitchy and I could sense that she wanted to ask for something else when she made me a cup of tea and brought it over.

"What do you want now?" I said, taking it from her.

"Would you wear it tomorrow? I want to see how it works when you wear it all day. You know, real world experience."

"Real world experience for your underwear?" Like a test drive?

"Rory, I have to make sure that these products work for real people. And you're a real person, so we've got to give it a test run. Please?"

I could sort of see what she was talking about, but I really wished she'd find someone else to do this. Still, she'd been really good to me lately, so I'd be a bitch to say no.

"Okay, okay. I just need to figure out what to wear over it so it doesn't show." Anything white was out, so I went with a black shirt and tan leather skirt and my red shoes. I laid them out next to the underwear outfit that night and sighed. The things that Sloane talked me into.

The next day I had a little secret under my clothes. I felt like people knew, even though that was impossible. I wished I could forget that I was wearing it, but every time I moved the ribbons caressed my skin and I remembered, and felt like I had the word SLUTTY HARLOT stamped on my forehead. Not that what I was wearing was remotely slutty or harlotty (if that's even a word), but I did feel a little naughty. It was definitely not office-appropriate underwear.

I was dreading seeing Lucas (Mr. Blaine, for the love of CHRIST), because I knew if anyone would figure out my little underwear secret, it would be him. He was the kind of guy who could see under your clothes whether you wanted him to or not. Like Superman.

Correction. I wanted him to see under my clothes, it just wasn't appropriate for the workplace. Any other place was fair game . . .

"Good morning, Miss Clarke." There was another bag on my desk, along with my coffee.

"You didn't tell me what you liked, so I got everything again today." Oh, hell. I was going to gain forty pounds if I didn't tell him.

"You have to stop doing that, Mr. Blaine. I can get my own breakfast," I said as I snatched the bag, pulled out a donut and handed him the bag back.

"Strawberry frosted donut. Noted." He grinned and took out the cherry Danish and I swore his eyes traveled up and down my body twice and my cheeks started getting red. HE KNEW.

"You look very nice today, Miss Clarke, if I may say so without incurring a sexual harassment reprimand." *Oh, aren't you Mr. Smooth?* He said it with one of those smiles that only lifted one corner of his mouth. Yum.

"Thank you, Mr. Blaine. You look very dapper yourself." He did, in a grey pinstriped suit with a dark purple tie. Not that many guys could pull off a purple tie, but he made it look easy. And sexy. Very sexy.

"Well, thank you for the breakfast. I'll get yours tomorrow. Cherry Danish? Black coffee?" I said, trying to dial my bitch level back a bit.

"Perfect." His eyes did another sweep, and I swore this guy had x-ray vision. I should start calling him Clark Kent, even though he looked nothing like Clark.

I gave him what I hoped was a composed smile as I headed into my office and closed the door.

By midmorning I was glad I had the sexy underwear on because it gave me a little more confidence when I had to deal with an asshole on the phone who was unhappy with one of our products and DEMANDED to speak to someone in charge.

Of course, he'd not only been using it on an ancient computer, but he'd bought the wrong model and was mad that it didn't do what he thought it should. Usually those calls got routed somewhere else, but sometimes they slipped through the cracks.

I finally got the guy off the phone and went out to get some coffee and cool down. I hated it when people got me riled up. I could usually handle myself, but that guy had just pushed my buttons.

I didn't meet Mr. Blaine's eyes, but I could feel him watching me. Great. Now he was going to think I was some stupid girl who couldn't deal with a phone call.

I got my coffee and sipped it, leaning against the counter in the break room and just trying to bring myself back to normal by doing some deep breathing with my eyes closed.

"Are you okay?" I knew he was going to follow me. I wasn't sure how I knew, but I knew.

"Yeah, fine. Just taking a breather." I didn't open my eyes, but I could hear his suit swish as he stepped closer. Sexy sound.

"You sure about that? You looked upset. Miss Clarke." The last part was added in a low voice and accompanied by a hand on my shoulder.

My eyes opened and he was right in front of me.

"I-I'm fine. Seriously." *Yeah, the stutter made that completely believable.*

He leaned closer and I could smell his cologne. Not too much, just enough to know that he was there and that he smelled incredible. This was entirely inappropriate work behavior, but right in that second, it was kind of nice.

I'd never had someone that I could vent to at work. I'd never wanted to because I didn't want to look weak, or like I was just a whiny princess that had gotten the job because of her Daddy.

"Okay. If you're sure," he said, his hand slipping down my shoulder and then moving across my stomach. I froze, even though there was no way he could know about the sexy undergarment I had on.

The second I flinched, he removed his hand, mistaking my flinch for one that meant I didn't want him to touch me. Well, I did, but he shouldn't. Those were two different things.

"I'm sure," I said, sliding away from him along the counter. He smiled and leaned over.

"Let me know if you're not later on. And I hope this isn't sexual harassment, because you do look incredible today." Before I could answer, he backed away, turned and was gone.

I was left to slump against the counter and wonder how long both of us could hold out before we had a repeat performance like the one in his apartment. Mr. Buzzy just wasn't doing it for me at the moment. I needed a real man. A real man with a real penis and real hands and a real mouth that could sweetly torture me all night . . .

Keep it in your pants, Rory. Get back to work.

My fortitude was tested again later in the afternoon as I brought Mr. Blaine with me to his first meeting. It was one of those boring ones about projections and loss leaders and economic terms I'd studied in school but hadn't bothered to keep in my brain after the test. I was forcing him to take notes for me in case I missed anything.

My thigh was practically touching his and I was trying to keep my lust bottled up for the hour and a half that I had to sit next to him in the darkened boardroom as our CFO droned on and went through chart after chart. Why did the room have to be so dark?

I shifted in my seat and re-crossed my legs under the table. Mr. Blaine shifted next to me and his leg brushed mine. Accidentally? On purpose?

I wanted to look at him, but he was on my right and the presentation was on my left so I couldn't without being terribly obvious about it. And then it happened again. He slowly dragged his leg against mine. I froze and waited. Then his hand brushed my thigh. It was so light I wouldn't have felt it unless all my nerve endings were freaking out right now. I squirmed a bit and stared at the presentation packet in front of me. Everyone else turned the page, and I hurried to follow. I had no idea what we were talking about.

The hand came back, and I almost slapped it away. I wrote *Stop it!* on my notes and slid it so he could read it. I swore I heard him laugh before he used his finger to write NO on my thigh. I could freak out. I could have his ass for harassment, or I could screw with him.

I chose the latter.

I uncrossed my legs and tipped them toward him, sighing just a little bit as I fiddled with the hem of my skirt, inching it upwards just a tiny bit. I was satisfied by a sharp intake of breath from the seat next to me.

Dad wasn't at this meeting because he was schmoozing a potential client, or else I never would have been this brazen. Everyone else was in "meeting mode" and totally absorbed in the charts and numbers and such.

Then I took the hand that had come back to rest on my thigh and guided it around my leg and in between, and then under my skirt. His fingers twitched and I could feel him wondering what the hell I was doing, even though I couldn't see him. Once his hand was completely under my skirt, I thought he could figure out what I was asking him to do as I shifted myself closer to his hand and put both hands on the table and stared at the presentation as if my life depended on it.

After only a moment of hesitation, his hand worked its way upward and came in contact with my over-sensitized flesh. Good boy.

His fingers fluttered for a moment on the very inside of my thigh before brushing across my center. I had to fight the sigh that almost escaped my lips. I felt him shift so he could get a better angle and then his fingers danced across me in a staccato pattern that was making things a little wet down there.

Have you ever been fingered during a tedious meeting and had to stop yourself from sighing in pleasure? Yeah, not easy.

The moment it was the hardest was when he moved my panties aside and started stroking my clit and fingering my entrance. I didn't know he'd take it quite that far, but it was my own fault for having this idea in the first place. As he stroked me toward orgasm, the meeting started getting hazy and I had to bite my lip to stay silent. I kept looking around, but everyone was still engrossed in the charts. Or whatever those were. My eyes couldn't really focus on them.

It soon became a struggle to keep my hips still as they wanted to thrust toward his hand and I knew that I had to put a stop to this. Against nearly every instinct in my body, I grabbed his hand and removed it slowly from under my skirt and placed it back on his leg. Out of the corner of my eye, I could see that he was staring at the presentation.

You'll finish this later I scribbled on the notepad and slid it toward him. It felt very much like we were passing notes in middle school again. He took the pad and wrote something before moving it back to me.

Where?

Hm, good question. Most of the places here were out of the question, seeing as how anyone could walk it in at any time. Which was kind of sexy, but would prove disastrous. Ah! We had a room that was reserved for overseas calls that was soundproof and locked when it wasn't in use, and I just happened to have a key. BOOM. This was happening.

Conference room. End of hall. After meeting. I have a key.

There was no reaction that I could see, but his hand caressed my leg and wrote one word. YES. And then he added what I could only interpret as an exclamation point.

I almost laughed and had to swallow it and make it a cough. Finally, the presentation ended and the lights came on. I saw that my notes were a little incriminating, so I scribbled them out and then crumpled them up in my hand. I'd put them through my mega shredder later.

Standing was a little tricky and then there was a hand to help me up.

"Good meeting, wasn't it, Miss Clarke?" Mr. Blaine said as I met his eyes and blushed.

"Yeah. Very good. Very productive, Mr. Blaine. I'm very pleased with the projections." Oh God, that sounded dirtier than I meant it. He just grinned at me and gathered up his notes.

"Is there *anything* else I can do for you?" I almost smacked him in the arm, convinced someone was watching us, or they could at least smell the aura of lust that hung over both of us.

"Why don't you type up your notes and then send me a copy so we can compare them?" I arched an eyebrow at him and hoped he got my meaning.

"As you wish, Miss Clarke." And then he bowed. He freaking bowed and I almost laughed out loud as he walked out of the room.

"How is he working out?" A voice said, interrupting my watching of Lucas as he walked away.

I turned to find Hal Marksman standing right beside me. One of the board members was asked to attend all relevant meetings, and it was his turn this week. Of course.

"Very well, Mr. Marksman. He learns fast and retains the information and he has common sense."

"Good, good." He nodded and I looked for my escape. "I have a very good feeling about that boy." Or man, seeing as how he's an adult.

"Me too. If you'll excuse me, I've been supervising him on a project and we're nearly finished, and I'd like to get it done today." I had no idea how I said this with a straight face, but I managed.

"Yes, yes, of course. Carry on." I seized my moment and scurried away. The hallway down to the locked room was empty, so I made a dash for it. I unlocked the door on the first try and shut it behind me, taking out my phone. I had Mr. Blaine in my contacts in case he ever needed to call me for any reason when we weren't in the office.

Count to 100 and then knock three times.

Yes, this plan was convoluted, but it was the only way to make it work unless we left the office, and we both had too much stuff to do today.

I waited what felt like hours with my heart pounding and my body still keyed up from earlier. I could probably finish myself, but that was so much less fun.

Knock. Knock. Knock.

I cracked the door open and yanked him in.

"Did anyone see you?" I said as I locked the door behind him.

"No. The hallway was empty." The room wasn't big, and it seemed to be getting smaller by the moment. I kept the lights off because I was convinced if we turned them on, someone would see and know that we were in here. Soft light filtered in between the window shades, so it wasn't completely dark.

Paranoid much? Yes, I was.

I turned to face him and he was a breath away.

"So," he said.

"So," I said.

And then his mouth was on mine, devouring it, and it was like he had more hands than just two because they were EVERYWHERE and my skirt was on the floor and my shirt was joining it and then his shirt followed and then he was bending me back on the desk and kissing me so hard I couldn't breathe, but I didn't think it really mattered.

"What's this?" he said when he finally pulled back enough to notice the lingerie. His fingers stroked the ribbons that crossed my stomach. "It's not my birthday, but it feels like it."

"My roommate made it," I said breathlessly as he traced the lines of the ribbons.

"She's very talented. It's almost too pretty to spoil. Almost. Shall I unwrap you?"

"If you don't, you're fired," I said and he laughed. "There are snaps." I felt the need to direct him so he didn't rip it or ruin it.

"Got it." He found the snaps and released the ribbon part, easing it off me before running his hands down my overheated skin.

"Happy un-birthday to me," he said before his mouth was on me again and he was climbing onto the table to join me.

"What do you want?" he said, pulling back for a second, his hand on his belt. It was such an honest question that I stopped thinking about my body's needs for a second.

"I want you to kiss me everywhere and I want to kiss you everywhere and I want you inside me until we're both satisfied, but we don't have time for that."

"What a shame," he said pinching one of my nipples through my bra. "But you are the boss, so I should probably satisfy you. Because when the boss is satisfied, everyone is satisfied." As he said it, his hands reached around, unclasped my bra and pulled it over my arms. The table was cold on my bare back, but the rest of me was on fire.

"I wouldn't want to get a poor score on my performance review." And then my panties were gone and I was naked and he was straddling me and kissing me fiercely, his tongue diving and tasting and conquering.

His hands, oh, his hands. Such wonderful hands. One was teasing my left nipple, making it hard and making my right nipple very jealous, and his other hand dived between my legs and started stroking. I was still wet from earlier and he smiled as he slid a finger inside me and I moaned.

"Music to my ears, Miss Clarke." His mouth left me and I whimpered, but then he kissed down to my breasts and spent some quality time on my nipples. I had no idea how much time had passed, but I seriously didn't care. He moved lower and, as much as I wanted him going down on me again, I felt bad that he was spending all our precious time on me.

"You, inside me, now." This time he didn't ask if I was sure. He just reached into his back pocket and pulled out a condom.

"For emergencies," he said as he tore it open with his teeth and shoved his pants to his ankles with my help and then rolled the condom on. He really did have a nice package. I should compliment him on it later.

"Quick and hard?" he said, teasing my entrance like he had the last time.

"Quick and hard," I agreed and he thrust into me so hard my back slammed into the desk with a thud. Good thing the room was soundproof.

I gasped as he pulled back and thrust again as his mouth assaulted mine, and then the two of us were lost and it was hot and rough and I never wanted it to end. I was going to have bruises and I didn't care one bit.

"Are you close?" he said, breaking the kiss for just a moment.

"So close." He reached a hand down and circled my clit, playing with my piercing as he continued to drive both of us closer and closer until . . .

I shuddered around him and then I felt him tense and come himself. Nearly simultaneous orgasms. I'd never had that happen before. Near the end of my relationship with Royce, I'd had to fake a few times and then get Mr. Buzzy to finish the job.

Lucas rolled off me and onto his back on the desk, which was sweaty from our combined efforts.

"Anything else I can do for you, Miss Clarke?" he said, his voice a little breathless.

"No, I think that about covers it, Mr. Blaine." I turned my head and he was grinning at me. "You get my approval."

"Does that mean this will be a regular occurrence? I just want to be sure I'm as prepared as I can be."

"Well, you did have a condom in your back pocket," I said, propping myself up on my elbow.

"I was a Boy Scout. Be prepared." He made the sign with his hand and I rolled my eyes.

"Well, I was never a Girl Scout." I reluctantly peeled myself off the desk. "Ugh, I think there are some cleaning wipes here somewhere." I found some, and also some tissues for Lucas so he could clean himself up. He put the tissues and condom in his pocket, which was probably a good idea. A used condom in the wastebasket was a wee bit suspicious.

I put my clothes back on, and wiped down the table and sprayed some air freshener that I'd also found in a cabinet for good measure. Hopefully no one would come in here for the rest of the day so it could air out. That's the part you never think about when you decide to have sex in the office: the cleanup.

I heard the zip of Lucas' pants and we turned to face one another.

"How's my hair?" I said.

"Honestly? Thoroughly fucked." I didn't have a mirror, but I used my hands to feel my head and it was definitely not good.

"Here," he said, motioning to me to turn around. He took my hair down from the hairband and started combing through it with his fingers.

"I have two nieces," he said in answer to my unspoken question.

"Oh." He smoothed my hair back, then gathered it and twisted it back into a low ponytail like someone who had done it a fair share of times.

"There." I reached back and it was an improvement.

"Thanks."

"Anytime. It's been a business doing pleasure with you." He gave me a quick smile and I realized that his hair was pretty fucked, too. I motioned for him to lean down and I ran my fingers through it, trying to get it back to how it looked before.

I gave up.

"Don't worry. It always looks like this." He kissed my cheek and then motioned for the door.

"I'll go first, yes?" I nodded and he slowly opened the door after I unlocked it. "Coast is clear." I gave him the go-ahead and he walked out of the room like he was just taking a stroll, then headed toward the break room. Smart. I left the door open a crack and waited, my heart pounding.

"Is there someone in here?"

My heart was no longer pounding; it had stopped. The door opened and it was Mrs. Andrews, peering in. I dropped to my knees.

"Oh, hello dear. I saw that the door was open, so I wanted to make sure everything was okay." I looked up and tried to look as calm as I could.

"Oh, I was just looking for one of my earrings. I only found one this morning, and I remembered I'd been in here last week and thought maybe I'd dropped it, but no luck." I sighed to really play it up as I got to my feet.

"Would you like me to help you look for it? Four eyes are better than two." She started to come into the room, but I knew if she did that she'd smell the air freshener and then there would be questions that I couldn't answer, or at least come up with a good enough story to explain.

"No, that's all right, I think I've combed this room a million times." I moved toward the door and she had no choice but to back up as I shut it and locked it again.

Sexcapade: Accomplished.

Chapter Ten

I scurried to the bathroom to check my hair after I nearly got busted by Mrs. Andrews and realized I needed to, um, actually do my job. I loved my job. It was challenging and interesting (for the most part) and I wouldn't trade it for anything.

Having an office tryst with Lucas was not going to change that. Or change me. I barely knew the guy, and I wasn't going to let having sex every now and then with him alter my life.

When I got back to my office, Lucas was back at his desk and he gave me a wink as I walked by. I glared a reprimand at him, but then I slowed my walk and wiggled my butt just a tad before going into my office and shutting the door.

Nothing was going to change, except that I would be sexually satisfied and that was a good thing for everyone.

"What's the verdict?" Sloane said the second I walked into the apartment that night.

"Can I just put my bag down?"

"Yes, but while you're doing it tell me how it went with the undies?"

I put my bag down and sighed. To tell the truth, or not to tell the truth? That was the question.

"Well, Lucas seemed to like it when he ripped my clothes off in one of the conference rooms and proceeded to bang me on the table." Sloane's mouth dropped open.

"Are you fucking serious? You had sex in your office?"

"Not in my office. But yeah, we did."

"You dirty slut!" she said slapping my arm, but it was a term of endearment. "I knew you had it in you. Oh my God, you have to give me details. Chlo is coming over by the way. She's been extra emo lately, so I told her she needed to stop moping and listening to Evanescence and come over." That was probably a good idea. I hadn't talked to her in a few days, but I knew Sloane called and texted her frequently to make sure she was doing okay.

"Poor thing. I've never seen her take a breakup this hard. We need to get her laid. Do you know any attractive single lesbians? Or anyone who's bi? We just need a rebound lay and then she should be fine."

"I work in a building full of men. So not really."

"Hm, we'll have to do something about that. But anyway, tell me about the dirty office banging. I want all the details. Who was on top?"

This was going to be a fun night.

It got even worse when Chloe arrived because she wanted to hear all the details as well, because she didn't want to talk about her breakup or rebounds or anything about herself, so I was forced to tell the story again, and against my will, I got hot and bothered and I just wanted to go to my room with Mr. Buzzy and relive the experience alone.

"Wow," Sloane and Chloe said at the same time as I finished my second retelling.

"Yeah," I said as I sipped my second glass of wine and grabbed another chip from the bowl and dipped it in hummus. Yes, we were classy bitches. We also had salsa, animal crackers a jar of frosting, and carrots and celery with ranch dressing. It was unofficial dip night.

"I'm jealous and I don't even like penises. You know, the plural should really be peni," Chloe said, grabbing another chip and popping it into her mouth.

"It should," I agreed.

"So are you going to make it a regular thing?" Lucas (I'd given up on calling him Mr. Blaine. Once a man's penis has been inside you twice, you can't call him that without feeling weird), had asked me the same thing and I really didn't know the answer. The stakes were pretty damn high, and I wasn't about to throw my career away on a fuck buddy.

"I don't know. I should say that I'm going to end it, but I seriously don't want to. And then I feel horrible for even considering it. I love my job and I would never do anything to put it in jeopardy and oh GOD, if my dad ever found out, I can't imagine what he'd say." I shuddered just thinking about it. That would be so much worse than the time I'd gone to an unsupervised party in my teens and gotten drunk and passed out on the front lawn, only to be discovered when the party holder's parents had come back from Martha's Vineyard a day early.

"I shouldn't even be considering if it's going to happen again. I'm a terrible person," I said, shoving my face into the couch.

"No, you're not. You just haven't gotten laid in a while and you need someone to clean out your pipes," Sloane said and Chloe and I made identical sounds of disgust.

"It's times like these that make me glad I'm a lesbian." We all drank to that.

"I don't know what to do. I mean, I know what to do, it's the doing that's the problem."

"Actually, it's the not doing, in this case," Chloe pointed out.

"Yes, that's so helpful. Okay, we did it once. It was great and I got it out of my system. But it's not going to happen anymore. I'm putting my foot down. No more."

"Hear, hear!" Sloane said. We all toasted again and pretty soon the food trays were empty and so was the second bottle of wine.

"Why couldn't he just be a regular guy? Why does he have to be my secretary?" I said, peering into my empty wineglass.

"Don't you mean sexcretary?" Sloane said with a giggle. Two seconds later I joined her and we all giggled helplessly.

"You should make him take a memo," Chloe added, and even though it wasn't that funny, we burst further into hysterics over it and then we started with an endless string of dirty office jokes.

"You should ask him if he'll put his file in your credenza!"

"Defrag your lady system!"

"Put his spam in your inbox!"

After a while we were all laughing so hard that there were tears and we were all gasping and rolling on the floor and I knew that my stomach, in addition to my back (from the vigorous table sex) was going to be sore tomorrow.

"Ass-istant!"

And we were off again.

Chloe had decided to crash on our couch, and getting her up was a chore, even when I wasn't a little hung over. Stupid wine.

"Get up!" I had resorted to smashing her in the face with pillows. That girl slept like the dead. Seriously, sometimes I had to check her breathing to make sure she was still alive.

She made a groaning sound and rolled off the couch. Well, that was a start.

Sloane was hunched over the coffeepot like Golem over the Ring and she growled at me when I asked her for a cup. I was running late, but I didn't care as much as I normally would have. There was that "almost late" period where if you hurried like a madwoman you could get there just a few seconds late and once you've passed that, you're late, so fuck it. This was one of those mornings. I knew I was going to be at least ten minutes late, so I was going to have to text Lucas and let him know so he didn't think I'd been hit by a taxi or something.

In the harsh light of day, things were a little less funny. I couldn't have a sexual relationship with Lucas. I'd been insane to even consider it for a moment. It was wrong, wrong, wrong.

Running late. We need to talk when I get in. I hit Send and waited for a response.

Don't forget my cherry Danish.

And that was it. I was left staring at my phone and thinking, once again, that boys are weird.

All three of us managed to get our butts awake and ready to go to work. One of the upsides of having Sloane as a friend was that she ALWAYS had extra clothes around, so lucky Chloe didn't have to do the walk of shame and instead got to go to her job as the manager of a spa looking like she just stepped off the runway.

"Have a good day at work, dear," Chloe said as I headed toward the T and she waved for a taxi.

"You too. Call me later."

"Not if I call you first." With a wink and a wave, she was off. Silly girl.

I was about to head for the T, but then I realized I had to get Lucas' stupid Danish, so I walked to the closest bakery and then grabbed a taxi.

I was still late, and stressed about talking to Lucas. I wondered if his family called him Lucas. Or Luke. Or Luc. It was a nice name. Especially paired with Blaine. It had a great ring to it.

"Is that my Danish?" The owner of the name with the great ring appeared in front of me as I'd been strolling to my office. Crap, I'd forgotten about him while I was thinking about his name. Which doesn't make any sense, but there you have it.

I held up the bag in front of him and gave him my best smile.

"Your Danish, Mr. Blaine. And here is your coffee. Black. Like your soul." *Shit, I wasn't supposed to be flirting with him. Bad Rory.*

"Thank you very much, Miss Clarke. I was informed by the message on my cellular phone that you wished to speak with me. Would you like to do that now, or would you like to finish your breakfast first?"

Curse him and his adorableness.

"I would like to finish my breakfast and then I will call you, Mr. Blaine," I said before pivoting in my heel and walking to my office.

I didn't let myself laugh before I shut the door.

Trouble. I was in trouble.

NO. I was sticking to my guns. Standing my ground. Putting up walls and fences and slamming my legs shut. A chastity belt might be a good idea right about now.

Sighing, I banged my head on the door. Why was this such a challenge? He was just a guy. Just a guy, like any other. Maybe if I pictured him with Hal Marksman's belly that would turn me off.

I closed my eyes and tried, but that just led to me picturing Lucas without his shirt and then I started thinking about his nipple ring and then I was a lost cause so I went to my desk, drank my coffee and ate my croissant. They were out of my donuts.

I ate slowly and sipped my coffee slowly and went through my inbox and got started for my day slowly. I was putting off talking to Lucas. I even opened one of the presentations that I was required to study and approve and be able to discuss rather than talk to him.

By 9:30, I realized I was becoming the equivalent of a kid hiding in the garage to avoid seeing her parents because she broke Grandma's vase.

I reached for the phone and dialed Lucas' extension.

"Hello, you've reached Aurora Clarke's office, how may I direct your call?" He knew it was me. He could see it on the caller ID, but he was screwing with me.

"Yes, would you mind stepping into my office for a moment, Mr. Blaine?"

I could hear him smirking.

"Yes, of course, Miss Clarke." I hung up before he could say anything else and there was a knock a few moments later.

"Come in." He walked in with authority this time.

"You said you wanted to see me?" He raised one eyebrow as if he thought this is going to turn into a sexfest on my desk. Think again.

"Yes. I wanted to discuss the thing that happened in the conference room yesterday and to tell you that it's not happening again. Ever." I folded my arms and crossed my legs to emphasize that my body was in lockdown. I might want to get a blinking NO TOUCHING sign.

He grinned at me, still thinking I was flirting. "Never, ever?"

"Never, ever. It shouldn't have happened the first time, or the second. It was wrong. Very wrong. So, from here on forward, there will be no touching, no licking, no kissing, no longing glances, no undressing via eye contact, no winking, smirking or lascivious stares of any kind. All of this," I said, motioning to myself, "is off limits. Understand?"

He stared at me for a moment as if he found me fascinating.

"You're so sexy when you think you're in control," he finally said.

"No. I'm not sexy. I'm your boss. And you're my employee, and any relationship other than a strictly professional one is against the code of conduct that we both signed. So enough of that. I'm not sexy."

"Yes, you are. You'll always be sexy." Ditto, buddy.

"Well, I don't know what to do about that, so you're just going to have to deal. The only physical contact we will have from this moment on will be a cordial handshake."

He leaned back in his chair and the studious look got even more . . . studious.

"Such a shame." Lucas shook his head slowly back and forth, as if he was lamenting a great loss. "Well, if that's how you want it, there's nothing I can do to stop you. I'll just take myself back to my desk." He stood, but instead of moving toward the door, he came around the desk.

"What are you doing?"

"I'm going back to my desk," he said, as if I'd asked an insane question. I turned in my chair and he was leaning over me, both hands on the armrests of my chair. Seriously, what was happening?

"This isn't your desk," I said, stating the obvious.

"Oh, it's not? I could have sworn my desk was around here somewhere. Perhaps you could . . . help me look for it?" He leaned closer and a smile danced across his lips.

"Mr. Blaine, stop. You are doing exactly what I just told you not to do. Anyone could walk in. And it's wrong. So—" I was cut off by his hand racing up my leg.

"Is this my desk? Is it here? Or maybe it's further up?" His hand goes higher and I grab his wrist to stop it from going under my dress. Maybe I should start wearing pants. Then he wouldn't have such easy access. That chastity belt would also be a good idea right about now.

"Stop."

He stared into me with those eyes and it was like he could see into every corner of me, to see the things I kept hidden, the things I didn't talk about, the things I wanted to forget. And then he pulled his hand back and stood up.

"I believe my desk is across the hall and I think I can find it on my own. I'll send up a flare if I get lost." Before I could respond, he was out the door and shutting it behind him.

It was time to take more drastic action.

"Sign this," I said a half hour later as I slammed a few sheets of paper down on Mr. Blaine's desk. He looked up in amused bewilderment.

Damn. Even that was sexy. Picture the belly. Gross beer belly with a crooked penis and saggy ballsack hanging . . .

Nope, still sexy.

"To what do I owe the honor of you bringing this to my desk and delivering it personally?" He kept his voice low as one of the other executives walked by for a cup of coffee from the break room.

"Read it. Sign it. Don't speak of it again." This time I was going to have the last word, so I stomped back to my office and purposefully left the door open to show him that I could do this. I could work in his vicinity without exploding into a lusty ball of . . . lust.

I went to my desk and got back to my real job even though I could feel it whenever he glanced at me. I did NOT look at him. Not once. Because I was a goddamn professional.

But then I had to look up when a paper airplane sailed through the air and landed perfectly on my desk. I snatched it and shot a glare in his direction but he was pretending he was busy with something.

I unfolded the paper, which turned out to be the Code of Conduct that I'd written earlier.

It was pretty lengthy, and added to my verbal list from earlier, greater defined what was off limits. He'd signed it, but folding it up into an airplane kind of defeated the purpose of that.

I slid the paper back and forth on the edge of the desk to smooth out the creases and then took it and held it up for him to see while tore it in half and then tore it in smaller pieces and then shoved it in my paper shredder, hoping the sound carried to his desk. Then I pretended to dust my hands off and went to get some coffee, my chin in the air.

"You didn't think you were going to get off that easy, did you?" He was close, but not too close. Still, my skin shivered in response to his voice. Like I was a robot programmed to react to him. How had that happened so fast? The sex probably had a little something to do with it.

I turned slowly, holding my coffee in front of me as if it could protect me. As a last resort, I could always throw it in his face, but that would probably result in a lawsuit.

"Look. This," I motion between us with the hand not holding the handle of the coffee cup, "can't happen. Period. It's best for both of us to just pretend nothing happened and move on. So, how are you coming with organizing those reports?"

He leaned against the counter and crossed his arms.

"I'm having a little trouble with some because they've been updated and I don't have access to the folders where they're stored."

See? We could do this. We were talking about reports and I didn't want to rip his pants off and mount him at all.

Well, maybe just a little. Or a little-lot.

"Hm, let me see what I can do about that. You're still technically in training until your three week review and then you can ask for additional access, but maybe I can fast track that. I'll talk with Mr. Clarke and see what I can do." I always called my father Mr. Clarke in front of other people. I'd been doing it for so long that I was used to it.

"Thank you, Miss Clarke, that would be fantastic." He sounded completely unenthused.

"Good. I'll get right on that for you, Mr. Blaine. Now if you'll excuse me." He stepped around me and went for the Keurig without another word. Ugh. I wanted to smack him in the back of the head, but that wouldn't be very professional, so I went back to my office and dialed my father's extension.

"Hey sweetheart, how are you?" I will always be my father's little girl.

"Hi Dad, I'm good. I'm actually calling you on official work business."

I proceeded to tell him about the issue with Mr. Blaine's access issue.

"Hmm, I'm not sure what I can do to speed that along. The auditors would have my hide if we didn't follow our written procedure. Let me speak with Laurie and I'll get back to you." Laurie was basically the Chief Rule Follower and it was her job to make sure we all followed the bazillion rules that we had to follow to stay in business and not piss off the government.

"Okay, great." Despite working just down the hall from one another, we sometimes went an entire day without seeing each other.

"So how is your new sidekick working out? It must be weird having someone other than Sal at that desk. I know it's strange for me."

Oh, Dad. If you only knew.

"He's been great so far. Quick learner and he finishes everything before I even know I want it." *Mind out of the gutter, mind out of the gutter . . .*

"I've been meaning to have a chat with him myself, but I just haven't gotten around to it. Why don't you send him down this afternoon?"

"Uh yeah, sure," I answered before I thought about how bad an idea that was. Hopefully Mr. Blaine could keep everything on the down low.

"There was one other thing I wanted to ask you about. Oh, remember how I asked you to look over those reports?"

I had looked at them in any spare moment I had, but hadn't come up with anything earth shattering. But, to be honest, I hadn't looked all that hard. It had been low on my priority list.

"Yeah, I haven't found anything that stuck out."

"Hm. Okay. We'll talk about it later. Listen, I have to get to a lunch, but I'll see you later. Bye, sweetie."

"Bye, Dad. Have fun."

I hung up and I could feel that Mr. Blaine was back at his desk. I picked up the phone and dialed his extension. He looked across the hall at me and picked up the phone.

"Hello, Aurora Clarke's office. How may I direct your call?"

"Hello, Mr. Blaine, this is Aurora Clarke. I just wanted to inform you that I have spoken with my father about your access issue and he is speaking to someone about it and will get back to me, and that he would also like to see you in his office this afternoon." I could both see and hear him smiling.

"You know what this reminds me off? Did you ever use two soup cans and a rope and make a telephone? My brothers and I used to do that . . ." he trailed off and it was almost like he'd blurted something out that he really wished he could reel back.

"No, I never did that. But it sounds like fun." Not that my childhood was un-fun, but that just wasn't the kind of thing I did.

"It was." Okay, totally weird moment. We locked eyes as we both held the phones to our ears.

He was the first to recover and clear his throat.

"Well, thank you Miss Clarke for keeping me apprised. I appreciate it very much, and I will be sure to see him later."

"You're welcome Mr. Blaine." There was nothing else to say, but I didn't seem to be able to hang the phone up.

"You hang up," Lucas said, and that made me smile.

"No, you hang up."

"I asked you first."

"I'm your boss."

"Fair point." Click. We both grinned like idiots at each other until someone walked by and broke our eye contact.

Chapter Eleven

I was nervous. I was nervous about meeting Fin for coffee. I mean, my palms weren't sweating, but I was definitely nervous. I'd arrived twenty minutes early and I had already decided to order herbal tea because I was keyed up enough as it was.

I chose a table near the front with a good view of the street so I could see him before he could see me. Between scanning the street for him and checking my phone to make sure he hadn't texted or called to cancel, I whiled away the time. And then it was five minutes until our meeting and I saw a man with dark wavy hair and a familiar nose stroll up the sidewalk and walk into the café.

Holy. Hell.

The scrawny guy with the greasy hair and the once-crooked teeth had undergone a transformation worthy of that television show that gives ridiculous makeovers. His blue eyes scanned the shop, and I pretended to be engrossed with my phone. Out of the corner of my eye, I saw him see me and start to walk over.

"Rory?" I look up and it wasn't hard to put on a shocked face. He was even more . . . wow, up close.

"Fin? Is that you?" Even back in the day, he'd towered over me. Now he was even more . . . formidable.

"It's me," he said, holding his arms out and then wrapping me in a hug. Whoa. I wasn't much of a hugger when it came to people I didn't know well, but I was forced to submit to it anyway until he let me go. He must have seen my hug reluctance.

"Oh, sorry. I'm kind of a hugger."

"It's fine. No big deal. Do you want to sit?"

"Have you gotten anything yet? What would you like?"

"Um, whatever they have for decaf tea is fine. And maybe a scone or something?" I started to rummage in my purse for some cash.

"It's on me. Be right back." He whisked away before I could stop him.

Hey, I tried.

I watched him as he ordered and flirted with the girl who wrote his name on our cups and waited for our orders. He definitely wasn't clumsy anymore. He'd grown into his body and he clearly knew how to use it.

What had my parents gotten me into?

I had to look back at my phone again so he wouldn't catch me watching him.

"Here you go, ma'am. Decaf peach tea and a cranberry scone." I took the tea and sipped it, burning my tongue.

"Thanks, Fin."

"My pleasure."

Enter awkward silence.

We both just sort of sat there, neither of us knowing where to start.

"So. This is terribly awkward." Thank you, Fin. We both laughed and I shook my head.

"So don't feel any pressure for this at all. I'm not expecting anything, if you were worried." Well, I wasn't until now. Why hadn't that occurred to me? He must have seen my look of horror.

"And I did that thing I do and made this already awkward situation even worse. I'm going for the record today." He shook his head at himself.

"Well, how about we move onto less awkward ground. How's your job going?"

He mimed shooting himself in the head.

"That good?'

"It's not the job, exactly. I enjoy it, and I like traveling, but I feel like it's time to stay in one place. I know that's odd for a guy to say, but I just wish I could stop living out of a suitcase and getting an email with a plane ticket and an order to be here or there in two weeks. Most of the time I don't even get to see anything, except from afar." He kept going and it was like I'd unleashed something that had been pent up inside him for a long time and he just needed someone to talk to about it.

When he finally took a breath, I realized we'd been talking for almost a half hour.

"Wow, I am not normally this much of a talkaholic. I am so sorry. I didn't mean to lay that on you." He stuck his scone in his mouth as if to stop any more words from coming out of it.

"No, it's fine. Really. Everyone needs to bitch every now and then. I feel honored that you chose me."

"Anything you want to talk about? Lay it on me." He finished the scone and sat back and I felt like this was some sort of date-slash-therapy session.

"Well, work is going well, I'm living with my best friend and I don't have much to bitch about." Something told me that he wouldn't really want to hear all the sordid details of my relationship, or whatever it was, with Lucas. Mr. Blaine.

He stared at me for a minute and then shook his head.

"You almost had me there. I almost believed you. But it's been my experience that when someone says everything is going great, it means the opposite, and when people say that things are terrible, it's the opposite. Not in every case, but in most cases. So, what is it that's got you down?"

He leaned forward and propped his head on his fists and gave me a sweet puppy dog face that made me burst out laughing, startling the people at the next table who glared at me as if my laughter had somehow disturbed their enjoyment of their double tall half-caff soy mocha whatevers.

"Come on, lay it on me." I took a deep breath.

"Okay. I'm about to share some very personal stuff with you, but sometimes it's easier to talk to someone you don't know very well than a best friend. So there's this guy in my office and we've been flirting back and forth and I've told him to stop, but he won't. It's not entirely his fault because I keep saying no, but then telling him yes in other ways."

I stopped for a moment to see if he was following me.

"Did you sleep with him?" Well, be blunt, why don't you?

"Yes. Twice. Once before we worked together and once in the office."

"Wow, bravo. I feel like I should be giving you a round of applause for that."

"No! What I need is advice on how to stop letting this happen. I've never let my personal life get in the way of my work life. I mean, I found out my fucking boyfriend cheated on me and the same day I had to make this huge presentation that millions of dollars rode on and I nailed it. When I'm at work, all that stuff goes away, but now that stuff is at my work and things are getting mixed together and I don't like it and I don't know what to do about it."

I put my head down on the cool table and then realized how many germs were probably now on my face, so I sat up.

"That is a conundrum. Have you thought about letting it happen?"

"That's not what I want." *Liar, liar, Spanx on fire.*

"Well, if saying no is that hard, then maybe you should say yes. I'm sure you're not the first person who's had an indiscretion in the office. And you won't be the last. Just don't get caught." He winked. Was he for serious?

"Are you always this good at advice? Because that's pretty much the worst I've ever gotten, except for that one time when one of my friends in high school told me to put vodka in water bottles because my parents would never figure it out."

"Hey, I'm just telling you what I think. You don't have to follow it. That's on you. It's also on you to figure out how to carry on this thing without anyone knowing, but you seem like an intelligent girl, so I'm sure you'll figure it out. If you want it to happen, make it happen."

"You sound like one of those motivational posters with a guy standing on top of the Grand Canyon with his arms raised."

"I get all my best advice from crappy posters. And bumper stickers."

I shook my head and finished my tea.

"I can't let the wants and desires of my ladyparts get in the way of my job. That's not me." Or at least it hadn't been.

"Maybe your ladyparts know something you don't. Or don't want to admit." He raised his eyebrows and I crumpled up my napkin and threw it at him.

"You are completely useless, Fin."

We stayed at the coffee shop for another hour, just talking about whatever. I could tell people around us thought we were on a date. Yes, Fin had turned into quite a male specimen, and I found him attractive, but not attractive in the way that I wanted to see him naked. He was funny and sweet and cute, but he just didn't make those feelings erupt.

I didn't believe that a straight man and a straight woman couldn't be friends without eventually having sex. Sure, if I was drunk, it might be a possibility, but only if we were both very drunk, and he would have to make the first move.

"So, how long are you going to be in town for?" I said as I walked him toward a cab.

"About two weeks, and then . . . who knows? I'm considering a radical life change, but I don't want to say anything about it yet."

"Okay, noted. So, maybe you want to do something next weekend? My friends and I go to this bar and they have open mic night and if you can stomach it, it's actually a lot of fun."

"Actually, that does sound like fun. Who wouldn't want to hear a thousand renditions of emo guitar songs? I mean, sign me up for that."

"Fine, don't come, but you're missing out." He looked at the cab and sighed heavily.

"If you're going to twist my arm, I *guess* I can come."

I told him I'd give him a call and tell him where and when, and then with a wave he was in a cab and I was strolling toward the T and turning over his horrible advice.

Chapter Twelve

Yes, it was horrible advice. I wasn't the kind of girl who was good with secrets, especially secrets like this. I also sucked at lying to my parents. They knew EVERYTHING. More so than most parents, I think.

Of course I had to tell Sloane every single detail and I told her about his advice.

"That advice sucks." *Yes, I know.*

"That is seriously, like the worst advice ever. Your parents wanted to set you up with this guy? He sounds like a moron." And then I showed her a picture of Fin I'd taken on my phone when he wasn't looking.

"Okay, so he's a very attractive idiot, but still."

I also told her about my plans to invite him to the bar with us.

"Hmm, I find this plan intriguing. You know what we should do, right?" I had no idea where she was going. Sometimes Sloane's mind went to different places than mine and she had to practically give me a map and a GPS to get me there, and sometimes even then I was still lost. This was one of those times.

"Look at him. Dark hair, blue eyes? Funny and slightly weird? Who likes all of those things, and who is in need of a good sexy fuckfest?"

I was still not following, so Sloane smacked me on the arm.

"Marisol!"

Okay, I had to admit that it made sense. Marisol was one of those adorable bubbly girls that everyone loved and I could absolutely see her and Fin together. But the only thing Marisol hated more than guys who spit in the street was being set up. She was all sweetness and light until you tried to make her do something behind her back and then the darkness came out. I'd seen that once and I never wanted to see it again.

"We don't have to actually do anything. Just make sure they sit next to each other. The God of Love will do the rest."

"The God of Love? We talking the Greek or Roman one?"

"The American one. Alcohol."

Another point well made.

"Oh, this is happening. I wonder if she'll let me give her some of my lingerie. I could totally make it in her size." One of the hazards of having a friend who made clothing was that she kept track of all your measurements, and was not above taking them in public if she thought you'd gained or lost a few pounds.

"I don't know. I can't see her wearing anything like the ribbon ensemble."

"Of course not, I'd make her something maybe white and cotton candy pink. What do you think?" She dashed off to her studio room before I could answer. Another hazard of living with someone who makes clothes was that bolts of fabric became décor in your home, because there were only so many places you could put them.

The rest of the evening was spent giving my opinion on what the design should look like, and how it would capture Marisol's "essence". Sometimes Sloane took fashion a little too far.

We had another movie marathon, this time with 80's classics. *Breakfast Club, Pretty in Pink, Sixteen Candles, Ghost, Dirty Dancing.*

"Why in the hell do we let ourselves watch this movie?" Sloane said, dabbing her eyes as we watched *Ghost.*

"I don't know," I said, grabbing for the tissues as soon as she was done with them. "We should have done them in better order." I blew my nose and then yawned.

"We're such suckers for this shit," Sloane said, tossing her tissue angrily on the floor.

"It's why Nicholas Sparks is so successful."

"Douchebag." I concurred.

"So what are you going to do with Fin's terrible advice?"

Ugh, we were back to that. I'd thought we put that baby to bed.

"I'm going to ignore it and keep trying to have a professional relationship, even though it's hard. I don't have a choice."

"Well, that's not true. You could say, 'fuck it,' and just do what you want. Not that I'm saying you should. I know how important your job is."

"It is important. I've been working my entire life to get where I am. I'm not going to give it up and not over this."

"You go girl!" She held her fist up and we bumped. "Solidarity sister."

"Amen."

"How was your weekend, Mr. Blaine?" I had come once again with his cherry Danish and black coffee. It seemed that we had an unspoken agreement that we would alternate who would bring breakfast and it felt like my turn.

"Lovely, Miss Clarke. Very relaxing. I partook in some golf and went deep sea fishing." I looked up from the pastry bag where I'd been trying to find another napkin.

His eyes were dancing with amusement.

"I'm kidding. I hate golf and I get seasick, so I ended up visiting my nieces. This is the first time in two days I'm not wearing a tiara or glitter on my face."

Once again, unexpected.

"How old are they?" I asked.

"Four and two. Gracie and Fiona." *Fuck you evolution for making a guy who is good with children so fucking attractive. Especially right now.*

"Those are good ages."

"They're great. So, how was your weekend?" *Oh, now we're talking about me again.*

"It was fine. Boring." I wasn't going to go into details. He didn't need to know details. We were keeping this professional.

"Sometimes boring is the best kind of weekend."

"Exactly." *Ugh, awkward moment.*

"Well, I should let you get to work. I wouldn't want to take up too much of your time, Miss Clarke." Oh, that was a dig if there ever was one.

I almost let it go, but I leaned toward him and whispered in his ear and ignored how nice he smelled.

"Don't be a dick."

"I seem to recall you sucking on mine. I can't seem to get the image out of my head. Those perfect lips wrapped around my c—" I didn't let him finish as I went to my office and shut the door.

Then I made sure my pants were smooth (thankfully, I didn't have an erect penis to hide), went to my desk, sat down and got my ass to work.

By lunch, I almost felt like my old self, pre-Lucas. We were getting ready to launch a new product in the coming months, and pretty soon I was going to be spending nights and weekends here while trying to make sure everything was on track and deal with the inevitable insanity that accompanied a new release.

I had to be extra bitchy, and I'd already yelled at three people who hadn't done what I'd asked them to for the third time. Everyone else was working hard, except for Mr. Craig, who had bailed for golf again. It was so cool that if I did the same thing, I would have been out on my ass a long time ago. Or maybe not. Dad probably would have given me a stern talking to and I never would have done it again.

I didn't actually mind the crazy and even looked forward to it. Everyone got hopped up on caffeine and went without sleep and lived on takeout, but it helped bring the team together to go through something like that. There's no other bonding experience like it.

There was only one problem. I didn't want to do any further bonding with Lucas. Mr. Blaine. We had bonded quite enough already.

But then there was a knock at my door and there he was, invading my space and talking with that voice and looking at me with those eyes.

"It's almost time for your meeting," he said, pointing at the clock above my door.

"I know."

"Well. I just thought I would let you know so you didn't miss it."

"Thank you, Mr. Blaine." I didn't point out that he could have called me to let me know. I expected him to leave, but he lingered, with only his head inside my office and the rest of him on the other side of the door.

"I'm sorry I was a dick." He shut the door before I could say anything.

Well, that was progress.

We made more progress over the next week, and I got to the point where I only got a lady boner every other time I saw him, and his lusty looks to non-lusty looks ratio went from 99:1 to 70:30. If we could get it down to 50:50, that would be great.

By the time Friday rolled around, I was ready for the weekend. All the girls and I were going out to the bar on Saturday and I'd messaged Fin asking him to come, but then I started second-guessing myself. I mean, it was going to be him and four women. Most guys would think that was some kind of fantasy, but when you actually put them in that situation, it would be completely overwhelming. I was sure Fin could handle it, but I didn't want him to get weirded out and then never hang out with us again.

"Any fun plans for the weekend?" Mr. Blaine said as we both walked toward the elevator. It was an innocuous question, but I could tell he was really interested.

"Oh, nothing earth-shattering." Or panty-shattering. Or ripping.

"Hm." The doors closed and the air suddenly got thin and hard to breathe, like we were on Everest or something.

Oxygen. I needed oxygen.

We didn't face each other and instead I stared at the numbers as they got smaller and begged them to go faster, knowing that wasn't going to happen.

"And you?"

"What?" He acted as if he'd forgotten I was there.

"Do you have any exciting plans this weekend?" I fiddled with my purse. It was always great having a purse that you could use to fool with when you didn't want to look at someone.

"Not really. You, uh, heading to the bar?" Oh, crap.

"Um, we might. But probably not. Why, you headed for open mic night again?" I still didn't look at him, but I saw him shrug out of the corner of my eye as the elevator door finally opened.

"Haven't decided. Maybe. Maybe not." He motioned for me to leave first, so I did.

"Well, have a good weekend, Mr. Blaine." We faced each other in the lobby.

"You as well, Miss Clarke." He almost looked sad as he turned and headed for the revolving door.

Boys. Are. Weird.

Sloane couldn't be dissuaded from her plan to hook Marisol up with Fin, so on Saturday morning she dragged me to the salon to get our nails done, because apparently going to the bar now required us to have perfect hands and feet. Marisol met us there too and I almost felt bad for her in her cute obliviousness.

"I miss you guys. I feel like we haven't hung out in forever, but I've been so busy." Marisol was our only friend who was still in school and getting her PhD in Education. She already had two master's degrees; one in Education and the other in Business. Yes, she was one of *those* people.

"I know," I said as we sat in massage chairs and soaked our feet. "God, I needed this. You have no idea."

"Oh, I think I have some idea," Sloane said on my other side.

"No comments from the peanut gallery, please."

"Wait, what did I miss?" I hadn't wanted to share the rest of the story with Marisol, seeing as how she was swamped with all her work. It seemed almost crass to call her up and be like, *Hey, what's up? Well, I'm banging my assistant . . .*

"Ugh, okay. I guess I'd better tell you before someone else takes it and embellishes it and makes it into more of a big deal than it is."

Marisol put down her magazine and gave me her full attention. Lovely.

I started from The Morning After, because she didn't know about that yet, and worked my way forward. Actually, it was weird that she hadn't asked me about this before now. Her lack of shock was also starting to make me suspicious.

"And then I told him that we couldn't do it anymore, which you already know," I said. Marisol feigned shock. An actress she was not.

"What? No, this is the first time I'm hearing about this. Go on." I turned and glared at Sloane.

"What? You never made me sign an NDA. That means everything is fair game. Besides, you would have told her eventually. I just told her sooner. And you know I'm better at telling stories anyway." She was right on the last count, and I would have told Marisol. Ugh, I hated it when Sloane was right. She always gloated way too much.

"FINE." My story time had been hijacked, so I just gave up and let Sloane tell the rest of the story.

Neither of us mentioned Fin, and I felt bad. We were totally ambushing her.

"So how's Chlo?" Marisol and Chloe lived only a block apart and saw each other almost every day. She had to work this morning, which was why she hadn't come with us.

"She's still . . . not good. We need to find her a rebound. If she doesn't get out of this funk soon, I swear I'm going to make out with her." That made the women doing our nails give each other shocked faces and the three of us smothered our laughter.

"There is this girl in one of my classes that definitely stares at my boobs in a lusty way. You know how you can tell if a girl's just jealous of your boobs, or if she wants to motorboat them." I had to shove my fist in my mouth and I swear the woman working on my feet looked like she was going to have a heart attack.

"I'll have to do some more covert ops to find out for sure, but she's definitely Chlo's type."

"So what week have we decided on for our trip?" I said, trying to change the subject. As much fun as it was to watch the manicurists to squirm, I didn't want them to charge us extra.

"Um, I can't do the 24th to the 31st anymore," Marisol said. "I'm sorry! I got roped into doing this charity thing." Marisol was always getting herself into that stuff. She had a hard time saying no to anyone.

"No, that's fine. We can reschedule," Sloane said, looking at her phone. We'd already rescheduled four times. When you try to take a trip with four women who have high-pressure jobs or school, things get tricky. We'd been planning on going together to Jamaica for at least a year. The ultimate Girls' Week. But it was proving more difficult to plan than figuring out Donald Trump's hair.

After our hands and feet were polished and pretty and the women in the shop breathed a sigh of relief, we went to lunch.

"So do you think he'll be there again tonight?" Chloe said.

"Seriously? Are we back to that?" I thought we were done. I'd relaxed and was enjoying my Lucas Blaine-free time.

"Oh, he'll be there," Sloane said, bumping my knee with hers. "He wants you. Bad."

Yeah, well, it was mutual.

"Are you blushing? Wow, do you really like this guy?" Chloe said, which made me blush even more.

"No, no. I mean, he's fine to work with and he's not bad in bed, but that's it. He may be funny and able to sing and have fabulous hair and a chin dimple . . ." I trailed off.

"Fuck," I said, before remembering that we were in a café and there were children around. "I like him."

Sloane and Chloe gave each other the same face.

"I love how you're the last to realize it," Sloane said. "For someone who's so smart, you can be pretty dense sometimes."

"I mean, I can like him without *liking him*, liking him." God, I sounded like I was in junior high again. Maybe I should pass Lucas (Mr. Blaine) one of those notes that was like, *Do you like me? Circle one: Yes, No, Maybe.*

Sloane and Chloe both laughed at my expense and I slumped in my chair.

"Shut up, both of you."

As the day wore on, I started to get more and more nervous. It was very similar to the feeling you have before a first date. Not knowing what to expect, worried you're going to make a fool of yourself. It had been a long, long time since I'd had first date jitters. I hadn't even had them with Royce.

Sloane was dressing me, and I was being shoved into another one of her lingerie creations. This time it was a beautiful black bustier with sapphire flowers embroidered all over it, and a matching set of panties with little blue bows on the sides. It was nothing I'd ever dare to wear, but Sloane was insistent, so I put it on under a tank top and layered a sheer t-shirt over it so hopefully no one would guess what I was wearing underneath. I paired that with my favorite pair of dark jeans, and high-heeled black boots.

"Fabulous! I really like this real-world testing. Between you and Chlo, I'm gaining valuable insight."

"That means we get a cut, right? Ten percent?" I said as I turned back and forth to make sure nothing was sticking out.

"Nice try, bitch."

It was worth a shot.

An hour later we were in the bar, and I was fiddling with my first gin and tonic. Fin had texted that he was running late, but I told him it was no big deal. We'd gotten an extra chair and piled our purses on it, so we could just clear it off when he got here. So far, there had been no Lucas Blaine sightings, but that didn't mean much.

"Terrible. That girl really should never ever sing again," Sloane said as a girl exited the stage to a smattering of polite applause. The really mean critics hadn't gotten here yet. It was good she went on early, or else she would have gotten ripped apart and probably left the stage crying. That happened at least once every time.

"Oh, come on. It wasn't that bad," Marisol said. "Okay, maybe it was. Maybe I want to bleach my eardrums so I can clean myself of that experience."

"Good plan," I said, finally sipping my drink. Most of the ice was melted, so it was pretty watered down.

"Calm down," Sloane said in my ear and squeezed my knee. I was pretty good at hiding my nervousness in the boardroom, but this was completely different.

And then it happened. It was like I heard him open the door, even though that was impossible. There was way too much noise, but I knew the second he walked in. It was almost supernatural.

"He's here," Sloane said in my ear, but I knew that already. Slowly, I turned my head and there he was, making his way through the crowd, his eyes locked on me. It was a bit like one of those scenes in a movie when all the sounds around me went down in volume and everything slowed and all I could see was this man walking toward me. This gorgeous man who only had eyes for me.

Yeah, I liked him.

"Miss Clarke," he said, stopping about three feet away. He was casual again in a black t-shirt with a faded emblem on the front and jeans.

"Hi," I said, dropping any pretense of formality.

"Nice to see *you* again," Sloane said, resting her head on my shoulder and smiling. Shameless. She was shameless.

"It's nice to see all of you again. Could I buy you ladies some drinks?" Sloane kicked me under the table and I kicked her back as Lucas took everyone's drink orders and went to the bar.

"Oh my God, he looks at you like he wants to do you right here in front of everyone. I wouldn't mind watching him in action," Sloane said, openly ogling him as he leaned over the bar to get the bartender's attention.

"Those buns are fresh and hot from the bakery." I smacked her on the arm.

"What? I'm just admiring. Don't worry." I wasn't worried about Sloane and Lucas. In fact, when Sloane was really into a guy, she didn't talk about all this stuff.

"He is pretty cute, Ror." Even Marisol was in on the action.

"If he had a vagina, boobs and longer hair, I'd be all over that," Chloe added.

"I don't know you people," I said, shaking my head.

Our ogling was interrupted by a voice behind me.

"Hey, sorry I'm late. I got held up with something," Fin said and we all turned.

"Oh, hey Fin," I said as he gave me a side hug. It was easier because I was almost at his level since I was sitting on a high chair.

"Everyone, this is Fin Herald. Fin, this is Sloane and Chloe and Marisol." He shook everyone's hand and I definitely saw Marisol blush, and Sloane kicked me under the table again. Pretty soon I was going to have bruises.

I moved our purses and Fin took the last available chair as two guys took the stage and did an awesome rendition of 'Fat Bottomed Girls' complete with a tambourine.

"Here we are," Lucas said, a tray in his hand with everyone's drinks on it. Oh, this could get weird.

"Fin, this is Lucas Blaine. We work together." Fin smiled at Lucas and extended his hand. Lucas paused and his eyes flicked from me to Fin and then he shook Fin's hand.

"Nice to meet you," Lucas said as everyone sipped their drinks.

"Nice to meet you as well," Fin said and I knew he knew that this was the guy I'd been telling him about the other day.

Sometimes I wish life had an Abort button. I'd be pushing it right now to get out of this situation.

"Fin's a friend from high school and he's back in town for a few weeks visiting. Our parents are best friends so they tried to set us up." No point in beating around the bush.

"Yeah, that wasn't awkward at all, was it?" Fin said with a laugh. Lucas still looked a little tense, and I could sense he was trying to figure out what the deal was between Fin and me. Not that it was any of his business. He wasn't my boyfriend.

"Would you like a drink, Fin? I didn't know you were coming, or else I would have gotten you one," Lucas said.

"No, I'm fine. I'm actually trying to cut back. I'm a bit of an all or nothing guy." He looked down and his happy façade cracked for a moment. Hmm. There was a story there, but now wasn't the time for it.

"Fair enough."

"Are you going to sing?" I said, trying to save the situation.

"I was thinking about it. I brought my guitar, just in case. It's in the back." I hadn't seen him with it, so he must have stashed it somewhere. Fin's phone rang and he looked at the screen.

"Shit, I have to take this. Excuse me." He weaved his way through the crowd and outside.

"I have to pee," Sloane announced.

"Me too," Marisol added.

"Wait for me," Chloe said, taking a gulp of her drink and then grabbing her purse before the three of them left me alone with Lucas.

"They're about as subtle as a punch in the face," Lucas said, watching them go. I shook my head and turned to face him.

"So," I said.

"So," he said. The last time we did that, we ended up having sex.

I touched his arm. "You jealous, Mr. Blaine?"

He leaned in so I could hear him better. "And why would you think that, Miss Clarke?"

"Because you look like you want to take Fin out back and rough him up a little even though you really have no reason to. My relationship, or lack thereof, with him is none of your business because our relationship is strictly professional."

"If you say so," he said, brushing some of my hair away from my face. I shouldn't have worn it down, but Sloane said it looked better and I was having a good hair day.

"Stop it." He sighed and his breath moved my hair again.

"Okay, Miss Clarke." He moved backward.

"Thank you for the drinks. You didn't have to do that." I didn't want him to go. But I didn't think he should stay.

"You're welcome Miss Clarke," he said with a little bow. I smiled and he smiled back as he made his way toward the stage and disappeared into the back room of the bar, presumably to get his guitar.

"Hey, sorry about that." Fin's voice cut through the haze Lucas had left behind.

"No problem," I said with another smile.

"So, uh, that was the guy, huh?"

"Yup, that was the guy."

Fin gave me a look.

"What?"

"I stand by my advice even more now. You want him. He wants you. Let it happen." He shrugged and winked at me. "I'm going to go get a glass of water. You want one?"

"Sure, yeah." He patted my shoulder and left me alone again.

"Where did your sexcretary go?" Sloane said as the three traitors came back.

"He was scared of you three and ran away," I said, downing my second drink. I was cutting myself off after that. The last time I'd had drinks in this bar and Lucas had sung, I'd ended up in bed with him, and that was something that couldn't happen again. Fuck Fin's advice.

"Shut up, he was not. Oh, there he is." The announcer said his name and he took the stage with his guitar and sat on a stool again. Be still my ladyparts.

"This is a little song you might remember, but I've decided to put my own twist on it," Lucas said into the mic and then sat back on the stool.

"This should be interesting," Sloane said in my ear. I batted her away as Fin came back with a glass of water for himself and one for me.

He started playing the guitar and I recognized the song immediately.

"Is that 'Total Eclipse of the Heart'?" Sloane hissed at me, and I glared at her as Lucas started to sing.

Somehow he'd taken an 80's ballad and turned it into a slower, sexier song that was something else entirely.

"Wow," Sloane breathed in my ear. "If you don't want him, I'll take him."

Lucas finished the song and opened his eyes. He always sang with his eyes closed.

"Thank you," he said, and got a round of applause and cheering and a few wolf whistles. I clapped along with everyone else, completely lost in his performance. He smiled and exited the stage to make way for the next performer.

"I never thought I would actually like that song, but that was pretty damn good," Fin said, nodding his approval.

"Get up," Sloane said, shoving me off my chair.

"Hey!" I had no choice but to give up my chair.

"Get out of here. Right now. Before I change my mind and go for him." She pushed me toward the back of the bar. I looked at Marisol and Chloe for help, but they were staring into their drinks. Fin just made a shooing motion with his hands and then turned to talk to Marisol.

"Go on," Sloane said, and I was powerless against her as she pushed me through the bar.

"And don't come home tonight," she said in my ear before smacking me on the ass and walking back to the table.

I was about to turn around and go back, but Lucas came out of the back and smacked right into me.

He caught me before either of us fell and smiled when he realized it was me.

"Coming to get an autograph, Sunshine?" He steadied me with one arm and had his guitar with the other. Shit.

"No. My soon-to-be-former roommate shoved me over here. So here I am." I crossed my arms and tried to put on my best Bitch Face.

"Ah, so you're here under duress. I'm so sorry about that, Miss Clarke."

"It's no big deal, Mr. Blaine. If you'll excuse me, I'm going to call a cab and go home." I turned to go, but he stopped me.

"Wait. Don't go." I sighed and turned back around. "Stay. Please."

"I can't, Lucas. We can't." He moved closer and I could see the desperation on his face and I could feel it inside of me. I wanted him so much.

"One more time. Please?" His voice was deep and it made me feel something unfold way down inside and I knew I was going to say yes, even as I tried to say no.

"Why did you have to sing? I could say no if you didn't sing," I said as he moved closer and pulled me into his chest.

He laughed and it rumbled through him.

"I'll keep that in mind. Come on. Come home with me. One last time."

Maybe I'd been going about this the wrong way. Maybe if I gave in, really gave in, for one night then I'd get it out of my system and it would take the forbidden nature away from our relationship. That was probably half the attraction anyway. Forbidden things were always more sexy.

Plus, I had fabulous underwear on.

"One night. I'm all yours for one night." I looked up at him and he stared down at me.

"One perfect night."

His hand slid down my back, squeezed my ass and then he twisted his fingers in mine.

"Let's get out of here."

Chapter Thirteen

This time we held hands in the cab on the ride to his apartment. He kept looking over at me and smiling, and I was getting the first date flutters again. I felt bad for abandoning poor Fin, but Sloane texted and assured me that he and Marisol had been deep in conversation and he hadn't even noticed that I'd left. Maybe I wasn't the only one who wouldn't be going home alone tonight.

Lucas traced the back of my hand with his thumb, and it was so sweet that I giggled.

"What's so funny?"

"Nothing."

"You're cute when you laugh." The praise made me blush and giggle again.

"Stop that. My reputation as a bitch is going to be shattered if you tell anyone that." He looked down at our joined hands.

"Well, we can't have that, can we?" He leaned closer and kissed me on the cheek. "I'll tell everyone at the office what a heartless bitch you are. Happy?"

I glared at him and he laughed.

"You're cute when you do that, too." He was exasperating. Why did I get in this cab with him again?

The cab stopped and Lucas paid the cabbie and helped me out, keeping his hand in mine.

"Hopefully I don't have any mishaps with the key this time," he said. We walked through the lobby and to the elevator, and this really did feel like a date. I just couldn't decide if it was the end or the beginning of one.

"Shall we?" he said as the doors opened.

"Here goes nothing," I muttered and I knew he heard me.

"One last night," he said, pulling me close and kissing me softly. Like a first kiss. Tentative.

"Okay," I said as we walked to his door. He put his guitar down and released my hand before getting out his keys and this time there was no fumbling.

"Do you want the tour, since you didn't get it officially last time, or do you want to skip it?"

I didn't really have to think about that.

"Skip the tour," I said and he closed the distance between us with one step.

"Thank God. I couldn't keep my hands off you one more second."

"So don't. I'm yours tonight."

Okay, so I wasn't into owning or being owned. I was a progressive woman. I believed in gender equality. But honestly, I was ready to be his tonight.

"And I am yours," he breathed into my mouth before kissing me. I took his lead and wrapped my legs around his waist and plunged my tongue into his mouth. He growled and backed up. I felt something new in his mouth and I pulled away from the kiss in confusion. He smiled when he saw my face and stuck his tongue out deliberately, presenting the silver barbell that pierced it before kissing me fiercely again, letting my tongue dance with his.

Fuck. Me.

Something told me that we weren't going to make it to the bedroom. He crashed into the refrigerator.

"Bedroom?" he said, taking a quick break from my mouth to kiss and suck on my neck in a spot that made me grind my hips against the bulge in his pants.

"If you can get there," I said breathlessly as I raked my hands on his back. Stupid clothes. Why must they always be in the way?

"I'll try," he said with a little laugh as he walked backwards with me toward the door and kicked it open.

"Can you get the light?" he said moving me near the switch. "I want to see you." Well, ditto.

I flicked it with my elbow and he made his way toward the bed and I unhooked my legs from around his waist so he could lay me down.

"I only get you for this one night, so I'm going to make sure you remember it," he said, and his words sent shivers up and down my spine.

"And I'm very much hoping you're wearing something similar to that ribbon number from the other day," he said as he straddled me.

"I guess you'll have to undress me to find out," I said, and I managed to sound a little sexy.

"I guess I will." His fingers played with the edge of my t-shirt, teasing me before I put my arms up and he pulled it over my head. I swore he seemed a little put out that I had a tank top on under it, but when he removed that, his eyes got wide as he took in the bustier. It was pretty damn sexy, and I felt sexy wearing it, even though I couldn't breathe that well, and my poor boobs felt like they were being squeezed to death.

"Lovely," he said as he moved his hands up and down and then undoing the button of my jeans and slowly sliding them down to reveal the matching panties.

"I am very, very glad we turned the lights on," he said as he joined his mouth with mine again for a deep kiss. I still had my boots on, but he didn't seem all that concerned. He was still fully clothed and I was having a problem with that, so I reached for his shirt and started yanking it over his head. We broke the kiss long enough for me to get it off.

He really did have a fabulous body. I ran my hands up and down it as he went to work on my boots, pulling my legs up so he could unzip them and toss them to the other side of the room before removing his own shoes. Then he slowly inched my pants down my legs until they were off.

"You're beautiful, Sunshine," he breathed. I loved the way he looked at me. Almost as if he were afraid to touch me. Almost.

"Thank you," I said, and then made a face.

"What's that face for?"

"It sounded weird. I mean, it sounds stupid. Like I'm one of those girls who thinks they're hot and everyone else does too. I'm not one of those girls." He was laughing.

"Why are you laughing?"

"Because you're adorable." No. I was not adorable. I could not be adorable in this bustier. Sloane would kill me.

"Just get over here so I can take your pants off," I said, reaching for his belt and using it to bring him closer.

"Yes, ma'am." I froze.

"I will not have sex of any kind with you tonight if you call me ma'am."

"Yes, sir," he said and moved to kiss me.

"No, I'm serious." And then he kissed me and pressed his hips against me and lost my train of thought. Belt. I had to get working on that.

I finally got it and started shoving his pants and underwear over his perfect ass. Ah, I'd missed that.

"As much as I love this pretty thing you're wearing, I'm more fond of what's under it," he said starting to unhook the bustier.

"You've done this before."

"No, I just know how to get what I want." He released me from the bustier and I took a deep breath.

"That feels so good. I never knew how nice taking a deep breath was until right now." He smiled and kissed down my neck, licking and biting, and with the addition of the tongue barbell, I was a quivering mess by the time he used it to stroke one of my nipples.

Somewhere along the line the panties went the way of all of my other clothes and we were both naked and sweaty and ready.

"I want your mouth on my cock," he said as he looked down at me. Hey, at least he'd said something first instead of shoving it into my face like some guys did. Nothing made me feel sexier than a penis and a hairy ball sack being shoved in my mouth when I least expected it.

"You do, do you?" I moved my hands down and stroked him.

"Yes," he said, and I scooted down and he moved up, and I took him in my mouth. Once again, I am not a blowjob master, but with my hands, I could do pretty well. I hadn't been going very long when he grabbed my chin and moved my head away.

"I don't want to come in your mouth. I want to be inside you." Aw, how considerate. I propped myself up on my elbows and he shifted me back up and laid my head on his pillows. He smiled before he moved down my body and settled his face between my legs. I was so looking forward to what else he could do with that tongue ring.

I parted my legs for him and he stroked my leg almost absentmindedly. What was he doing? I wanted his mouth on me. RIGHT NOW. He couldn't tease me like that and then not follow through.

"If you don't lick me right now, you're fired," I said and he laughed against the inside of my thigh.

"I was just making sure that was what you wanted, Miss Clarke," he said before he licked me up and down.

Every curse word and expletive exploded in my brain and I fisted the sheets as he licked me again before taking my piercing into his mouth. My piercing was designed to stimulate me in that area already, but in addition with the little ball on his tongue ring, I was coming undone in only a matter of moments.

"Are you enjoying your coffee, Miss Clarke?" he said smiling up at me and that almost did it.

"Get back to work, Mr. Blaine," I said, stroking his hair.

So he did. Moments later I was in the grips of a powerful orgasm. He let me ride it before going back again, and wringing a second out of me right away, one even more powerful than the first.

"*Fuuuuck*, Lucas."

"Lucah," he said as he kissed his way back up my body. "Just for tonight, could you call me Lucah?" He stared at me and I watched a storm swirl in his eyes.

"Please say it for me."

"Lucah," I said and before I could ask him why he wanted me to call him that, his mouth was on my mouth and he was reaching into the drawer for a condom.

Then he was inside and I would call him whatever the fuck he wanted. The sex was faster this time, but not quite the pace of when we'd been in the conference room.

"Come for me, Sunshine," he growled before another orgasm tore through me and I came calling his name. Or the name he'd asked me to call him. I don't really remember. I could have yelled out some combination of the two for all I knew.

He held me and we locked eyes with him still inside me.

"Can I get a raise?"

Chapter Fourteen

When I said only one night, I meant it, which also meant that we had a lot of sexual ground to cover in a short time. Lucas (or Lucah) was open to anything, so we did it. Sometimes it didn't work out and we'd end up giggling and kissing, but when the sun finally started to come up, we'd had each other in almost every way you can have a person, and my body was exhausted. I also really, really needed a shower. And coffee. And sleep.

"Are you awake?" Lucas whispered in my ear before kissing my earlobe.

"No. You've even fucked the sleep out of me." I rolled toward him and smiled.

"Then my job here is done, Miss Clarke." He stroked my arm and the sun lit up his hair like fire. He kissed my shoulder.

"Are you hungry? I can make some breakfast if you want to shower."

"Are you a mind reader now, too?" He kissed my cheek, slapped my ass and then went to the kitchen. I rolled my eyes and crawled out of bed. Huh, my legs did work. A few hours ago, didn't think I was ever going to be able to use them again.

I stumbled to the shower and ended up using his products since they were my only option. Besides, I liked smelling like him. I cut the shower short and went back into the kitchen in a towel. He was still naked and doing something with a frying pan.

"Isn't cooking naked a little dangerous? Flaming grease and all that?"

"I cook my bacon in the oven and I think I can handle pancakes without bodily injury. Did you enjoy your shower?" He kissed my hair and sniffed it, smiling.

"I did. And thanks for the extra toothbrush. That was very nice of you."

"I thought I should have it. Just in case."

"In case for me, or in case for someone else?"

"In case for you." I kissed his shoulder and stood next to him as he flipped a stack of fluffy and golden pancakes onto a plate.

Before we ate he put on some boxers, and I put on one of his shirts and we sat on his couch to eat. He flipped the television on and handed me the remote.

"I know how women are with the remote, so I'm handing over control now."

"Um, excuse me? How are women with the remote?"

He looked at me like I was dense.

"Women always want to control the remote. It's easier if I just let you have it than fight over it. I gotta pick my battles." He shoved a bite of pancakes in his mouth.

“Um, I’m pretty sure that’s bullshit because men are the ones who always want control of the remote.”

“Only because women are bad at using it.” Oh, he was baiting me and I knew it, but I didn’t care.

“Yeah, well I’m going to use this remote to bash you in the head,” I said before I changed the channel. I skipped around until I found a channel that showed old cartoons. Wile E. Coyote was busy chasing the Roadrunner and I laughed and set the remote back on the coffee table.

“Cartoons?” Lucas said.

“You have a problem with how I use the remote *and* what I pick?”

He shook his head. “No, actually. This is what I would have picked.” A beat of silence passed and it felt like it meant more than we picked the same thing to watch.

“I used to watch these when I was a kid. Every Saturday morning. My parents told me I wasn’t allowed, but I kept the volume down and turned it off when they came in the room. I was very stealthy. Or at least I thought I was,” I said as Wile E. Coyote bought yet another anvil from ACME. “You’d think he would stop buying products from ACME. I mean, nearly every one is defective.”

“He should call the Better Business Bureau and report them,” Lucas finally said, rubbing my knee.

I really shouldn’t have let him, because I’d said it was just one night, and it definitely wasn’t night anymore. I should have waited until he was asleep and snuck out.

We finished our pancakes and bacon and coffee and I leaned against his shoulder and he stroked my drying hair.

It felt . . . sweet. And normal. Like this was our life. But it was only temporary. We were vacationing in this space and it was almost time to go back to reality. I knew that, which was why I'd turned my phone off as soon as I'd gotten into the cab with him.

Against my will, and probably against his, we fell asleep together.

The next time I woke up, the sun was hanging low in the sky and the television was still on, but it was playing different cartoons. I moved and that roused Lucas, who blinked his eyes open and smiled when he saw me.

It was almost Sunday night and I'd said it was just going to be one night, but that one night was getting stretched and if I didn't put my foot down, that one night was never going to end.

Oh, but I didn't want it to.

I liked him. I really, really liked him.

I'd been kidding myself when I'd thought we could go back to a strictly professional relationship after having sex. Well, maybe we could have after the first time, but now feelings were involved, at least mine were. I didn't know how he felt about me, and I sure as hell wasn't going to ask.

"I should go. I have dinner with my parents soon," I said, peeling myself off his chest. My hair was all over the place because it had dried without the help of a brush or any styling products.

"Okay," he said, helping me up. I didn't say anything as I went back to his bedroom and put everything back on but the bustier. I needed another person to get into that thing, and I wasn't going to ask Lucas, because then that would lead to us starting up again, and I couldn't. This had to be it.

Why did I feel like I wanted to cry?

I shook my head at myself and folded up the bustier and shoved it in my purse. Then I got dressed the rest of the way and pulled my hair back.

I was not looking forward to going back and getting the third degree from Sloane, but I had to. I had to go.

Lucas wasn't in the living room when I went back out. Where the hell did he go? I found a note on the counter.

See you tomorrow, Sunshine.

-Lucas Blaine

There were a few other doors in the apartment, and I didn't know what they were for, and he clearly didn't want to say good-bye in person, so I took the note and put it in my purse, right next to the bustier.

The apartment was quiet when I got back and another note greeted me, this time from Sloane, saying that she'd gone in to work for a few hours. I sighed and looked around the big empty apartment.

One of the reasons I loved living with Sloane was that I was never alone. Growing up as an only child had been rough; add to that the fact that my parents had a lot of money, and I'd been extremely isolated.

I got dressed in my favorite sweats, the ones I wore when I was sick, put on some music and grabbed one of my favorite books. It was hard to read with Sloane around, because she was always interrupting me, or reading over my shoulder and asking me what the book was about. It kind of killed the enjoyment.

I had only read about fifty pages when my eyes started closing again and I fell asleep with the book on my chest.

"Hey, Rory." A hand shook my shoulder gently and my eyes opened to find Sloane peering at me.

"Hey," I said, sitting up and causing the book to fall to the floor. "What time is it?" The apartment was dark. I must have slept for hours.

"It's six. Are you okay?" I must look really terrible or else Sloane would be on me for details about the date and the sex and the bustier.

"I think so. I mean, I told him it would only be one night and it was only one night. I just needed to get him out of my system." Sloane set some bags down on the counter and came to sit on the couch with me.

"And did you? Get him out of your system?" Honestly?

"No," I said, and against my will I started to cry. "I mean, I feel like I'm breaking up with him, which is stupid because we're not dating. I've only known him for a few weeks. I shouldn't feel this way after a few weeks, and a few sexual encounters."

"How are you supposed to feel?" Sloane took my feet into her lap and started rubbing them. One of her other talents was great foot massages, but she only gave them in emergencies. I'd had quite a few when I'd broken up with Royce.

"I'm supposed to be able to move on with my life. To see him at work and not feel butterflies whenever he smiles or says my name. To not think about him and want him all the time. I'm better than that."

"Better than what? You're attracted to him, he's attracted to you. That's not a sin, Rory."

"It is when you work together."

We both sighed at the same time.

"I'm fucked," I said.

"Yeah, you kinda are. I wish I could help you."

"You can distract me. Tell me about Fin and Marisol." Sloane's eyes lit up.

"Well, I'd say that the chemistry was definitely there. But you know how she is. No kissing on the first date, let alone sleeping with a guy. I mean, I would get her drunk to test it out, but that doesn't seem like the best idea. But, they did exchange numbers and eye fuck each other for several hours after you left. I think we have a match."

"Good. Someone deserves to be happy." Sloane gave me a sympathetic face.

"I'm making you breakup cake."

"But we weren't dating."

"I know, but I think you need it." Sloane always made a cake when one of us broke up with someone. It wasn't any particular type of cake, just whichever one was our favorite. She made it in heart-shaped pans, which was more of a sick joke than anything. My favorite cake was German chocolate with coconut frosting.

"It's too late cuz I already got the ingredients. You sit there and find something trashy to watch and I'll make us some dinner, okay?" She kissed my forehead and I nodded.

"Hey, I texted you a million times. Did you turn your phone off?"

"Shit, I did. Can you hand it to me?" Sloane fished in my purse and tossed it to me. I knew she saw the bustier, but didn't comment.

I turned my phone on and was inundated with messages.

"Fuck!!!" It was Sunday night and I was supposed to be at my parents' for dinner. I had three missed calls from my mother. Oh God, they probably thought I was dead.

"What?"

"I completely forgot dinner with my parents! What am I going to say?" There was no way I could tell them the truth.

"Give me your phone," Sloane said, and I handed it to her. She hit a button and put the phone to her ear.

"Mrs. Clarke? Hello, this is Sloane. Yes, I'm calling about Rory . . . No, she's fine, she's just very under the weather. We went out for breakfast and I think she had some bad eggs or something. She was puking all morning . . . No, she's sleeping now . . . I think she just needs to sleep it off and get it out of her system . . . Yes, I will. Okay, Bye." She handed the phone back to me.

"Done."

"I feel like I should call and explain," I said, looking at the phone. I hated lying to my parents.

"Call them later. Or tomorrow morning. It's no big, she was just worried and once she knew that you were indisposed, she was fine."

"Okay, I guess." I still felt shitty about it.

"Go back and sit down." Sloane shoved me toward the couch. I sat down with a sigh and turned on the television, finally settling on a marathon of a show about picking wedding dresses. I knew Sloane would love it. Her running commentary was worth the price of admission.

An hour later, I was inhaling enchiladas with pico de gallo, and a black bean and corn salad, and the German chocolate cake was baking in the oven. Sometimes, you need to eat your feelings.

"Oh my God. I can't watch. I can't watch. Tell me they're not going to put her in a mermaid gown. Tell me this is not happening," Sloane said, covering her eyes with her hands.

"Oh, it's happening. Her mom always dreamed of her in the mermaid dress, so she's wearing the mermaid dress." On most people, a mermaid dress would look good, but on this girl . . . not so much.

I grabbed another enchilada from the pan and some more salad. Sloane peeked behind her fingers. "Oh thank God. That's much more suited to her."

The timer dinged and Sloane raced to get the cake out of the oven and set it on a rack to cool while she made the frosting.

Once the cake was finished, we didn't even cut it, just used forks and dug in. My internal clock was messed up from the all night fuckfest and then the huge nap I'd taken. Tomorrow was going to be rough.

"Men suck," Sloane said with her mouth full of cake.

"They do." I took another bite. I found it interesting that Sloane was so focused on everyone else's love lives, but was doing nothing about her own, and I was starting to get suspicious, but I was going to wait a little while before I asked her about it.

Besides, I had some more wallowing to do.

Chapter Fifteen

I didn't get breakfast for Lucas on Monday morning, but I got my own. I kind of hoped he would see that as a statement, but maybe he wouldn't.

In the elevator up to my office I was trying to gain my normal ice-cold composure, but it wasn't happening. I couldn't snap the wall in front of my emotions. All because of Lucas Blaine and his stupid magical tongue and lovely penis.

I got out of the elevator and walked right to his desk, my heels clicking on the floor, which helped steady my nerves just a little bit. There was a bag on top, as if it was waiting for me. Mr. Blaine was already typing away.

"Good morning, Miss Clarke. Your strawberry donut and coffee are right there and I've already gone through and flagged your important emails." He didn't stop typing or look up at me.

"Thank you Mr. Blaine." I waited for him to say something else, but he didn't, so I grabbed the bag and my coffee and headed to my desk. I hoped he didn't see that I'd already gotten my breakfast, so I now had two.

I just had to get through the rest of the day. And then the next after that . . .

I threw myself into work, and it seemed that Mr. Blaine had done the same. All our discourse was clipped and short and without any longing or lusty staring. At least on his part.

He seemed to be doing fine, and that made me feel even worse. Clearly, he'd taken me seriously about the one night thing. We should have done this originally. Then maybe I wouldn't be in this predicament. Even though it was torture, I left my door open and it took any leftover concentration I had to not look at him as he worked.

His face was so serious all day. I'd never seen him that way, and it was just as sexy as his smile. There was something unbearably attractive about a man when he was on a mission. That was how he'd been last night when he looked at me. Like he was going to possess me. Own me. I'd let him, and I'd done my best to him back.

I tried to block him out, but later in the afternoon he was on the phone and I couldn't ignore it. He was arguing with someone, and it didn't look like something work related. I looked up from my desk and saw him pinch the bridge of his nose as if he was losing his patience.

I wished I could read lips, but I couldn't, and he was too far away and talking too low for me to eavesdrop; but something was definitely not okay. He smacked his hand on the desk and then looked around, as if he was aware that he might be making a scene. I quickly flipped my eyes to some papers on my desk, but I knew he saw me.

He hung up the phone and I could feel his eyes on me. Great. I'd gotten caught. I picked up my phone and dialed his extension. He picked up after one ring.

"Everything okay?" I said. He sighed and he looked defeated. It's a strange thing when you can see the face of the person you're talking to on the phone. Puts a whole new spin on it.

"I'm sorry if I disturbed you. I didn't mean to. It won't happen again." He sounded depressed and dejected and I wanted, more than anything, to reach through the phone and put my arms around him.

"Is there anything I can do?"

"No," he said as he shook his head. "Nothing anyone can do."

"Is it bad?"

"No. Nothing that won't take care of itself. Don't worry about me." His voice was soft and it reminded me of the way he'd spoken the other night in bed. *You're so beautiful.* Sloane hadn't asked me to wear any more of her creations, and I was relieved. Wearing them just for me wasn't as much fun as seeing Lucas' face when he looked at me in them.

"Okay. Please let me know if I can do anything."

"Thank you, Miss Clarke. That won't be necessary." His cordial voice was back. He was shutting me out again. I should be glad, but it was almost as if he'd slammed a door in my face.

"You're . . . you're welcome, Mr. Blaine." He hung up the phone and went back to work.

Questions swirled through my head and made it hard to think. What had the phone call been about? Was it personal? He hadn't mentioned anything about his personal life, other than his nieces and brothers. He'd never spoken of his parents.

And that opened up other questions. I had his résumé, so I knew where he went to school and when he graduated, but what had it been like? Did he have a lot of friends, or was he a loner? Had he liked school? What did he do in his spare time, other than singing?

And why did he ask me to call him Lucah on Saturday night?

The questions weighed heavily on me and made me tired. I locked the screen on my computer and walked down the hall to Dad's office. I'd seen him this morning already and told him all about my illness, which was easier than I thought it would be, and that made me feel even worse than I already did.

I knocked on the door and waited. He was on the phone, but he hung up and told me to come in.

"Rory, what are you doing down this end of the hallway? Not that I'm not pleased to see my girl." He got up from his desk and gave me a hug. I must have looked like I needed it.

I definitely did.

"Why so blue?"

"Oh, I think I'm still worn down from the food poisoning. Nothing a few good nights of sleep couldn't cure. Or maybe some more coffee. Lots of coffee." I breathed in his aftershave and cologne. It was a special blend Mom had made for him every Christmas, and I'd smelled it since childhood. It was home. And safety.

"So since I didn't get to interrogate you at dinner, tell me how your outing with Fin went," he said, leading me to a chair and handing me a glass of water. I took it, if only to have something to do with my hands.

I gave him the sanitized version and told him that despite having a lovely conversation with him, and him being very good-looking, it wasn't going to be producing love or babies anytime soon.

"Ah, I thought so, but your mother was convinced. And there isn't another special young man in your life?" I shook my head, probably a little too vigorously.

"Nope. I'm married to the job right now. When the right one comes along, I'll know." God, I sounded like a Disney character. I should be twirling around in a field and singing while woodland creatures cleaned my house.

"Well, I don't want you to turn around forty years from now and regret that you missed out on something. The job will always be here for you when you want it. People say I'm a nepotist, and I am. There will always be jobs for those I care about. Why would I hire anyone else?" He gave me another hug.

"Dad? Don't tell anyone that I was in here. I have to keep my persona intact." He laughed.

"I won't breathe a word. Come talk to me anytime, Rory." With one last kiss on my head, I left, feeling a little bit better, but no less confused.

I made it through the day, and Lucas left a few minutes before me, so I didn't have to ride the elevator down with him.

The next morning he brought my breakfast again, and he was deep in work when I got there. It was almost an exact repeat of the day before.

The next day was the same. And the next.

A whole week went by with his cordial words and emotionless looks and I felt myself getting more and more bogged down with work and stress. I'd wanted this. I'd demanded it, and now that I had it, I just wanted to go back to the time when he'd come up behind me in the break room and whisper something dirty in my ear, or when I could feel him ogling my ass as I walked away, or even when he'd smile and I knew he was happy. He didn't seem happy, and then it was time for his three-week evaluation. It was my job to do this one, but all other evaluations would be done by the head of Human Resources.

If he lasted that long.

I picked up the phone and dialed his extension. He picked up without looking up at me.

"Would you please come into my office and close the door, Mr. Blaine?"

"Of course, Miss Clarke." We hung up and he straightened his desk and locked his computer before walking around his desk and into my office, shutting the door softly behind him.

"Please, sit down." We hadn't been alone like this and I knew it wasn't going to be easy. My body reacted to his. That's just the way it was. He flipped a switch in me whenever he was around.

"As you know, you've been with us three weeks now and so it's time to evaluate your progress. So, how do you think you're doing?" I folded my hands on my desk and thanked whoever had written a sheet of questions for me to ask so I had something to look at other than his face.

"I enjoy my job. It is challenging and exciting; I feel like I get along with everyone here and I think I'm contributing." Well said, but with about zero emotion.

This wasn't him.

I cleared my throat.

"Well, I agree with you on all of those points. You're a hard worker. You're on time and you finish everything you start and—" I was interrupted by him using his hand to smother a laugh. That caught me completely off guard.

I looked up from my paper and saw that his face was red and he was still trying not to laugh and failing.

"I'm sorry. Go on." He coughed and tried to put his serious face back on.

"As I was saying, you finish everything you start and—"

Cue laughter. This time he couldn't stop, and I caught it.

"Oh, you are such a perv." I grabbed a pen and threw it at him. "Of course you would take something as simple as an evaluation and make it dirty. Typical guy." Yup, any semblance of professionalism went out the window.

He shook his head. "I'm sorry, you just looked so serious when you said it."

I looked up from his evaluation form. "Hey, I'm not the one who's had serious face on all week."

"Yeah, well your bitch face has been getting quite a workout. Every time I check you've got it on. I mean, it's just as sexy as your not-bitch face. If you were trying to not be sexy, it didn't work."

"Yeah, ditto."

He leaned back and his face relaxed and mine did too.

"So," he said.

"So."

"We sucked at that, didn't we?" he said.

"Sucked at what?" He put his hands behind his head and I pushed the evaluation sheet aside.

"At the one night plan. When . . . when I woke up and found you in my arms . . . I knew that I couldn't have just one night. I wanted more. Still do."

Oh, these were all the things that girls want boys to say to them, but they were wrong in this context.

"Just because you want something, doesn't mean you can have it," I said.

"Actually, it's been my experience that it does. I always get what I want, even if I have to work for it." He was incorrigible.

"Why are you making this so hard on me, Lucas? Oh, and why did you ask me to call you Lucah?"

That caught him off guard. Hmm.

"It's . . . it's a nickname I had when I was young. Only certain people are allowed to call me that."

"And I'm a certain person?"

Our eyes met and locked.

"You are."

I took a shaky breath.

"I can't deny that one night wasn't enough for me, but I can't let this, or whatever it could be jeopardize my job. This is my life. I've known I was going to work here since I could crawl down those hallways. I took my first steps outside Dad's office. This is who I am and I don't know how to add you to the picture without wrecking everything." He waited, because he knew there was more.

"With that said, how about we continue our . . . nights outside the office. Just nights. And then we'll come in the next day and we can function, because right now, I don't feel like I'm functioning. I'm still doing my job, but it's not the same." I didn't mean to tell him all that, but it was pointless to try to hide how I was feeling.

"I know. I'm . . . I'm so sorry about all of this." What did he have to be sorry for? I could have slapped him with a harassment suit at any time and tossed him out on his ass. But then he could have thrown it in my face, since I was his boss and in a position of power to leverage him for sex.

"It's not your fault. We just have to figure out how to work around this. Maybe . . . maybe I can get you transferred to another department. Then at least we wouldn't have to stare at each other all day long."

He half smiled. "But I like staring at you all day long."

I bit my lip. "Yeah, me too. I mean, staring at you. I don't stare at myself."

That elicited another real smile from him.

"Nights?" he said, the smile widening and becoming more wicked.

"Nights. Only nights."

He got up from his chair and walked around my desk, then turned my chair to face him.

"Well, it's night in England right now. And you know, this country was founded by Englishmen, so as far as I'm concerned that makes it night here by proxy." He got down on his knees so our faces were at the same level.

"Is that some twisted way of saying that it's five o'clock somewhere?"

"More or less." His mouth was so close to mine. I felt like I hadn't tasted it in so long. I could have a kiss, right? Just one little itty bitty kiss.

He stopped with his face only an inch away from mine and our noses almost brushed. He crossed his eyes at me and I couldn't help but laugh.

And then my phone rang, shattering the moment. He groaned and I saw that it was one of the other executives, so it was important.

"I need to take this." He nodded and stood up, but didn't leave. I gave him a look and he put his hands up as if he surrendered and backed out of the room as I answered the phone.

He left my door open, and I swiveled my chair back around so I could watch him as he sat down at his desk. The call was quick, something that could have been taken care of via email, and I spent most of the time rolling my eyes and miming shooting myself as Lucas tried not to laugh at his desk. Whenever someone walked by we had to stop looking at each other.

I hung up from the unnecessary phone call and immediately dialed Lucas.

"We didn't finish your three week evaluation."

He hung up the phone and walked back into my office and shut the door.

"You rang?"

How could I be serious with him?

"You know that you're doing well, and that there isn't anything that's a major problem. So just keep doing what you're doing. The next time you'll be evaluated, it will be in three months and I won't be the one doing it, so you're not going to be able to get away with all the stuff you're getting away with right now. Don't screw it up and don't make me look bad. Here's a copy of your evaluation to look over and sign. Now get out of my office," I flung the piece of paper at him and pointed to the door.

"Bitch," he said grabbing the paper and pretending to storm out, but when he got to his desk he stuck his tongue out at me, minus the silver bar. I still needed to ask him about that.

I picked up the phone again.

"When did you get your tongue pierced?"

"You know, telling me to leave your office and then calling me back sends a bit of a mixed message."

"Just answer the question and get back to work."

"In my wild youth. Good-bye, Miss Clarke." He chuckled and hung up. I glared at him and shook my head. And then I went back to work.

Chapter Sixteen

"So," he said as we got into the elevator at the same time that night. I knew he'd totally planned this, but I wasn't complaining.

"So."

"Your place or mine?" he said, moving closer to me and taking my hand. I pulled mine away, because we were still in the building and I wasn't taking any chances.

"Well, I have a roommate, sooo . . ."

"Ah, right. My place then. I'd like to see your place though." I didn't want him to see it until I'd cleaned it and then the housekeeper had come and then I'd cleaned it again.

"Maybe sometime. But do you mind if I go home first and get some things? Not that I don't love using your shower gel, but your shampoo sucks."

He nodded and the elevator reached the ground floor and we exited together.

"See you . . . in an hour? Don't worry about eating. I'll take care of dinner." Ah, a man who took charge. Sexy.

"Okay."

"Okay." There was a pause, as if both of us wanted to kiss the other good-bye, but we couldn't. People walked around us, oblivious.

I ducked my head and headed out the door and he followed behind me and then we went our separate ways.

My phone rang a few seconds later.

"Hello, Miss Clarke." I turned around and he was still visible about a hundred feet down the sidewalk.

"Hello, Mr. Blaine. Was there something you needed?"

"No. I just wanted to ask you what you wanted for dinner." I swore I could see his smile shining at me from this distance.

"Surprise me. Good-bye, Mr. Blaine. I'll see you in an hour." I ended the call and kept walking toward the T.

About ten minutes later, my phone buzzed with a text message from him.

How do you feel about pizza?

I shook my head and typed a response.

Pizza and I have been in an intimate relationship for many years. I would marry pizza if I could.

I sent it and waited for a response as I walked back up to the street level and started toward my apartment. My phone buzzed with a response.

Who am I to stand in the way of true love? Pizza it is.

I smiled and put my phone away. Texting and walking was a dangerous sport and I didn't want any part in it.

Sloane wasn't back yet from work, so I texted her and she said she was stuck at the studio and might be pulling an all-nighter. That wasn't unusual when she was working on something new, or preparing for a show, so I told her that I was sending her imaginary coffee and if she did get home I wouldn't be there because I was also stuck at the office. And by stuck, I meant having sex and by office, I meant with Lucas.

I'd fill her in tomorrow. I just didn't want to get into why this was such a bad life decision now. Lucas was waiting.

I spent most of the hour away from him trying to pick out the best set of underwear I owned. I still had the two pieces from Sloane, but he'd seen them already and I felt kind of weird wearing them again. So I chose a simple white lace bra and white panties. They were sweet and comfortable and I hoped he liked them.

Since we were having pizza, I figured the night was going to be casual, so I went with a comfortable t-shirt that made my boobs look great, and black skinny jeans. I took my hair out and put up again in a loose ponytail. I did one last check in the mirror, made sure I had enough supplies in my bag for any emergencies (tampons, toothbrush, deodorant, birth control) and I was off.

The entire cab ride to Lucas' I alternated between giddy excitement and telling myself what a terrible idea this was, while picturing scenes in which he and I were caught in the act and there was a dramatic firing and my Dad just shook his head in shame at me.

The cab stopped outside Lucas' apartment and I paid the fare and got out, my legs a little wobbly.

My phone rang, and I had kind of expected it.

"Hello, Aurora Clarke. If you'll proceed to the front door, just tell the doorman who you are and you can come right in." I looked up at the building, but there was no way he could see me from his place unless he had night vision binoculars. Well, that was a creepy thought.

"I'm standing in the lobby. I can see you," he said, as if sensing my reluctance.

I looked into the lobby and saw him through the glass doors. He waved one hand and I waved back, feeling a little foolish. The doorman let me in when I said my name and Lucas came forward to meet me. He was casual as well, in another band shirt and faded jeans.

"You look great, as always," he said, kissing my cheek.

"Thanks." He took my bag from me, and grabbed my hand as we walked toward the elevator.

"This feels like a date," I said.

"Do you want it to be a date?" I looked at him as the elevator started to rise.

"No. I mean, if this is a date, then that means we are dating, which means that we need to put a label on it, and that's not what this is. You and me, we're nights. Just nights. I have to draw the line."

"Okay, then this isn't a date. But I have a few requests for this nights-only arrangement."

"Proceed."

"Call me Lucah." I still wanted to know why he wanted me to, but I knew he wasn't going to tell me why. This man was a deep well and I didn't think he was going to let me see the bottom. Not that I should try. He wasn't my boyfriend and I wasn't falling in love with him.

"Okay, I can do that. Anything else?"

"I don't think we should discuss work or the office."

"Yes, that's another good one. I also think we should keep this arrangement to ourselves. I told Sloane that I had to work all night, so that's where she thinks I am."

"Agreed."

"Agreed."

"Do you want to put this in writing and then shred it?" I poked him with my elbow.

"No, I think I can trust you."

"Ah, that will be your misfortune. I may suddenly but inevitably betray you." Wait. Hold up.

"Did you just quote *Firefly*?" I said.

He kept a straight face as we walked toward his door and he unlocked it.

"I have no idea what you're talking about."

His apartment was spotless as usual. He had a very minimalist decorating style, and it worked for him, but I wished there were more personal items around so I could get a better sense of him. No pictures, no little knickknacks from trips or any extraneous things. It was a bit odd, but I guess he was just that kind of guy.

"So you said you loved pizza, but have you ever tried it with truffles?" That must be the amazing smell that had taken over his apartment. There were two pizza boxes on the counter and a few other containers with things in them.

"I haven't, but my roommate makes truffle mac and cheese and that's to die for." He took my bag and set it in the bedroom, then came back and put his arms around me.

"I've been wanting to do that all day. Do you know how hard it is not to cross the space between us during the day and put my arms around you? And my hands on you?" As he spoke his hands traveled down my back and cupped my ass.

I shook my head and pulled away.

"You're not supposed to talk about the place-that-must-not-be-spoken-of."

"How could I have broken that rule already? Are you going to punish me?" he said with a wicked smile.

"Maybe. I might make you get on your knees for it." I moved my hands down and squeezed his butt. It really was the bee's knees of butts.

"That wouldn't be a punishment," he said, and I could feel him getting hard. Hmm, pizza might have to wait.

I moved my hands from the back of his jeans to the front and stroked him.

"Now?" he said, his voice hoarse.

"Now." He shoved me up against the front door and attacked my mouth and oh, help me, he had the tongue barbell in again.

I'd thought after doing this a few times that some of the heat would cool, but it was like each time made us want it even more.

He gathered my wrists and put them above my head and I put my legs around his waist. Kissing down my neck, he moved his hands under my ass to hold me up. We weren't even going to get naked this time. I was definitely ready. I'd been thinking about this all day and I wasn't sure how much longer I could hold out. I quickly moved my hands down to unzip my jeans and shove them with my underwear down low enough.

"Inside me. Now, please." He fumbled for just a moment to get the condom out of this back pocket, and I had to stand again, but I helped him roll it on this time and then he was picking me up and with a move that I would have to figure out later, he slid inside me.

"I've. Wanted. This. All. Day," he said with each thrust and I clung to him as he set a frenzied pace that we both craved.

"Oh God, Lucah. Me too." In the very back of my mind I knew we were making quite a racket and every time he thrust into me, my back banged against the door. I came hard and fast, and it was all I could do to keep my legs wrapped around him as he came, growling my name in my ear. He lowered me slowly and pulled out, and we held onto each other, trembling with aftershocks.

We were both trying to catch our breath as he rested his head on my shoulder and kissed it.

"Wow," I said.

"Yeah," he said. We started both started laughing. And then there was a knock at the door.

I ducked my face into his shoulder and bit it to stifle my laugh as Lucah looked over my head through the peephole.

"Maybe she'll go away," he said low in my ear. The knock sounded again.

"Mr. Blaine? Is everything okay? I thought I heard banging." Oh, she definitely had.

He looked down at me and tried to keep a straight face.

"Yes, Mrs. Parks. Everything is fine. I was just doing some exercises. Sorry to have disturbed you. It won't happen again." I snorted and tried to keep it together so she didn't hear me.

"Oh, okay." She didn't sound convinced. We both waited and he looked out the peephole. A few seconds later he breathed deeply.

"She's gone. God, I swear anytime I breathe that woman is knocking on my door. She's divorced and older and lonely and I think she wants me to be her pet."

I made a growling sound and moved my head from his shoulder.

"Down girl," he said and stepped away from me. "If you'll excuse me, I need to clean up and then we'll have to reheat the pizza.

"Hurry back," I said and he gave me a quick kiss on my forehead. When he was gone, I straightened my clothes and tried to get myself together. My hair was a mess from its contact with the door, so I took it out and flipped my head down to fix it.

"That's a nice view," Lucah said as he came back in. My ass was in the air, so I wiggled it and he dashed forward and smacked me.

"Hey now, I'm trying to fix the hair that you ruined." I stood up and gave up on my hair, just letting it go everywhere.

"It looks fine. I like seeing you like this. When we're at work, it's always pulled back and I can't do this," he said, running his fingers through it.

"You did it again. That's two strikes." He pressed his forehead against mine.

"I guess I owe you a lot of knee time." Mm, I really liked the sound of that.

"Pizza first," I said.

"Since this isn't a date, I didn't feel the need to get out candles, but I do have wine and the nice glasses are clean," he said as he took the truffle mushroom pizza out of the oven. He also had a gorgeous chopped salad, but he wouldn't tell me what dessert was.

"I also have this," he said, moving over to a cabinet, which revealed a classy stereo with speakers that I'd noticed around the apartment. He hit a button and a song I wasn't familiar with surrounded me. It almost reminded me of the Beatles.

"What is this?" I said as he poured me a glass of wine.

"'Brighter than Sunshine' by Aqualung," he said with a smile as we took the pizza over to the couch. He had a dining table, but that felt too much like a date. I'd rather be comfortable.

"It's nice. I like it," I said after I'd listened to a little more of the song. I sipped the wine. It was light and crisp and went well with everything else.

"So where's your guitar?" I said as I munched on my salad.

"In my music room."

I almost choked on a cucumber.

"Music room?"

"Yeah, it's right over there," he said, pointing with his fork at one of the doors I hadn't been behind yet.

"I'd really like to see it," I said.

"Well, I'd love to see your apartment. Show me yours and I'll show you mine." I rolled my eyes.

"You've already seen mine. Several times."

"Yes, I've seen your body, but you're more than just your body. A lot more. And I'd like to see it."

"That sounds awfully like something a guy who wants to date me would say." I pointed my fork at him and he shook his head.

"No. It's not a boyfriend thing that I want to get to know you. That could just be me wanting to get to know you. Not so I can date you, just so I can know you."

He was fumbling and it sounded like bullshit to me, but I was going to let it go.

The song changed and I recognized Bobby Darin's, 'Beyond the Sea'. Very classy.

We started the pizza and it was amazing. I would have to tell Sloane about this so she could make it.

Or maybe not. Then I'd have to tell her about the nights-only arrangement and we'd already agreed to keep this on the down low. God, this was complicated. But when he reached out and wiped some cheese off my chin, then winked and licked it off his thumb while my stomach did little flips, I knew that maybe it would be worth it.

Once we were stuffed, we sat on the couch with my head on his shoulder and sipped wine. The music kept playing and it was . . . eclectic. I'd heard Queen, Adele, Simple Minds, The Black Keys, Cole Porter and Jamie N Commons and a bunch of others that I didn't know well enough to name.

"What's for dessert?" I asked.

"You." I pinched his non-pierced nipple with my fingernails.

"Bad girl. We're having s'mores."

"Really?" I hadn't had one of those in a very long time.

"I mean, unless you don't like s'mores in which case, there's the door." He pointed and his face was serious.

"You mean to tell me that if I didn't like s'mores, you'd kick me out?" I raised my eyebrow.

"I don't want anyone in my house who doesn't like s'mores."

"Well, it's a good thing for you that I do."

"Thank God." He motioned for me to let him up and went back to the kitchen as the song changed again to Muse's 'Starlight'.

"Do you need any help?" I hadn't seen a fire or anything, so I was wondering how this s'more thing was going to happen.

"No, I've got this, just relax. You're only the boss during the day."

I held up three fingers. "Three strikes."

"More knee time. Whatever shall I do?" I watched him from the couch as he brought out something from under his cupboards and brought it over to the coffee table. It was a hybrid of a fondue set, but without the pot on top, so it was basically like a little tiny fire. He lit it and then brought over plates of chocolate, graham crackers and marshmallows.

He handed me a metal skewer with a little handle and took one for himself.

"Ready?"

"Um, yeah, I've made these before, but never inside. It's nice that I don't' have to worry about mosquitos. Or smoke in my eyes."

"Did you go camping a lot?" he said as we rotated our marshmallows to evenly brown them.

"My parents have a summer place in Maine, so we used to go a lot. We'd be at the house and then Dad would just start packing a bag and tell us we were going camping. I mean, it was *real* camping. Sleeping on the ground, outhouse, bathing in the river, the works. It was the only time I ever saw my dad wear flannel, or my mom without her lipstick. It was great." I waited for him to tell me something about his childhood but he seemed intent on his marshmallow.

"Did you go camping as a kid?" I finally asked.

"Not very much." Okay, childhood questions were out. My marshmallow was done so I grabbed my graham cracker and chocolate and slid the marshmallow off and in between the crackers. Apparently, making a s'more was like riding a bike. Or having sex. It all came back to you.

I was eating my first s'more when Lucah's first marshmallow got too close to the flame and went up. He tried to blow on it, but that only made it worse.

"Aw, you lose. Want some of mine?" I held my s'more out to him and he took a bite before he pulled the burned part from the marshmallow and ate it anyway.

We both went for our second marshmallows and I saw that Lucah had marshmallow smeared in the corner of his mouth.

"Hold still."

"What?" He went to wipe his face.

"No, I just told you not to move." I leaned forward and licked the marshmallow. I tried to pull back, but he grabbed my chin and kissed me. He tasted of chocolate and graham crackers and sweet melted marshmallow and underlying it all was the taste of him that I never thought I was going to get enough of.

"I like a little you with my dessert," he said, pushing my hair back.

"Same here."

We ate a few more s'mores and kissed a little more, and he slowly removed my clothes and I removed his and then he carried me to the bedroom and fucked me so slow and so sweet that I held onto him afterwards and didn't want to let him go.

He looked down into my eyes and smiled and then rolled so we were both on our sides and pulled out.

"Any second thoughts?" he said.

"A few. But I'm ignoring them."

He ran his hand over my shoulder.

"I could quit."

"No, you don't have to do that. I can't let you do that for me. We can make this work. This is only the first night. It's going to take some adjusting."

"I don't want to put you in this position. It isn't right of me to make you take chances, Sunshine." I put my hand on his mouth.

"It's not for you to decide. I'm the one who told you to put your dick inside me. Repeatedly. And I also told you that I would fire you if you didn't do it. Jesus, I made you finger me in the middle of a meeting. I'm not innocent in this."

He circled his finger on my shoulder.

"No, you're definitely not innocent, but I like that about you."

"Oh, you like that? What else do you like?" I smiled and moved closer to him.

"I like your bitch face. And I like that you always wear high heels. And I like that you care so much about your job. And I like this . . . And this . . ." He moved his hand from one breast to the other and then slid it down my stomach and moved and thumbed my clit and flicked my piercing.

"Oh, I definitely like this." I was so sensitive from the recent contact with that area that it didn't take much for me to want him again.

"I like your hair, and your eyes, and this," I said, putting my finger in his chin dimple. "And I like this," I said tapping his nipple ring. "And I guess I like this," I said, moving down to his dick.

"You seemed to like it a few minutes ago."

"I guess. It was okay." He growled and lunged at me until he was straddling me again. I screamed and he nuzzled in my neck.

"Speaking of that, I need to take care of it." He reached over to grab some tissues and tossed the condom. I needed to get up and pee, so I did that and then came back and crawled back into bed with him, snuggling under his arm.

"I like this," he said, pulling me close.

"I like this too." I liked it a lot. A lot, a lot. I yawned even though I tried not to.

"Go to sleep, Sunshine. We'll have other nights." I didn't want to, but he had really nice pillows, so I let myself rest against his chest and the sound of his breathing lulled me to sleep.

An alarm blared in my ears and it felt like it was stabbing my skull with sound.

"Oh my GOD, that needs to stop," I moaned and rolled over. I'd been sprawled over Lucah's bare chest and his arms and legs had been all twisted with mine.

The blaring stopped abruptly and I looked at him as he blinked his eyes open.

"I wanted to make sure you had enough time to shower and get to work. Sorry about the early hour, Sunshine."

He kissed my forehead and I squinted at him.

"No big. Why don't you get up and make me breakfast, or get it, or something and I'll just lay here for a little while and . . . get myself mentally ready."

"You're not a morning person, are you? I thought you would be."

"Why? Because of the name? I think that was wishful thinking on my parents' part. Besides, nobody really calls me by my full first name, not even my parents."

He got up and pulled his boxers back on before he leaned over me.

"I'm going to get some breakfast ready. If you're not in the shower in ten minutes, I'm coming in here and throwing you in." He nipped the end of my nose and I put the pillow over my head.

"Get up, Sunshine," he said, ripping the covers off me.

"Douchebag!"

His only answer was to laugh as he banged around the kitchen. Well, if the alarm didn't get me up, the noise in the kitchen did. I grabbed my bag and went to shower. One of these mornings I wanted to shower with him. Or nights. Just nights. Maybe tomorrow.

I blow dried my hair and got it up before I put on my work attire. I was back to my pencil skirts and buttoned shirts and I had my red heels on. His back was to me as I walked into the kitchen, but the moment he heard my heels on the tile floor, he turned.

"You're trying to end me, Sunshine. There's no way I can work today. I give up." He held his hands up, one of them holding a spatula.

"Don't be so dramatic, Mr. Ginger." I walked closer to see what he was doing. Looked like omelets in one pan and fried potatoes in another. I'd never been so spoiled with breakfast before.

"Hey, I'm very sensitive about my hair color. Be careful there, Miss Clarke." I grabbed a handful of his hair and tugged on it.

"What are you making?" I made sure to keep my distance from the pans so I didn't get grease on my white shirt.

"Omelets and potatoes. Which reminds me, what would you like in your omelet? I have peppers, cheese and tomatoes."

"All of the above. One of these mornings, I'm going to make you breakfast. Sloane has taught me a thing or two in the kitchen."

He flipped one of the omelets.

"Will you do it wearing nothing but those heels and an apron?"

"We'll see," I said, going for the coffeepot. He'd already put out the cream and sugar for me.

"I'm still going to have to buy you breakfast to keep up appearances," I said as I sipped the coffee and felt instantly better. I knew it couldn't affect me that quickly, but damn it was good stuff.

"I don't mind second breakfast," he said with a little smile, almost as if he was enjoying an inside joke.

"What's so funny?"

"Oh, nothing." He scooped my omelet out of the pan and onto a plate, then added some potatoes. I went to the fridge and searched around until I found some ketchup.

"It should be illegal to eat potatoes without ketchup," I said, squirting some on the side of the plate.

"What about potato chips?" he said, making up his own plate and declining my offer of ketchup.

"I eat those with ketchup too." My omelet was really good and filled with extra cheese.

"I hope you like me thick, because if I keep eating breakfast like this, there's gonna be more of me." He shrugged.

"I've never liked girls with nothing to them. There's nothing attractive about fucking a skeleton." I made a face.

"Nice description."

"Hey, it's true."

We finished breakfast and it was time for our night to be over. I took my bag and he walked me to the door.

"See you at the-place-we-won't-name," I said, giving him one last kiss.

"See you later, Miss Clarke." I walked backwards as he closed the door slowly.

I had to fight a deep sigh as I walked toward the elevator. I was joined by a woman with a giant box in her hands so I held the door for her.

"Oh, thank you," the woman said, and I recognized her voice. It was the woman who'd knocked on Lucah's door last night. But she didn't know who I was.

That didn't stop me from fidgeting and blushing the entire ride down to the lobby. The woman smiled at me as she exited and I left after her, still blushing.

Chapter Seventeen

I swung by a coffee shop and got our second breakfast before I hopped in a cab and headed to the office. Somehow, Lucah (I'd have to remind myself to call him Lucas out loud at work) beat me there and I smoothed my facial expression and tried to walk normally as I approached his desk.

"Good morning, Mr. Blaine. I thought I would bring you breakfast." I set the bag on his desk and he gave me a cordial smile.

"Well that was very nice of you, Miss Clarke. I was just sitting here and kicking myself that I had neglected to eat breakfast this morning."

"You're welcome, Mr. Blaine," I said and walked to my office, sat down and gave him a huge wink. He stuck his tongue out at me and I turned my computer on and started checking my messages.

I had quite a few. It seemed that overnight one of our servers had gone down and they were still working on getting it up and running. Even in a building full of people who knew everything there was to know about computers, we still had problems. If the problem persisted, we were going to have to look at maybe getting a few more backup servers, which weren't going to be cheap. Lovely. If the fight about the pens had been bad, this was going to be even worse.

I scarcely had time to glance at Lucah because I was so busy doing damage control the entire day. I was starving by one thirty, and I knew there was no way I was going to leave the office at this rate.

I picked up the phone and dialed Lucah.

"I'm so sorry, but it doesn't look like I'm going to get to leave my desk to pee, let alone eat, so could you get me some lunch?" It was perfectly within his job description, but I felt like a bitch asking.

"What do I get in return?" he said in a low voice.

"Um, nothing, seeing as how this is part of your job, Mr. Blaine. Don't make me write you up."

He sighed.

"Fine. But you owe me a blow job." I gasped and he laughed. "What can I get you, Miss Clarke?"

I had barely left my desk by the end of the day, and it felt strange to stand after sitting for so long. I was exhausted.

And then I saw Lucah sitting at his desk and waiting for me. That was all I needed to not feel so tired anymore. Amazing sex was better than coffee. Or maybe having amazing sex while drinking coffee.

Probably not. Sounded dangerous. Crotch burns didn't sound fun.

"Oh, Miss Clarke, I just had a message for you," he said, handing me a sticky note.

I'm fucking you in those heels tonight.

-Lucah

I tried to keep my face impassive as I read it and then folded it up and put it in my purse.

"Thank you for the message, Mr. Blaine. I will take that under consideration."

"Have a good night, Miss Clarke."

"You as well, Mr. Blaine."

The minute I stepped off the elevator I had a text.

One hour.

I shook my head and typed a response.

One hour.

"Oh my God, I feel like I haven't seen you in two years!" Sloane threw herself at me.

"Whoa, buddy. It's only been 24 hours." I hugged her back, which was hard because she was so tall.

"I know, but I felt like I was missing a part of myself. How's work?"

"Oh, it's . . . stressful. You?" I only had a short while to prepare for going to Lucah's and I wanted to pick out the right underwear, but Sloane was top priority at the current moment.

She started talking about work and telling me about how the company that did a bunch of her sewing had gone out of business, so she'd had to hurry to find someone else and do new contracts and bills of lading and so forth.

"It's been a complete nightmare. You have no idea. I'm running on no sleep and pure caffeine right now. Can you tell?" Just a little. Her eyes were wide and she was pale and frenzied.

"Uh, no. Not at all. Listen, we need to talk." I led her over to the couch and sat down. Lucah was just going to have to wait. Chicks before dicks. I sent him a quick text saying that I was going to be a little late.

"I'm having a . . . nocturnal sexual relationship with Lucas. Lucah, actually. He wants me to call him that, for whatever reason. So that's where I'm going tonight. And that's where I was last night." Sloane's mouth dropped open and she smacked me across the shoulder.

"No fucking way! You dirty hussy! I have a whole new view of you now. Give me some love." She held out her hand for a fist bump and I bumped my fist with hers.

"It's a terrible idea. It's probably the worst idea I've ever had, but for the first time in my life, being bad feels really good." And I gave her a rundown of the previous evening, including the door sex and the s'mores and waking up next to Lucah.

"Aw, I'm getting jealous over here. It sounds so amazing. You really like him, don't you?" I couldn't lie to Sloane.

"I do. That's the problem. I feel like I'm getting closer to him, but then there are these big holes and mysteries he's hiding from me. I know all these intimate things about him, but then I don't know if his parents are still alive, and he shuts me down any time I ask anything. It's so frustrating." I pulled my knees up and set my chin on them.

"Aw, hun. I'm sorry. You sure you want to go see him?" Sloane rubbed my shoulder.

"Yeah, I know it's wrong but he makes me feel good. He makes me happy, and it's not just because of the mind-blowing sex. Although that would be more than enough reason to go over."

"Good?" She raised her eyebrows up and down.

"Very good."

"That's why you're all glowy. It's pretty disgusting." I got up and gave her a hug.

"Thanks a lot. I've got to get ready." She followed me to my bedroom and sat on my bed as I pulled off my work clothes and picked out a new outfit.

"I have another piece for you, if you want to wear it." I had been going through my underwear drawer and I was having the same problem as I did last night, not finding anything that I wanted to show him.

"You do?"

Sloane nodded like a bobble head on crack and then dashed to her room and came back with a gold bra and panties with black designs that almost reminded me of Victorian wallpaper. Both pieces were absolutely beautiful.

"Put it on." Sloane was bouncing up and down and I wished I could turn her down a few notches, so I put my hands on her shoulders and forced her to turn around so I could get dressed without her critical eye adjusting me before I even had my boobs in the bra.

I got everything in and where it was supposed to be and told her to turn around. She gave me the once over and poked and prodded and got everything the way she wanted it and then clapped her hands.

"Good girl. I think this one's a winner. Now we'll just have to see what the boy thinks."

"You sure you're okay with me leaving?"

"Um, if I was leaving you to go have fabulous sex with a hot guy, would you stop me?"

"You wouldn't let me stop you," I said as I pulled a tank top over my head and then a cropped short sleeve cover over it.

"Exactly." Sloane handed me my jeans and I pulled them on, then jumped a few times to get my ass into them and make sure they were going to zip. It was almost period time for me, so I was a little fat this week.

"So go get it on. Work that booty." She did a little booty shake with her nonexistent butt and I had no choice but to join her and we had an impromptu booty shaking dance party.

"Okay, I gotta go." I shoved some fresh clothes in my bag and Sloane gave me a kiss on the cheek.

"Be dirty." Oh, she had no idea.

"I told Sloane about us," I said a few hours later as I rolled off Lucah. We were on the floor in the living room, not having made it to the bed. Per his request, I had the red heels on, even though they hadn't gone with the gold and black set, but he didn't seem to notice.

We both caught our breath and I moved onto my side and faced him, propping my head on my elbow.

"And?" He did the same, mirroring my position. "I thought we were keeping this on the down low."

"Yeah, well, I can't spend every night here and lie about where I am. It's just not feasible for me to do that. She's on your team, by the way, as long as I give her plenty of details. I really need to find her a man. You know anyone?"

"None that Sloane would want." He got up and I stretched on the floor. I felt like he'd been giving me a better workout than the gym ever had. More fun, too.

"Do you have any guy friends?" He'd never talked about anyone.

"Yeah, a few." He sat down next to me wearing boxers.

"Why haven't I ever heard of them?"

He shrugged one shoulder.

"I don't know. I just don't talk about them with you, that's all." I reached for my bra and put it on.

"Why are you always so closed, Lucah? I'm not asking for your entire history. I'm asking you to share some things about your life. Just basic information a friend would know. Aren't we friends?" I came over and put my chin on his legs.

"Friends who work together and fuck together," he said, holding my face.

"Strike four."

"Didn't I already take care of at least one of those strikes?"

"One. Just one." I held one finger up, and he stuck it in his mouth and sucked on my finger. "But now you're trying to distract me."

He gave me my finger back and sighed.

"I'm sorry, Sunshine. There are just some doors that I need to keep closed. Understand?" I shook my head.

"God, you're stubborn."

"I'm also a bitch. How do you think I got where I am at Clarke Enterprises? My pretty face?" I puckered my lips at him. "I'm not asking for the world. Just a little more information. Just a bit."

Putting his head back he looked at the ceiling like he was praying for me to drop it.

"What do you want to know?"

"I'm an only child. I wanna know about your siblings. Obviously since you have nieces, you have at least one brother or sister, and you mentioned playing with brothers, so you have at least two. Come on, tell me, tell me." As great and fabulous as the sex was, I also liked just talking with Lucah.

"I have two brothers. One older, one younger."

"Aha!" I couldn't stop myself from saying.

"Whoa, what was that for?"

"You have middle child syndrome. See? This explains so much now. Keep going, this is fascinating."

"You're ridiculous."

But he didn't stop talking. He told me about his brothers, Tate and Ryder, and that they were close when they were growing up. Tate had a wife, April, and the two little girls, Gracie and Fiona. He saw them nearly every weekend since they lived not that far away in Cambridge. He didn't elaborate much on Ryder and I could sense there was brotherly tension, so I let that go. I was afraid to say anything or interrupt him, because this was the first time he'd voluntarily talked about himself.

Well, the first time he'd talked about himself under duress.

Then he talked a little bit about school, and then he asked me about school and I found myself telling stupid stories that I'd never told anyone else. Maybe it was the nudity. I hadn't gotten to put my panties on, just my bra.

We talked until my voice got tired and he took me to bed, removing my bra. I wanted to have sex again, but we were both too tired, so we just lay there and he stroked my hair and fell asleep and I felt for the first time that I was starting to unwrap the mystery that was Lucah (Lucas) Blaine.

Chapter Eighteen

I spent every night of the following week at his place, and Sloane didn't seem to mind and I didn't mind and Lucah certainly didn't mind.

My stuff started making its way to his place and when my period arrived, tampons made their way into his bathroom. He made no mention of it and I was happy that our extra-sexular activities didn't slow in the slightest. Royce wouldn't even go near me when I was on my period, but Lucah wanted me as much as ever.

The sex. Je-sus Christ, the sex. I felt like I walked around in a constant state of post-coital glow and even though I wasn't sleeping for as many hours, I was getting better quality sleep and I felt better.

We'd also finally sort of got our working relationship on solid ground, or at least ground that we both felt comfortable walking on. We practiced speaking cordially to one another when we were naked sometimes and we always just ended up laughing, but no one seemed the wiser in the office.

As long as we kept our interactions in front of others on the up and up, I was pretty sure we were fine. He did do little things to let me know that he was thinking of me. Like asking me if I wanted "coffee" via a sticky note on a stack of files, or brushing against me in the break room, or sending me naughty text messages. As long as he didn't do anything overt, I didn't mind. In fact, I kind of looked forward to those little things.

I had lunch with my Dad on Friday because our schedules finally synched up and we had the time.

"You look good, Rory girl. Happy. I haven't seen you smiling so much in a long time. Any particular reason?" This was going to require more evasive maneuvers on my part.

"Not really. I've just been feeling really good lately. Maybe it's all the cake Sloane's been making." Sure. Blame it on cake. Cake was responsible for the fact that I looked like I was on mood enhancers all the time.

"She does make a good cake. I haven't seen Sloane in a while. You should bring her to dinner." My parents adored Sloane. Mostly because Sloane could charm anyone.

"I'll ask her and see if she'll make some coconut cake for you." That was Dad's favorite. I changed the subject and we talked about a trip my parents were taking for their anniversary and the difficulties of me planning the girls' trip to Jamaica.

"You could always bring them up to Maine. The house is yours to use whenever you want. Or you could go camping."

He'd offered a bunch of times before, but I just couldn't see my friends roughing it, not to mention camping. That would be a hell no. Especially not Sloane. She would die without access to a shower, hot water, and her extensive makeup collection. Marisol or Chloe weren't that much better.

"Thanks, Dad, but we'll work it out."

I finished my soup and salad and we split a piece of double chocolate cake, but I could tell he wasn't done with me.

"Are you sure there isn't someone special in your life?" I swore he could smell the sex on me, but that was gross and ridiculous.

"No, Dad. I don't need a man to be happy, do I?"

"Absolutely not. I just feel like there's something you're not telling me. But if you say there isn't, then I believe you." Ugh. That was the worst.

"Maybe I'm just finally glad I got rid of one," I said with a wink. Dad had never liked Royce, but since he came from a good family and had money, he couldn't really say anything or else risk alienating a few of his friends. Rich people were complicated. Yes, I knew I was technically part of that group, but I never really felt like I was a member of it.

"Yes, I think we're all a little happy about that, to tell the truth." He gave me the last bite of cake and sat back in his seat. The waiter came back with our check and he ordered both of us tea. I thought we should get back to the office, but I wasn't complaining.

We sat and sipped and enjoyed the hum of the restaurant around us. Or rather, he did and I chewed my lip and felt like crap about lying to him, but there was absolutely zero way of explaining this to him in a way he would understand, or a way that wouldn't make him ashamed of me.

Yes, my parents knew I wasn't a virgin, but having them know that and have them know that I was engaging in an almost purely sexual relationship with someone I worked with was something else entirely. They'd probably call in a priest and break out the holy water. Or at least have some sort of intervention.

And Lucah would be out on his ass before you could say "Daddy's little girl." I didn't mind taking the heat for this, but I didn't want it to go on him. If it were only about me, I could take it.

I cared way too much about him. I wished it would be possible to freeze a relationship and keep it the way it was. Because right now, things were great. I just didn't know how long it was going to last.

"Ready to get back to work?" he said, bringing me out of my own head and back into the restaurant. He looked at his phone and then sighed. "It seems Mr. Craig has a new car that I simply *must* see when we get back." I rolled my eyes.

"Well, take a ride and tell me how it is," I said, as he gave me his arm and we walked toward his car.

"Love you, Rory."

"Love you, too, Dad." He gave me a big hug before we put our professional faces on and went back to the office. My phone rang as soon as I sat down at my desk.

"How did it go?" He knew I'd been worried about lying to my dad. It was actually kind of sweet.

"It was fine, thank you for your concern, Mr. Blaine. If I'm not mistaken, it's time for your lunch break."

"Why thank you Miss Clarke. It seems that it is. Am I going to see you tonight?" As much as I wanted to see him, I really needed a girls' night, sans penis.

"Um, so how would you feel if I went out with the girls?" I braced myself for him to be pissed.

"I'll be honest and say that I would rather have you to myself, but I'm not one of those guys who doesn't know how to share. Middle child, remember?" He kept his voice low because there were a lot of people walking back and forth. I also kept my eyes on my computer.

"Good. I was hoping you weren't going to be one of those possessive guys who doesn't want his woman out of his sight."

"You're not my woman," he reminded me.

"True enough. But I swear, I will more than make it up to you. Saturday night? I'll text you with details."

"Does this mean I finally get to see your place?" I grinned and hoped that he saw it.

"Maybe. Wait and see." I hung up without further ado.

Sloane and I had been talking about the situation and she said she was completely supportive, and to show that support, she was giving me the apartment for the night, and she was going to make us a fabulous dinner.

Have I mentioned she was the best friend ever?

She was having so much fun with her new lingerie line that she wanted to pull an all-nighter at her studio and get a collection together to send to her new manufacturer so they could pitch it to her existing clients.

I had something potentially sexy and potentially silly in my head and I was going to ambush him with it when he came to my place. Plus, the extra night off gave me a chance to make my apartment so clean and sterile, you could eat off every surface. I also removed anything that I didn't want him to see, like stupid fish-faced pictures of me Sloane had taken, and shoved half of my shoes to the back of my closet. Guys were weird about shoes, as in they always thought women had too many, but I say that there was no such thing.

Sloane thought I was being ridiculous, but it was a big deal for me to show him my place. She just didn't understand.

"So how's everything going with that guy from work?" Marisol said as we sat at the bar and waited for open mic to start.

I'd made Sloane swear to keep her trap shut, and so far she'd kept her word.

"Oh, it was one and done." I couldn't deny going home with him the last time we'd been here, but I had decided to tell them that was it, and we were back to our working relationship. It was easier.

"Bummer. Was it bad?" Far from it.

I shrugged and hoped I sounded convincing.

"I was drunk the first time and sober the second and it just wasn't worth potentially ruining my career over. Plus, can you imagine if Dad found out? I think I'd die of embarrassment." Yup, probably would. Which was why Dad could never find out.

"Too bad," Chloe said, pouting. "Is it weird working with him now? I don't think I could ever screw someone I was working with."

"It's not too bad. We're both adults enough to make it work."

The three of them burst into laughter.

"You are so full of shit, Rory," Marisol said, holding onto Chloe. "Tell us the truth."

I took a sip of my drink and Sloane nudged me under the table. She really had to stop doing that.

"It's awkward, okay? It's like we don't know what to say to each other, or how to act normally. I feel weird asking him to do things, even though it's his job. So there. Are you all happy now?" I pretended to pout and sat back in my chair.

"Well, that's what you get for eating where you . . . how does that expression go?" Chloe said and then she and Marisol spent the next ten minutes trying to figure it out as the first victim took the stage. It was a girl we'd seen before and she didn't fare any better the second time around.

"Anyone else thinking a lobotomy would be a good idea right about now?" Sloane said, squeezing my knee and then changing the subject. A few seconds later I got a text from her.

Got your back. I didn't message her back, but I volunteered to get the next round and that was as good as a thank you.

Chapter Nineteen

"Have you shaved?" Sloane said, sitting on my bed as I got ready for Saturday night.

"Yes."

"You're waxed, yes?"

"Sloane. This isn't the first time he's seen my downstairs. He's seen it a lot. So I'm pretty sure he's cool with how it looks." He had actually informed me that he thought it was very nice and that it would make a lovely portrait. I hoped he was kidding about the last part.

"True, but you don't want to let yourself go this early in the relationship. Keep up appearances for a little bit longer."

"We're not in a relationship."

"Then what the hell is it?" She grabbed one of my pillows and tossed it at my ass.

"It's two people having sex and dinner and dessert and spending time with one another. Not necessarily in that order. Sometimes we don't get to the dinner part." I had a feeling tonight was going to be one of those nights.

"You'd better get to my dinner. I slaved away at that for you, bitch." Another pillow followed the trajectory of the first.

"Okay, okay. Dinner before sex. I got it." I put on the outfit that he'd first met me in, along with the red pumps, and slicked my hair back into a bun. The only thing that was different was the underwear, which was another Sloane creation, this time in red that matched the shoes, with green vines twisting all over it and even snaking up the straps.

"You promise?" she said, getting up and glaring at me from her height.

"I promise. But I can't make any promises for Lucah. Once he decides what he wants, he sort of goes for it."

"Well, you'll just have to stop him." I sighed and looked at the clock.

"He's going to be here soon." I still had a lot to set up, but I wanted to do it when Sloane wasn't here.

"Okay, okay, I'm leaving." She backed out of my room and then got her purse and an overnight bag. "Have fun. Enjoy the food and when he leaves tomorrow you have to call me and give me details." I agreed and gave her a hug and she slapped me on the ass before she left. So violent, that girl.

I got all the food set up and looking fancy. I didn't even bother pretending that I was responsible for it, because there was no way I could take credit for Sloane's cooking. She'd outdone herself with a sweet potato bisque, a fruit salad and steak wrapped around asparagus, with roasted red potatoes. Everything was ready and keeping warm in the oven, and she'd set the table for me as well. I lit some candles and then went back to the bedroom to get everything ready.

Ten minutes later, my phone vibrated and I dashed out to the door to buzz him up.

I unlocked the door and tried to arrange myself in the sexiest possible pose, but ended up feeling like a moron, so just leaned against the counter with my hand on my hip.

A knock on the door made my heart leap and I lowered my voice.

"Come in, Mr. Blaine," I said in what I hoped was my Sexy Voice. I didn't really know what that meant, so I worked on emulating the sexy voices of women from old movies. Mae West had nothing on me.

He opened the door and took in my attire. Ha. Speechless. That was what I was going for.

Lucah didn't look bad himself in a pair of fitted black pants and a white button down shirt. I'd asked him to wear something nice. He shut the door and crossed his arms, and shook his head.

"It's a miracle I didn't take you during that job interview. I had to keep adjusting myself so you wouldn't see me getting hard whenever I looked at you." I hadn't noticed.

Slowly, I walked forward.

"Is there anything I can do for you, Mr. Blaine?" I'd made a button and pinned it to my shirt and I could tell he was trying to read it.

"Aurora Clarke, Sexcretary? Is that what that says?" He asked, coming closer and leaning down to read it. I put my finger under his chin and moved his head up so he was looking in my eyes.

"Tonight, I work for you. So, is there anything I can do for you, Mr. Blaine?" I clasped my hands behind me and stuck my boobs out.

"Oh, that is a very, very long list, Miss Clarke. But how about we start with dinner? I don't know how Sloane got my number, but she texted me that if we had sex and let her dinner get cold, she would never forgive me." Freaking Sloane. I shook my head and walked to the kitchen and started getting things out of the oven.

"Please sit down, Mr. Blaine and let me serve you. Would you like some wine?" I had a few bottles to choose from because I didn't know which he'd like.

"Yes, please, Miss Clarke." His gaze burned over my skin and I really wanted to forget the dinner, but I didn't want to incur the wrath of Sloane.

I handed him a glass of wine and he reached out and pulled me in, his hand reaching up my skirt and caressing my panties.

"You are a remarkable woman, Aurora Clarke. I don't know why you came into my life, but I'm damn glad that you did." I smiled down at him and I wanted to kiss him, but if I did, then it would turn into something else and then Sloane would kill me.

"Same here, Lucah Blaine. Now sit there and I'll get your dinner for you." He removed his hand and I made up his plate and carried it over and then made up mine. We'd never eaten dinner at an actual table. It felt formal.

I made sure to keep a napkin in my lap and eat carefully so I didn't get anything on my shirt.

"How is everything?" I asked.

"It's really good. You weren't lying about her cooking skills."

"She's one of those people who excels at whatever she decides she wants to excel at. It makes me kind of hate her sometimes, but she's the best friend I could ask for, so I can't hate her too much." We stuffed ourselves and afterward I tried to clear the plates, but he wouldn't let me.

"I'm your sexcretary. I'm in charge of this part of the evening." He shook his head and took the plates to the sink anyway.

"You're undermining my position, Mr. Blaine," I said in my sexy voice.

"Oh, I think you'll get over it," he said with a wink as he scraped the plates and then started filling the sink with water to rinse everything. I got up and stood behind him, running my hands up and down the front of his pants.

"Are you sure there's nothing I can do?" He may have told me he was doing the dishes, but his pants were telling me a different story.

"Traitor," he said, and I think he was talking to his dick. Then he dropped the plate he was working on, spun around, grabbed my face and kissed the daylights out of me as his hands worked on the buttons on my shirt.

"Whoa, red light," I said into his mouth as I pulled away, but hooked my fingers on the waistband of his pants and pulled him toward my bedroom.

"I have to show you something first." We reached my door and I swung it open to reveal that my bed had been covered with pens, papers, sticky notes and lots of other office supplies.

It took him a second to get it, but then he smiled.

"I think I'm picking up what you're putting down, Miss Clarke," he said and walked over to stand next to the bed.

"Oh no!" I said, pretending to be shocked and doing a terrible acting job on purpose. "My bed has turned into a desk. I guess we can't use it." I pouted and then Lucah took his arms and swept everything off my bed and onto the floor.

"How did you know I've always wanted to do that?" He said as he grabbed me and threw me on the now-clear bed.

"It's my job," I said, grabbing him and pulling him onto the bed on top of me.

A little while later, I was lying in my bed-turned-desk-turned-back-into-bed and Lucah was having fun with the sticky notes. I had ones all over my breasts that said *kiss me* and ones on my shoulders that said *bite me* and then he was working his way down and putting quite a few *lick me* and *suck me* notes in other places.

"You're still hijacking my job, Mr. Blaine," I said as he slapped another note on my thigh.

"I don't care, Miss Clarke. I'm the boss and this is what I want you to do, so stay still. This is a very important project I'm working on here." He did look like he was concentrating. That cute little crease between his eyebrows was back and I wanted to kiss it, but I wasn't allowed to move.

It took a while and two packs of notes, but he pretty much covered my entire body with the little yellow notes. Just FYI, those things don't stick too well to skin—he kept trying to get them to stay and getting frustrated when they didn't.

"Now that you've got me like this, whatever will you do with me?" I said as he admired his work.

"Well, I must follow what all these notes say. They're very important." He took one last one that said *kiss me* and stuck it on my mouth.

And then he proceeded to remove and follow the directions on every single note until I was screaming his name and thinking that this whole sexcretary thing had been my best idea ever.

"So, Mr. Blaine. Is there anything else I can do for you?" I was exhausted and my room was filled with discarded sticky notes.

"Not a thing, Miss Clarke. Just stay there." He got up and found the dessert, a non heart-shaped German chocolate cake. He carried the entire thing in, along with some forks and we ate it on my bed and he smeared me with frosting and I smeared him and we kissed and licked it off each other.

He was looking at me strangely as we fed each other bites of the cake.

"What is it?" That was a serious face if I'd ever seen one.

"I don't just want nights, Sunshine." He put the fork down and continued to look at me with such intensity it was almost hard to look back.

"I don't want just nights. I want mornings. And mid-mornings and late mornings and noons and afternoons and evenings and everything in between. Sunrises and sunsets and twilight. I want it all." I put down my fork.

I knew what he was saying, but I didn't know what he was saying.

"I want to be with you. Definitions and everything. I want to call you mine."

Shit. That was not part of the plan. I knew I was falling for him, but I didn't count on him falling for me, too.

"I know this puts both of our jobs in jeopardy, but . . . I just can't go on like this anymore."

"But we've only known each other for a few weeks." That wasn't the biggest issue, but that was what came out of my mouth first.

"It doesn't matter. I knew I wanted you the first time I saw you. Then I got to know you and I wanted you even more. I go after what I want."

I knew that. He'd been so persistent in that first interview and then after.

"Lucah . . ." I trailed off, not knowing where to start or what to say.

"You don't have to agree to anything. I just wanted you to know where I stand." He grabbed the cake and the forks and started to get up, but I put my hand on his arm to stop him.

"It's not that I don't want to, Lucah. I do. I really do. I like spending time with you and being around you. You make me happy and I haven't had that much fun at work in a very long time. But what happens if we don't work out? If we go for this . . . and what we feel burns out?"

He listened without comment and then brushed his thumb across my lip.

"Let's just enjoy the rest of tonight then, Miss Clarke."

"Okay." I could push it aside for now, but I was going to have to think about it tomorrow, and we were going to have to talk, and things were going to change. I didn't want them to change. I didn't want us to change. Yes, we had moved to Us Territory. We'd moved there a long time ago. Bought property, moved in, put up a fence and a bunch of garden gnomes.

I didn't want things to change, but they were going to, and I was going to have to choose. He already had.

Chapter Twenty

I made him breakfast the next morning wearing an apron and my heels like I promised and brought it to him in bed. I was trying to keep on a happy face, but it wasn't easy when I knew that he was going to leave in a little while and then I'd be all alone with my thoughts. I didn't want them for company. I'd much rather spend that time with Lucah in bed, or even just talking, or watching cartoons again.

After we finished breakfast, he made me let him do the dishes and stack them in the dishwasher and then we put on clothes and sat on the couch and he rubbed my feet and we watched whatever was on television.

"Spend the day with me," he said, pinching one of my toes.

"Lucah—" I started to protest, but he threw himself on top of me.

"Spend the day with me. I know you want to. I'll be your sexcretary this time." I wanted to, so much. So, so much . . . One day couldn't do any more damage, could it?

"Okay, Mr. Blaine. I will spend the day with you. But we should probably go out, or else Sloane will come home and creepily watch us and I'd rather not be creepily watched if you don't mind."

"I would also prefer to not be creepily watched. Since you planned last night, does that mean I get to plan today?"

"Sure, why not? As long as there is no public humiliation involved."

"I would never publicly humiliate you. Or at least not on purpose." He smiled and held my feet up so he could get up.

"Come on, Sunshine. Let's go somewhere."

A half hour later, we were standing in front of the Boston Museum of Science.

"This is where we're spending the day?" I looked up at the building with the metal letters on it. I hadn't been here since I was ten, and even then it was a class trip and we hadn't stayed long.

"I bring my nieces here all the time. I think sometimes I get more out of it than they do. So," he said, holding out his hand. "Shall we?" I smiled and took his hand.

"Yes. We shall."

Who knew how much fun you could have at the science museum? I definitely hadn't had this much fun when I was a kid, but maybe who you were with that determined the fun level. We'd done nearly everything from taking pretend horrified pictures at the foot of the dinosaur models to ruining our hair with the static electricity machines. I'd allowed him to take pictures of us on my phone. I would put them in a secret folder on my computer when I got home. I also didn't worry about us being seen together because there wasn't a less likely place for us to run into anyone from the office.

We even went to the gift shop where he bought me a "Pluto: Revolve in Peace" t-shirt and a stuffed animal that was shaped like the common cold virus. He also picked up two stuffed frogs for his nieces. I insisted on buying him a CD that was all songs designed to boost your positive thinking and a baseball cap, which I promptly shoved on head and made him take a duck-faced selfie with me while he was wearing it.

We had lunch at the café surrounded by screaming kids and frazzled parents trying to wrangle them.

One little boy ran by us and tripped, wiping out right next to our table. Lucah was on his feet and picking the little guy up faster than you could say "boo boo" and was checking him for injuries as his mother rushed over and tried to assess the damage.

"I think he's okay. Just startled. You're okay, right buddy?" Lucah handed the kid to his mom and held his hand up for a high five, which the little boy gave him, a smile breaking out on his tearstained face as his mother took him away, making promises of ice cream.

"What?" Lucah said, catching me watching him.

I shook my head. "Nothing."

"I know what women say." He sat down and gave me a look as if I was in on some kind of conspiracy.

"What women say about what?"

"What women say about men who are good with children."

I played dumb. I knew exactly what he was talking about because I'd thought it about him before.

"And what is that?"

He raised one eyebrow and I mirrored him, but he didn't crack a smile.

"That men with children are very attractive. It's some sort of primal instinctive thing that's supposed to help the species continue and all that. Don't you find men who are good with children more attractive than men who can't stand them?"

"No, not at all," I said with as much seriousness as I could muster. Men who were good with kids were fucking attractive and anyone who said otherwise was either a liar, or wasn't interested in men anyway.

"You're a terrible liar, Miss Clarke," he whispered, leaning over the table. I threw a French fry at him and he finally broke out that smile I adored so much.

His phone rang, interrupting us. He looked down at it and the smile instantly vanished.

"I need to take this, excuse me." He didn't wait for me to respond before he got up and walked to a quiet corner of the café. He answered the call and I could tell whoever it was, Lucah didn't want to talk to. I knew him well enough now to recognize when he was agitated and trying to hide it. He was arguing and trying not to make a scene by raising his voice, but he was losing his temper. I tried not to watch, but it was hard not to.

Lucah threw his head back like he had so many times before, like he was looking directly at God and asking for patience, or intervention. Then he said something else and hung up. I looked down at my plate and pretended to be very interested in it as he composed himself and walked back over.

"Bad news?" I said, hoping maybe he would confide in me.

"Nothing. Just . . . nothing." He put his phone back in his pocket and stared at his plate as if it had been the one to piss him off.

"You can talk to me, Lucah," I said, trying something different. I reached across the table and tried to take his hand, but he pulled back.

"Okay, fine. Be a clam. See if I care." I crossed my arms and looked away from him.

We sat in silence for a few minutes as I waited for him to cave. I hadn't cultivated my bitch persona for nothing. I could wear it all day if I had to, and I often had.

"It's my brother. He's gotten himself into trouble, again, and he wants me to bail him out, again, and I won't. He's had too many chances and he's burned all his bridges and he needs to get his shit together, because I'm done. I am completely done." He lowered his voice when he swore because we were surrounded by children and families and it was probably frowned upon.

"Drugs?"

"Among other things. He just has a tendency to jump into things and then he gets into trouble. He also has a hard time saying no to people, which is another reason that he gets himself screwed over. Anyway, he's been calling me and calling me and begging for money, for a place to stay, for whatever. I can't let myself get involved with him again." He shook his head and for a moment he looked completely exhausted. And older than his twenty-five years.

"Anything I can do to help?" I had no idea what I could possibly do, but that was one of those things you say when you didn't know what else to say and you feel bad for someone you cared about.

"No. He's my stupid brother. I'll probably end up caving in like I usually do. Anyway. Enough about him. I don't want him crashing our day. You ready to explore some more?" I didn't want to drop the brother thing, but he did, so I let him.

The rest of the afternoon was spent watching a bird expert bring out a few rare birds, and then we took in a 3D show at the Omni theater. Lucah seemed to be having a good time, but I could tell he was thinking about his brother. Sloane had been blowing my phone up all day, and if I didn't get home tonight and take care of her, she was liable to explode. I also had dinner with my parents to fit in somewhere.

We held hands as we walked toward the T and headed back to my apartment. I knew Sloane was there, so the plan was to leave Lucah in the hallway, grab his stuff, throw it at him and have him leave without being accosted and then interrogated.

Of course, that was not what happened, because as soon as Sloane heard me fumbling with the door, it flew open.

"Hello lovebirds!" She was clearly wired again from being up all night and I had thought maybe she'd have crashed, but no such luck.

"Hi, Sloane," I said, trying to give her The Signal with my eyes.

"What's wrong with your eyes?" she said, completely missing The Signal. So much for that.

"Okay, well Lucah has to go home, so I'm just going to get him his stuff and then he's going to go. I'll be *right back*." I poked Sloane as I passed her.

"Ow!"

"Be nice!" I said as I hurried to my bedroom for his stuff.

"So, you're banging my best friend, huh?" Ugh! Did she not hear what I just said?

"Sloane!" I yelled.

"What? It's a legitimate question. And we're all adults here. Oh, and how did you like the steak? I wasn't sure if it was going to turn out because the asparagus hasn't been very good this year, but it turned out okay, right?"

I hung back for just a second, listening.

"It was wonderful, thank you so much for doing that. You're a great friend to Rory, and any friend of hers is a friend of mine."

"Uh huh," she said and I could tell by the tone of her voice that she was still evaluating him. It was time to dash in and rescue Lucah.

"Here you go," I said, coming out and shoving his bag at him. "I'll see you tomorrow at the place?"

"See you tomorrow, Sunshine." He didn't kiss me good-bye, because we'd agreed no kisses good-bye after our nights now. He walked down the hall and waved before taking his hat out of the bag and putting it on his head.

I smiled and closed the door.

"Oh my God, you have got the fever, Rory." Sloane fanned herself.

"I do not."

"You are so totally and completely in love with him."

"I am not," I said, walking into the living room and avoiding eye contact with her. She just followed me, grabbed my shoulders and sat me down on the couch facing her.

"You love him, Rory." This was a statement, not a question.

"No. Not yet. But . . ."

"Yeah, you do. Admit it. You wanna marry him and make little ginger babies and continue the ginger species. They're dying out you know, which means you're probably going to have to have at least ten. Come on. You can admit it to me. I won't tell anyone, I swear.

Scout's honor." Sloane hadn't been a scout either, so she just gave me a peace sign with her fingers.

"Sloane," I said. "Just don't push, okay? I've got a lot to figure out right now and I really don't want to talk about it." She searched my face, and she knew me well enough to know when I shouldn't be pushed. This was another quality that made her such good friend material.

"Okay, Rory. You got it. But I still want details about what you did." So I talked about the night and the sticky notes and going to the museum and before I could stop myself I told her about the phone call and the brother.

"A brother? A bad boy brother? I wonder if he's got red hair as well . . ." She stared off into space as if she was trying to conjure the brother with her mind.

"Sloane." I snapped my fingers in front of her face.

"What? I was just thinking. Anyway, so it was good? You're happy? You seem happy. I catch you smiling all the time. You didn't smile that much with King Douchebag. And at least this guy hasn't made you cry."

Yet.

I rolled my eyes and went to take a shower before I headed over to my parents'.

Chapter Twenty-One

"You have to stop doing that in the office, Mr. Blaine," I said as his arms came around me as I stood at the counter of the break room. I stepped away from him and moved toward the Keurig, popping in one of the cups.

"Okay, okay. I'll give you five feet." He slid down the counter so there was space between us.

"Are you drinking coffee tonight?"

"Yes. At the usual time."

"Sounds good." He was undressing me with his eyes, which was against the rules, but I let him get away with it anyway.

"You're being bad, Mr. Blaine," I said with my voice low. Mr. Craig walked in, interrupting the sexytimes. Cock blocker. What was the girl equivalent of that? There should be one.

"Hello, Rory. How are you?" All of the older men in the company had watched me grow up here, so they all got to call me by my first name. I'd tried to put a stop to it a while ago, but it had been useless. These guys didn't change their habits.

"I'm fabulous, how are you?" I smiled as the coffee brewed into the cups and Lucah started washing his hands in the sink so he would have some reason for being in the break room. He dried them quickly and without saying a word to Mr. Craig, he left, not looking at me. Well, that was suspicious.

"How's your new assistant working out?" Mr. Craig said.

I made some generic compliments about Lucah and then told him that my dad was waiting for his coffee, so I had a reason to escape when he started talking about his new car and what a crime it was that they had redone his favorite golf course.

I actually decided to visit Dad, since it had been a while since we had talked about work-related items. I'd also been watching the expense reports, and I had noticed another spike in ordering. Subtle, but it was still there. Dad was busy and didn't have a chance to talk, so I just wrote him a note that it could wait. The spikes could be completely normal. I was probably just being paranoid.

I went back to my desk and found a dirty text from Lucah. He'd been sending me a lot of those lately. I typed an equally dirty response and sent it to him. I drew the line at naked pictures, but imagined the look on his face if I closed my office door and took one and sent it to him. A seductive thought, but I knew it would come back to bite me in the ass.

This was going to be a long week.

Something was up with Lucah the next morning when I got out of the shower. He made me breakfast, but he almost seemed grumpy, and I tried to ask him what was wrong, but he didn't say anything.

We hadn't discussed what he'd told me about wanting to be with me all the time since Sunday. I was going to put it off as long as possible. I'd also been subtly searching out to see if we had any positions in other departments that I could put him up for. I had no doubt that it would be easy to get him in somewhere else with my recommendation and the support of the board. I still hadn't figured out what that was about.

"You sure you're okay?" I said as I got dressed.

"Hm?" He looked up from where he was sitting on the other side of the bed putting on his shoes. I walked over to him and stood between his legs, then gently knocked on his head.

"Anyone home in there? What is up with you, Lucah?"

"Family business," he said, putting his head into my stomach and hugging me around the waist as if he didn't want to let me go.

"Your brother?"

He sighed and lifted his head.

"He's a pain in my ass that won't go away," he said. "I'm lending him some money so he can get his own place and so he'll get off my back. I also volunteered to help him get a job, which was an incredibly stupid thing for me to do. So that means that some of my time with you will be given to him, and I resent him for taking me away from you. And then I feel like a dick for resenting my brother for not having his shit together and for my parents dying and not being here to deal with it." He seemed to realize that he just mentioned his dead parents for the first time and then ducked his head again.

"I didn't know that about your parents," I said, stroking his hair back.

"It was a few years ago. House fire. The smoke detectors worked, but they didn't wake up."

"Oh, Lucah. I'm so sorry." I wanted to cry, but I held back.

"I know you are, Sunshine. You're one of the only people that I know truly means that. So anyway, Tate has given up helping with Ryder, so it falls on me."

"Family comes first, you know how crazy I am with mine. You have to do what you have to do. I'll be fine. I'm not one of those girls."

"You're the best kind of girl," he said into my stomach.

"Aw, thanks," I said, leaning down to give him a kiss. "Okay, I have to get to that place. See you in a little while."

"See you," he said, making the kiss linger and make me want to call both of us in as "sick". Yeah, that wouldn't be suspicious at all.

He was late. If there were two things I knew about Lucah Blaine, it was that first, he was an oral sex god, and second, he was never late.

I called his cell phone, but he didn't answer. When he was ten minutes late, I was freaking out and I'd called and texted and was about ready to start using skywriters or smoke signals or Morse code.

Then I got a text back from him.

Almost there. Dealing with brother. Oh thank God. My mind had gone to worst-case scenario and I was about to start calling hospitals.

Need time off? He'd never asked for any before, but if he needed it, I'd get it for him, especially for this.

No. Be there soon. Need LOTS of coffee tonight.

I typed back a smiley face and put my phone down and counted the minutes until he walked in. I motioned for him to come in my office, and he did, closing the door.

"Is everything okay?" He didn't say anything, but came around the desk and kissed me hard. Then he pulled back and rested his forehead on mine.

"I needed that." He backed away and sat down.

"Yes, I'm fine." I got a smile that wasn't quite convincing, but I couldn't ask him about it again or else I would risk making him mad, so I just smiled and told him to get his ass to his desk.

"Coffee. You and me. Later," I said as he closed the door.

"Yes, Miss Clarke."

I spent the rest of the day putting out fires, looking at expense reports and wondering when the hell I was going to meet this mysterious brother. I mean, part of me didn't want to meet him, but part of me really did. But I sure as hell wasn't going to ask Lucah about it and bring a sore subject up.

Chloe and Marisol had come over to have dinner with Sloane, so they were all there when I got home and they had clearly been talking about me because they froze when I walked in the door like three deer in a set of headlights.

"Well, don't stop talking about me just because I walk in," I said before one of them could recover and make up a story about what they'd been talking about.

"I told them," Sloane said, not looking at me. "But to be fair, they figured it out. It's your fault for having smart friends." Yeah, that was exactly the problem. I guess I hadn't been as stealthy as I thought.

"It was really obvious," Marisol said.

"What she said," Chloe echoed. Je-sus Christ.

I set my bag down and joined them on the couch with a huge sigh.

"So you knew? The whole time I've been pretending and you already knew?" What a waste of time lying had been. Oh God. If they hadn't been fooled then maybe Lucah and I were really terrible liars. What if people at the office . . .

"What's wrong with you? You look like you're going to pass out," Sloane said, coming and putting her hand on my forehead like I was a kid with a fever.

"Was I that bad at lying?"

"No, it wasn't that. We just saw the chemistry between you two and we knew that it wouldn't be over after just one night. And honestly? Telling us he wasn't that great in bed? Huge red flag, woman," Marisol said, rolling her eyes.

"Amen. Plus, I knew that you had to be somewhere at night and I knew it wasn't at the office, so you had to be with a guy and what guy would you be with that you wouldn't tell us about? Process of elimination, really," Chloe said. Damn. I did have smart friends.

"Okay, well now that's out in the open, I need some advice." I gave them the rundown of Lucah and the brother situation and the developments from this morning.

"It's such a sore subject right now, so I think I should avoid it, but he says that he wants to be with me, and if we're going to be together, I think I should meet his brother, right? That's how relationships should work."

They all agreed, but then said that it was shaky ground and that maybe I should wait until the situation had settled before I asked about it. I agreed, and then it was time for them to treat me like a Barbie and dress me up to go see Lucah.

I ended up wearing a lot more makeup than I would have, and wearing a more-flashy outfit than I normally did, and they also packed me a nightie. Most of the time I just wore Lucah's shirt or nothing at all when we slept, but he might enjoy that, so I took it with me.

They all wished me good sex and I wished I had time to ask Marisol about any Fin developments, but I didn't. Fin had texted me a few times, but he was off in Europe again, so the messages were few and far between. Lucah asked me if I had heard from him, but I said not really and I could tell he was happy about that.

Lucah may not be one of those guys who would punch another guy for looking at me, but he was definitely glad Fin was in Europe.

Lucah attacked me as soon as I walked through the door. No hello. No greeting. Just shoved me up against the door, shoved his tongue in my mouth and a few minutes later his dick was shoved inside me as well. What a greeting.

"Hello. Is. Customary," I panted as he pounded into me and I bit his shoulder to contain my screams. I didn't want his neighbor knocking on the door again.

"Hello. Miss. Clarke," he said as he stiffened and then came. I hadn't, but I knew he would more than make up for it later. I slid down him as I unlocked my legs from around his waist.

He rested his head on top of mine and I could tell he was upset.

"What's wrong? Not that I don't enjoy ambush door sex as much as the next girl, but you seem down." He stepped away from me without a word and went to the bathroom.

Uh oh. I'd never seen this side of him and I didn't really know how to handle it. Somehow I didn't think a blowjob and/or me making jokes was going to help. I went to the bathroom and knocked on the door.

"Lucah. Please talk to me." The door opened and he let me in. I sat on the edge of the tub as he paced. There wasn't a whole lot of room for pacing, but he was doing it anyway.

"It's not just this thing with Ryder, Rory. There's a whole bunch of things that . . . I didn't mean . . . Why did it have to be you?" He stopped in front of me and then put his hands on both sides of my face.

"Why did you have to be you?"

"Is that a trick question?" I said as he stared at me so deep that I felt like he could see all of my secrets and there was one that I wasn't ready for him to know yet.

"No, Sunshine. Forget it." I didn't want to. He was going through something and I wanted to help. I just wanted him to talk to me. And then it seemed as if whatever had him pacing a moment ago was pushed aside and he frowned.

"Why are you wearing so much makeup?"

Chapter Twenty-Two

We were avoiding. Don't get me wrong, avoiding talking about commitment by having fabulous sex was fun, but sooner or later . . .

I loved him. Over the moon, past the stars, couldn't breathe, smiled whenever I thought about him, couldn't keep my hands off him, pictured a wedding and ginger babies and growing old and rocking chairs love. He drove me crazy, made me laugh and understood me in a way that few people did.

I fucking loved him and I wanted everyone to know it. Except Lucah, of course. He was the last person I wanted to know that I loved him. Second only to my dad.

So I told Sloane.

"I knew it. I told you so. How's it feel?"

I answered truthfully.

"Awful."

We both laughed.

"Yup, that's love. Ah, I'd forgotten how much it sucks. You have my sympathies." I was going to need them. "Are you going to tell him?"

"I'll have to, at some point. He's not a moron, he's going to figure it out. So I love him and I can't say the words out loud and he's still hiding things from me and not sharing them with me and it pisses me off because I love him and want to have his ginger babies."

Sloane gave me a sympathetic face and a hug and offered to make more breakup cake, but I didn't think that would help. She made the cake anyway, and I was not going to turn down free cake.

There was a knock at the door as I stuffed myself with chocolate, and Sloane went up to get it.

"Emergency girls' night!" Marisol announced, holding up two bottles of wine. Chloe came behind her with a bag full of movies and the game Cards Against Humanity.

I almost started crying as they forced a glass of wine into my hand and started making even more fattening and delicious snacks.

I could avoid for a little bit longer. He seemed to be doing it.

Lucah texted me when I was on my third glass and I was a wee bit tipsy.

Have to deal with family tomorrow night. Sorry, Sunshine.

I didn't really have a response for that, so I just typed out **Ok, see you tomorrow.** I wasn't drunk enough to not be able to text, but I was getting there.

We had somehow turned Cards Against Humanity into a drinking game, but I was still unsure of the rules, so whenever someone told me to drink, I did.

By the time we got to the second bottle of wine, I was definitely buzzed and feeling good. Warm and fuzzy and kind of in love with everyone. I wouldn't stop hugging Chloe and she kept threatening to make out with me if I didn't stop.

"We need more wine," Sloane said as she poured the last into my glass. I tossed it back and she stumbled to the kitchen and found another bottle.

"Score!" We all cheered as she filled up our glasses again.

An hour later, I was completely toasted. I hadn't been this gone in a very long time. Maybe not since college. It was kind of nice. My phone buzzed and I picked it up. It was another text from Lucah.

Missing you.

I had an impulse and hit his number and before I knew it, he was picking up and saying, "Hello?"

"I love you. I love you and it sucks because now I'm going to lose my job and all our kids are going to have red hair and I want at least one of them to be blonde, but they'll probably all have red hair and you're keeping secrets from me and I love you." I hung up before he could say anything and he called me back a second later, but I tossed my phone on the table and ignored it.

"You tell him!" Sloane said from her position on the floor. She had been sitting on a chair, but now she was on the floor. I found this wildly funny and we all laughed until we forgot what we were laughing about.

"I'm drunk," Marisol said.

"Me too." Chloe moaned and put her head on my shoulder.

We were all drunk.

"Fuck you, sun," was the first thing I heard the next morning. We'd ended up either on the couch or on the floor.

"Why did we do that?" I finally opened my eyes and instantly regretted it.

"Fuck you, sun," I said as everyone else moaned and groaned and tried to get up.

We all had to work today, but we were all hopelessly hung over. Damn wine. My phone buzzed and I reached for it, squinting at the clock.

"SHIT!" I was supposed to be at work five minutes ago.

"Why is there screaming?" Chloe moaned as I struggled to get to my feet while my head pounded and my stomach heaved. Nothing short of a miracle was going to get me into the office today. I hadn't called in sick in two years, but there was absolutely no way I could go in. I grabbed a glass of water to wash my mouth out with and then called my dad.

"Hey, Dad. I just wanted to let you know that I can't come in today. I'm just not feeling well." This wasn't a lie at all and I hoped he heard it in my voice, and didn't figure out what caused it.

"Oh, Rory. Are you sure you're okay?"

"Yeah, just need another day. Will you let everyone know?"

"Of course, of course. You never take a day off and I always worry that you're going to burn out before you're old enough to burn out. You take some time and we'll take care of everything here."

"Thanks, Dad. Love you."

"Love you, too." He hung up and I saw that I had about twenty texts and missed calls from Lucah. How had none of us heard my phone? I scrolled through the messages and then it came back to me.

Oh . . . SHIT.

JE-SUS CHRIST.

I had told Lucah I loved him. Also that I wanted to have his ginger babies. I TOLD HIM THAT I LOVED HIM.

My stomach finally woke all the way up and I had to run to the bathroom. I wasn't sure if it was the wine or the unintended declaration that made me puke, but I ended up in the bathroom for the next hour, with Sloane and Marisol taking turns holding my hair and bringing me water.

I told him that I loved him.

Fuck.

"Are you feeling any better?" Sloane tiptoed into my room in the late morning. She was better off than I was, but she'd decided to take the day off and take care of me. I didn't know which was worse: the hangover or the fact that I'd accidentally told Lucah I loved him when I was drunk.

"No. The only way I'm going to feel better is if you find a time machine and can take me back to last night and tell me not to drink. That would be fantastic. Thanks." She sat down on the edge of my bed and held out a cup of lemon ginger tea.

"I'll get right on that, babe." I took the tea from her and sipped it. The ginger would be soothing on my stomach. I really didn't want anything in my body right at the moment, but I drank it anyway.

"Why didn't you stop me?" I squinted at her and she looked fantastic, as usual. She had the kind of hair that worked curly or straight and her large curls from yesterday were still intact.

"Hey, you were on a roll. And it was bound to come out eventually. They have that quote about the truth being in wine for a reason. Now that it's out, you can talk about it and deal with it and then realize that you're both idiots and you belong together."

"How do you know that we belong together?"

"The same reason I know how to make a flan just by reading a recipe once. Pure instinct." She did have good instincts, but I was still humiliated.

"You just gotta decide what's more important. And I'm guessing that forty years down the line, you're not going to regret that you chose love over your job." She patted my foot and left me with my tea and my thoughts.

When I finally felt a little bit better, I found my phone and stared at it. I needed to call Lucah and explain myself. He'd been texting me all day asking if I was okay. He didn't mention the love thing because he was great like that.

He was so concerned about me even when he had a ton of crap to deal with and that only made me love him more. It really was like a sickness and it multiplied the more I thought about it and the more I thought about him.

Finally I took a deep breath and called him. I knew he'd be on lunch so he'd be free to talk.

"Hello, Mr. Blaine," I said, sitting back on my pillows.

"Hello, Miss Clarke. How are you feeling this afternoon?" His voice was soft, and I could hear him walking away from some other voices. He must be out getting food.

"A little worse for wear. How are you?" His voice instantly made me happy, even though I felt shitty. Yup. That's love.

"I'm just concerned about you."

"Yeah, same here. How's everything with your brother?" I didn't want to talk about me. And because he was such an awesome guy, he talked about his brother and how he was trying to get him a lease on an apartment and also his failed attempts to get Ryder a job.

"He's not really qualified to do anything. He never finished college, just started a bunch of times and never got all the way through. He's one of those people who knows how to do a bunch of things, but not enough to get a job. I don't know what to do with him."

I couldn't imagine what that must be like, but even though I didn't have any siblings, I had friends and that is similar. Luckily, my friends had most of their shit together.

"We have a few positions open at Clarke. I mean it's nothing glamorous. The mail room, billing. If he wants to come in for an interview, I could set it up. Just a thought."

"Thanks, Sunshine, but I don't want to put you in that position. Plus, I don't think Ryder would last a day in an office. He'd probably end up jumping out the window and taking off. Trust me, he's done it before."

"He jumped out a window?"

"Yeah. It was on the first floor, but still." There had been days when I wanted to go out the window, but since my office was so far up, I would end up dying and I wasn't that desperate.

"So am I ever going to get to meet this elusive brother?"

"I don't think so. Not right now. Maybe sometime. He's just . . . a lot to take." Had he met Sloane?

"I think I can handle it, but it's up to you."

"Thanks. Now, have we talked about enough other things that we can go back to the drunken phone call I received from you last night?" Crap. Fuck. Hell, crap, fuck, Jesus.

"What phone call?"

"Nice try, Sunshine, but I know you remember and I know you don't want to discuss it; but since you said it, I feel the need to say something too." He took a deep breath and I cut him off.

"I was drunk. You don't have to say anything. I . . . I didn't mean to say it like that. I didn't want to say it, but there it is. I wish I could go back and unsay it, but I can't, so there it is. But I don't know if I'm ready to say it sober yet. Which doesn't make any sense." I was rambling again and I wasn't even drunk. I waited for him to say something.

"I love you, and I'm completely sober and I've wanted to say it for a while now, but I didn't know if you'd say it back."

It shouldn't come as a shock to me when he said those three words, but hearing them in his voice was a whole different thing than I thought it would be.

"I'm not ready to have your ginger babies. But I love you." I said it in a whisper, as if it was less true if my voice wasn't that loud.

He sighed.

"I wish I was with you right now." I wanted to reach through the phone, grab him and pull him into my room. Why hasn't science made this possible yet?

"I wish you were here."

"I can come over." Even as he said it we both knew it wasn't possible. It would look too suspicious if we were both out, and I wasn't willing to risk it.

"No, you can't. Not right now, but you can later. After work." It killed me to say that, but I had to.

"Why must you be the voice of reason, Miss Clarke?"

"Because I'm your boss. And you're my sexcretary."

"We're going to have to talk about that. I think we need to have some more trade off nights. I have some more dirty uses for office supplies that I want to try out."

Mmm, that sounded really, really nice. As long as staples weren't involved. Ouch.

"We'll talk later. I'm going to go shower because I'm pretty gross right now." I sniffed my armpit and was actually glad that he wasn't here to witness it.

"You're never gross, Sunshine. Or at least you're not gross to me. But I'll see you later. As long as my brother doesn't have a disaster between now and then."

"I've got my fingers crossed," I said and then wondered how we were supposed to end our phone conversations now.

"Am I allowed to end this conversation by saying that I love you and I'll see you later?" he said.

"You're asking my permission?"

"Not really. I was going to say it anyway."

"Well, I'm not going to stop you. I love you, too." I almost had a giggle fit after I said it and it made my toes curl under thinking about seeing him tonight.

I set the phone down and fell back against my pillows with a happy sigh. And then my door flew open and Sloane came barreling across the room and jumped on my bed with a scream.

"You totally love him!" She pulled me up on my feet and started jumping on my bed and I had no choice but to jump with her with.

"You love him!"

"I know!" We jumped until we were both out of breath and I was worried about the structural soundness of my bed.

"I'm sorry, I just felt that needed to be celebrated." She held up her hand and I smacked it with mine.

"Now that you're in love, you're not going to turn into a disgusting sap that I can't stand to be around, are you? Because then I will have to vagina punch you."

"I don't think I'm going to become any different than I already am. I mean, I was sort of in love with Royce. Or at least I thought I was." I hadn't been, even though I'd told him the words. This felt completely different. Love with Royce felt . . . obligatory? Love with Lucah was something I couldn't control, and something I didn't want to control. Loving him was letting go. Surrendering.

I didn't want to make Sloane leave when Lucah came over, so she decided to make us dinner and then vacate so we could have some "ooey, gooey lovey sex", according to her. But she wanted to officially spend time with my "lover" so she was going to force us to eat dinner with her. I knew there was no point in arguing, so I said it was fine and sent Lucah a text so he wouldn't be thrown off when Sloane attacked him, as I knew she would.

He said he was okay with it, so he must really love me.

Sloane buzzed him up while I was getting ready, and beat me to the door.

"Hey, lover boy! Come on in. Any lover of Rory is a lover of me." That probably didn't sound the way she meant it, but she didn't seem to care. Lucah just smiled and let her hug him.

"I am so sorry in advance for anything that she says. I am not responsible for her, as you well know." I pinched Sloane and she yelped.

That was just payback for her kicking me all those times. I hoped she had marks.

"I think I can handle it. Hi," he said, turning his attention to me and letting the sweetest smile pass over his lips. When he spoke I saw the metal flash of his tongue barbell. How I loved that thing and what he could do with it.

"Hi," I said and he gathered me into his arms and pulled me off my feet.

"I wanted to get you something, but everything I found seemed silly, so I went with this," he said, handing me a small box that he'd set on the counter.

"Oohh, what is it?" Sloane said, leaning over my shoulder. Yeah, that wasn't annoying at all.

"Well, I don't know yet because I need to open it." I reached through the tissue and pulled out what I determined was a paperweight shaped exactly like my favorite red shoes. There was also a coffee cup that said WORLD'S GREATEST BOSS on it. Ha, I didn't know he was a fan of *The Office.*

"And I am now realizing the present is silly anyway. There are also some sticky notes in shoe shape in there as well." He was blushing and it made me laugh.

"It's so sweet, Lucah. Thank you. I love it. This is a million times better than flowers." Now I would always have a little piece of him on my desk and no one would know. That was the best part.

"I never knew office supplies could be so adorable, but this is really cute, Ginger. Also, nice brown nosing. Well done." She really had to stop calling him ginger. I gave Lucah a kiss right in front of

Sloane and she made cheering noises and then a pot started boiling over on the stove and she had to go tend to it as I led Lucah to the couch and sat down with him.

"So you like it? You're not just sparing my feelings. I swear, I can take it." He pulled me into his lap and I stroked his hair. I loved this hair and the man it belonged to.

"I love it. Really. If it sucked, don't you think I would tell you?"

"Yeah, you would."

"She would," Sloane called from the kitchen. I took the paperweight out and set it on the table and stared at it.

"I love you." Now that I'd started saying it, I didn't want to stop. Those three little words were like little bits happiness that seemed to want to spew out of me at random times. It was like I was a love spaz.

"I love you, Sunshine."

"Okay, enough, we get it. Get a room before I throw up in your dinner," Sloane said.

"You wouldn't dare," I yelled at her and she make puking noises until I got up and threatened to beat her to death with a wooden spoon. Lucah just watched us like we were some sort of comedy show and then started clapping.

"You two should really have your own show. It would be a hit." I glared at him and he stuck his tongue out at me and then I had to look away because he was turning me on and I was waiting until Sloane left to have any kind of "coffee".

Dinner was actually fun. Sloane didn't tone herself down at all, which was actually a good thing. No sense in toning it down only to shock him later. Throw him to the wolves now.

"Well, dessert is in the oven, and I have some things I need to take care of at the studio, so the place is yours for the night. Have fun, sex monkeys," she said, and sauntered out of the apartment, blowing a kiss as she left.

"I like her," he said when the door shut.

"Well, if you like her so much, then why don't you marry her?" I said, teasing.

"She's not my type. I like blondes who wear red shoes and are in positions of authority and have secret piercings. That's my idea of the perfect woman."

"Hate to break it you, Ginger, but I'm not the perfect woman." He was definitely the perfect man, though.

"I can think you're perfect if I want." He threw me on my back on the couch and then climbed on top of me.

"Fine, you can think I'm perfect," I said as he kissed behind my ear, making me tingle all over.

We didn't remember the dessert until the smoke detector started going nuts.

"At least we know it works," I said as Lucah and I waved brooms in front of it to dissipate the smoke from the now-black cheesecake.

"Sloane is going to kill me. Or maybe you for distracting me so much."

"I am prepared to give my life for yours, my lady love," he said in a dramatic fashion as the beeping finally stopped. We both breathed a sigh of relief, but then there was the black cake to think about.

"We could just eat it," I suggested.

"I will if you will." It wasn't a large thing, only about five inches round, but it was pretty gross looking. I got out two forks and handed him one.

"One, two, three!" We both grabbed a bite and shoved it into our mouths.

And proceeded to run for the sink and spit it out.

"Oh my God, it's like zombie cheesecake," I said, rinsing my mouth out as he made the most hilarious faces I'd ever seen.

"Zombie cheesecake?"

"Like cheesecake that died, was buried and then rose again from the dead." I shuddered and stared at the offending cheesecake.

"There's only one thing to do." I found a garbage bag and tossed the thing in it and Lucah and I made a trip down to the Dumpster.

Since we didn't have dessert, we just got to the sex faster. I'd started keeping condoms and plenty of lube and so forth in my nightstand drawer, but as Lucah went in for a condom, he found something else I forgot I had put back there after using it the other day.

He pulled out Mr. Buzzy and raised one eyebrow at me.

"What? You've never seen a vibrator before?"

"Oh, no I have. I just didn't know you had one. Why didn't you tell me?"

"Why, are you jealous?" If he was jealous, I was going to be pissed. Men and their stupid fragile egos.

"Hell no. I'm just mad that I didn't know about it earlier, and that you would be cool with using one."

"So you're cool with it?"

"That's an understatement," he said, trying to turn it on. "Show me how you use it." I grabbed the batteries from the drawer and put them in.

"You want to watch me?"

"Once again, understatement. There's nothing sexier than a woman who knows what she wants and can get it for herself. Show me." Well, if that was what he wanted . . .

I put Mr. Buzzy through his paces while Lucah watched and it was the single sexiest moment of my life. He was mesmerized and I felt like a goddess as he watched me. I loved it and I loved him. When I came, I called his name anyway, and he took Mr. Buzzy away from me and entered me with one sharp thrust and I felt like I had been destroyed in that one moment.

"I. Love. You. So. Much. I. Almost. Can't. Stand. It."

"Same. Here," I said as we both came again.

I realized that there was a buzzing in my head aside from the afterglow, but it wasn't ecstasy. Mr. Buzzy was still going nuts on my floor from where Lucah had tossed him.

I rolled over, picked him up and turned him off.

"You're amazing, and someday, you're going to teach me how to use that on you."

"Sure thing." I patted him on the shoulder.

We lay together quietly for a while, and I had to bring up something that had been burning in the back of my mind.

"What are we going to do about work?" His fingers walked up and down my stomach.

"I don't know. Do you have any brilliant ideas in that sexy brain of yours?" he said.

"Nothing that doesn't involve one of us getting a different job, and that's a sacrifice I don't think I can make. I feel like if I were to leave, or change my job that I'd end up resenting you and I can't have that. I want us to work, and if one of us resents the other, it won't. It would eat away and soon we'd be doing nothing but fighting."

"True. Okay. So is there any way to get around the no-dating policy? Is there anyone who's done it before?"

"Um, yes. There were two people who worked in customer service that tried to date in secret and then got found out. They had to declare their relationship and one had to switch departments. They broke up within a few months at the company Christmas party. It was ugly. People still talk about it and that was four years ago." I did not want that to happen to us.

"But those people aren't you and me."

"True."

We were coming up empty.

"Have you thought, I'm just going to throw this out here, that maybe you could tell your dad? He might have some advice and he would be able to keep it on the down low."

I shook my head without even considering it.

"No, I can't put Dad in a position like that. He'd end up lying to everyone and . . . no. I can't. Besides, he would probably kill you. Or fire you. Or both."

"I'm not that scared of the firing, it's the killing that makes me a little nervous. Okay, so that's out." I rolled over and flicked his nipple ring.

"So we're left with one option. Keeping this a secret until something changes. As soon as you get promoted, which you will, then we can go forward. But for right now we're secret lovers." He started humming the song and that made me laugh, but we still had the specter of keeping our relationship secret.

"I feel like I should get that contract out again and make you sign it," I said.

"That was pretty funny. I'll never forget your face when you shredded it. I think I fell a little in love with you right then. Who knew a shredder could be so sexy?"

"Yeah, well, you concentrate really sexy. Like when you're reading something and I can see you making calculations in your head, Ooohh baby." I fanned myself.

"I don't know how I'm going to contain my affections for you, but I'll do my best, boss."

"You'd better, sexcretary."

I set my red shoe paperweight and my WORLD'S GREATEST BOSS mug on my desk the next day and made sure they were in full view for Lucah to see them. He brought over some reports and there was a note on the top of the stack that said, *nice mug.* I assumed he was talking about the boss mug, but I couldn't be absolutely sure.

Dad called me again and asked me to come down when I had a moment. The end of the month reports had just been posted, so I was sure that was what it was about. I got up from my desk and stopped at Lucah's before I went to see Dad so he didn't worry.

"Be right back. Meeting with Dad. Don't panic." I gave him a wink before walking down the hall and knocking on Dad's door.

"Come in."

I walked in and he was staring at piece of paper.

"End of the month report?" He looked up as if he just realized I was there.

"Hm? Oh, yes."

"Anything bad?" He squinted and then handed it to me.

"I'm not sure. Looks like things are back to normal. As I said, I didn't want to mention anything unless I had a reason to. No sense stirring up trouble unnecessarily. Have you noticed anything?"

"Just a few spikes here and there, but nothing that couldn't be explained. It seems to fluctuate a lot, especially when we have a new launch. If you hadn't pointed it out, I doubt I would have taken notice."

"Ah, well. I'm sure I'm just being paranoid. Like daughter like father. Anything else you wanted to talk about?" I had to be careful sometimes with what I said to him, because he was the president after all. That was something I'd learned very early on, that things I said to Dad weren't always confidential when it came to the welfare of the company. It was also why I had pretty much zero friends at the office. Lucah was about the only person who sought me out to talk to me, and even then I made him leave so people didn't get suspicious.

One day I envisioned a time when the two of us could have lunch together and bitch about office politics, but that day wasn't today, and probably not tomorrow either. I might have to wait a while for it.

"No, everything else is going well, so I'm expecting a disaster any moment."

"That's my girl."

He was busy, so I left and headed back to my desk and gave Lucah a quick smile before settling back down.

Mrs. Andrews knocked on my door a few minutes later.

"Sorry to disturb you dear, but this got put in your father's inbox by mistake, so I thought I would drop it off."

"Oh, thank you." I took the folder from her, and breathed a sigh of relief.

"I thought I'd lost this and I was about to go down to the file room and spend the rest of the day searching. Thank you so much. Now I don't have to look for it." This would save me a hell of a lot of time I didn't have to spare anyway.

"What an adorable paperweight," she said, pointing to my red shoe. "It reminds me of Dorothy's ruby slippers. Are you a fan of *The Wizard of Oz*?"

"Oh, yes. I love that movie." The truth was that I did like the movie, but not enough to buy a paperweight. But if she wanted to think it was in homage, then she could go ahead and think that.

"How sweet. Well, I'll see you later, dear." I said good-bye and went over the file, which had all the information I needed, but hadn't been able to find on the computer. We were still in the process of taking all our old files and scanning them to our database. You'd think this wouldn't be a problem at a technology company, but such is life.

Lucah got up from his desk and came in, and I loved the way he walked and breathed and the way he picked up my coffee mug and told me I needed a refill and he was going to take care of it.

I loved the way he came back and our hands brushed as he handed me the mug and I loved the way he winked those stormy eyes.

If anyone else had told me this stuff, I would have wanted to slap them. Or at least roll my eyes and avoid them. If it wasn't me, I'd say I was insufferable.

Stupid love. Love made you want to punch yourself in the face.

It also made you so distracted that you didn't get as much done at your job as you should because you were too busy fantasizing about your stupid guy and his magical penis.

It made you spend meetings trying not to draw little hearts, or see what his last name would look like with your first name.

Love made you into a fucking twelve-year-old girl.

I couldn't ask Lucah if he was suffering from the same thing because it was just too ridiculous a thing to say out loud.

But then in the afternoon he picked up the phone, said, "I want to fuck you on your desk right now and it kills me that I can't," and then hung up. Well, he could, but it would definitely get us both fired. Although desk sex might be worth it . . .

Love made you consider losing your job for a little desk sex. Love made you a fucking idiot.

Chapter Twenty-Four

"So you seem to be getting along very well with your assistant, your father tells me," my mother said that Sunday night at dinner. I choked on my wine and spewed it all over the white tablecloth. I coughed and grabbed my glass of water to clear out my throat.

"Are you okay, Rory?" Both my parents looked at me in concern as my eyes watered and I tried to breathe normally.

"Fine," I rasped. "Just went down the wrong pipe. What did you say?" Maybe I'd heard her wrong?

"I was saying that your father said you seemed to be getting along very well with your new assistant. I'm interested to meet him next month at the Employee Ball." Shit. I had completely forgotten about the Ball.

Most companies had a yearly party to reward the employees, but Dad always threw a ball. There were themes and everyone dressed up and he rented a fancy place and it was a great time and I looked forward to them all year long. But of course, love had put it out of my mind.

"Right, the Ball. What's the theme this year?" I couldn't recall it for the life of me. Love was taking up too much space in my brain.

"It's black and white this year. Very classy, very chic. I'm thinking about getting these giant chess pieces made and doing the floor in black and white tiles. What do you think?" Mom was the party planner extraordinaire. Seriously, my birthdays were so fabulous, they belonged on one of those television shows about fabulous parties. Renting an elephant or an entire theme park was the norm for us.

"Sounds great."

"You know, I heard from the Heralds that Fin will be back in the area by then. I'm sure he'd love to go with you," Mom said, giving Dad a look. Subtle. Why didn't she just invite him and not tell me and then shove him at me? Or better yet, put him in a box with a bow on it, and then roll him out and have him pop out of it?

"Eva, I believe that ship has sailed," Dad said, coming to my rescue. It was about time.

"Are you sure? You would look so beautiful together. Dark and light." Yes. Like we were a pair of lamps.

"Mom. It's not going to happen. In fact, I'm pretty sure he's smitten with Marisol. They've been texting while he's been gone." I wasn't sure if I should share this with them, but I wanted Mom to drop it. Even if I hadn't been in love with Lucah, I wasn't ever going to be in love with Fin. It just wasn't going to happen.

My mother practically pouted, but then smoothed it behind a smile.

"Well, I will hold out hope that he will change his mind." Lucah thought I was stubborn. Well, the apple didn't fall far from the tree in this case.

Dad just shook his head. He knew how to pick his battles after this many years of marriage. I had a moment of bliss picturing myself in my mother's place and Lucah in my father's. That led me to thinking about us having sex, which led to me thinking about my parents having sex and then I just shut that line of thinking down.

I got out of there as soon as I could and took a cab to Lucah's.

"Honey, I'm home," I said as I came in. He'd left the door unlocked for me. I was here enough that it seemed silly for me not to have a key, but I didn't want to ask for one. He was still so secretive about those rooms. I still hadn't seen them, and I tested the doors once when he was in the shower and found that they were locked. Whatever he had in there (please God, let it not be bodies), he wanted to keep it hidden, even from me.

Love also made you stop questioning things for fear of causing tension or ruining perfect moments.

"Hello, dear, how was dinner?" he said, putting his arms around my waist. I put my arms on his shoulders and twisted his hair in my fingers.

"It was fine, except I completely forgot about the Company Ball next month and my mother wants me to take Fin."

"I think I heard about that once or twice. Is it a big deal?"

"You have no idea. It's a huge deal. The theme this year is black and white, so you'd better have something fancy in one of those colors." I hadn't gone searching through his closet, but he was always so impeccably dressed that I was pretty sure he'd have something on hand.

"It sounds fancy. What are you going to be wearing?"

"Whatever Sloane makes me," I said with a smile. She'd made my last three Ball gowns and each one had been more spectacular than the last. She was going to be sad about the color choice, but I knew she would make up for it by making something unbelievable.

"Lucky girl. So, I'm going to take a shot in the dark and say that I'm not allowed to take you as my date, correct?"

I'd thought about that, but it seemed like a recipe for disaster.

"Lucah."

"I know, I know. But at least save me a dance. Or a few. I can dance with my boss, can't I?"

"Yes, you can dance with me." He started swaying back and forth and humming. "Are we practicing now?"

"Why not? I know how to waltz."

I rolled my eyes as he moved his hands into waltz position with one on my waist and the other clasped in my hand.

"Of course you do."

He waltzed me around the kitchen, humming a tune I wasn't familiar with that I was pretty sure he made up on the spot. Because he was the kind of guy who could make up a tune to waltz to. Because he was the perfect man.

"Well aren't you Mr. Smooth?"

"Yes, that's what they call me." He spun me under his arm and then we did a dip and he kissed me.

"My mother taught me how to waltz. She said that a man should always know how to waltz with a woman." He let me up and we continued to sway.

"She sounds like a smart woman."

"She was," he said, and I thought he was going to talk more about her, but he didn't. He spun me out and spun me back in and then kissed me in a way that made me forget about waltzing. Well, at least vertically waltzing. We could do a great horizontal dance as well.

"So I have something else for you," he said, reaching into his nightstand.

"It better not be your penis. Because I've already had that gift."

"No, it's this." He held up a key and it glinted in the light. "I had an extra key made for you." I took it from him and turned it over in my hand. I was excited about the key, because it seemed like he'd read my mind, but I wanted to know if this was going to open all the doors, and not just the front one.

"Does this open every door in your apartment?" His eyes narrowed for a split second.

"I told you, Sunshine. There are some doors that need to be kept closed. I love you . . . but there are things that I can't share with you. I wish I could, but I can't. Someday maybe I can tell you, but right now, those doors are shut and they're going to stay that way." His voice was almost harsh and I pulled the blanket across my body. He was keeping those closed doors between us and I didn't like it.

"I wish you could explain it in a way that I could understand. But if you say that you need to do it, that's what you need to do. I wish there was something I could do to change that, but it's really up to you." I tried not to sound bratty and bitter, but failed on both counts.

"I'm sorry, I'm not trying to be snotty about it, seriously. Can you understand where I'm coming from?" He pulled the sheet back down and pulled me so I was under him.

"I do. Believe me I do. If there was something I could do, Sunshine. Oh, you don't know what I would do to fix it."

The more he talked, the more confused I got.

"Just tell me it's not a roomful of dead bodies. Or something creepy. Or a shrine of some other girl. Or something else illegal, or creepy, or gross."

"It is none of the above, I promise. It's just something that I can't share. Okay?" I sighed.

"Okay." For now. I was okay for now. Just the fact that I had a key was something. Now I had to get one made for him.

"Big step, giving me a key," I said, tugging on his hair. "Does this mean I get a drawer?"

"Sunshine, you've already taken over half my dresser and most of my bathroom. You can have whatever space you want." He was right. I had kind of started taking over.

"But I don't mind. I like having to move your shampoo to find mine, or accidentally reaching for a toothbrush and getting yours instead of mine."

"What about my tampons? You cool with those?"

"I am cool with your tampons."

"Good."

"Cool."

The next morning he let me use my new key to lock the door when I left and I got a little thrill about putting it on my key ring.

At lunch, I ran to a locksmith and got one made for him since the only extra keys I had were in Sloane's possession. She may have been great at making flan and lingerie, but she was terrible at not losing her key.

When I got back I saw Dad talking to Lucah and I immediately panicked. Dad had his back to me and Lucah was facing me so he saw the panic on my face and shook his head very subtly back and forth.

What did that mean? Did that mean things were okay? Did that mean I should panic? WHAT DID THAT SIGNAL MEAN? We hadn't worked out our signals yet.

I had to walk by Dad to get to my office so I did it in such a way that he saw me out of the corner of his eye.

"Oh, Rory. Just getting back from lunch?" I put on a smile and walked up to them.

"Yes, which means it's Mr. Blaine's turn." Dad and Lucah shared a look that I couldn't decipher and then Lucah excused himself and headed off to lunch.

"What was that about? You trying to steal my assistant?" I joked, trying to make light of the situation.

"Oh, no. He's all yours," he said, and it felt like a double meaning, but that was probably just me. "No, I was just stopping by to see how things were going for him. He's a bright young man you've got there." Was it just me, or was Dad acting shifty?

"Oh, well, he's a hard worker and never complains." I was floundering and I needed to get out of there. He seemed to sense that as he cleared his throat and looked around.

"Well, I need to get back to work, but I'll see you later?"

"Absolutely." We had another meeting this afternoon and I was already not looking forward to it. Lucah would have to sit next to me and we'd have to keep our hands to ourselves. Most of the time I told him not to come with me just because it was too much temptation, but this one I was out of luck because there was so much involved that I needed to remember that I needed another set of notes to supplement mine and he took really good notes when he wasn't trying to shove his hand up my skirt. Or maybe he could do both. I sure as hell couldn't.

I texted Lucah the second I got back to my office.

What was that about? Every second it took him to respond freaked me out even more. I was probably being paranoid, but when you were having a secret love affair with a guy you were not supposed to be having a love affair with, then it kind of went with the territory.

Nothing. I swear. Just asking about the job. Relax, Sunshine :)

I couldn't see his face or hear his tone via the text, so I had no way to tell if he was just trying to calm me down, or if it was really nothing. I'd have to ask him when he got back.

Love made you paranoid.

I was biting my nails and flinching every time someone walked by my door until Lucah got back. I motioned him into my office and he closed the door. I was willing to take the risk just to make double sure that we were still flying under the radar.

He smiled at me and shook his head.

"I told you that we were fine. I think he was checking up to make sure I was doing you justice and not slacking off. It was all work talk, honest."

His voice was sincere and his face was too. Okay, crisis averted. Freak-out aborted.

I took a deep breath.

"You need to stop stressing so much. It's not good for you." He reached out and stroked my face just as there was a knock at my door. Crap, it was time for the meeting.

"Rory dear? It's time for the meeting." Mrs. Andrews' voice made Lucah freeze with his hand on my face. Then he dropped it and we both got up. There was nothing to do but leave the office together. If we both played it cool, then no one would know anything.

"Be right there," I said, and Lucah got up and opened the door open for me as I walked through. He followed a second later with two notebooks and pens, which, of course, I'd forgotten.

He followed too closely behind me and I knew that it was going to be a herculean effort to get through this, although Dad was in this meeting, so there would definitely be no funny business, even if I wasn't already paranoid. I had to draw the line somewhere.

I actually did focus on the meeting and when it was over, I realized that Lucah hadn't touched me once and his notebook was full of his small neat handwriting. My handwriting was terrible and I was jealous of his. If only you could go back in time and relearn how to write. But it was probably too late to do that now. Oh well. It just wasn't one of my talents.

He was keeping his distance, and I knew it had to do with the fact that he thought Dad was watching him. It would have been kind of funny if it wasn't so terrifying. We barely made eye contact for the rest of the day, which only made it sweeter when I unlocked the door to his apartment later and he kissed me like he hadn't seen me in weeks.

"It is torture not being able to look at our talk to or touch you all day, but I felt like we were being watched, so I decided that your paranoia was warranted."

"So you're saying I'm right?" He laughed and bit the tip of my nose.

"Yes, I'm saying you were right." I raised my fist in victory and did a little victory dance, complete with booty shaking and he clapped and urged me on.

"God, you're sexy," he said when I was done. Clearly, he loved me because only someone who loved me would think that display was sexy.

"You just keep telling me that. I haven't heard it enough today." I felt seriously deprived so he made up for it in quite a few ways. Plus, I'd packed Mr. Buzzy in my bag and we had some fun with him as well.

"Does this count as a threesome?" he said, and I smacked him with a pillow.

"Not if the third person is powered by batteries."

"What about a robot?"

"Are you asking me if we had sex and a robot joined us, would that be considered a threesome?" I propped myself on my elbow and gave him a look.

"I'm just saying. I think it could count. If the robot had human emotions."

"Do you understand that we're talking about robot sex?"

"Yes. Because you're an amazing woman and I love you." He kissed me and that was enough of discussing robot sex for one evening.

Chapter Twenty-Five

Lucah and I kept our distance, difficult as it was, for the next week. It made our reunions every night all the sweeter, but parting every morning that much harder. Yes, it sounded like I was bitching but that was what love did to you. Turned you inside out and made you into a person you never thought you'd be. Love turned you into a whiny bitch.

Lucah seemed to be having just as hard a time as I was, which made me feel a little better, even if the situation still sucked.

There was no mention of Fin at dinner the next Sunday and I wondered if Dad had a little chat with Mom about pushing Fin on me, and how that was not going to work, as much as she wanted it to. I didn't need to know, as long as I was sure she wasn't going to ambush me again when the time came for the Black and White Ball. She was already starting to go nuts with the planning and had roped me into helping, so I spent a few Lucah-free afternoons and evenings with her working on invitations and decorations and picking the menu.

Lucah was still dealing with brother drama. Apparently Ryder had gotten a job at Starbucks, but had been fired for cursing out an asshole customer. Lucah told me the story, and I had to say that I couldn't blame Ryder. The customer had sounded like a total jerk. I wasn't sure if I'd have been able to keep my cool. I'd cursed out a customer on the phone once or twice. That was why it paid to be the boss' daughter.

I got Lucah his key, giving it to him by placing it in my navel one morning when he slept over so he saw it when he opened his eyes.

He was thrilled, and I told him that he could have a drawer if he wanted, so I ended up clearing out half my lingerie and shoving it in a lower drawer. Lucah's stuff was more important than another pair of lace panties. He might argue with that, but I wanted him to have his own space at my place. I also slowly brought out the things I'd hidden when he'd first come over because honestly, he'd seen it all and he was still here, so I didn't think there was much that he was going to find out about me that might send him running.

I got a call from Fin on Friday while I was out at the bar and I went outside to take it.

"Hey World Traveler!" I was happy to hear from him, because Marisol had been keeping her trap shut about him and changed the subject whenever we mentioned him.

"Hey, Rory. What's new? I just had a spare moment, so I thought I'd and see how things were going." I hadn't updated him on my relationship with Lucah, because I knew he was going to gloat about being right, or at least think that I'd followed his insane advice.

"Things are good."

"Wow, could you be more vague? How are things with the coworker? And you know the one I mean." I could just see him wiggling his perfectly arched eyebrows. For a guy, he had great eyebrows.

"He's fine. I'm fine." That wasn't going to be good enough for him.

"From the fact that you're avoiding topic, I'm going to go out on a limb and say that you did in fact take my advice and are now so disgustingly happy that I want to reach through the phone and throttle you. Am I warm?"

"Maybe," I said.

"You can drop the act. I heard the happy in your voice. So things are good with him?" Oh, he could hear happy now? Ugh, was I that obvious?

"Things are good as long as we can keep it in our pants in the office and no one finds out. I hope there aren't any other people who can hear happy."

He laughed.

"I'm just more perceptive than most. Hey, you wouldn't by any chance be able to pass along a message to Marisol for me?" It seemed weird, but I wasn't going to question it.

"Yeah, sure. I'm with her right now."

"Can you just tell her 'Tom Hanks'?" Um, what?

"Did you just say 'Tom Hanks'?"

"Yeah, just tell her that. Okay, I gotta go, Rory. Talk to you later." I hung up and shook my head.

Boys are fucking weird.

I went back inside and delivered the message to Marisol. She blushed and then rolled her eyes and refused to tell any of us what it was about, no matter how much we pestered her. Oh, and we definitely did, no holds barred, no mercy, but she stuck to her guns and stood her ground. I should take some lessons from her.

I had no problem telling Lucah I loved him and it came out at the oddest times. Once he was just in the kitchen cleaning up when he grabbed a cup and started moving and tapping it, and I was reminded of a game I used to play at camp.

"I love you," I blurted out as he performed tricks with the cup. I mean, it wasn't anything you hadn't seen in a million YouTube videos, but I thought it was pretty awesome.

He just smiled and flipped the cup on the air and caught it behind his back as I clapped.

Love made you easily impressed by things that you wouldn't normally be impressed with.

The paperweight and mug became regular fixtures at my desk and when anyone asked about them, I just said that a friend had given them to me and let them draw their own conclusions.

We'd somehow found a routine and a pattern, and, of course, as soon as we got used to it, things changed.

Lucah disappeared one Friday afternoon and I couldn't find him. He went on lunch and didn't come back. First he was a half hour late. Then an hour. Then two. Then three.

I was trying to stay calm, but inside I was freaking out and picturing all the worst case scenarios and then trying not to do that so I wouldn't jinx it while still trying to prepare myself for the worst in case it was the worst. I called and texted his cell phone and his home phone and I was about to start calling his favorite lunch places when he called me back.

I shut the door so my hysterics wouldn't carry down the hall.

"Where the hell have you been? I've been going crazy here."

"I'm so sorry. I just . . . I got busy doing something and I turned my phone off. I'm so sorry, Sunshine. It will never happen again. I didn't think it was going to take me this long."

"What? You didn't think what was going to take you this long? You can't keep secrets from me and then vanish. I love you and that makes me think that you're dead on the street somewhere whenever you're a second late. Loving you makes me into a crazy person, and I would think that you'd understand that." It took all my strength not to scream at him, and I definitely wiped a few tears away. It was a fine line between angry and relieved. I wanted to throw my arms around him and I wanted to throw my knee into his crotch for doing this to me.

"I'm sorry, Rory. I'll be back in a few minutes. We'll talk tonight." And he hung up on me.

WHAT THE FUCK?!

He thought he had seen my bitch face. Oh, no. He hadn't seen my bitch face, but he was going to get it.

He hurried in about fifteen minutes later and came right into my office, shut the door and got down on his knees in front of me.

I was torn by the need to make sure he was okay and the need to strangle the life out of him. I did neither. It wasn't just about not telling me where he was. It was all the secrets. I thought I could deal with them, but I couldn't. We had keys to each other's apartments, but there was a corner of his life that he wouldn't let me in. How can you say you love someone, yet keep secrets from them?

I'd thought of everything it could be. From bodies, to a secret love child, to some sort of kinky sex room, to an obsession with My Little Ponies. Whatever it was, it wasn't worth hiding.

The only thing was that I didn't know who he was protecting. Me or himself.

"All I can say is that I'm sorry. I'm so, so sorry. You have no idea how much this kills me. To keep things from you. It's not that I don't want to tell you. I do. I've wanted to say, 'fuck it' so many thousands of times, but I can't. My hands are tied. This is bigger than you and me and I wish I could. But I can't. I wish I could for you. If anything would make me want to, it's you, Sunshine." He was a wreck. His eyes were red, his hair looked like he'd been tearing his hands through it and his suit was all over the place, his tie nearly coming undone, probably from him yanking on it.

I'd never seen him like this, and his honesty made me feel a bit better, but still.

"I love you, and you say you love me, but . . ." He put his hand on my mouth to stop me, and I almost bit his fingers, but let him speak. He was the one who had all the explaining to do.

"I do love you, but this isn't about us."

"Are you in the CIA?" I said, and my voice was muffled by his hand. He moved it and I repeated the question.

"I wish, but even if I was, I couldn't tell you." He was serious. I'd kind of been joking when I'd asked.

"Are you in the CIA?" I watched to see if his eye twitched or something to give me an indication I was on the right track. Nothing. And still, what would the CIA want with our company? Unless they thought we were funneling money to unsavory characters overseas, or making WMDs in our basement, and I knew that neither of those things was happening. At least I thought so . . .

Now my head was spinning with even more possibilities.

"Shit," Lucah said.

"What?"

"I can see your head working right now, which means I've said too much." He'd barely said anything. He got up and sighed.

"Are you still angry with me?"

"Yes," I said, even though I didn't sound convincing. I really was pissed at him, and I was going to make him work to get back in my good graces.

"Well. I think I can do something about that. You know there's the stockholder meeting this afternoon and that they're going out. No one is going to be in the office. Even Mrs. Andrews is going for the free food. So. We have more than enough work here and we should stay behind and get going on it and they can save us a pastry. What do you say to that?" He put both hands on the arms of my chair and leaned down.

Was I still pissed at him? Yes. Was I going to let that stop me from having amazing office sex again? Nope.

"I say that you'd better be absolutely sure this is going to work and then you'd better be absolutely sure that I am more than satisfied at the end of it," I said, trying to keep my bitch face on.

"Yes, Miss Clarke. I will let you know the details later." His face was close enough to kiss, but he didn't. Instead he smiled and strolled out of the office as if he was very pleased with himself.

He'd gone from a man on his knees to a man that was practically skipping because he knew he was going to bang me on my desk. Not that I wasn't looking forward to it, but that he could flip so easily was a little disconcerting.

And then he rushed back into my office, shut the door, came over and looked into my eyes.

"I'm so sorry, Sunshine. I hope you can forgive me." And then he was gone again, nearly crashing into Dad as he walked past my office. Dad gave him a strange look.

Being with Lucah was anything but boring and it was about to get really interesting . . .

"Are you coming to the meeting? You know they're serving those little crab puffs you love," Dad said later on his way past my door to go to the meeting. I tried to look as frazzled and stressed as I could and didn't glance up from my computer.

"Would you hate me if I didn't go? I'm absolutely buried right now. I have about twelve fires I'm trying to put out."

"Sure, I just didn't want you to miss anything. Why don't you send Mr. Blaine along to take notes for you?"

"I need him," I said, and then immediately realized how that sounded. "I need him to go down and get some of the old files for me. We're kind of double teaming this right now, so it would just make more work if he left." I typed faster and still didn't look up.

"Oh, of course. It's nothing earth shattering. Probably it will turn out like all the others with lots of golf talk and discussion on the Red Sox' chances this year. I'll give your excuses. Have a good rest of your afternoon. I'm headed home after the meeting." I said good-bye and didn't look up until the entire office went silent. I glanced at Lucah's desk and made a thumbs-up sign and he did the same.

Coast was clear, but I had to make absolutely sure, so I knocked on every single office door and made sure we were the only two people left.

Lucah leaned against his desk as I did one more check.

"Is anyone here?" he yelled and I shushed him. He put his hand to his ear. "Nope, nothing but echoes." He grabbed my shirt and pulled me closer.

"So," he said.

"So," I said.

"Your desk or mine?" he said, kissing me and backing me up so I was against my office door.

"I have reports all over my desk," I said as he kissed me and started unbuttoning my shirt.

"There are reports all over *my* desk," he said. He kissed my collarbone and I moved my hands down his back to un-tuck his shirt from his pants.

I didn't want to have sex on reports that were going to go back into files. That was just . . . not okay.

"How about we go over here?" he said, pulling me with him to the boardroom. There was a big huge table and it got cleaned every night and it also had a lock.

"You're so smart. I love that you're so smart."

"I love that you're so sexy," he said, opening the door, slamming it and then locking it.

Before I knew it, he was bending me back on the table and kissing me. I missed the tongue ring and he stopped and pulled back for a moment.

"I almost forgot something," he said, reaching into his pocket and pulling something out. He held his hand open and I saw that it was his tongue barbell. He stuck his tongue out, slipped the barbell in and screwed the top on. It looked a lot easier than it probably was.

"You are the perfect man," I said as he kissed and licked my neck with his magic tongue.

"Turn around," he said, and I did. He reached his hand up under my skirt, testing and teasing me.

"Do you want me inside you?" He asked me this nearly every time and the answer was always yes.

I heard the rip of the condom wrapper and then he was entering me from behind and we were both mostly clothed. It was deep and hard and he bent me over until my face was on the table and I turned my head to the side as he thrust into me and I met him with my hips. It was primal and felt almost forbidden. The combination of that and the location and the fact that anyone could walk in had me coming fast, with him right behind me.

He lay on my back and kissed the back of my neck.

"I'm sorry about earlier."

"I know," I said, looking at him with my peripheral vision. "I'm still going to make you pay for it." With that, he got off me and flipped me over, pushing me until I was sitting on the table with my legs dangling. I knew exactly what he was doing and the anticipation made it all the more delicious. He took care of himself, zipped up his pants and kneeled before me, spreading my legs open.

Hooking my panties with his fingers, he pulled them over my hips and pushed my skirt up. I was wide open to him and my skin puckered with goosebumps.

Lucah ran his hands up the inside of my thighs, stopping just short of where I wanted him. Then he stuck his tongue out and licked the path his hands had just taken, stopping short again. My legs were trembling, waiting. He was paying me back, but he was also going to take his sweet time about it, which almost made it worse.

His tongue circled my clit, his piercing clicking as it hit mine and my hands went in my hair and then I was flying higher as his mouth and tongue and hands brought me up, up, up . . .

"Oh God, Lucah. I love you." I couldn't come without telling him this now. His mouth was otherwise occupied so he didn't answer, but when he made me come again a few minutes later and I collapsed on the table, the cool mahogany causing shivers to break out on my skin. He grinned and pulled himself up to sit next to me, his legs actually touching the floor whereas mine weren't even close.

"You're forgiven," I said, clumsily patting his shoulder. I didn't think I could move. He was going to have to carry me back to my desk and prop me up in it for the rest of the day.

"I'm still sorry." He put his hands behind himself and leaned on them. I turned my head to watch him.

"I know. It's not like you're hiding a secret lovechild, or you're cheating on me. You're not lying because you're trying to save your own ass. I can respect that. I'm a reasonable person." I waited for him to snort about the last part, but he didn't. He seemed lost in thought.

"You don't have a love child, do you?" He finally looked at me.

"No. No children here." Not even any scares. "Hey," I said and rubbed his arm and sat up, resting my chin on his shoulder. I shimmied my skirt down and made a note to find my underwear before we left.

"It hurts so much, not being able to tell you. So much that it's like a knife sometimes." I kissed his shoulder.

"It's okay, Lucah. I swear. I'm fine now. Just give me a heads up next time, or at least try to get me a telegram or a smoke signal or something. Anything. I was really worried about you and I don't like being worried like that."

"I don't like to make you worry like that. I'll make sure it doesn't happen again." He leaned down to pick up my panties and got off the table, leaning down to put them back on. I hopped off the table and he slid them back into place. Such a shame.

"So how was it for you, Miss Clarke? Do I get a performance evaluation?" His playful side was back and I was glad. Not that I didn't like his serious side, but it worried me sometimes when he was too serious for too long a time.

"Hm, I think I'll have to see some more of your work before that happens." I wrapped his tie around my wrist and used it to pull his mouth down for a kiss. And then we heard the sound of a door closing.

Lucah and I froze, mid-kiss and my eyes flew open. I clung to him and we listened. The chances of someone coming in this room were slim, but you never knew. I started thinking about my options. The door was locked on the inside, but if someone tried to open it, we were screwed.

I could hide under the table and Lucah could say that he had to get something, or he could hide under the table. Or we could both hide under the table, but then the person would need a key to open the door and if we were caught, we were definitely beyond in trouble.

In limbo, we waited.

"Do you want me to peek?" he said low in my ear. I shrugged one shoulder, scared to speak less the person hear us. Lucah walked as quietly as he could to the door and put his ear in the crack between the door and the frame. I held my breath and waited. And waited.

The suspense was killing me and I could swear my heart was beating loud enough for it to echo through the entire building. Lucah put his finger up for me to wait. So I waited some more.

Then he nodded and went to unlock the door. Was he insane?

"It's okay, I heard the elevator," he said at normal volume and I nearly leaped across the room and tackled him. He unlocked the door and the sound was so loud it was like a gunshot.

"I'll go first. If I don't make it, know that I love you and I hope you pine for me for the rest of your life. But first, one last kiss." He kissed me and then strolled right out into the hallway and turned around, holding his arms out.

"See?"

And then my heart felt like it had been replaced with a bomb that was then detonated in my chest.

"Mr. Blaine, I thought you would be at the board meeting." Mrs. Andrews came out of my father's office with his jacket. Dad was always forgetting his jacket. Then she saw me and I had never wished for a mysterious sinkhole to open under me and swallow me up as I had in that moment when I saw her putting two and two together.

"We were just—" I started to say.

"We—" Lucah tried to say.

She started laughing. Like, throw-your-head-back, eyes-watering, beg-for-mercy-from-Jesus kind of laughing.

Lucah looked at me and I just gaped at Mrs. Andrews as she gasped for breath and then wiped her eyes. She walked forward and patted my cheek like I was an amusing child.

"Oh, my dear. I wasn't born yesterday. Your *secrets* are safe with me." She winked at Lucah and then walked to the elevator, humming a tune I didn't recognize.

"What the—"

"I have no idea," Lucah said, shaking his head as the elevator doors closed.

So much for being stealthy.

"She's not going to tell anyone, right? I mean, the woman has known me since I was in diapers. She's not going to expose us. Right?" Now I was the one pacing. Lucah and I had gone right to his place after work, mostly because I was freaking out and I needed to be alone. Well, alone with him.

Lucah just watched me pace. I was still in my work clothes and I thought he liked watching me walk in heels. He had kind of a glazed look, as if he was picturing me naked and pacing in heels. I wish he would freak out more about this with me. It was uncomfortable to be freaking when your significant other was not freaking. It made me feel like I was freaking too much, which only made me freak out about freaking out.

My life was exhausting sometimes.

"Would pacing naked help? I know it would help me." Yup, I called it. I whirled around and glared at him.

He tried to look innocent. "What? I really think it would help give me some insight on the situation."

"And by 'situation' you mean my ladyparts."

He pretended to be shocked.

"I am offended that you immediately jump to the conclusion that I only want you to pace naked for my benefit. That's not giving me much credit." He was trying to distract me and it was working.

"You don't deserve credit, Mr. Blaine," I said, leaning over the back of the couch and wrinkling my nose at him.

"She's not going to betray us, Sunshine. From the way she talked, it seems as if she's known for a while and hasn't said anything. Stop worrying." He pressed the spot between my eyebrows that I knew was all wrinkled up from stressing.

"Well you don't worry, so I have to worry for both of us." He reached out, grabbed my arms and pulled me over the back of the couch and into his lap. I screamed and he started tickling me until I breathlessly begged him to stop.

"She's *not* going to tell. Trust me," he said again. He must have thought that if he said it enough times I'd eventually believe it. "Now can we talk some more about the naked pacing? I don't think we really discussed that fully."

Despite Lucah's assurances that Mrs. Andrews wouldn't narc on me to anyone, I was a WRECK when I went to Sunday dinner that weekend. Sweaty palms, racing heart, the whole nine yards. Whatever that meant. What the hell did that mean?

"You're going to be fine," Lucah said, kissing the top of my head as I did my makeup in the mirror, interrupting my wondering about yards.

"I swear if you say that one more time, I'm stabbing you with my mascara brush."

He just laughed and pinched my ass.

"Be careful or you're not getting any tonight." I was full of shit and we both knew that. He just laughed and walked back into the kitchen where he was making dinner for one. It pretty much sucked that he couldn't come to the dinner with me, but that completely defeated the purpose of hiding our relationship. We'd jokingly thought of scenarios where he could just happen to drop by and could join us, but there was no way to do it without making it completely obvious.

He texted me when I was in the cab with a picture of himself sticking his pierced tongue out and it made me smile, but didn't help with the nerves. I messaged him back and then it was time to face my parents.

"You look pale," was the first thing my mother said to me. Yeah, hiding my nervousness was going really well.

"Oh, I'm just tired. I've been having trouble sleeping." *Because of all the sex I've been having with my assistant.*

"What about chamomile tea? That always used to work when you were younger," Mom said as we sat down at the table. Somehow I didn't think tea was going to help in this situation.

"I'll try that," I said anyway. Mom swore by tea as the cure-all for everything. Upset stomach? Ginger. Can't sleep? Chamomile. Need a jolt? Black.

Luckily, Mom was full of details about the Black and White Ball, so I didn't have to talk much. Dad seemed quiet, but he was probably just exhausted by Mom talking about the ball.

"Has Sloane started your dress yet?" The second I'd mentioned the thing, Sloane had run to her drafting table and started sketching. She'd made at least five potential sketches and I'd picked one and she'd started working on it in her spare time. First she was going to make a dummy dress out of muslin to fit it to me and then we were going together to pick out the fabric. Maybe this year she'd actually take my input.

"Yes, and it's going to be black. We thought a white dress was way too wedding."

"Well, you should decide who you're taking and see what color he wants so you can match exactly. I'd love to see both of you in white," she said and I dropped my fork on the floor. Of course I'd taken Royce to the last Ball, which had been a Garden of Eden theme. I'd worn red and he'd worn a green suit. The apple and the snake. Yes, I knew it should have been obvious that the snake was inside the suit, but I was blind.

"I don't think I'll be taking anyone." I'd had years where I didn't have a date. Granted, they'd been when I was a gawky teenager, but still. There was no rule that I had to have a date to the ball. This wasn't a prom in 1953.

"Oh, but you have to bring a date," Mom said as if I'd suggested coming to the event naked.

Dad cleared his throat.

"She doesn't have to bring a date, Eva. It's not a social disgrace for a woman to be single at an event anymore." See?

"I know that, Walter. I just thought that she might have someone in mind that she could bring. Just as a friend." A someone named Fintan Herald. I could see what was going on in my mother's head as if I was watching a movie.

Me, in a fabulous black gown. Fin, also in black. Our eyes meet across the crowded ballroom. Everyone stops and stares at my beauty as I walk in slow motion across the room to meet him. Our eyes lock as the string quartet starts a waltz and everyone moves out of our way as we glide across the floor. Everyone remarks about how lovely we look together. Fin compliments mean and I blush attractively and duck my head modestly. When the dance is over he gives me his arm and we stroll onto the patio and he spouts magnificent poetry and plucks a rose from the trellis and . . .

"I don't need a date. I've had a date for the past few years, and clearly, it didn't work out for me. So I'm going alone."

Mom sighed as if I was the most defiant child ever but then she smiled as if an idea had struck her.

"Well maybe you'll meet someone there."

I looked at Dad and he just shook his head. You couldn't stop Eva Clarke once she got started.

"Or maybe I'll trip, break my ankle and there will be a cute paramedic that comes to my rescue," I said with a smile as I speared a tomato from my salad and popped it into my mouth.

"We can only hope," Mom said.

"So you would let me break my ankle just to meet a man?"

She waved her hand as if I was being ridiculous. "Don't be dramatic. You could just twist it and make it look convincing." She looked down at her salad and I shared a glance with Dad. Insane. The woman was insane.

Luckily, the heat was taken off of me as Dad started talking about politics and then he and Mom got in a heated discussion about the economy. I know most kids hated when their parents fought, but for them it was more like a debate between two fiercely intelligent people so I kind of loved it.

I just sat back and watched the words fly, and sipped my wine while I calmed down. Lucah was waiting for me and I was pretty excited about that. You'd think after however many rounds of sex we'd had that we'd get bored, or one of us would stop having orgasms, but that wasn't the case. We got each other off each and every time and it always felt new. There was no way this could go on forever. Sex wasn't always that magical, not in real life.

When my parents had finally agreed to disagree as they always did, it was time for dessert and I did whatever I could to get out of there without Mom bringing up the date business again.

I succeeded and texted Lucah as the cab drove me back to his place. He just sent me back a smiley. I'd thought he was going to rub being right in my face, but he wasn't that kind of guy.

"Didn't I tell you it was going to be fine? Why don't you listen to me, Miss Clarke?" he said when I walked in. Or maybe he was that kind of guy. I just rolled my eyes and let him kiss me, but didn't kiss him back.

"Aw, did you think I would be above gloating about being right? Think again, Sunshine." He winked and I stuck my tongue out at him.

"You are definitely not getting any tonight," I said, pulling my shoes off. I now had at least five pairs that had taken up residence at his place, but I didn't want to bring too many and take over like some kind of shoe fungus.

"That's okay. I'm cool with cuddling. I'm going to cuddle you so hard." He put his arms around me from behind.

"Yeah, that's why your dick is pressing into my ass. You're that excited about cuddling." I turned in his arms and he pressed further into me and against my will, I was getting turned on. Stupid libido.

"I am crazy about cuddling. I'm going to cuddle my cock right into your—" I put my hand over his mouth.

"That is not cuddling and you must think I'm an idiot if you think I'm going to fall for—" This time I was interrupted by him grinding his hips into me and turning me on further.

"Fuck it," I said, grabbing the back of his head and wrenching it down to meet mine. We could cuddle with his cock inside me. It was way more fun that way, anyway.

Chapter Twenty-Seven

Monday morning Mrs. Andrews gave me a wink as she walked by my office and I smiled back at her. I was surprised that she hadn't told anyone. I mean, Dad was her boss and it was almost like she was lying to him. I wondered how many times she'd lied to him in all the years they'd worked together. Probably not many. I felt bad making her do it, so I stopped by her desk on my way to the break room for my second cup of coffee.

"I just wanted to thank you for not saying anything," I said in a low voice. Her desk was right where everyone walked by, so I didn't want anyone to overhear.

"Oh, you're welcome dear. Mum's the word." She pretended to zip her lips and gave me another smile as she answered the phone. I guess that was that. I took my WORLD'S GREATEST BOSS mug and went to get my coffee.

There was only one other thing that had been nagging me, but I hadn't mentioned it to Lucah because I knew he would say that I was being paranoid again, and I didn't want to have that discussion over and over and over.

Mrs. Andrews knew about us. My friends knew. Yes, they knew me well and had seen us together, but were we that obvious? I'd thought we were being careful, but maybe love hung over you like a smell and anyone could spot it. Like B.O.

But if that was the case, then why hadn't anyone called us out? That was the only thing keeping me from saying anything about it to Lucah. Yes, I was the boss' daughter, but there were plenty of people working here that would be more than happy to see me tossed out on my ass so they could have my job.

So either my friends and Mrs. Andrews were just that perceptive or whoever knew about it hadn't said anything. I thought about chatting up some of the other people and feeling them out to see if they were just keeping their mouths shut, but I'd probably seem really suspicious and then it would backfire.

I was terrible at this covert relationship thing. I was much better at making a software presentation to a new client, or getting through a hundred emails in two hours.

"Your messages, Miss Clarke," Lucah said as I walked back to my office. He'd started listening to my voicemails for me, taking down the gist of each message and ranking them in order of importance. He really was damn good at his job. I wished he would have been terrible at it and then I could have fired him and we wouldn't have to exchange dirty sticky notes, or have sex in the boardroom when everyone was gone and get caught as we snuck out.

"Thank you, Mr. Blaine," I said, being overly cordial. It was sort of our inside joke and it was almost sexier that way. Forbidden. Dun, dun, duuuuunnnn.

Love made you crazy.

I made sure to give him a quick thumbs-up to share that everything had been okay with Mrs. Andrews. He drew a smiley face and put it on the stack of messages. I had to stifle a giggle as I went back to my office.

"I thought I would let you know that I will be absent this afternoon, Miss Clarke for several hours. I most likely will not be coming back to the office, so I thought I would let you know." I looked away from my computer and across the hall at him, but he wasn't looking at me.

"Well thank you, Mr. Blaine, for letting me know so I don't worry."

"You're welcome, Miss Clarke." He hung up and two seconds later another airplane sailed onto my desk. I hadn't even seen him throw it and when I looked at his desk, he was typing like he nothing had happened.

I unfolded the paper airplane and there was a note on it.

Your boobs look great today.

-Lucah

I tore the note up and put it through my shredder just as my phone rang. I picked it up and didn't even bother saying hello.

"Didn't like my note?" I fought a smile.

"How old are you? You are a grown man."

"Grown men can't use the word boobs?"

"They shouldn't."

"What am I supposed to call them? Mammary glands? Love pillows? Jugs? Hooters?" I burst out laughing and had to hang up the phone because I didn't want anyone catching either of us talking about other words for boobs.

I hadn't had this much fun at work in my entire life, and Lucah was mostly responsible for that. Our banter helped the day go faster and when I was working on something I didn't want to work on, he always found little ways to help out, or make me smile. Not that my job was bad before, but he just took it into awesome territory.

I missed him that afternoon. I kept looking at his desk and he was missing and it kind of made me sad. Not that I was moping. Or pouting.

But I did my work and got through the day and headed to my apartment to spend some time with Sloane before going over to Lucah's.

"Hey, do I know you?" Sloane said when I walked in the door. Yes, I deserved it.

"I know, I know. I'm sorry." She put her hand up and turned her head away from me.

"Your words are empty. Here I am, using all my extra time to make the most beautiful dress for you and you can't even be bothered to spend any time with the person you claim is your best friend."

"Sloane . . ." Uh oh. She'd been neglected and it was going to take a lot of groveling and doing things for her to get back in her good graces. There would be backrubs and chocolate involved, and probably some sort of girls' weekend with no boys allowed. I was willing to make the sacrifice for our friendship. She'd done a lot for me, and I did owe her. I'd done what I promised never to do: let a boy come between us.

"I'm sorry I let him take up all my time. You're important to me, Sloane. Chicks before dicks, right?"

"Well you're gonna have to show me you mean that," she said, slowly turning around.

"Name it."

"Well, firstly you're taking me out to dinner. Then you're buying me a massage. And maybe after a shopping trip we can talk. But for right now, you can put on the new piece that I made for you today." She finally busted a smile out and I knew that I would be forgiven. Sloane wasn't one to hold grudges, unless they had done something against someone she cared about. Case in point: Royce. I was pretty much over him, but she still wanted to go and let the air out of the tires of his beloved BMW and then key it, in addition to a lot of other illegal things. Sloane had a twisted mind and I never wanted to be on her bad side. Her idea of revenge scared the crap out of me.

"I can do all of that. Tomorrow night for dinner? This weekend for the shopping trip and massage? I'll make an appointment for both of us. I could use one too."

"I'm sure your back is worn out from all the sex," she said, not sounding bitter at all.

"Hey, I'm not stopping you from getting laid."

"You're not helping me at all. I work in an industry populated by bitchy women and gay men. You work in a building full of men. Smart men."

"Yeah, men who are good with machines and coding, but not good with people. I mean, not that all guys who are good with computers are nerds who can't hold a conversation, but most of them are married, or aren't single, or guys you wouldn't want. Don't you think I would tell you if I knew someone?"

She knew I was right. If there was anyone who I thought would be good for her, I'd be all over it. I wanted her to be happy. I also had a tendency to think that no one was good enough for her. It would take a special kind of man to keep up with Sloane and I hadn't met him yet.

"I suppose," she said and I put my arms around her. She let me hug her but didn't hug me back.

"Okay, okay, get out of here. Oh, but put on what I laid out for you." I dashed to my bedroom and saw another awesome lingerie set. This time it was green, with a snap on lace panel that was like the first bow outfit I'd worn. Lucah was getting very good at getting me out of them by now. I put the lingerie on under a cute shirt and jeans. It didn't seem to matter what I had on over the lingerie. Although, I was going to make sure to have my eyes locked on his face when he saw me in the dress Sloane was making. I knew it would be worth it.

"Are you sure you're not mad at me?" I said before I left.

"No, get out of here, you crazy kid."

Yup. Best friend ever.

"I am going to have to abandon you to have Girl Time this weekend with Sloane. Oh, I also have to take her out to dinner tomorrow night and I think I should actually spend the night at my own apartment. You know, because I live there." I made sure I said it after sex.

"I don't own you, Rory. You don't have to ask my permission to do anything. Well, I would be a little upset if you had sex with another guy. Just a little."

Oh, but he did own me.

"I know, but I just wanted to make sure. And I'm not having sex with anyone else. Just you. I wouldn't have the strength. You're always wearing me out." Ain't that the truth.

"Good. Because if you were, I'd probably find the guy and pummel him into yesterday."

"Caveman." I'd pay to see that. There's something kind of erotic about seeing two men beat each other up. Why is UFC so popular? Sloane loved to watch two hot sweaty guys go at each other and I had to admit that I enjoyed it too.

And then something occurred to me. "You're not having sex with anyone else, are you?"

"No, Sunshine. I would rather wake up with you than go to bed with anyone else." He kissed my nose and I couldn't help but smile. I loved it when he said things like that. It made me feel all warm and fluttery inside. Like I was going to bust.

"You're sweet," I said, twirling his hair around my finger. I loved watching the colors change in the light. Sometimes when we were out in the sun his head looked like it was on fire. In a sexy way, of course.

"You're sexy," he said, running his hand over my hip and hitching it over his leg.

"You're sweet *and* sexy." He flipped me so I was straddling him and brought my face down for a kiss.

"You're everything." Yup. My happy was about ready to explode. Gross.

"You're full of shit," I said.

"Liar," he said and I kissed him again because I was totally lying.

"I hope you know I plan on buying the most expensive mixed drink on the menu. And the most expensive entrée," Sloane said the next night when we were at dinner.

"Go nuts, girlfriend." This night was going to put me in debt, but oh well. Gotta make sacrifices for friends.

Sloane moved her foot up my leg under the table.

"So what are my chances of getting lucky on this date?" She put her elbow on the table and leaned in, lowering her voice and pretending to be seductive. I leaned in and played along.

"If you play your cards right."

"Ooh, baby." The waitress chose that moment to appear and she cleared her throat. Ha, she probably thought we were on a date. Well, I didn't care and I knew Sloane didn't. It would be kind of fun to keep up the charade.

"You want to order first, babe?" I said to Sloane, hoping she'd play along.

"Thanks, darling. I will have the escargot to start, and then I will have the surf and turf as well as the seafood stew, and I will also have the most expensive mixed drink you've got. I don't care what it is. She said she was going to spoil me, right baby?" she cooed.

"Only the best for my girl," I said, blowing her a kiss. I ordered shrimp cocktail, salad, and mussels with lemon garlic sauce in linguine, plus my gin and tonic. I knew there was no way Sloane could eat all that food, and was definitely going to be bringing it home and eating it for the next few days, all on me. She knew how to work the system.

The waitress came back with our drinks, and Sloane took a sip of hers without asking what the hell it was. I waited for the verdict and she made a face as she swallowed.

"How is it?" I asked and she pushed it across the table at me.

"I think I just drank gasoline mixed with nail polish remover." I took one whiff of the thing and decided to pass.

"I'm good, thanks. But you'd better drink that entire thing. I'm not paying for you to throw away good alcohol." She glared at me and took her drink back.

"I will drink it."

"Yeah, you will," I said, smirking at her. She'd made her bed so she was gonna lie in it. Or drink it, in this case.

Our food came and Sloane looked at the snails as if they were going to bite her.

"Hey, you ordered them," I said when the waitress left.

"I know, because they were expensive and I figured they were fancy. Rich people eat snails."

"Um, my parents have never eaten snails. Or, at least not voluntarily."

"Your parents don't count," she said, picking up the device used to hold the snails as you forked the meat out.

"My parents don't count as rich people?" This was news to me.

"Yeah, but they're normal people. They don't act like rich people." I wasn't even going to step into that minefield to figure out what the hell she was talking about. I just ate my shrimp and shook my head.

Every time the waitress came back, we pretended that we were on a date.

"God, if we keep this up much more I'm gonna wind up having my way with you in the cab on the way back," Sloane said as we ordered dessert. She went with the tiramisu and I got the same. The waitress brought the bill and I didn't even look at it as I handed her my card and then signed my name when she came back. The gratuity was already in there, so I wouldn't see it until I checked my online statement tomorrow. And at that point, I would avoid it.

"Just remember to use protection. I can't afford to get knocked up at this juncture in my career," I said, downing my third drink. Yeah, I was a little tipsy. Sloane had finished her drink and there was apparently a high alcohol content in it, because she was pretty far gone.

"Are you implying that I have a penis?"

"A really big one. Jumbo-sized. A porn star penis." I knew my voice was loud and the topic of conversation was completely inappropriate for this type of restaurant, but I didn't care at this point.

"You know it," she said with an exaggerated wink.

We finished our desserts and stumbled toward a cab, Sloane dropped her doggie bag along the way and abandoned it on the sidewalk. Some homeless man was going to have a very lucky night.

We both fell onto the couch when we got home.

"That was nice," Sloane slurred.

"You're not a cheap date, Sloane Harris."

"You spread that around." We ended up changing into pajamas and spending the rest of the night sobering up on the couch with lots of water and microwave macaroni and cheese.

"See? This is just as much fun as going out. Actually, it's more fun because you can wear what you want and you don't have to be humiliated if you fart or something." I moved away from Sloane on the couch. We'd lived with each other long enough that we'd seen it all, but that didn't mean I wanted to be close to her if she let one rip.

"So are you going to move in with Lucah?"

"I can't. What would I tell Dad? What if he wanted to come visit? It would never work. It's just too risky."

"That sucks."

"Tell me about it." I scraped the bottom of the bowl for the last remnants of melted cheese product. It might not be real, but that stuff was damn tasty.

"You think I'm ever going to find someone?" I did a double take. Sloane almost never wanted to talk about stuff like this. Must be the alcohol.

"Of course. There's someone for everyone."

"That's just what happy couples say to single people to make them feel better. Not everyone finds their one true love, and what if only some people actually fit together? Like, what if some people are meant to go together, like puzzle pieces, but the factory screws up a few and they don't have a match? What if I'm a bad puzzle piece?"

"You're not a bad puzzle piece, Sloane." I moved closer to her and made her look at me. "You are smart and you're sexy and you're funny and you're so freaking talented and anyone who ever meets you adores you. I know this is all the stuff a friend is supposed to say, but it's seriously true. I wouldn't bullshit you."

"Not to my face."

"Yes, to your face. You know I would." She finally relented.

"Where is he? I'm just worried that I'm going to be old and look back on my life and there wasn't anyone to share it with. I want to share my life with someone." I smacked her in the shoulder.

"Um, what about me? You're sharing your life with me right now. Yes, it may not be in a romantic way, but you need all kinds of love in your life, not just that. I love you and so do Chloe and Marisol and everyone at your studio loves you, for the most part, and my parents even love you. Your life isn't devoid of love, and you're not alone, okay?"

"When the hell did you get all good-advice giving?" I had no idea. Normally I sucked at advice.

"I have no idea."

"Must be love. Makes you smarter and more insightful."

"Um, I think it does the opposite. Love makes you an idiot. So I didn't tell you that Mrs. Andrews knows about me and Lucah." I proceeded to inform her about the boardroom sex and then the getting caught. I'd been so stressed about it until I'd talked to Mrs. Andrews that I hadn't even wanted to bring it up at all.

"You are such an office slut! Remind me not to touch any surfaces if I ever visit you." That earned an eye roll from me.

"We haven't had sex everywhere, Sloane. I'm not that bad."

It was her turn for an eye roll.

"Yes, you are, and I love you anyway. Maybe your love karma will rub off on me." And then I had a fantastic idea.

"Be my date."

"Um, we kind of just did that."

"No, be my date for the Black and White Ball. Then you can look over all the guys from my office and decide if you want to take a chance on any of them. They'll all be there, and you can make yourself a great dress and then my parents will get off my back about inviting a guy."

She stroked her chin like she had a goatee and narrowed her eyes as if she was thinking about it very seriously.

"Interesting. Very interesting." I waited and she dragged it out before diving at me and shoving me back into the arm of the couch.

"Ow!"

"Of course I want to go! Oh my God, yes!" She screamed in my ear and I was immediately second guessing this once brilliant idea. This was going to be . . . Jesus, what did I get myself into?

"This is going to be awesome. I've been dying to go to this thing and I've been hiding my jealousy for years." This was news to me. Guess she was good at hiding jealousy.

"Well good. I'm sure my parents will hide their disappointment that you're not a man and will be thrilled to see you."

"I could pretend I was a man. Wear a suit and put my hair back and all, and I could stick Mr. Buzzy in my pants." I was now regretting I'd ever told her that my vibrator had a name.

"Yeah, that would go over real well." She finally got off me and ran to her workroom, then came back with a sketch that she shoved in my face.

"What do you think?" Clearly, she had designed this dress for herself. It was long and had a gorgeous cutout in the back and a cutout in the front that was made more modest by sheer fabric underneath.

"I thought I could do it in black and white, maybe with black flowers or something."

"It's gorgeous, Sloane, and it will be gorgeous on you." Because that bitch was tall. I could never in the history of ever get away with something like that. It would cling to all the wrong places and would be way too long anyway. Such was life as a short girl.

"You're gonna be the hottest girl there."

"Damn right I am, baby." She dashed back to her room and got started on making a pattern. When I finally went to bed, her light was still on.

Chapter Twenty-Eight

I didn't get a chance to tell Lucah about my girls' night until I was at his place the next night. I was dreading Monday, so I was hoping the weekend would last as long as possible. Work had been insanity as I was preparing for a presentation that Dad had handed off to me because he was going to be traveling and didn't trust anyone else to do it. Or at least that was what he'd told me. I had no idea what he told the other people he could have given it to. They were probably pissed, but I didn't care. I'd stopped caring if other people got upset about stuff like that a long time ago.

"So you know how I said I wasn't with anyone else? Well, I think you might have to fight Sloane for me now. She's going to be my date for the Black and White Ball." I watched his face as I told him and he smiled. I didn't think he would actually be jealous.

"Then I'll have to save her a dance too. Speaking of the Ball, I'm not sure if I should bring someone or not. You know that I don't want to bring anyone but you, but maybe I should bring someone just to keep up appearances." I knew this wasn't some kind of underhanded way to date another girl. Too bad he couldn't bring a guy friend without making himself look gay. Or maybe he didn't care.

"You could bring your brother."

"If you don't mind someone filching people's wallets, or getting really drunk and crashing through a window. Or getting caught having sex with the help in the kitchen. Or doing karaoke even though there isn't karaoke happening."

Wow.

"Yeah, Ryder has done all of the above. Never all of those things at the same party, but he would probably take that as a challenge. Plus, it would be a little odd. Do you know any girls who wouldn't mind going with me and wouldn't get any romantic ideas?"

Actually, I did.

"I can ask Chloe if she wouldn't mind. No worries about romantic ideas at all. Plus it would be more fun to have as many friends there as possible. Maybe we can escape and have a party within a party. As long as we don't do anything illegal or at least don't get caught, we should be able to have a good time."

"As long as I get to dance with you, I'll be happy. You still haven't told me about your dress."

I shook my head slowly. "It's bad luck to tell you about the dress before the ball."

"Sunshine, I'm pretty sure that's just for weddings."

"Oh, I think it should also apply to balls. Also, because I want to savor your facial expression when you see me sweep down the staircase in it." I got up from the couch and practiced sweeping down the stairs and did a little curtsy.

"Will there be stairs to sweep down?"

"Yes, there are. They remind me of stairs from *Gone With The Wind*."

He got up and bowed. "So am I Rhett Butler or Ashley Wilkes?"

"Oh you're Rhett. Definitely Rhett. What kind of a question is that?" Ugh, Ashley Wilkes was the worst. Plus, I knew it was an old fashioned name for a guy, but still. I couldn't be attracted to a guy named Ashley.

"Just making sure," he said before he took my hands and twirled me around. "Rhett was the better dancer. And he didn't emotionally cheat on his wife."

"Ashley kissed Scarlet, remember? So he actually cheated on her. Douchebag. He reminds me a little of my ex." He also had a stupid name.

"That's right. I haven't watched that movie in a long time. I'd forgotten." He moved his hands around my waist and we started slow dancing instead.

He finally hummed a tune I recognized.

"Is that the song by the Rembrandts that was the intro to *Friends*?" I couldn't be sure because he'd slowed it down a bit.

"Maybe." But he said it with a smile so I knew I was right.

"Well if you invite Chloe, then that means Marisol is left out and that's not right."

"I could invite her, too. Have a lovely lady on each arm."

"Like a pimp."

"You said it, not me."

We danced for a little bit more.

"It's not a bad idea," I said. "Bringing the three of them. It would be a lot more fun. And I know they're not going to turn it down. Do you want me to ask, or do you want to do the honors?"

"I'll handle it," he said and kissed me.

"You're awesome."

"I know."

I got two all caps text messages the next day, one each from Marisol and Chloe. Apparently, Lucah had sent beautiful flower arrangements to each of them with a note asking them to the ball.

They were both ecstatic, even Chloe who claimed she'd never been on a date with a man, but was willing to make an exception. Sloane texted me and she was less enthused because they each wanted dresses and that was going to be hard to finish in time, with the event only a little more than two weeks away. Sloane thrived on pressure, but she bitched about it every step of the way. I had no doubt in my mind that she'd finish. I'd just have to hear her whine and complain the entire time, but I guess that was part of the fun of living with her.

I texted Lucah and told him, and he grinned over his desk at me and sent a message back.

What can I say? The ladies love me. I sighed loud enough for him to hear and texted him back.

Don't let your head get too big or you won't be able to hold it up.

That earned me a snarky text back and then my phone rang and there was an issue with a PowerPoint presentation and I had to go figure that out. I swear, PowerPoint was created by Satan to ruin lives.

I got the problem sorted out and that afternoon I had to put on my nice face and present to some potential new clients. I had my favorite heels on and I was confident in my material, and the best part was that Lucah got to come watch me.

His eyes were locked on me the entire time and it gave me even more confidence. I could have done the entire thing naked and rocked it out. Afterwards they shook my hand and said how impressed they were with someone so young. Dad beamed and told them I was his daughter. Lucah gave me a wink and I couldn't tell who was more proud, him or Dad. I was floating on post-presentation high and I wanted nothing more than to pull Lucah away and screw him somewhere, but that was completely impossible. Hopefully I could hold out until tonight.

He called me the second I got back into my office.

"I am so fucking proud of you and you are so fucking amazing and I wish I was fucking you right now, and I've said fuck too many times but I feel it is warranted in this situation." He hung up and I did a fist pump and he pretended to clap. Then we had to stop because there were people walking by.

I was beaming the rest of the day. Things were actually going well. Lucah and I were ridiculously in love, all my friends were coming to the ball, we'd potentially just made a multi-million dollar deal and Mrs. Andrews was keeping our secret.

Something had to go wrong soon to balance things out. Not that I was cynical, but it was my experience that when things are perfect, that's when reality comes and bites you in the ass and reminds you that life isn't like that. It's a series of ups and downs and the downs sometimes come when you least expect them.

Chapter Twenty-Nine

"What do you think?" Sloane said as she zipped up the side of the dummy dress. We were at her studio because she had better mirrors and she could make alterations on the spot.

I turned slowly in front of the three-way mirror and then stopped. This was not a dress. This was something else entirely.

"You're not saying anything," Sloane said, her eyes bugging out from lack of sleep and too much caffeine and anticipation. "You hate it. It's too much. Will you just say something?!"

"It's the most beautiful thing I've ever seen, and this is just the mock up. I just . . . I mean, look at it." The top was a bodice with a sweetheart neck that made my boobs look lush, but not like they were busting out and then the skirt . . . oh, the skirt. The bodice dipped into a V and the skirt started just at my hips and flowed out, but not in a cupcake way. There was an underskirt and so forth to help it stay out, not that it needed any help. This was a Ball Gown.

It was like Sloane had sculpted the dress out of some sort of non-fabric substance. I moved in it, but it didn't lose its shape, and it wasn't heavy at all. That might change when we got the real dress done, because the fabric would probably weigh more, but damn.

I felt like Scarlet O'Hara coming down the staircase at Twelve Oaks while Rhett Butler ogled me in front of everyone.

"You are the absolute bestest friend in the entire world, Sloane. I would hug you, but I don't want to hurt the dress." Her face finally burst into a smile and she crushed me in her arms before picking me up and whirling me around once.

"It's just the practice dress, it doesn't matter. I could make another one in my sleep. I'm so glad you like it. I wanted it to be spectacular."

"Mission accomplished, Sloane. Really. Lucah is going to lose his mind." I couldn't wait to see it.

"Speaking of him, what is he wearing? Black or white?"

"He won't tell me. Since I won't tell him about my dress, he refuses to tell me about his tux. I mean, I know he's gonna look sexy, but I kind of wish I knew what color it was." I'd been trying to use my feminine wiles to get it out of him, but no amount of blowjobs would get him to tell me. He could keep a secret, but I knew that already.

Sloane helped me out of the dress and I put my work clothes back on. I'd come straight from the office and I was heading home to order food before Lucah came over. Sloane was so busy making ball gowns that she'd spent the last few nights at the studio so Lucah and I could have all the dirty screaming sex we wanted at my apartment. It was lovely.

"Have you told your parents yet that you're bringing me? She said as she wrestled the dress back on the dress form.

"Uh, not yet. I don't think Lucah has told them about the two dates thing, either. I mean, it's going to look a little weird that he's bringing my friends. We didn't consider that when we originally made this plan, so breaking the news is going to require some finesse on both our parts. I definitely don't have it, but maybe I can borrow his. I mean, it's not like Dad doesn't know that Lucah and I get along, and maybe I used him as a reason to get my friends to the event and had had to agree because I'm his boss. I think that's the way I'm going to play it." I'd thought about this a lot. It seemed that spare moments in my life were spent trying to come up with feasible stories for my interactions with Lucah. It was a better hobby than knitting.

Lucah was late, but he texted me letting me know he had brother drama again. I kept picturing a snotty little kid throwing tantrums, even though I knew his brother was twenty-three. Lucah still hadn't given me physical descriptors, so I built an image of him in my head that was probably completely wrong.

He finally walked in and he was in a mood that I didn't think any amount of sex or cuddling or anything else was going to lift, so I took his hand, led him to the couch and made him sit.

"Talk to me. That's an order, Mr. Blaine." I thought he was just going to shake his head, but he didn't.

"I don't know what to do, Rory. I'm out of ideas. Short of planting drugs on him and calling the cops, I've got nothing." He put his head in his hands.

"All he does is get himself into trouble. It's a wonder he hasn't gotten arrested yet. Seriously, it's a fucking miracle. He always seems to find a way to get out of it. He's smart, and he knows it. I just wish he'd find something constructive to do with it. He seems bent on destruction right now, but he's not a kid anymore. He's an adult and I'm thinking about just telling him that I'm done until he gets his shit together." I had no idea what to say or do to make it better, so I just sat there and listened.

"I know he's broken up about Mom and Dad, but he was having problems before that. I don't think he's addicted to drugs, but maybe rehab would help? I just don't know what to do." He finally lifted his head and I'd never seen him so anguished before. It absolutely broke my heart.

I reached out and pulled him into my arms and held him. That seemed to be the only thing to do, since I didn't have any magical solutions. I stroked his hair as he breathed and I could tell he was on the verge of tears. It was an intense thing, seeing someone break down like that. It only made me love and ache for him more.

"Are you sure there isn't anything I can do. I just feel awful."

"I know. I'm sorry that I'm dumping this on you at all. I didn't mean to, but I don't have anyone else to talk to. Tate has pretty much cut ties with him so Ryder burned that bridge already. I don't blame him, because he has the girls to think about, but it's just hard sometimes."

"I know, I know. We can talk about something else if you want." He sat up and his eyes were red, but dry. "Tell me about your parents," I asked tentatively. I expected him to shut me down, but he didn't.

"We were poor. I mean, not that we didn't have enough food, but there were times when we ate cereal dry for dinner because that was all we had in the house. My dad was a good man, but he had the worst employment luck ever. He'd get a good job and then the company would go bankrupt, or it would burn down, or he'd get laid off when the jobs went overseas. It happened so often that Mom kept an emergency fund for when he was out of work. She had health problems, so she couldn't really keep down a job. We lost our house a more than once and had to live in a one-bedroom apartment for a few months one summer. But Dad made it like we were having an adventure, so he strung a tarp up in the living room and we got to pretend we were camping." He smiled at the memory and I was shocked. I had no idea that Lucah had grown up like that.

It made me think about my own upbringing and how lucky I'd been. Not that I ever forgot, but when you heard someone else's story, it really made you think about your own life.

"The only way out was school, so I did the best I could so I could find a way out. I remember seeing a man in a suit, and he drove a beautiful car and looked like he had the world at his feet, so I made the goal to be a man in a suit. And here I am."

He smiled and his mood did seem a bit lighter.

"I dressed as my dad for Halloween when I was three. I insisted on using his briefcase, even though it was almost as big as I was and I had to drag it on the ground behind me. It was a really expensive briefcase and when I came home with it full of candy, and all dirty, he just laughed and said it was mine now. I didn't really have any concept of what he did, but I knew that was what I wanted when I grew up." When other little girls had been obsessed with their astronaut and princess Barbies, Dad had gotten me one that was probably supposed to be a secretary. Instead, he told me she was CEO Barbie and he somehow found a doll-sized desk for her, and I made her hold meetings with all my other dolls and stuffed animals.

Yes, I was an only child and didn't have a lot of friends.

We talked more about our childhoods, and even though they'd been so different, there were so many things we had in common. Childhood was pretty similar no matter how you grew up, I guessed.

I was hungry and ready to order food, and Lucah seemed better.

"Thank you, Sunshine. I don't know what I'd do without you."

"Same here." We smiled like idiots at each other and I realized something else. Yes, I loved him, but not just in a romantic way. He'd become one of my best friends. Even if we never had sex again, I would miss his presence in my life if he were gone. I couldn't get rid of him now, even if I wanted to.

"You're my favorite," I said as he pulled me to my feet and then into his arms.

"You're my favoritest of favorite things," he said.

We didn't talk any more about his brother that night, but I wanted to make it a regular thing for us to talk more about growing up and our pasts. I still felt like there was so much I didn't know.

"I'm not good at opening up," he admitted, at last, the next morning as we showered together. If we didn't hurry, we were both going to be late.

"Why Lucah, whatever do you mean?" I said, rinsing the shampoo from his hair so it didn't get in his eyes. My shower was enormous, which was one of the reasons I'd fallen in love with this apartment. There was nothing worse than trying to be sexy with a guy in a shower that was too small.

"Yes, I deserve that." I squirted some conditioner and ran it through the ends of his hair and he did the same with mine. I'd taught him well by now.

"It's self preservation, most of the time. And fear. Fear that if I open up to people they won't like what they see."

"You're silly," I said, making his hair into a mohawk. "Why wouldn't someone like you?" I was sure there were people, but they weren't anybody I would want to be friends with anyway.

"There are a lot of people that are not fond of me, Sunshine. It's a longer list than you could imagine."

"Okay, now I'm intrigued," I said as he tipped his head back to rinse the conditioner out and then we switched places so I could do the same.

He laughed but didn't elaborate.

"Hey, don't leave me hanging like that," I said, but he just shook his head and started massaging my back as the hot water pounded down on me. That felt amazing, and even though I knew he was using it as a way not to continue our conversation, I was going to let him. I could ambush him later when he least expected it.

We ended up both getting to work on time, but as soon as Lucah sat down on his desk, he pulled his phone out and looked at it, frowning. He quickly typed something and then waited for a response. I figured it was something about his brother so I tried not to eavesdrop by staring at him and turned my computer on while I started to figure out what I had to get done immediately.

My phone rang and I answered it without looking to see who it was. Before I could say hello, I hear Lucah's voice.

"Listen, there are some things I need to take care of today, so I need to leave. I'm so, so sorry, but this has to get done." I looked across the room and he really did look sorry. It absolutely totally and completely sucked and I wasn't thrilled, but I also wasn't a total bitch.

"Are you sure you can't tell me what this is regarding?"

"I wish I could, but I can't." I was getting really tired of hearing him say that over and over, but it wasn't going to change anytime soon.

"Okay. Okay. Just . . . just be careful and I'll see you later. Bye." I didn't wait for him to say anything. I needed to get off the phone before I said something that I couldn't take back. I wrote a smiley face on a sticky note and put it on top of some files and went to drop them off on his desk without saying a word. I hoped he wasn't mad at me, but I could only take so much.

"I want to take you out somewhere," he said that night as we lay in bed. We'd pushed aside the unpleasantness of earlier. I'd spent the day completely stressed out that he wasn't there, and wondering where the hell he was and what he could possibly be doing and if maybe I should fire him, and then that would solve everything. But then I knew it wouldn't, so I resigned myself to doing nothing again.

"Where?" We'd never actually gone out just the two of us, other than the Museum day. I think both of us were worried about being seen together. I didn't seem to be the only paranoid one on that front.

"I don't know. Don't care, really. Just want to go somewhere with you on my arm so everyone will see my girl." Aw, well that was just adorable. I wanted people to see me with him, too.

"How about dinner? I know that sounds so typical, but it would be fun with you. And the movies? We could sit in the back and mock whatever it was." This was one of our favorite things to do together now when we found a crappy movie on television. Mock the crap out of it.

"Perfect. How did you know that was exactly what I would pick?"

"I'm psychotic," I said with a serious face.

"I think you mean psychic, Sunshine."

"Yeah, that too." He just shook his head at me. Hey, he was the one who wanted to be seen in public with me. You could dress me up but you couldn't take me out.

"So when is this going to occur?" I asked as he rested his head on my stomach. He didn't seem to mind that it wasn't exactly flat. Probably was more comfortable on his head that way.

"How about tomorrow night?"

"You're not going to be disappearing again, are you?" I didn't mean to say it, but it came out anyway.

"No," he said, kissing my belly button. "I think the disappearing is going to be slowing down. Hopefully. I have my fingers crossed."

This was news to me, but good news.

"Will you tell me what it was? Someday?" I asked.

He let out a breath.

"Maybe someday." That wasn't enough of an answer, but I'd have to take it.

Chapter Thirty

"How about here?" Lucah and I stopped outside of another restaurant. We'd decided that we wouldn't pick a place beforehand, because it was more fun to walk around and then decide together. More spontaneous, too. I had a few favorite places, but I wanted to try something new.

The restaurant was lit with a soft glow, and all the walls were brick. It looked semi-Italian and cozy.

"Perfect," I said as he opened the door and I walked through. We were seated in a corner booth, and it was kind of quiet, which was great. Soft music played through hidden speakers, and I was reminded of the spaghetti scene in *Lady and the Tramp*. I bet if I asked him, Lucah would reenact it with me, but I wasn't going to ask him to. That would be silly.

"I would pull your chair out for you, but seeing as how it's a booth, I can't really do that. But I would. If I could."

"You're forgiven," I said, reaching across the table and patting his arm.

The waiter came and we ordered garlic knots for an appetizer and a pizza with the works, and a bottle of cheap red wine.

"Shit," he said.

"What?" He looked like he was reaching for something under the table.

"You're too far away for me to grope. I was hoping to feel you up during dinner, but I can't reach." Something touched my knee, but couldn't go much further.

"Stop that. You don't have to grope me in public," I hissed at him.

"But I want to grope you in public," he said and he was almost pouting. Impossible. He was impossible. The waiter came back with the garlic knots and I tried to smack Lucah because he was groping my knee now and it tickled.

"Stop that," I hissed when the waiter left us again. He just smiled and grabbed one of the garlic knots and dipped it in sauce, but he did stop touching my knee. I took one of the garlic knots and dipped it in sauce as well.

"No double dipping," he said as I took a bite and went to put it back in the sauce.

"Are you serious? I have had your dick in my mouth. I don't think double dipping is that big a deal." He was opening his mouth to argue when a female voice invaded our little bubble.

"Tyler?" If she hadn't been standing right beside our table, I would have just ignored her, but she was and she was staring at Lucah like he was a ghost. She was tall and leggy and dressed like she was going clubbing in a silver skintight dress. A definite glamazon.

I gave her a WTF face, but the color drained from Lucah's face and his expression froze.

"Oh my God, Tyler!" The woman's face broke out into a smile and she leaned down to try to give him a hug. He just sat there as she kissed him on the cheek.

What. The. FUCK.

"Stef, wow. Long time no see," he finally said and it was like he had to choke out the words. He stood up and let her really hug him. Okay, so clearly he knew this girl, but she had called him Tyler. I knew that wasn't his middle name, or a nickname, or any other name that I'd ever heard him ever use. So now I had to wonder why this woman knew him as Tyler and what that meant.

"Oh my God, what are you doing here?" The glamazon named "Stef" hadn't even looked at me. I knew I was short, but I wasn't fucking invisible. I wanted to say something, but I had no idea what that should be until I could figure out what the story was.

"Oh, I'm just traveling." He sat back down and he didn't look at me either. HAD I TURNED FUCKING INVISIBLE AND I WASN'T AWARE?

"I can't believe this!" Stef was gushing and I wanted to punch her in the face, even though I didn't know her. "What has it been? Almost a year? Where are you working now?" Lucah cleared his throat and she FINALLY looked away from him and saw me. Her smile dropped for a second as she glanced down at me, but it was back on a second later, although it was tight and not as friendly. Fake.

"Oh, I'm such an idiot," she said with a fake laugh that made my ears burn. "I'm Stefanie. I used to work with Tyler out in LA." Okay, first of all, his name isn't Tyler. Second, nothing in his résumé had mentioned LA. NOTHING.

The three of us were suspended in the moment, none of us knowing what to say. I was waiting for someone to explain what the FUCK was going on, Stefanie seemed to be waiting for me to leave so she could have a joyous reunion with "Tyler" and Lucah (or Tyler) seemed to be waiting for the world to end.

"Okay, since I'm clearly in the dark, I'm going to go ahead and say it. What the fuck, Lucah?" I turned my anger and confusion on him and his face turned red.

"Tyler? I can come back. Or you could call me." *Shut up, bitch. I don't care about you.*

"I think that would be best, Stefanie." She smiled and waited for him to give her his number, but he was staring at me.

"Okay, well. Here's my number." She fiddled in her purse and pulled out a card and set it on the table, then waited for him to say something else, but he didn't so she slinked away.

Thank God and good riddance.

"Explain," I said, crossing my hands on the table.

He put his head in his hands.

"I don't even know where to start. Fuck, I knew this was going to happen." The waiter came back with our pizza, but I ignored him as he set it in front of us and then, sensing the tension, hurried away.

"Let's start with why the hell she called you Tyler? How about that?" The pizza smelled good, but there was no way I could eat now. A sinking feeling had entered my heart and a little voice said, *I told you so.* The secrets that he'd hidden from me? They were starting to come out.

"Because that was my name when she met me."

"Why?" He took the world's biggest deep breath. "Are you sure you want to do this here?" He looked around as if someone was going to jump out and come and bail him out, but he was shit out of luck.

"Oh no, we are doing this here, Mr. Blaine. Why does she know you as Tyler?" Maybe I was overreacting about the name, but I knew it was all part of what he was hiding from me and I wanted to know the truth.

"Stefanie knew me as Tyler because that was the alias I was using in LA."

AHA!

"So you are in the CIA!" I said it so loud that half the restaurant turned and stared at us. Oops.

"I am not in the CIA," Lucah (or whatever his name was) hissed in a whisper as his face turned red again.

"Then why did you have an alias? Is Lucah an alias? What other reason would you need an alias for than being in the CIA? And why the hell did that girl act like you knew each other REALLY well?" I knew how a woman looked at a man she'd slept with and that was the look on her face. We'd get to that later.

"One question at a time, Sunshine."

"Don't you dare call me that until after you've explained." I crossed my arms and leaned back against the booth.

He looked up at the ceiling and then at me.

"I need an alias because I am, for lack of a better term, a corporate mole. I'm a freelancer and companies hire me to infiltrate and do undercover investigations, anything from embezzlement to fraud to sexual misconduct. I've gone undercover in companies all over the United States and whenever I go to a new one, I get a new identity. New name, new résumé, new life. So Stefanie met me when I was Tyler Keller. That time it was a Public Relations firm that had a problem with missing money, and several of the executives were funneling drugs and using the company events to do it. Stefanie and I . . . had a relationship for a few months. It was nearly a year ago and it ended the second my job was over. I never thought I would see her again. I had no intention of ever seeing her again." He took the card and ripped it up in front of me.

"I wish I had your shredder right now," he said with a tiny smile. Oh no, he could not dump all that info on me and then make a joke. No fucking way.

"That is a lot of information, Lucah."

"I know."

"What is your real name? Am I allowed to know it?" This wasn't the most important thing he'd lied to me about, but a name was an important thing.

"My real first name is Lucah. I went with Lucas because it was close to my real name and I was tired of trying to be someone else. My real full name is Lucah Jacob Blythe. I'm from New Hampshire. I went to Dartmouth. I'm twenty-five and I'm in love with a girl named Aurora Abigail Clarke. Those are the only things you need to know."

No, that sure as hell wasn't all I needed to know.

"You lied to me," I said as an enormous silence stretched between us like it was pulling us apart.

"I had to," he said. "I am so sorry."

"So those locked rooms in your apartment?"

"All of the things from my real life. In boxes. I ship them with me wherever I go so I can remind myself who I am once in a while. I couldn't let you see them because I couldn't jeopardize my job." That led me to another question.

"Why are you at Clarke Enterprises?" Jesus, what was he investigating? Who had hired him? My brain was about ready to blow up.

"I can't tell you that. Like I said, there are a lot of things at stake, and it's not just about you and me. I've just broken every single rule by telling you anything at all. It puts the entire investigation in jeopardy." Investigation . . . That made something click. The Board of Directors. Dad. They'd be SO ENTHUSIASTIC about him and had basically told me to hire him. Had Dad known about him? No, that was impossible. He wouldn't have lied to me.

"Are you investigating ME?" There was no way.

"No! No, of course not." He was definitely telling the truth about that. Well, that was a little bit of a relief. Not that there was much relief happening for me in that moment. Knowing the truth was almost worse.

"You lied to me." He might not be the only one.

"I know." He didn't make an excuse this time. Yes, I knew that it wasn't his choice, and that it was his job, but that didn't make it hurt any less.

"You *lied* to me."

He didn't answer, just reached across the table for me, but I pulled back even more. I didn't want him to touch me right now.

"I think I need to go home. Alone. I need some time to think." And I got up and left, grabbing a cab and going back to my apartment.

"What are you doing here?" Sloane said when I opened the door. Then she saw my face.

"What happened?"

I'd been holding myself together in the restaurant and in the cab, but here, in my apartment, I finally let myself fall apart.

Chapter Thirty-One

I told her everything. I knew I probably wasn't supposed to, but I didn't give a shit. My boyfriend had lied to me and I needed to talk to my best friend about it.

She sat on the couch and stroked my hair and listened as I cried and poured my heart out.

"Wow. That's unbelievable," she said when I was finally done.

"I know. I wouldn't believe it unless he'd sat there in front of me and told me the whole thing."

"So he's investigating the company? How do you feel about that?"

"It's fucking crazy. I'm actually pissed off about it, because I know the Board went behind my back, and maybe behind Dad's. I have no idea why they thought they could do this without telling us this."

Sloane's hand paused for a second as she played with my hair. "Are you *sure* your dad doesn't know?"

"No, no. If he knew he'd tell me. Dad isn't that good of a liar." But honestly, I wasn't sure about anything right now. My world had flipped upside down. If the sky was green tomorrow, I wouldn't be surprised.

"But he told you his real name."

"But he lied to me about everything else. And that girl, my God, you should have seen her."

"But it's not like he cheated on you like Royce. He was just doing his job. It's not like he meant to fall in love with you. It's actually kind of ironic, if you think about it." It wasn't ironic, not really. I didn't know what it was, but ironic wasn't the word that I would use.

"Or maybe it's more tragic than ironic," Sloane said.

"Sloane?"

"Yeah?"

"Stop talking, please." She did and started humming. That didn't help because it just reminded me of Lucah, so I asked her to stop doing that too. I knew I was being a pain in the ass, but I didn't care. Then she turned on the television and *Mystic Pizza* was playing.

"Julia Roberts' hair is ridic in this movie," Sloane said.

"Yeah, it is," I said in agreement.

I had literally no idea what was going to happen when I went into work the next morning. I considered calling in sick, but there was no way I was going to do that. If I stayed home, then I would just mope. I wanted to be out and have something else occupy my mind other than Lucah. Only problem was that I didn't know if I would see Lucah at work. He'd tried to call me last night, but I'd ignored him.

To tell the absolute truth, I had no idea how I felt. It was like I had too many emotions and my body had gone into some sort of shock because it was overwhelmed. I hoped it was on vacation somewhere nice. A tropical island would be great.

I pulled myself together on the T and tried to act as normal as I could when I exited the elevator and walked toward my desk.

There he was, pastry bag and cup of coffee waiting for me. I walked right past it, into my office and shut the door. I hadn't eaten this morning, but I didn't feel like it. I hadn't eaten last night either. This was one of those times when eating your feelings wasn't going to work.

My phone rang and I checked the caller ID before I picked up. It was Lucah and I didn't answer. Instead, I turned my computer on and started answering emails.

My phone rang again. Nope. Wasn't answering him. He couldn't harass me in the office, not without blowing his cover, so that was another good reason to be in the office.

Then he started blowing up my cell phone, so I put it on silent and kept working.

Ten minutes later, there was a knock on my door.

"Who is it?" I said. I didn't want to ignore it if it was someone important.

"It's me," Lucah said. He couldn't really beg me to open the door without arousing suspicion as to why he would be begging me to open my door.

"I'm busy," I said and waited to hear him move away from the door. Then something slid under the door. I waited until I was sure he was back at his desk before I got up to retrieve the note. I couldn't read it right now, so I shoved it in my purse. I'd read it on my lunch break. If I could handle it.

I hunkered down in my office the entire day, leaving only to retrieve coffee and pee. I avoided eye contact and small talk with everyone. No one really seemed to notice, except Mrs. Andrews.

"How are you, dear?" She ambushed me in the break room, so I had no escape. There was only one way out and she was blocking it. Once again, I wished for a sinkhole, or maybe a secret portal to open up and suck me into another dimension. A dimension where the man I loved hadn't done what he did.

The absolutely insane thing was that I knew I was being horrible to him about it. I knew he had secrets. He'd told me. I'd said I accepted it. And then, when he'd been forced to tell me about it, I'd gotten mad at him. I was mad at the situation and I was taking it out on him. Besides, if Dad knew, then Mrs. Andrews had to know. So she might have been lying to me as well. Something I couldn't comprehend.

"I'm fine. Just busy." She patted my shoulder, then glanced to make sure we were alone and closed the door.

"Did you and Mr. Blaine have a falling out? I sensed some tension between you two." Yeah, I bet. I was surprised more people hadn't felt it.

"It's nothing," I said. I'd gone into it with Sloane, but I couldn't break Lucah's confidence further.

"Oh, Rory. Work it out. Don't let that boy get away from you. He's one of the good ones and they don't come around very often. You've got to grab onto them when they do and make sure you keep 'em. My husband was one of the good ones and once I knew that, I wasn't letting him go and I never did." Her husband had died a few years ago from a heart attack, and she hadn't remarried. I'd never asked her, but I figured it was because he was "it" for her.

She patted my face and gave me a sympathetic look.

"Ah, sometimes youth is wasted on the young." She laughed and then opened the door and went back to her desk. I grabbed my coffee and went back to mine, avoiding looking at Lucah, even though I could feel his gaze burning my skin. It was different than when he looked at me when we were naked. That made me feel beautiful. Now it just made me . . .

Sad? Angry? Frustrated? Negative. It was all negative.

But yet . . . I was still head over fucking heels in love with him. He might be a liar, but he was my liar. He was my Lucah. Despite not knowing his real name, I knew other things.

I knew what he looked like when he woke up first thing in the morning. I knew what he wanted to hear when we were having sex. I knew where all his freckles were. I knew the curve of his shoulder and that he liked Bugs Bunny cartoons and truffle pizza and s'mores. Were those more important than what I didn't know?

I left the office at lunch and took the letter with me as I sat outside at a café with an iced tea and a ham and cheese croissant. I was finally hungry again.

I opened the letter and saw Lucah's neat handwriting had covered pages, front and back. I started to read and I realized it was more of a list than a letter. A list of all the things I didn't know about him.

When I was twelve, I had my first kiss with a girl named Cassidy. It was during Spin the Bottle at my first boy-girl party. She tasted like bubble gum and our noses bumped.

My first girlfriend was Annie. We started dating when I was fifteen and we stayed together for six months. She started dating my best friend a week after breaking up with me, and they dated all through high school and then got married. They have three children and still live in my hometown.

I lost my virginity to a girl at my first party. I was sixteen and I have tried to remember her name, but I can't. She was from another school and we were both drunk and I don't actually remember much except that we definitely had sex and it definitely lasted about thirty seconds.

I've never really loved a girl the way I love you. I thought I had, but I had no idea what it was before you. I've told exactly five women in my life that I loved them. You, my mother, my nieces and Annie.

I can't stop thinking about you, even if I wanted to. I never believed in fate, and I didn't believe in love at first sight either, but I have no other way to describe the feeling that went through me when you walked down that hallway and I saw you for the first time. Oh, yes, there was lust. I knew I wanted you, and I wanted to be inside you. I also knew that I shouldn't pursue you. It is very, very against the rules. I'd been with other women when I went undercover before, but that was different. Those were strictly physical no-strings.

He went on to tell me so many other things, some I wanted to know and some that were hard to read. Like his parents, and how it felt to lose them. I couldn't even begin to imagine what that had been like for him, but I kept reading, even as tears started to fall down my face and the page became blurry.

Lucah had poured his pain and his past into this letter, and the only way it wouldn't have affected me was if I didn't have a heart. Well. I'd had a heart but I'd given most of it to him. That was what love did to you. Made you give parts of yourself to someone and they could do whatever they wanted with them and there was nothing you could do about it.

I finished the letter and went back and read it again. And then a third time. And then I put it down and went to a secluded corner outside the café and cried. It would be much better if I could go home and cry, but I had to actually go to work. Dad was out of town for a few days, so the company was kind of in my hands. Yes, there were other people that shared the burden, but he was my father and I had more of a burden of responsibility. It also meant that I couldn't confront him about Lucah until he got back. That wasn't something you did over the phone. I was going to put that off as long as possible.

I got myself together and popped back into the café to fix my face. My eyes were puffy, but my crazy expensive mascara and eye makeup were still in place. They should put that in the advertisement; will withstand heartbreak and ugly crying.

There was nothing I could do about my puffy eyes, so I wet a paper towel with cold water and put it under my eyes for a few minutes. A few other women came and went, and some stared at me and some made sympathetic faces and others just glared at me for taking up space in front of the mirror.

Why couldn't I cry like girls in the movies? Even if those bitches were sobbing, they always looked cute doing it and their eyes were never red afterwards. So many people said they wanted a man from a movie, or a house, but I wanted to cry like girls in the movies. That would be great.

The cab ride back to the office didn't feel long enough and when I walked into the office, I wanted to turn right back around and go home.

My head hurt from the crying and my heart was torn to shreds and I just didn't give a fuck about work right now. But I straightened my jacket and walked to the elevator.

Chapter Thirty-Two

Lucah wasn't at his desk when I walked by it. There was a note on the edge of it.

Had a meeting. Be back later.

-Lucas Blaine

He couldn't put more detail in it in case someone walked by the desk and saw it, and he signed it with his alias.

His alias. I really hadn't sat down and thought about that. How many times had he done that? How many names had he had? How long had he been doing this corporate investigator gig? How did he get into it?

Even after that massive letter, there were still questions, but I couldn't talk to him. I was actually relieved he wasn't here, because then I didn't have to shut my office door.

I checked my phone and saw all the missed calls and texts. The last one was explaining that he had to meet with the Board of

Directors and give them his evidence and what he'd found. I stared at the message for so long I didn't hear someone calling my name.

"Rory?" It was Mr. Craig. Ugh, not now. I did not want to hear about his stupid car, or his stupid golf course or his stupid summer home in Bora Bora.

"Oh, yes? Sorry, I guess I'm busted." Cell phones other than for work purposes were prohibited. I tried to laugh casually, but it sounded deranged, but he didn't seem to notice.

"I just wanted to know if you father had left any files with you? I needed something in one of them." I stared at him blankly for a second and then remembered that Dad had left me some files. I really needed to get my shit together if I was going to get through the rest of this day.

"Oh, yes, sure. They're right here." I handed him the stack of files and he thumbed through them.

"Thank you very much, this is just what I needed." He was absorbed in the files and kept staring at them as he left my office. Guess I wasn't the only distracted one.

When I finally got home after the longest day in the history of long days, Sloane was waiting right by the door with a glass in her hand.

"Don't say anything, just drink." Usually we had wine, but this was hard liquor. And I tipped the glass back and swallowed as it burned down my throat. I wasn't going to ask what was in it.

"I needed that. Thank you." I took my drink and walked to the couch as I shucked off my heels. Sloane grabbed a glass, joined me and waited for me to speak.

"He wrote me a letter. This big long letter telling me all these things about his life and his past and things I didn't know and he talked about losing his parents and Sloane . . . I . . ." I had to set the drink down because I was going to lose it again and I didn't want to spill all over the floor.

"Oh, honey." She pulled me into a fierce hug and let me cry some more. Couldn't I be done with the crying? At this point, I had no idea where the tears were coming from, or what they were for. My emotions were on overload and something had to give.

"And even though he lied and he wasn't who I thought he was, I still fucking love him. I love that son of a bitch," I said through my tears.

"Of course you do, Rory. That's what unconditional love is."

"But I don't want to love him," I said as she handed me a tissue so I could blot my running nose. "I want to hate him. I do, a little, but not enough to stop loving him. I mean, he didn't cheat on me, he didn't do anything technically wrong. He was just doing his job and he didn't choose to fall in love with me. Asshole."

Sloane laughed and I glared at her. This wasn't funny.

"I'm sorry! I can't help it." I smacked her in the arm, but I could feel a smile starting on my face.

"Are you done being dramatic now? Ready to build a bridge and get over it and have fantastic makeup sex which may or may not cause you to get knocked up with a ginger baby?" Well, when she put it that way . . .

"No. I still need some time to think and process. I have no idea how this is going to work. I mean, he's not in the CIA, but his job would make things kind of hard. What about the next time he goes somewhere? I can't follow him. My life is here. He's a gypsy and I'm not. This is home to me. I can't imagine living anywhere else but Boston."

"Oh, I wouldn't worry about that," Sloane said as if she knew a secret that I didn't.

"What are you talking about?"

"Honey, that boy is never going to leave your side. Where you go, he will follow. Like a puppy." I gave her a look.

"What? It's true. Wherever you go, he'll find you."

"Now you're making him sound like a stalker." She shrugged.

"Stalker, boyfriend. Kind of the same thing." Uh, no. Not really.

I got up and threw away my disgusting tissues and tossed back the rest of my drink while Sloane made me another. I kept staring at my phone, waiting for him to call, or text, or anything, but it was silent.

When I finally went to bed, I was still staring at my phone. I couldn't sleep, so I just scrolled through Lucah's texts. I could almost feel the desperation in them, and I finally decided to call him.

He picked up right away.

"Hello? Rory?" Oh my GOD, I'd missed his voice and it had only been a few hours since I'd heard it.

"Yeah, it's me." He let out a breath and I did the same. It was such a relief to finally be with him, even if it was just on the phone.

"Did you read my letter?" he asked.

"I did. Three times."

"And?"

"And it made me cry and fall in love with you and hate you and wish I'd never met you and then thank God that I did and want to call you and punch you and kiss you and fuck you."

He didn't say anything right away.

"Can you come downstairs?"

I sat up.

"What do you mean?"

"I've been outside your building trying to talk myself into going up for about two hours, and if I'm not careful, I'm going to get arrested for acting like a creeper." I vaulted out of bed and ran from my room to the elevator. It didn't matter that I was wearing a pair of shorts and a tank top and no bra or shoes. It didn't matter that I didn't have my key to get back into my apartment. I ran through the lobby, out the front doors and right for him, diving into his arms. Luckily, he was ready and he caught me. I wasn't the only one wearing their pajamas. We were a matched pair.

"Oh, Sunshine," he said before our lips locked and I never wanted to let him go.

Chapter Thirty-Three

Now, having sex on the sidewalks of Boston was generally frowned upon, but Lucah and I were pretty close to going ahead with it anyway.

"Come home with me," he said into my mouth.

"Okay," I said and he waved his arm for a cab before he picked me up in his arms. "I don't want you to hurt your bare feet," he said as he put me inside. The cabbie had probably seen a whole lot weirder things than a girl wearing her pajamas and no shoes. Lucah gave him the address and then pulled me onto his lap and held me close while he kissed me. His hands started moving under my clothes and I didn't care there was a cabbie just a few feet away.

I let him touch me and it was the best cab ride ever; even better than the first one, when I'd "kissed" him.

He carried me out of the cab and through the empty lobby of his apartment. He didn't even set me down when we were in the elevator. I was worried about him getting tired of holding me, but he didn't seem to mind. I didn't know if this was because I wasn't as heavy as I thought I was, or maybe he was just really strong.

My feet didn't touch the ground at all, even when he unlocked his door. He'd mastered the art of holding me and using his key at the same time. This was a valuable skill to have.

Instead of throwing me on the bed, he set me down slowly, as if he was afraid I was going to break. He was rarely this gentle with me, and it was almost like he was hesitant. Like I was going to run away if he pushed too hard.

"I'm not going anywhere," I said as he lay down over me, careful to hold the majority of his weight with his arms.

"You'd better not, Sunshine," he said, giving me another light kiss. What the crap was up with that? "Remember that first night when I said we would take it slow? Well, we never did, so I think tonight is going to be a slow night. We are going to make this last." I had a feeling he was talking about more than just the sex, although I was fine with making that last too.

"Make it last. I like that," I said as he started kissing from my lips to my cheeks and then down the side of my neck. Soft kisses, barely there kisses that were somehow just as thrilling.

Inch by baby inch he kissed his way down my body, all the way to my feet before he lifted my shirt an inch and kissed my stomach. Then another inch. By the time the damn shirt was close to my breasts, I was wound so tight that I was ready to lose it.

I got frustrated when I tried to touch him and he wouldn't let me. I pouted and he just laughed.

"Slow. We'll take care of you first, Miss Clarke." I guess I couldn't argue with that, really.

Once I was completely undressed, he sat back on his heels and stared at me, shaking his head. The suspense was killing me.

"What's the face for?" I fought the urge to cover myself with my hands, or at least move a little. It wasn't like he hadn't seen all of it before, but when someone looks at you like that and you are naked at the same time, you FEEL naked.

"I'm just trying to freeze this moment in my mind so I never forget it. I never want to forget how I feel, and how you look, right here, right now. Naked in my bed and ready for me."

"I am ready for you. I've been ready for a while. Not that I don't love slow, but can you go slow while you're inside me?" I reached for his boxers, and he was about ready to bust right out of them.

A slow smile spread on his face and I swore that his eyes darkened.

"You're the boss." He pulled a condom from the band of his boxers and I couldn't help but laugh.

"You are always prepared, Mr. Blaine." Then I realized that wasn't his name, and then I realized it didn't matter as he slid inside me and I put my legs around him and we joined together.

His name didn't matter. His past didn't matter. Nothing mattered except that we were perfect together.

We were anything but slow and we both finished quickly as we threw everything into each other, into this moment.

"I missed you, Lucah Blythe," I said as my back arched and I came.

"I missed you, Aurora Clarke," he said moments later.

We both rolled onto our sides and I kept him inside me.

"We suck at slow," he said, stroking my back.

"That probably means we should try again."

He grinned and shifted his hips and I knew it would only be a few minutes/short time before he could go again.

"You called me Lucah Blythe."

"It's your name, silly."

"Yes, it is."

"To mangle Shakespeare, a Lucah by any other name would be as sexy," I said and he rolled his eyes at me.

"That poor man is rolling over in his grave right now." I shrugged one shoulder. Right now I didn't give a fuck about Shakespeare.

"Oh, shit I hope Sloane isn't wondering where I am," I said when the sun came up the next morning. We'd stayed up all night talking, laughing and fucking. I called him by his real name over and over and he beamed every single time.

"You might want to text her," he said, but I realized I didn't have my phone. I'd tossed it on my bedroom floor in my hurry to see Lucah.

"Use mine," he said when he realized I didn't have mine. I texted Sloane that it was me using Lucah's phone and that we were busy making up. She just texted back a bunch of really suggestive emoticons. I deleted the text before giving the phone back to Lucah.

We'd made up, we were on the same page about wanting to be together, but now the question was how the hell that was going to work.

"So are you done with what you needed to do now?" We'd avoided this topic for the most part. I also hadn't asked him if my Dad knew. I just couldn't go there yet.

"Yes, I am. So that means I'm supposed to sever all ties, get rid of my cell phone and disappear without a trace." My heart jumped into my throat for a second.

"But that's not what you're going to do. Is it?"

He looked at me as if I had lost my mind.

"Did I not just spend the entire night telling you that I was never leaving you again? You couldn't get rid of me if you tried. You're stuck with me." He was still inside me, so technically this was true at the moment.

"But what about your job? Your corporate spy job?" I liked thinking of it that way.

"I'm not a corporate spy. I'm a freelance corporate investigator," he said and finally pulled out.

"But what about it? How . . . how is that going to work?"

"Well, it'll work because I'm going to quit. I've been tired of doing it for a while, but the money was too good and I didn't have a reason to stop. Now I do. You." He tweaked my nose and I willed myself to believe it was true.

"Really?"

"Really with extra really on top." It couldn't be that easy. He'd done so much to hide this from me and it was all working out too easily.

"You're just going to give up your job? Just like that?"

He nodded and snapped his fingers.

"Just like that."

"So you're going to give up your job and stay here in Boston with me."

"If you want me to."

Well of course I wanted him to. I wanted to move in with him and then someday get married and make ginger babies. I saw it flash in my mind and I could picture it for the first time in my entire life. When I'd thought about my future when I was younger, I'd always pictured myself in an office with a beautiful desk. I'd never dreamed of wearing a wedding dress. Not that I didn't imagine getting married, but the pictures were always blurry and hazy, and there was never a guy.

Love made you picture your wedding with the man you were lying in bed with, and it felt right.

"So it sounds like you need a job, Mr. Blythe," I said, moving some of his hair out of his face. It was all over the place and fucked to perfection. Mine was probably pretty spectacular as well, but it didn't matter in the slightest.

"I do need a job, Miss Clarke."

"Well, I don't know of any place where there are any available jobs, so I can't help you out with that," I said with a completely serious face. "So I guess you're shit out of luck, Lucah Blythe."

"I guess I am. Maybe I'll become a gentleman of leisure. That would be quite pleasant." That brought up another question.

"Do you have a lot of money?"

"Sunshine, don't you know you're not supposed to ask people that?"

I didn't answer and just waited for him to confirm or deny. His apartment was better than mine, and he had the very best tailored suits and his watch was definitely not cheap. Nothing about Lucah was cheap.

"Yes. I have a lot of money. Probably not as much as you do, but yes. I have a lot for someone my age. I could do without a job for a while and still maintain my lifestyle. But I'd rather work for my money. I was born with nothing, so everything I have, I worked for."

I suddenly felt cold. I didn't think he meant to imply that I'd had everything handed to me, but in the back of my mind, a little voice told me he did.

My face must have fallen.

"Oh, Sunshine, I didn't mean you. You've worked hard to get where you are. Yes, you have had advantages other people haven't, but it would have been so easy to just rest on your laurels and coast. You didn't."

"What does that mean? Is a laurel a plant? Why would that be a good place to rest?" I said, completely derailing what he was trying to say.

"I have no idea, but did you hear the rest of what I said?"

"Yes, I did. Thank you. I appreciate that."

"You're welcome."

It was officially morning and it was officially time for me to get my butt to work.

"I have to go to work. So I'm guessing you're not going to be there with me?"

"I can't. It would raise too many questions. Until arrests have been made, which should happen in a week or so, I have to vanish. My desk will be cleared out and there will be no trace of me. So. I will be here waiting for you when you get back."

I started to pull away from him, but he wouldn't let me go.

"Um, I need to go to work. You have to let me go." His arms didn't budge.

"One last kiss." I let him kiss me, but then his hands were going in places that weren't going to allow me to leave the bed, so I pinched his nipple and twisted and he yelped while I made my escape, diving for the shower before he could catch me.

I jumped in and a second later he joined me.

"You're not going to let me go to work, are you?"

"No, I will. I just want to savor my last few minutes with you, and I'd like to savor your body and those sounds that you make when I touch you," he said, using his hands to follow his words.

"I'm terrible at saying no to you," I said, bracing myself on him as he pushed a finger and then another inside me, and used his thumb against my piercing. The water wasn't the right temperature, but I couldn't adjust it. I also needed to wash my hair, but, whatever. My brain shut down and I just thought with my body.

"Come for me, Sunshine." Oh, well, if you insist.

I came apart around his hand and he laughed.

"You're not letting me go, are you?"

"Never."

Chapter Thirty-Four

I was late, but I did make it to work. Before I'd left, Lucah had coached me on what to tell people when they asked why he wasn't there. The story was that he had called me and quit. No reason, no notice. I was to tell everyone that he was gone and not coming back and I didn't have any other details than that. It seemed simple enough, but lying almost never was. I was also going to have to see Dad and figure out if he knew, and if he didn't, how I was going to lie to him about it.

I spent most of the morning repeating the story so many times I wanted to write it down, make copies and then just hand them out. I decided to send a mass email instead, because now that I was an assistant short, I had a shit ton of work to do.

I got a few responses and a few questions, but for the most part people didn't say much.

Staring at Lucah's empty desk all day was more depressing than I thought it would be. I'd gotten so used to looking across the room and seeing that face with the freckles and the chin dimple smiling back at me.

Mrs. Andrews came into my office unannounced and closed the door before coming to sit in the chair on the other side of my desk.

"So I hear Mr. Blaine has flown the coop."

"Yes, he called me last night and handed in his resignation. I have no idea why, but I'm not very happy. Now I have to hire yet another assistant." I sighed and rolled my eyes.

"Rory," she said, giving me a look that told me she could see right through my bullshit.

"Okay, okay. It's a long story and I'm not supposed to go into it," I said and she raised one eyebrow.

"I see," she said in a cryptic way. "Well, it's a shame and I think we're going to miss him. But if you want to talk about it, I'm here." She stared at me as if she was trying to convey something else as well. I didn't know if it was because of my relationship with Lucah, or if she knew about what he was really doing here.

Je-sus Christ. I couldn't deal with these people.

Dad came right to my office when he got back and gave me a big hug, even though the door was open.

"Oh, I missed you. I also heard you are one assistant short. You want to tell me about that?" He pulled back and studied my face. I looked into his eyes, which were just like mine and . . .

I told him everything.

Not all the sexual details (oh hell no) but that Lucah and I had a relationship behind his back and that we'd been seeing each other. I waited for his reaction, and for him to tell me that he'd known all along about why Lucah was here.

Dad watched me and listened with a completely emotionless face. I knew I was blushing for some of the story, but once I finished, I was freaking out to know what was going on in his head.

"Are you completely ashamed of me?" I said in a voice that made me feel like I was a kid again and I had broken something important to him and had to 'fess up.

"Rory Abigail. Do you think that I didn't know that you were having a relationship with him? I think I knew what was happening before you knew. I saw how you looked at him and I saw how he looked at you. And I also caught him passing you notes in a meeting. I know you were trying to be discreet, but you didn't do a very good job."

Oh, I needed to sit down. I sunk into my chair.

"Does everyone know?" I said as he pulled my other chair around so he could sit across from me. I was having trouble breathing. I needed to open a window, but I couldn't move.

"Oh, I think everyone else was too wrapped up in their own little lives to worry about you. I also deflected a few times for you. I'm not ashamed of you, Rory. You're my daughter and you met a nice boy and he just happened to work with you. Yes, it is against the rules, but some rules are meant to be broken. What does your gut tell you about him?"

"That I love him." There was no point in lying about that, even if I could get away with it.

"Then that's all that matters." He shrugged and acted like it was nothing. Who was this man? I had memories of him taking people's asses and handing them back with a smile for much, much less. He'd been harder on his employees when he was younger, but still. My

Dad made sure that everything was up to par and he didn't accept anything less than perfection from his employees.

"Did you know about him?" I ask in a small voice.

"Yes. I did. I was the one who found him and hired him."

"Who else knew?"

"Mrs. Andrews, Hal. A few more on the board. I'm not surprised he told you." He shook his head back and forth and smiled at me.

"Well, I kind of forced it out of him." He hadn't really had a choice when I confronted him at the restaurant.

"That's my girl."

"Are you going to fire me?" I didn't know if he could even do this, since we were family.

"Would you like me to fire you?" Okay, remember what I said about special treatment? Forget that.

"No!"

"Well, you did break the rules and you signed a Code of Conduct that stated you would be terminated if you violated it. So, what would you like me to do?" Have amnesia? Pretend he hadn't seen anything? Set the building on fire? Build a time machine?

"I can see that mind of yours working. So, what's the verdict, Rory girl?"

"I don't want to leave. I don't want to lose my job and I don't want to lose him. I want to have it all. I want my flipping cake and I want to eat it." Or have sex with it. Did that make Lucah the cake?

I wasn't thinking about the important things at the moment.

"Then I guess that means that I have never seen any misconduct on your side or on his. Neither has Mrs. Andrews. And this is the last time we'll talk about this particular issue, seeing as how he is no longer employed by this company, and technically wasn't in the first place, since he was using an alias. If you were to start seeing him after his termination, then that wouldn't violate any rules. So."

"So," I said, letting out a breath. "That's it?"

He put his hands out.

"That's it."

That couldn't be it. All that and no big deal? All the worrying and freaking out and all of it for nothing?

"I need to sit down," I said, forgetting that I was, in fact, already sitting. Dad just laughed.

"I just remember the trials and tribulations I had to go through to get your mother. The hardships that you have to go through to be together make it worth it in the end. I only hope he can prove that he deserves you, Aurora." He leaned forward and I hugged him again. There's nothing like a hug from your Dad. I don't care how old you are.

"Thanks, Dad."

"Anytime. You're my only girl and I'd move the earth for you. But if you date someone else in this office, I'll fire you. Got it?" I couldn't tell if he was joking until he winked and kissed my forehead before leaving me alone in my office with a hell of a lot of thoughts.

I was still swimming in those thoughts that afternoon as I looked over another presentation, when there was a commotion in the lobby that carried through the entire floor. I got out of my desk and went to my door to peek out.

And then I saw the cops strolling past my office and a flustered Mrs. Andrews following after. She gave me a look when she went by my door and I got up from my desk. Damn, they'd called in the big guns. The cops looked like they spent half their time working out and the other half thinking about working out.

Everyone else was popping their heads out of their offices to see what was going on, but no one seemed to know. I shot a questioning look at Mr. Dunlap across the hall and he just made a shrugging motion.

This probably had something to do with Lucah's investigation. Well, I was curious to see what was going to go down, so I left my office and started walking down the hall as they stopped in front of Mr. Craig's door and knocked. His door was the only one that wasn't open.

The cops weren't messing around as they knocked again and then busted the door open. Dad was trying to take control of the situation, but the cops passed him a warrant, so his hands were tied, but he calmly sent Mrs. Andrews into his office to contact the company lawyers. People were starting to edge closer to get a better view as the cops smashed the door in and dragged Mr. Craig out.

He went quietly, not wanting to make a fuss and the drama was over as quick as it had begun.

Or that was how I thought it was going to go.

Mr. Craig did not go gently into that cop car. He went kicking and screaming and dragging his feet and begging for mercy and cursing and asking all of us to help him.

It was almost tragic, really. I'd never seen a grown man behave like that outside of a bar, or a sporting event. Dad came and found me and motioned for me to come into his office. I had a feeling I knew what he was going to say to me.

He closed the door behind me as Mrs. Andrews dashed past me to go back to her desk. Or maybe to do some damage control as everyone dropped whatever they were doing to gossip and chat about the insanity that had just gone down.

"That was ugly, but it had to be done. Mr. Craig and at least eight other people were using money from this company to funnel drugs over the border from Mexico," he said, rubbing his eyes as if he just wanted to go to bed. I didn't blame him.

Stealing money from the company AND drugs? How stupid could you be? I always wondered at criminals. They always seemed so stupid when they got caught.

"Do you want me to leave you alone?" I said after a few minutes. The voices chattering outside were distracting.

"No. Yes. I think I need to call a meeting." He hit a button on his phone and Mrs. Andrews' voice came through the speaker.

"Please let everyone know that we are having an emergency meeting right now. Mandatory for all Senior Management." She agreed and then Dad put his arms out and I gave him a big hug. He needed it.

Chapter Thirty-Five

The meeting was nuts, with everyone talking and asking questions at once. I stayed in the back and kept my mouth shut and my eyes on the floor. Dad didn't mention me, or Lucah or anything, just that there had been an internal investigation and if anyone had any questions they could ask him and that there would be no talking of the issue outside of the office, or else there would be severe consequences.

We'd never had a scandal like this before, so keeping the lid on it was going to be quite a job. We had a PR team, and they stood up with Dad and talked about how there would be a statement they would email around to all of us about what we could and could not say to anyone outside the office, including the press.

God, I didn't even think about that. This was going to explode in the media. Lovely. That was going to be fun to deal with. Not to mention what would happen once this got out and our existing clients heard. Oh, fuck. Shit, fuck, crap, fuck.

I nearly passed out when I thought about that prospect. While we were still talking, I swore I could hear everyone's phones ringing off the hook. Everyone downstairs was probably also freaking out.

What a fucking mess.

Any work for the rest of the day was shot to hell. I didn't even leave my desk or put down the phone. I knew Lucah was waiting for me, but everyone was doing damage control, and that included me. I wasn't going to bail on everyone so I could go have sex with my boyfriend.

Boyfriend. I could finally call him that, think of him like that. In all the suckage, that was the one bright little spot. I had a boyfriend to go home to whenever I could get the hell out of the office. If that ever happened.

I texted Lucah that I was going to be super late and as the night got later and later and still, I didn't see an end.

At seven thirty, Dad came into my office and ordered me to go home. I tried to protest, but then he yelled at me and I got the hell out of there.

The cabbie couldn't drive fast enough to get my exhausted ass to Lucah's apartment.

This time when he opened the door, I was the one who pushed him up against the door and started ripping his clothes off. And by ripping, I wasn't exaggerating. Buttons went flying and I nearly tore the zipper out of his jeans. He didn't even have time to put a condom on as he lifted my hips up and I slid down on him.

"Fuck yes," I said.

"Hello to you too," he said as we started moving together, setting a pace that we both craved. It was quick and hard, and soon I was sliding off him and he was carrying me to the couch.

"Rough day?"

"Something like that. And it's all your fault. Nine arrests. Fuck you very much, Mr. Blythe." I smacked him in the chest and then went to the bathroom to clean myself up. I didn't have to worry about much since I was on the pill and we'd both been tested, but I was still paranoid about pregnancy, even with my precautions.

I was a paranoid person in general, apparently.

Figuring I was going to spend the rest of the night naked, I stripped down the rest of way and left my clothes in his bedroom. Then I walked out into the living room wearing just my heels. That led to him getting all the way naked and me working out more of my frustrations with the awful, terrible day.

The next day at work was even worse. There were actually people with cameras and microphones and so forth camped outside the building the next morning. I was grateful I was having a good hair day, because they definitely took pictures of me and asked me questions that I responded with, "No comment." I'd kind of always wanted to say that, but it turned out it wasn't all it was cracked up to be.

More phone calls. Word had gotten out to some of our clients and I basically got screamed at all day, and repeated the same thing over and over until I had to check my face to make sure it wasn't blue.

I didn't get a lunch because I didn't have an assistant to bring me one. Fortunately, Dad ordered out and had sandwiches delivered for everyone. I inhaled two of them and then went back to getting yelled at.

I missed Lucah. He was the only thing that could have made this not horrible. I could just picture him making faces at me, or throwing paper airplanes, or texting me dirty things. I looked at my shoe paperweight and my WORLD'S GREATEST BOSS mug and I texted him saying that I missed him. He refused to tell me what he'd done all day the day before, but I had so much else on my mind I didn't have enough energy to try to get it out of him.

Want me to come and make it better?

If only that were possible.

I wish. But you can't. I'll see you tonight.

He answered me back, but I had to answer the stupid phone, so I didn't see his response until a half hour later.

I'm naked and waiting . . .

And this was accompanied by a shirtless picture of him on the couch, making a kissy face.

I gigglesnorted and put my phone back in my desk. I'd be getting a penis shot next if I wasn't careful. Not that I didn't want one, but I didn't think I'd be able to handle it at work if I had to pick up the phone and be professional two seconds later.

I was actually able to get away by six, without Dad having to come and throw me out. But I was so exhausted that I hoped Lucah didn't expect much from me in the sex department. I might fall asleep mid-coitus.

When I walked in, he greeted me wearing nothing but one of his ties and posed seductively against the back of his couch.

"Welcome home, Miss Clarke." He fluttered his eyelashes and I burst into laughter because I was so tired and stressed and he was so sweet and ridiculous and I loved him.

"I am so tired right now, it hurts to laugh," I said, slipping off my heels and stumbling over to him.

"Aw, Sunshine, you do look tired."

"Thanks," I said and rested my head against his chest.

"Hold on, I have a plan. You come and sit here." He dragged me over to the couch and I collapsed on it, closing my eyes and resting my head on one of the pillows. I heard him walking around and I also heard water running.

I was so tired that I didn't even think I could fall asleep, but just closing my eyes was bliss.

"Come here, Miss Clarke," his voice said a few minutes later, and I propped my eyes open. It was not easy. He was still naked and tieless this time. "Put your arms around my neck." I did and he picked me up and carried me to the bathroom. The lights were off and there were a few scented candles burning.

"When did you buy scented candles?" I asked.

"Shh, don't ask questions." He set me down and started removing my clothes. The tub was full of steaming water and he must have added salts or something to it, because the water was frothy.

He got me naked and then helped me into the tub. Then got in behind me, pulling me into his chest.

"Oh my God, this feels unbelievable." The warm water immediately went to work on my tense muscles and the steam made me feel a little more alert.

"You feel unbelievable." He got out a loofah that I could tell was brand new and started working it up and down my arms and across my chest. I closed my eyes again and he started humming, his chest vibrating against my back.

"Rory?" he said.

"Hm?" I turned my head so I could see him out of the corner of my eye.

"I love you." He said it so seriously, like it was the first time he was saying it instead of the hundredth.

"I love you, too."

"I want you to move in with me. I want to see you all the time." That was definitely mutual.

"I want to move in with you, too. But what about Sloane?" He smiled as if he had been hoping for me to ask that.

"Well, I discovered that there is a vacancy in your apartment building. It also happens to be an apartment right down the hall from yours. So either we can live there and Sloane can have yours, or the other way around. Whatever you want to do, we have to act fast." He beamed, clearly pleased with himself.

"You have been busy, Mr. Blythe. I'll ask Sloane and see what she wants to do. So you don't want to live here?" His apartment was pretty nice. Nicer than mine, even if it was smaller.

"This isn't my home. The only time it feels that way is when you're here with me." Aw, he was just the sweetest sometimes.

"Besides, your apartment is bigger, and the spare room would make a good place for my stuff."

"What stuff? Your secret room stuff? Can I finally see that now? I mean, not right now, but maybe later?" I'd almost forgotten about Lucah's secret room in all the insanity.

"You can see it whenever you want. They're all unlocked now."

"When did you do that?"

"A few days ago." I flipped around so I was facing him. "I don't have anything to hide anymore. No more secrets, no more lies. Whatever you want to know, I'm an open book."

I liked the sound of that.

"How did you get started in corporate espionage?" I knew that wasn't what his job was called, but that was what I was going to call it.

"It's a long story, but basically I wanted to make money and I wanted to be someone else. I spent a lot of time running from my past. I guess that was just another way to keep doing it." One of the candles guttered out, making it even darker.

"Why?"

He sighed and shifted under me.

"Because I didn't want eat cereal for dinner. Ever again. And I didn't want people to know that was where I came from. My parents never tried to put the burden on me or my brothers, but I remember going to the food bank and understanding at a very young age that we didn't have things that other people had. I didn't want life ever to be that hard again."

It made sense, and I could understand wanting to run away from your past.

"This one time in college, I changed my major for a day. I also went by my first and middle name when I introduced myself to people."

"What did you change your major to?" The water was starting to get cold, but my muscles were all loose and I didn't think I could get up. He was going to have to carry me.

"Photography. It sounded cool, even though I didn't even own a freaking camera. I just wanted to do something else. Of course then I woke up in the middle of the night and pictured Dad's face when I told him I didn't want to work for the company and I was waiting at the guidance office before they opened the next morning to change it back. I never told my parents." It had been a moment of insanity, and I'd never told anyone about it, not even Sloane.

"I can't picture that, but I'm sure you would have been a great photographer." No, I would have been bad at. I couldn't even take a decent selfie with my phone.

I shrugged and another candle went out.

"We should probably get out before the water gets too cold. Are you hungry?"

"Yeah. I barely ate anything today." It was a miracle that my stomach hadn't growled yet.

"Well, we'll have to do something about that." He got up and got a towel before he pulled me out of the tub and wrapped me in it, rubbing the water from my body before he wrapped one around his waist.

"I can walk. I think." I might have moved a little slower than normal, but I made my way back to the couch and slumped on it. Lucah brought me some clothes and I got dressed as he made dinner in his boxers and a t-shirt.

"Can I look at your rooms now?"

"You can look at them anytime you want." He stirred spaghetti into a pot of boiling water and jerked his head at the three doors. It felt weird looking at these rooms with him here, but I got up and went to door number one.

It was just a closet, really, and was stacked with boxes. None of them were labeled, and despite what he said, I didn't feel comfortable going through them, so I went to the second door. This room was a little bit bigger, more of a small office size, but it too was filled with boxes, and his guitar. I walked in and shut the door behind me.

I pulled open one box and found there were a bunch of books in there. I skimmed some of the titles and they were some of my favorites. The next box had pictures in it and I flipped through some of them. They were of Lucah when he was younger and oh, boy. This was some quality blackmail material. I made a note to come back and look at those things later.

The rest of the boxes were also books and photographs and some yearbooks and other little things like band shirts and sweatshirts and so forth.

His life was in these boxes, his past, who he really was. Packed and locked away. It was almost tragic, that he had to keep this hidden. I found a few framed photographs with him and two little girls who had to be his nieces, and I gathered them into my arms before going back out into the living room.

Lucah didn't comment as I placed the pictures on the coffee table and then went back and got some more of his stuff and put it out. I went into the third room and found even more stuff and put that out.

When I was done, all three doors were open and his apartment actually looked like a home. I went to the kitchen and put my arms around him from behind.

"You're not going to comment on my redecorating?" I said as he stirred some spaghetti sauce so it didn't burn.

"I haven't lived in an apartment with my things all out in four years. It's . . . it's going to take some getting used to. But it's nice to see my pretty girls again. Now we just need to put some pictures of you around." Ugh, I didn't. I wasn't that fond of pictures of myself. But if he would be in them with me, that would be okay.

"No nude shots, okay?"

"Oh, I have some of those already," he said, pouring the sauce over the pasta and stirring it together.

"Shut up, you do not." I smacked him and he turned around and gave me a smile.

"Maybe I do and maybe I don't." I narrowed my eyes. I didn't want any naked pictures of me to exist. I pinched his butt, and he just kept smiling.

"Asshole," I said as he carried the spaghetti over to the coffee table which was now cluttered with photographs and other things. I'd also brought out his guitar and propped it against the wall. I was hoping for a performance later. That would be the only thing that would make this night better.

Chapter Thirty-Six

"What do you think?" Sloane said as she adjusted the skirt of my dress.

I was officially wearing the most beautiful dress in the history of dresses. Eat your heart out, Scarlet O'Hara. That bitch had nothing on this.

The fabric was black with almost a flower pattern on it that you could only see when you got up close. I swiveled my hips back and forth and listened as the dress swished and moved like a bell.

"Is it possible for me to wear this every single day for the rest of my life? Because I'd love for that to happen." I would clean in this dress. I would sleep in this dress. "I'm never taking it off."

"Well, I'm pretty sure Lucah is going to want to take it off you. And it's going to get pretty funky if you don't wash it." She played with the skirt again and I spun all the way around. I wasn't wearing a tiara, but it didn't matter. I felt like a princess. Where were the woodland creatures to help me with all my chores?

"Okay, now that you're set, wanna see my dress?" She wiggled her eyebrows and I had been afraid of this.

"Okay, so we have to talk about that. I know I said I was going to take you as my date, but that was before Lucah got done, and now he's not going to be able to go, so that means Marisol and Chloe are out as well." I'd been trying to think of a solution to that, but I didn't have one and the event was next week.

"So basically you're telling me that you're going to invite your boyfriend and bail on me," she said as I stepped away from the mirror.

"No! No, I'm not saying that. I'm just trying to figure out how I can still get all of you in. So. I'm going to ask Dad if I can just invite all of you. Sure, it's probably going to piss people off, but I don't give a shit. I want all of you there." Sloane beamed and hugged me, being careful not to smush the dress. It was going to get smushed when I danced, but I wanted to keep it perfect until then.

"You are awesome! Okay, let me just put my dress on and then you can tell me how fabulous I look." She dashed into her changing room and came out a few minutes later wearing a dress that was even better than the drawing she'd shown me. The cutouts were more daring, and plunging, but there was black sheer material that covered her (sort of) so she didn't look like she was wearing anything too revealing. The rest of the fabric was silk and white with large black tropical flowers printed on it. She spun slowly and I got a look at the back.

"You're gorgeous and you know it, Sloane. You don't need me to tell you that." Sloane wasn't vain. She was just confident and she was gorgeous. Anyone who said different was jealous or lying or both.

She came and stood in front of the mirror with me.

"I love you," I said. "And thank you for being the best friend I could ever ask for." She put her arm around me and gave me a hug.

"I love you too, bitch." She stuck her tongue out at me in the mirror and I did the same.

Once we were back into our other clothes, I told her about Lucah's plan.

"So it's up to you, whatever you want to do." I knew she could afford the apartment and had been talking about maybe getting one for a while now, but we liked living with each other so much that neither of us wanted to make a move.

"If I move down the hall, do I get to keep my key and come in whenever I want?" she said with an expression that I really didn't like.

"Within reason, Sloane. I don't want to be in the middle of having hot sex and look up and see you standing there. We're close, but we're not that close." Sloane made a face.

"I love you, but that is not something I would want to witness, thank you very much. I was just thinking of sneaking in early in the morning and gluing all your furniture to the ceiling, or hiding your shoes, but you took it totally dirty, you perv." Oh, like she hadn't thought about that.

"Shut up," I said, and we shared a cab back to our apartment. Lucah was at his place, packing his stuff back up to start bringing it over to my place. It felt weird to be fitting him in, but it also felt right.

Oh Jesus, where was I going to put my shoes?

Lucah came over with a few boxes and had dinner with Sloane and me so we could talk about the apartment situation.

"On the one hand, I'd get to start over with a brand-y new place. On the other, I'd have to move all my shit. So. Do you mind if I stay here? I'm kind of attached to this kitchen."

"The kitchens are identical," I pointed out.

"I know, but every stove is different. I like this stove. We know each other and we get along." She went over and stroked the stove and then kissed one of the knobs.

"She really likes the stove," I said to Lucah and he just shook his head at her.

"Well, you can keep the stove. So I guess that means we're moving, huh, Sunshine?"

"Guess so," I said. That was going to be a bitch, but hopefully Sloane would help us? Yeah, probably not.

"Maybe I can commandeer my brother to come and help us." I swore Sloane's ears perked up at the mention of the brother.

"Is he a ginger as well?" She tried to sound uninterested, but definitely failed.

"Yes, he is. Sort of. It's more brown with red highlights. And yes, he is single and no, he is completely off limits. My brother is a time bomb and you don't want to be around when he goes off. Trust me." Lucah was smart, but he didn't know Sloane. The fastest way to get Sloane to do something was to tell her not to do it. If he had just kept his mouth shut about Ryder, Sloane probably would have lost interest, but now . . .

Sloane's eyes sparkled at me, and I gave her a warning glare. She just skipped back to the table with a satisfied look on her face. I texted Lucah.

You have no idea what you've done.

His phone buzzed and he read the text and then typed a response.

She doesn't want him. Trust me.

"You'd better not be sexting with me right here," Sloane said and we put our phones away.

"You're insane," I said to Lucah, because he still wasn't getting it. He just smirked back at me. This was going to be a disaster.

"So, I have a question," I said that Sunday at dinner with my parents. I felt bad for asking Dad when he was so tired. I'd never seen him look so worn out. He wasn't as young as he used to be and I wondered if the drama had taken more of a toll on him than he would admit.

"What's that, Rory?" Mom said.

"Well, I need a favor. I want to bring four dates to the Ball." I didn't look up from my plate to see their reaction.

"Four dates?" Mom was the one to drop her fork this time. I glanced up and pretended like it was no big deal. "Who on earth are you bringing?"

"Sloane, Chloe, Marisol and Lucah," I mumbled, especially on the last name.

"You want to invite all your friends?" Mom acted like this was a ridiculous request. "This isn't an eighth grade sleepover. This is your work event."

I glanced at Dad and he looked like he was thinking.

"I know it's a work event. So do they. I just thought it would be nice to invite them. They've always wanted to come and I want to invite them." It wasn't the best reason, but I didn't have a whole lot of ammunition to fight this battle.

Mom opened her mouth to protest, but Dad put his hand up.

"She can invite them if she wants." He smiled at me and I smiled back. "If my daughter wants to bring her friends to her work party, then my daughter can bring her friends." I wasn't going to point out that it was actually my three friends and my boyfriend. I hadn't told them that Lucah and I were seeing each other, but they were smart people.

"Well, then if she's going to invite who she wants, then I think she should invite Fin. She doesn't have to go with him as a boyfriend, but I think he should come." Mom just wouldn't give up.

"Fine," I said. That would work out perfect. He could accompany Marisol.

Now that we'd gotten that straightened out, I had to tell them about my move.

"So I'm going to be moving into the apartment next door and Sloane is going to keep the other. She needs more space for work and um, I like more space as well." Or uninterrupted sex. That was really what I wanted.

"I always told you that place was too small, but you wouldn't listen. Why not just get a better apartment in a nicer building?" We'd had this conversation a million times already and I didn't want to go into it again.

"Are you sure you want to do that, Rory? That's a big step." Dad wasn't talking about moving into my own place. He knew the only reason I would do that was to move in with Lucah.

"I'm ready," I said simply. I was practically living with him anyway. Besides, if disaster struck, I could just hop back in with Sloane. Not that I didn't think it wasn't going to work, but just in case.

"Then at least let me call some men to move all of your things. I don't want you hurting yourself moving anything, even if it's just down the hall," Mom said. I kept my mouth shut even though I already had at least two guys to help me move. I glanced at Dad and I could tell he knew about that too. Smart man.

"I'm going to leave some of the stuff with Sloane. I can always buy new furniture." Then Lucah and I could go shopping together, or he could bring in some of his own things. My apartment was definitely more feminine than masculine. Not that I was going to be letting him bring in a basketball hoop, or a beer cap collection, but we could man things up a bit.

"Well, just let me know if you want to go shopping, or if you need any help with anything," Mom said and finally went to get out dessert. Phew. That went as well as I could have expected.

Lucah and I were moving in together, he was coming with me to the Ball and other than the shit show at work, and the fact that Lucah was unemployed, things were looking up. Plus, I had a fabulous gown in my possession. That would make the very worst day better.

Chapter Thirty-Seven

"Moving sucks," I said the next night as we started packing up my stuff to move it down the hall. Lucah and I had signed the lease that morning, after slipping the building owner a fifty to let us move in early. Sloane was gleefully talking about what she was going to do with all the extra space and pretending to be helpful, but actually doing the opposite.

I'd texted Chloe and Marisol, but they were busy. Or they just didn't love me that much. Or a little of both.

I joined Sloane and sat down on one of few packed boxes. I was sweating and we'd barely done anything. You never know how much stuff you have until you try to move it.

Sloane sighed and got up to get two bottles of beer from the fridge. I had no idea why we had beer because none of us drank it. I gave Sloane a look when she handed me one of the bottles.

"What? Beer felt like an appropriate moving drink. You know, the working man's drink." This was one of those times when I knew she had some reason for her crazy, but I couldn't figure it out.

The key sounded in the door and Lucah walked back in, but he wasn't alone.

"Rory, Sloane, this is my brother, Ryder. Ryder, Rory and Sloane." Lucah was NOT happy about the introduction. I could see from the way he held his shoulders that he was stressing out.

I slowly looked at Ryder and immediately saw that he was Lucah's brother. They had similar features, but Ryder was more . . . rugged. He also had a few scars here and there, the biggest one on the side of one of his cheeks. His hair was darker than Lucah's and he was a lot bulkier, with tattoos roped around his arms. There was a look in his eyes and that look said a few things to me.

Trouble. Danger. Stay away.

"Hello, Rory. It's so nice to meet you, I've heard *lots* of things about you." Ah, so he also had his brother's dirty sense of humor. He shook my hand and almost crushed my fingers with his calloused hand. Then he turned to Sloane and I waited for the fireworks.

"Hi, I'm Sloane." She said it slow and low before she got up and walked forward. Ryder watched her the whole time and I wanted to scream at Lucah. Sloane was working it and he was taking her in.

"Sloane. Very nice to meet you. I can't say that my brother has mentioned you. Or if he did I wasn't paying attention. I am now." She giggled and I knew that laugh. She only laughed like that around a cute boy. Oh, Sloane. Lucah had been right about this guy, he looked like he was only going to bring her heartache. Not that I could judge just from the five minutes I'd seen him in person, but Lucah had told me plenty of stories that backed up my initial impression.

Lucah started picking up boxes, stepping right between Sloane and Ryder. Good boy.

Then he shoved one at Ryder and told him to take it down the hall. Ryder gave Sloane a lingering look and she ducked her head and hid a smile. Seriously?

Lucah gave me a look and I gave him one right back. This was his fault. Making things forbidden made them more attractive.

I knew I was being a hypocrite for not wanting Sloane to be with Ryder when I'd had a forbidden relationship with Lucah and she'd been so supportive. But I didn't want anything bad to happen to her. I didn't want her heart to get broken. I couldn't take that.

"He's fucking hot," Sloane hissed at me while Lucah followed Ryder down the hall.

"Be careful," I hissed back, but I could see by the look on her face that she was going to take my advice with a grain of salt.

By the time we got most of the stuff moved, it was late, I was exhausted and Sloane and Ryder had eye fucked each other way too much.

"Well, I think I'm going to head out. Unless you need anything else?" Ryder said and I knew there was a double meaning behind that.

"No, I think I can take it from here. Thanks for the help," Lucah said, patting him on the shoulder.

"Oh, you're welcome. Anything for my big brother," he said with a wink at Sloane.

"Really, thank you," I said, interrupting more eye fucking. "It was so nice to meet you." He said good-bye and I think Lucah breathed a sigh of relief when he was gone.

"Oh my GOD," Sloane said, slumping against the kitchen counter. "*That* is your brother? Holy hell." She fanned herself and Lucah shook his head.

"I told you. I told you. I told you," I said to him. "There's no stopping it now."

"It was bound to happen eventually. No sense putting it off any more." He shrugged and went to the fridge to grab a beer.

"Oh, you like beer now?" I said as he popped it open.

"Sometimes in life, you just need a beer. This is one of those times." He sighed and went to sit on the couch.

I sat next to him, putting my head on his shoulder.

"Hey."

"Hey." He gave me a tired smile and I kissed him on the cheek.

"We're moving in together. We need to buy furniture. Aren't you excited about that?" I said.

Finally he really did smile. Sloane skipped off to her room to give us some privacy.

"Buying furniture. That's a big step. You ready for chairs and ottomans and maybe even a few lamps?"

"I don't know. Ottomans are pretty serious." He leaned his face forward and I knew what kissing him would lead to, even though we were both gross from moving stuff and exhausted and I had to work the next day.

"There's only one piece of furniture I want to talk about right now and that's your bed," he said, getting up and pulling me up after him as he lead me toward the bedroom.

"Hm, I'm not sure if I know what you're talking about. You'll have to show me."

"Oh, I will show you how best to use a bed, Miss Clarke."

"Looking forward to it, Mr. Blythe."

The next week the hours when I wasn't at work were spent with Lucah buying furniture and moving furniture and boxes, boxes, boxes.

And any other time I had free from that was spent with Sloane. I was literally moving a hallway away, but I felt like we weren't going to have as much girl time now that I was living with Lucah.

"So is he just going to be a bum now?" Sloane said on Thursday night when Lucah was out getting groceries.

"No, he is not going to be a bum. He's looking for a job. His actual résumé is pretty impressive, so I think he'll be fine." I wasn't worried at all.

Unfortunately, I still needed an assistant. I'd had no luck finding anyone and with the recent scandal at Clarke Enterprises, the qualified applicants were even fewer than before. I'd called a few people in for interviews, but no one seemed right. I'd have to try again with an advertisement and hope for the best. I fucking needed an assistant.

I didn't ask Sloane about Ryder. He'd been back once more, and I'd caught them talking, but Sloane hadn't said anything about him, which meant that she really, really liked him.

I was adopting a "wait and see" attitude. I'd talked to Lucah about it, but he just got mad whenever I brought it up, so I made a note to not do that very often. Eventually we were going to have to deal with it, but for right now, things were still in the beginning stages. Yup, wait and see . . .

On Friday at work, Lucah texted me to come out to the elevators. I quickly messaged him back, asking what was going on, but he didn't answer. I called him, but there was no answer. So I locked my computer, got up and went out, where I found Mrs. Andrews beaming at me from her desk, and Lucah standing and looking very pleased with himself.

He had the suit on that he'd worn when he'd first come in for an interview, complete with his diamond stud earring.

"Well, Mr. Blythe, you look very dapper. What are you doing here?" He'd obviously been waiting for me to say that.

"I work here, Miss Clarke."

My mouth dropped open.

"You're kidding." His smile got even wider and Mrs. Andrews laughed.

"You're looking at the newest member of the research and development team. Which means I am part of the Clarke Enterprises family, but not in your department. In case you were wondering if that would be a problem with us moving in together." I really wanted to throw my arms around him and squeal in delight, but there was no way I would do that in the office where everyone could see. So I just stood there and said, "That's wonderful, Mr. Blythe. I can't imagine how you swung that, but I'm happy that you are employed."

"I had a recommendation from the president, so I think I was a shoo-in." My mouth dropped open again.

"Dad?"

"He did. And now that I'm a member of the company, that automatically gives me an invitation to the ball. I just don't know who should go with me."

"Oh, I don't know. I can't think of anyone who would want to go to a Ball with you. Let me check—" I was silenced by Lucah closing the space between us and lifting me off my feet.

"You. I'm going with you and I'm not taking no for an answer, Miss Clarke."

I sighed dramatically.

"Well, then I guess I have no choice but to go with you, Mr. Blythe." And I kissed him right there in front of the elevator. I was sure there were people who saw us, but I finally stopped caring. If I wanted to kiss my boyfriend, I was going to kiss my boyfriend.

"You got that right, Sunshine," he said, setting me down. "Come on, I'm taking you for coffee." The tone of his voice told me that he wasn't talking about the kind you made and put in a mug.

"Coffee sounds perfect."

Epilogue

I stood at the top of the stairs in my unbelievable black gown and it was a bit like a dream. I looked down, but everyone was busy with their own conversations. So much for everyone being in awe of my beauty.

But there was one face that was staring right at me, and looking completely captivated.

I inhaled quickly as I saw that he was wearing a white tux complete with white shirt and a pale silver tie. I'd never used the word breathtaking to describe a man, but he was. I ascended the stairs and saw the three other people who were happy to see me. Sloane, in her black and white flowered dress, who was already attracting attention from some of the married and unmarried men. Marisol, stunning in a black dress that was gathered on one side and cut to reveal a white underskirt with Fin in a black tux by her side, looking at her as if she'd hung the moon. Chloe, who had a mod creation with a white panel down the front and black panels on the sides. They looked awesome and I waved as I started walking.

I glanced around and found my parents and they were beaming at me, and Mom made a motion to tell me to stand up straighter. No matter how old I was, she'd always treat me like her little girl. Dad tipped his glass in my direction and I gave him a thumbs-up. That wasn't exactly ladylike, but I wasn't going to put on a front just because I was here.

I walked until I was standing in front of Lucah and dipped slowly into a curtsy as he gave me a deep bow.

"May I have this dance, Miss Clarke?"

"You may, Mr. Blythe." He took my hand and led me to the black and white checkered dance floor as the quartet started playing a waltz that sounded an awful lot like the song "Clarity". His hand went to my waist, the other stayed in my hand and then, with a nod, we danced.

"You look ravishing, Sunshine," he said in my ear.

"You don't look so bad yourself." I looked at his face and he gave me a wink before sticking out his tongue to show me that he had the silver barbell in.

Some things never changed.

Playlist

Signed Sealed Delivered ~ Stevie Wonder
Sooner Surrender ~ Matt Nathanson
Let's Get It On ~ Marvin Gaye
Fat Bottomed Girls ~ Queen
Total Eclipse of the Heart ~ Bonnie Tyler
Brighter Than Sunshine ~ Aqualung
Beyond the Sea ~ Bobby Darin
Bohemian Rhapsody ~ Queen
Make You Feel My Love ~ Adele
Don't You Forget About Me ~ Simple Minds
Howlin' For You ~ The Black Keys
It's De-Lovely ~ Cole Porter
Rumble and Sway ~ Jamie N Commons
Starlight ~ Muse
Secret Lovers ~ Atlantic Starr
Clarity ~ Zedd (feat. Foxes)

The Noctalis Chronicles

Nocturnal (Book One)
Nightmare (Book Two)
Neither (Book Three)
Neverend (Book Four)

The Whisper Trilogy

Whisper (Book One)

Fall and Rise

Deeper We Fall (Book One)
Faster We Burn (Book Two)

My Favorite Mistake
(Available from Harlequin)

My Sweetest Escape (January 28, 2014)
For Real (November 14, 2013)

Thank You

This is my first foray into Adult Contemporary Romance, and there are quite a few people I have to thank for going with me along this new journey.

First to my family, Mom and Dad especially. I'm sorry I wrote a book that I used dirty words and wrote about sex. I hope you can forgive me.

To my friends who have inspired me (even if they don't know it): Caroline, Colleen, Liz, Rachel and Meridith. You are my reality check.

To my beta readers, Magan and Laura, thanks for catching my (numerous) errors and inconsistencies and helping make this book better. I couldn't do it without you.

To my editor, Jen Hendricks, who must be sick of me forgetting the difference between dessert and desert.

To all the authors who have held my hand (mostly online and via text message) during this process and offered their advice and (figurative) shoulders: Chelsea Fine, Tiffany King, Gennifer Albin, Heather Self and Karina Halle. Thanks for putting up with my crazy.

To all the book bloggers and other online friends who have ridden the roller coaster that writing this book was. I couldn't mention all of you. It would take too long, but I lovers all of you.

To my FABULOUS publicist, Jessica from InkSlinger PR, I wouldn't know where my head was if you didn't text me and remind me it was atop my neck.

To YOU. Yeah, In know it's cliché to thank you, but I'm going to do it anyway. You all deserve WORLD'S GREATEST READER mugs. And shoes. I'd get you all red shoes.

About Chelsea

Chelsea M. Cameron is a YA/NA New York Times/USA Today Best Selling author from Maine. Lover of things random and ridiculous, Jane Austen/Charlotte and Emily Bronte Fangirl, red velvet cake enthusiast, obsessive tea drinker, vegetarian, former cheerleader and world's worst video gamer. When not writing, she enjoys watching infomercials, singing in the car and tweeting. She has a degree in journalism from the University of Maine, Orono that she promptly abandoned to write about the people in her own head. More often than not, these people turn out to be just as weird as she is.

Find Chelsea online:

chelseamcameron.com
Twitter: @chel_c_cam
Facebook: Chelsea M. Cameron (Official Author Page)